祝福及其

THE NEW-YEAR

AND OTHER S

中國現代文學中英對照系列
Bilingual Series on Modern Chinese Literature

中國現代文學中英對照系列

Bilingual Series on Modern Chinese Literature

祝福及其他
The New-Year Sacrifice and Other Stories

中英對照版

Chinese-English Bilingual Edition

魯迅 著

楊憲益、戴乃迭 英譯

Original Chinese Text by
LU XUN
Translated by Yang Xianyi and Gladys Yang

The Chinese University Press

《祝福及其他》（中英對照版）
　　魯迅 著
　　楊憲益、戴乃迭 英譯

© **香港中文大學** 2002（中〔繁體〕英對照版）

中〔簡體〕英對照版2000年由北京外文出版社以《魯迅小説選》為書名初次出版

國際統一書號 (ISBN) 962–996–043–5

出版：中文大學出版社

　　　香港中文大學・香港 新界 沙田
　　　圖文傳真：+852 2603 6692
　　　　　　　　+852 2603 7355
　　　電子郵遞：cup@cuhk.edu.hk
　　　網　　址：www.chineseupress.com

The New-Year Sacrifice and Other Stories (Chinese-English Bilingual Edition)
　Chinese text by Lu Xun
　Translated by Yang Xianyi and Gladys Yang

© **The Chinese University of Hong Kong**, 2002 (Traditional Chinese-English
Bilingual Edition)

Simplified Chinese-English bilingual edition first published in 2000 by
　Foreign Languages Press, Beijing under the title *Selected Stories of Lu Xun*

ISBN 962–996–043–5

Published by The Chinese University Press,
　The Chinese University of Hong Kong,
　Sha Tin, N.T., Hong Kong.
　Fax: +852 2603 6692
　　　+852 2603 7355
　E-mail: cup@cuhk.edu.hk
　Web-site: www.chineseupress.com

Printed in Hong Kong

出 版 人 的 話

　　近二十年，中國與外界接觸日趨頻繁，影響所及，華文作家在世界文學圈中益受注目。二〇〇〇年諾貝爾文學獎由高行健先生獲得，或許並非偶然。

　　中文大學出版社一向秉承促進中西方文化交流的使命，故於年前開始籌劃「中國現代文學中英對照系列」，邀得鄭樹森教授出任編輯委員會主席，及幾位國際著名學者出任成員，挑選中國著名作家之重要作品及現有最好之英譯本，以中英文雙語對照排列出版，計劃每年出版五至六種書目。間或有版權問題未能解決的，則另邀請翻譯界的高手操刀英譯。每位著名作家及其作品亦會由圈內名家作序介紹，以為導讀。

　　本社謹對編輯委員會及其他曾出力人士之鼎力協助，致以熱切謝忱。

Publisher's Note

　　It is a recent phenomena that authors of Chinese origin have been attracting more international attention in the literary world of late, probably as a result of China's more frequent cultural interactions with the outside world in the past two decades. As such, it was not coincidental that the 2000 Nobel Prize was awarded to Gao Xingjian, an author of Chinese origin.

　　With the mission to bridge the gap between the Chinese and Western cultures, The Chinese University Press is uniquely qualified to play an active role in this area. Thus, this *Bilingual Series on Modern Chinese Literature* has come into existence. Under the able guidance of Professor William Tay and other members of the Advisory Committee, it is planned that five to six titles will be added to the list annually. They will be important works by major authors and will be presented in a bilingual format for cross-cultural appreciation. This means the Committee has either to identify the best existing translations, or to commission experts who can do the job well. Each author will also be introduced by a noted scholar in the field to put the work in the proper perspective.

　　The publisher appreciates the invaluable advice of the Advisory Committee, and sincerely thanks all those who have helped to make this series a reality.

Contents

目 錄

Introduction

It would be difficult to find a Chinese person who has not heard of Lu Xun and, given a secondary school education, read some of his works, too. While in other countries several literary figures in any period of the twentieth century compete for eminence, he stands head and shoulders above his contemporaries in reputation, at least in mainland China. This eminence does not rest purely on critical consensus, however; it is partly owed to political promotion. And such political promotion was made possible by his engagement in the great conflicts and debates of his time of highest activity, namely the 1920s and 30s. He stepped then into the traditional role of the scholar-intellectual as guardian of the nation's conscience and morals.

The bulk of Lu Xun's publications consisted of essays and translations. The translations have been superseded, as he expected them to be, and the essays are progressively less understood as knowledge of their historical context fades. The most accessible of his work is now his fiction. He was a pioneer in China of the modern short story. Modernity was in fact a key concept in all his thinking; not modernity as a fashion, but as a basis for China to first survive, then prosper. Lu Xun's own life story is that of the evolution of China's modern man.

Lu Xun was born in 1881 as a subject of the Great Qing Empire.

前言

　　今天，要找到一個從未聽聞魯迅大名的中國人實在不容易；教育程度在中學以上的中國人就更必定讀過他的部分作品。二十世紀，別國文壇也許名家輩出，各有千秋；但在中國，至少在中國大陸而言，魯迅的文名可說傲視同儕。然而，魯迅的盛名並非單靠口碑，中國大陸的政治宣傳亦功不可沒。政治宣傳所以湊效，多少在於魯迅曾在其創作全盛時期，亦即二十至三十年代，展開過連串大規模的文壇論戰，繼而擔當起文人學士作為民族衛道者的傳統角色。

　　魯迅的作品以散文與翻譯為主，其中的翻譯作品，一如譯者本人所料，至今已大多過時；至於其散文作品，則隨着背景資料的散軼而日趨難懂。最平易近人的還是他的小說作品。魯迅是中國現代小說創作的先鋒，其實現代觀念在魯迅思想中佔有極重要的位置；但他心中的現代觀念與趨潮流無關，而是中國賴以求存以至富強的基礎。魯迅一生正是中國現代人成長的最佳寫照。

　　魯迅生於1881年，當時中國仍是大清皇朝的天下。這個末代皇

The Qing was to be the last imperial dynasty to rule China: it was overthrown by a nationwide rebellion in 1911. In its heyday it was remarkably successful. It started in the seventeenth century, when the Manchus, a tribe originating to the north-east of the Great Wall, conquered the existing Ming Empire, and went on to expand its frontiers. In the long reign of the Kangxi emperor the whole population of the empire was moulded together, and the native Han people, reconciled to their conquerors, came to take equal pride in the military might of their Qing Empire and the glory of its civilization. The Manchus themselves became sinified, while the Han Chinese, after some initial resistance, adopted the Manchu queue, or pigtail, as the natural and proper way of dressing the hair for men.

Permanent peace and prosperity was, however, impossible to maintain over such a huge territory, and internal revolts became frequent in the latter half of the dynasty. In the nineteenth century the empire also found itself having to ward off interference from foreign powers. This interference brought not only demands for privilege and authority, but also the challenge of a different way of life. The Great Qing Empire was ill-equipped to respond to that challenge. It had, after all, owed its survival to conservatism. To win the allegiance of its Chinese subjects it had embraced the settled ways of Confucianism, to which the notion of progress was alien: the ideal society was set in the past. China was therefore much slower to learn how to defend itself against the industrialized Western nations than the Japanese, who following the example of Britain and France inflicted a military defeat on China.

By the time Lu Xun was born, the foreign powers had established enclaves (usually called "concessions") under their own jurisdiction in China's major ports, and foreign missionaries had built churches and schools. Chinese books and journals, chiefly published in Shanghai, were also busy propagating the "new learning" of the West.

朝雖然最終在辛亥革命中被推翻，但當其全盛時期，確曾有過一番
豐功偉績。滿清十七世紀崛起於東北，及至滅明之後版圖不斷擴
大；在康熙長期統治之下，全國各族歸於一統；漢族俯首稱臣之
後，亦對滿清皇朝的文治武功感恩戴德。滿人逐漸漢化，漢人初則
抗拒，但最終亦隨滿俗，男子一律以束辮為髮式。

　　但滿清帝國版圖遼闊，要長治久安絕非易事；清朝末葉即已內
亂頻仍。到了十九世紀，滿清帝國更疲於應付西方列強的侵擾；權
益的需索而外，西方生活方式的入侵，對中國傳統亦構成威脅。這
一切，實遠非靠維護傳統支撐大局的滿清帝國所能應付。其實，為
了爭取漢族臣民對其效忠，滿清更全盤以儒家思想治國。但儒家思
想不思進取，而只知以先王的社會為典範。因此，中國在抵禦西方
工業強國方面遠不如日本反應迅速；而日本則緊隨英法之後戰勝中
國。

　　魯迅出生之時，西方列強已在中國主要港口設立租界，外國傳
教士亦已在中國建教堂辦學校。主要在上海出版的中文書刊，亦標
榜西方的「新學」。但這一切文化上的巨變，對魯迅故鄉紹興影響甚

xii   *Introduction*

Yet little of this cultural revolution reached Lu Xun's hometown of Shaoxing, and even less penetrated the high walls of the clan mansion where he lived. Shaoxing was then a sizeable town in the south-east province of Zhejiang, situated on a plain intersected by rivers and canals. The surrounding countryside provided an abundance of "fish and rice," and the town itself was a centre for textiles, pottery and handicrafts, besides the distilleries that produced the famous Shaoxing rice wine. A new feature was the Christian churches, but they were beneath the notice of Lu Xun's clan, which was wholly orthodox in its beliefs and observances.

Our author's real name was Zhou Shuren. "Lu Xun" was a pen-name, adopted in 1918. His Zhou clan belonged to the land-owning gentry, and lived in three mansions in town, each divided into "houses" for the various branches. Once extremely prosperous, the clan saw its fortunes decline in the nineteenth century, but appearances were kept up. No member of Lu Xun's house would stoop to engage in trade or get his hands dirty, and the ambition remained an appointment in the imperial bureaucracy, to be obtained by passing a series of examinations. But as the career of Lu Xun's grandfather showed, that road could lead to bankruptcy.

This grandfather, Zhou Fuqing (1838–1904), brought glory on his house when he passed the Palace Examination, the highest in the empire, in 1871, but his subsequent career was a failure. Many years of waiting and lobbying in the capital Beijing cost a great deal of money, but brought only a lowly post. Instead of restoring his family's fortunes he ran down its land holdings to a level of bare sufficiency. The worst blow he inflicted on his family was to involve himself in a plot to bribe a chief examiner to pass local Shaoxing candidates, including his own son Zhou Boyi, Lu Xun's father. For that crime Zhou Fuqing served eight years in prison, from 1893 to 1901. The effects were devastating: sale of possessions, incurment of debt, and loss of respect.

微，更越不過魯迅家族深院大宅的高牆。紹興當時是浙江省東南面一大市鎮，位處平原地帶，河道縱橫，四周農村盛產魚米；除了以釀造紹興米酒聞名的酒廠以外，也是紡織品、陶瓷與手工藝品中心。雖然天主教堂建築亦已成為該市一大特色，但魯迅家族信仰的仍是中國古老傳統那一套。

魯迅原名周樹人，「魯迅」是1918年以後採用的筆名。周家本屬地主階級，在紹興市分居三處，同住一處的家人又分成好些「房」。曾顯赫一時的周家，雖然到了十九世紀已家道中落，但對外仍得繼續維持門面。周家子孫均矢志於士途，而不甘從商或以有失身分的方式謀生；不過，魯迅祖父雖在士途上堅持到底，但卻落得慘淡收場。

魯迅祖父周福清(1838–1904)1871年中進士，本應光耀門楣，但最終仍失意於士途。多年在京奔走，花錢無數，亦只不過求得一個卑微的官職；不獨未能興家，尋且因變賣田產而使周家上下要過緊日子。後來為求魯迅父親周伯宜等紹興考生過關而賄賂考官，就更令家族蒙上莫大的羞辱；周福清本人亦因此飽嘗八年(1893–1901)牢獄生涯。周家亦得變賣所有財產，甚至舉債度日，名譽掃地。周伯

Zhou Boyi fell into depression, took to opium, and died in 1896. Lu Xun himself, then in his teens, felt the disgrace keenly. In the change in people's attitude to him he saw "the true features of his fellow men," as he was later to write. In return, he looked with less than kindly eyes on his fellow townsmen, as is evident in his stories.

Despite the financial hardship, Lu Xun was able to continue his education in Shaoxing's best school, a small establishment run by an upright and dedicated scholar. There, as in all Chinese schools of the time, he had to memorize the Confucian classics, and latterly write essays to expound their teachings. The education also included writing verses and couplets in classical Chinese. This literary language, similar in status to Latin in medieval Europe, was in fact the only language that pupils were required to read and write. A literature in the spoken language, known as *baihua*, did exist, but traditionally it was used only for popular fiction. Lu Xun also read those novels privately in his boyhood, but the particular attraction for him was their illustrations: his most absorbing hobby was tracing and copying them. Out of this interest in the graphic art grew his support of the socialist woodcut movement in the 1930s.

Lu Xun's first step outside this provincial world came in 1898, when he enrolled as a student of the Naval Academy in Nanjing. This was not considered a good choice, but the new military schools set up by the Qing government had the advantage of providing a small stipend in addition to charging no fees. Since the aim of the training was to catch up with the European powers, foreign languages were taught from the outset. At the Naval Academy Lu Xun started to learn English; when in 1899 he switched to the Army School of Mines and Railways he had to drop English for German. His classes there introduced him to the natural sciences, and his extracurricular reading acquainted him with the revolution in political thought and the humanities that by then was well under way in China. Even wider

宜大受打擊，從此意志消沈，更染上鴉片毒癮，死於1896年。父親死時魯迅年方十五，卻深深感受到奇恥大辱，在後來的著作中更表示當時從人情冷暖中看透了「世人的真面目」。對於同鄉中人，亦少了一分善意；這一點在魯迅的小說中亦有具體的表現。

不過，生活雖然艱苦，但魯迅仍能就讀於紹興最好的私塾，背誦四書五經學寫八股文章以外，還學做舊詩對聯，打下古文根基。當時白話文只見於流行小說，難登大雅之堂，魯迅小時候雖亦暗地裏看過，但最教他感興趣的卻在於小說中的插圖；魯迅後來更以蒐集白話小說插圖為最大嗜好。魯迅也正因為自己對平面藝術的愛好而對1930年代鼓吹社會主義的木刻版畫運動大力支持。

魯迅1898年入讀南京水師學堂，是他踏出家鄉的第一步。雖然這在時下眼光看來並非明智之舉，但清政府辦的這個水師學堂不單免收學費，更為學員提供津貼。設立水師學堂既然是為了在海軍實力方面趕上歐洲列強，學堂一開始也就設有外語科目。魯迅原先在水師學堂學習英語，後來在1899年轉往江南陸師學堂附設的礦路學堂，就改為學習德語。魯迅就讀於礦路學堂期間除了初次修讀自然科學學科以外，還從課餘讀物中接觸到當時已席捲中國的政治及人

horizons opened up when he went on for further study in Japan on graduation in 1902, again at government expense. The occupation of Beijing by foreign forces sent to relieve the siege of the Legation Quarter in 1900 had finally persuaded the Manchu court that wholesale reform was inevitable, and because of its proximity Japan was the first choice for students to go and learn advanced skills.

For Lu Xun the first stage of education in Japan, at a Tokyo language school, was not very strenuous. He had ample leisure to read, write, and attend meetings of radical political societies. In published essays he expressed patriotic sentiments, and also attempted to spread scientific knowledge; one of his endeavours was translating Jules Verne's science-fiction (from a Japanese version). It was at this time that he took up his life-long habit of reading and writing well into the night, smoking one cigarette after another. In 1903 he cut off his queue, partly to make life in Japan easier, partly as a gesture to signify the end of subservience to Manchu rule.

When his language course came to an end, Lu Xun should have gone on to study mining and metallurgy, but university places were scarce, and he chose instead to take up medicine. One of his teachers recommended this course because medicine had led the breakthrough of modern science in Japan, and could do the same in China; a personal reason for Lu Xun was that he blamed the death of his father on the unscientific doctoring he received at home. As it turned out, that choice was a bad one. At Sendai University, where he enrolled, he was far from all his Chinese friends, felt himself the object of contempt as a Chinese, and found the method of instruction exhausting and deadening. He withdrew in his second year, returned to Tokyo, and registered at the German Institute, where he could attend classes or not as he pleased. He was now resolved to take literature as his vocation, to "cure minds" instead of bodies.

文學科思潮。魯迅1902年官費留學日本，就更眼界大開。1900年八
國聯軍攻陷北京，使滿清政府終於意識到改革勢在必行。日本毗鄰
中國，也就成為中國留學生學習西方先進技術的首選之地。

　　魯迅入讀東京弘文學院之初功課不多，也就有充裕的課餘時間
閱讀寫作並且參加激進的政治組織；所發表的文章除了抒發愛國情
懷之外，還志在傳播科學知識，致力於 (根據日語譯本) 翻譯凡爾納
的科幻小說。徹夜讀書寫作、煙不離手的習慣，也正是在這時期養
成。魯迅1903年把辮子剪掉，除了是到了日本入鄉隨俗之外，也在
於表示不再臣服於滿清的統治。

　　魯迅在弘文學院畢業之後，本應繼續進修礦務冶金，但礙於大
學學位有限，唯有轉而學習西醫。他的一位日本老師勸他學醫，原
因是新醫學對日本維新大有幫助，相信對中國也理應發揮同樣功
效。但魯迅學醫還有個人的動機，就是他一直認為父親的死實為中
醫所誤。但後來卻證實對魯迅來說，學醫實非明智之舉。在他學習
西醫的仙台醫學專科學校，他不但遠離中國友人，自己的中國人身
分又飽遭歧視，更發現醫科教學沈重而刻板；於是學醫學了一年，
第二年就退學返回東京，進當地的德語學院修讀德語，但僅隨興之
所致選修部分課程。這時魯迅已下定決心以文學創作為職志，治療
國人的心靈了。

In the summer of that year, 1906, he returned to Shaoxing and went through a marriage ceremony with one Zhu An, a bride whom he had not seen, chosen for him by his mother. This marriage was against his will, but in family matters he was very traditional, and would not defy his widowed mother's wishes. Zhu An's family was of comparable social standing to Lu Xun's own, with the unfortunate consequence that, as custom decreed, its daughters were instructed in domestic duties but not taught to read, and had their feet bound. Both those things were tokens of feudalism to Lu Xun, and effectively he rejected her as a wife, though he supported her as a member of his household. He even referred to her as his mother's wife, not his own.

Having gone back to Tokyo with all despatch, Lu Xun put into operation the plan for his first literary enterprise, a magazine significantly named *New Life*. He had as collaborators his younger brother Zhou Zuoren, who joined him in Japan, and two fellow students. Unfortunately the promised finances failed to materialize, and the magazine never appeared. However, he was able to publish his prepared essays elsewhere. The reach of his ambition as a commentator can be gathered from the titles: "The History of Man," "The Power of Mara Poetry," "The Lessons of the History of Science," and "The Lopsided Development of Civilization." Taken as a whole, these essays display a deep scepticism about the motives and breadth of mental horizons of those who were then advocating reform in China. This scepticism, verging on instinctive hostility, would persist in his attitude to all establishment figures in later life. On the positive side, hope is expressed in the free-thinking, free-speaking superior individuals whose emergence the theory of evolution seemed to guarantee. They would light the way to a higher stage of civilization, but they would meet with strong resistance as they went about their task.

As his second venture Lu Xun published in 1909 a collection

　　1906年夏天，魯迅回到故鄉紹興，跟素未謀面的朱安女士結婚。這純粹是母親一手包辦的婚姻，雖然魯迅並不願意，但在家事上魯迅卻十分傳統，因此絕不會違抗寡母之命。朱安與魯迅可算門當戶對，只可惜在大家閨秀的傳統下，朱安只知料理家務；更不識字，兼纏足。在魯迅看來，不識字與纏足兩點，正是封建制度餘孽；他視朱安為家庭成員，實際上卻從不把她當作妻子看待，甚至稱之為母親之妻，與自己毫無關係。

　　魯迅匆匆趕回東京之後，就馬上開展個人的文藝事業，辦起雜誌來，並且語重深長，將雜誌命名為《新生》。跟他一起辦雜誌的還有其弟周作人，以及另外兩位同學。可惜後來答應出資者未能兌現承諾，雜誌的計劃唯有胎死腹中。不過，他為雜誌預備的文章卻找到發表的園地。從《人之歷史》、《摩羅詩力說》、《科學史教篇》、《文化偏至論》等論文題目，亦足見魯迅作為評論家的不凡抱負。總的來說，這些論文在在表現出魯迅對當時鼓吹改革者動機與識見抱有極大的懷疑。這種跡近本能仇視的懷疑意識，在魯迅日後對當權派的態度中亦始終揮之不去。至於論文樂觀的一面，則寄望於思想開放而又敢言的優秀人才；根據進化觀點，他們似是注定要出現的一群；他們將為更高層次的文化發展指引前路，雖然在達成使命的路上他們將要遇到極大的障礙。

　　魯迅第二部作品是1909年發表的《域外小說集》，這部小說集裏

entitled *Stories from Abroad*. Translated by his brother and himself, these short stories were drawn mostly from the literature of "oppressed peoples" of Eastern Europe, the biggest contingent being from Russia. A large number of copies were printed, but only about twenty sold. Neither the selection nor the type of classical language in which they were rendered appealed to the public. So this undertaking was also a failure. It was as a disappointed young man that Lu Xun returned to China in the same year, driven by economic necessity.

Back in his home province of Zhejiang, Lu Xun relied on the natural sciences he had studied in Nanjing and Sendai to teach school, first in Hangzhou then in Shaoxing. He was not very happy in Hangzhou, and was even less so in Shaoxing. His feeling of frustration in Shaoxing was such that he wrote in a letter in January 1911 that he would not mind if all those in power and office there "drowned in a flood." When Shaoxing went over to the revolutionaries in November 1911, the improvement was only temporary, as the new military governor soon adopted the style of his imperial predecessors. Lu Xun's bitter comment was that the greatest benefit the revolution brought him was that he was relieved of the embarrassment of not having a queue.

In fact the revolution did bring him one very material benefit: it rescued him from his provincial backwater. The new republic had to set up a bureaucracy staffed by men of modern education. As one such, Lu Xun secured an appointment in the fledgling Ministry of Education, situated in Nanjing, in February 1912. When the ministry moved to Beijing, he followed, in May 1912. He was to stay in the capital until 1926. Cai Yuanpei, the first Minister of Education, and also Lu Xun's patron, was a man of ideas and vision, but he soon resigned, and Lu Xun had nothing but contempt for his numerous successors. Like most of his colleagues, he kept his head down, and devoted a large part of his office time to harmless hobbies in order to avoid suspicion in the intrigue-ridden capital. Having left his wife

的作品由其弟與他執筆翻譯，內容是東歐「被壓迫民族」的文學作品；其中主要源於俄羅斯。這部小說集雖然印量不少，但最終卻只能售出二十本左右。無論小說題材以至小說所用的古文，對一般讀者毫無吸引力。因此，第二次嘗試亦以失敗告終。出於經濟的考慮，年輕的魯迅唯有帶着失望的心情於同年回國。

回到家鄉之後，魯迅以其在南京和日本所學，先後在杭州與紹興兩地中學教授自然科學。但魯迅在杭州的經歷並不愉快，紹興的情況就更糟，從他在1911年1月寫的一封信中，更可見他的失落之情：「上自士大夫，下至台隸，……湮以洪水可也」。1911年11月革命軍進佔紹興之後，情況雖有改善，但亦只是曇花一現；新軍政府都督隨即擺起前清皇朝的排場。魯迅自嘲道革命為他帶來的最大好處，只在於免去他剪掉辮子的尷尬。

但革命確實為魯迅帶來好處，就是讓他遠離落後的故鄉。新成立的國民政府當時亟需物色受過現代教育的人才，而魯迅正具備這樣的條件，於是在1912年2月就獲得教育部的一份差事；後來更於同年5月隨教育部遷往北京，並一直留在北京，直至1926年。教育部首任部長蔡元培是魯迅的贊助人，雖然極有理想抱負，但不久也被逼辭了職。他的繼任人魯迅沒有一個放在眼內；魯迅也像部裏的同僚一樣不問世事，在辦公時間寄情文玩，以逃避國民政府監視者的耳目。魯迅與在紹興的妻子分隔兩地，過着獨身的生活，只跟與他有

behind in Shaoxing, he led a bachelor existence, mixing only with a few friends from his province and from his student days. In terms of activity the years that followed were fallow, but his extensive reading in ancient Chinese literature, his collating of texts and copying of stele inscriptions, endowed him with formidable erudition that he was able to put to good use later. His high salary also allowed him to make his family a comfortable allowance. About his only personal indulgence was the purchase of books.

Lu Xun was drawn out of his isolation by the arrival of his brother Zhou Zuoren in Beijing in 1917 and the launching of the New Literature movement shortly thereafter. He secured a position for Zhou Zuoren at Peking University through his connection with Cai Yuanpei, the new head of the university. Peking University became the powerhouse to overturn "feudalism" in thought and create a new literature in the spoken language along Western lines. Lu Xun was recruited to the brotherhood because of Zhou Zuoren's membership. His first contribution to the new guard's flagship magazine *New Youth* was in the form of a short story. For his model he resorted to the Russian authors he had translated in 1909. He signed this story, "A Madman's Diary," with the penname "Lu Xun," which then became his new persona: he quickly shed his identity of a civil servant for that of a writer. A stream of short stories, essays, translations and scholarly works came from his pen — or rather his brush, for that is what he always wrote with. From 1923, when his first collection of short stories came out, he published on average close to two books a year up to his death in 1936.

Growing fame brought new opportunities. From 1920 he taught part-time at Peking University and other colleges, and edited small magazines as stables for young writers and translators. At the same time he retained his post at the ministry, though he put in little time there. When he was relieved of his post in 1925, it was not for neglect,

同鄉或同學之誼的人來往。雖然在北京一直韜光養晦，但魯迅卻能善用時間鑽研古籍，並且藉着抄古書古碑，使學問大有進境，日後更大派用場。教育部優厚的薪俸，也足以讓他的家人過着寬裕的生活。他唯一的花費只在於買書。

魯迅孤立無援的困境，随着1917年周作人到了北京以及隨後不久發生的新文學運動而得到解脫。當時蔡元培出任北京大學校長，魯迅藉着與蔡元培的關係為周作人在北京大學覓得一份差事。北大已成為推翻封建參照西方模式提倡白話文學的大本營，魯迅亦因周作人是運動一分子而加入其行列。魯迅首次交該運動代表刊物《新青年》發表的是一部短篇小說，所根據的是他曾於1909年翻譯過的俄國作家作品。他把這部短篇小說命名為《狂人日記》，並署名「魯迅」。「魯迅」這個筆名，也給他帶來了一個新面目，而他自己也由公務員搖身一變而成了一名作家。此後在他的筆下，也就是他所慣用的毛筆之下，產生出連串短篇小說、論文、翻譯以及學術著作。1923年，他的第一部短篇小說集問世；自此之後，他每年平均發表接近兩部著作，這情況一直維持至他1936年去世為止。

有了名氣，機會亦隨之而來。魯迅從1920年起更在北京大學及其他院校兼任教職，還編過好幾本小雜誌，作為培養年青作家及譯者的園地。他同時繼續任職於教育部，但卻少花時間在部裏。他1925年給解除教育部的職務，並非因為玩忽職守，而是因為在北京

but because he publicly sided with the students of the Women's Normal College in their conflict with their principal. The personal element in his partisanship was that he had fallen in love with one of the chief student rebels. Her name was Xu Guangping, and she was then aged twenty-seven.

To explain Lu Xun's domestic situation, he had bought a large compound in Beijing in 1919. His whole family — mother, wife, two brothers with their wives and children — all moved there from Shaoxing. But a sudden rupture with his brother Zhou Zuoren in 1923 made Lu Xun move out, and when he became friendly with Xu Guangping he was living with his mother and wife in a small house he had bought elsewhere. After Xu Guangping satisfied herself that Lu Xun's marriage was an empty one, she embarked on an affair by correspondence with him: the letters they exchanged were published with some revisions in 1933. By the end of 1925 they were committed to each other, but it was not until 1927 that they set up home together, in Shanghai. Thereafter Xu Guangping was Lu Xun's acknowledged "wife," though no divorce from Zhu An had taken place.

Lu Xun's departure from Beijing in 1926 was occasioned by anxiety over personal safety as well as domestic considerations. On 18 March garrison troops had fired on a student demonstration, with great loss of life. Lu Xun's condemnation of this outrage was the most powerful of those published, and he was put on the government blacklist. He left the capital for the south, accepting an invitation to teach at the university in Xiamen (Amoy). He stayed only briefly there before moving in January 1927 to Sun Yatsen University in Guangzhou (Canton), where Xu Guangping was. Unfortunately that was not a safe place either, for in April 1927 the Nationalist Party (Guomindang) turned on its Communist erstwhile allies, killing them in the streets. Lu Xun and Xu Guangping repaired to Shanghai in the autumn. In Shanghai the foreign concessions could

女子師範大學師生衝突事件中公開表態支持學生，其中的個人原因是他與女師大一個女生相戀，這個女生就是許廣平，當時二十七歲。

至於魯迅當時家中的狀況，他1919年在北京給家人置下一座大宅，母親弟弟和弟婦侄兒都從紹興搬到大宅中居住。但1923年跟周作人發生齟齬之後，魯迅就自行遷出；魯迅與許廣平相熟之時正與母親及妻子居於他的另一個物業。當許廣平確信魯迅的婚姻名存實亡，二人就以書信展開一段戀情，後來彼此往還的書信略加修改之後，更結成集子於1933年出版。到了1925年，二人已私訂終身；但要到1927年二人才在上海共賦同居。自此之後，許廣平就等於成為魯迅的「妻子」，但魯迅與朱安始終沒有離婚。

魯迅1926年離開北京，除了出於人身安全的考慮以外，還與家事有關。同年3月18日執政府衛隊向示威學生開槍，導致大量人命傷亡。魯迅以當時最嚴厲的言辭譴責是次暴行，於是給官方列入了黑名單。他應廈門大學之邀離京南下往該校任教。他在廈門只作短暫逗留，然後在1927年往廣州中山大學，與身在該校的許廣平會合。可惜廣州也不安全，1927年4月國民黨對前度盟友共產黨倒戈相向，並公然在街上殺共產黨人。魯迅和許廣平於是在同年秋天前往上

always be a refuge in times of trouble. Lu Xun stayed there the rest of his life.

Lu Xun's career as a writer of fiction proper had ended with the publication of his second volume of short stories in 1926. For the purposes of this volume the last period of his life can be presented more briefly. Having lost hope in the Nationalist Party as an agent of progress, he gave his support to the beleaguered Communist Party, which seemed to have the right ideas. He lent his name to communist front organizations, the one in which he was most deeply involved being the League of Leftwing Writers (1930–1935). He had already mastered the art of the polemical essay, known as *zawen*, and it was that form of literature that he practised almost exclusively in his last years, commenting on current affairs and cultural matters. When first published in magazines these *zawen* were signed with different pennames, but when reprinted in collections they bore the name "Lu Xun." Hence he was always in the public eye. When in 1929 and 1932 he took trips to Beijing to see his mother, he gave lectures to packed audiences at universities. As an open dissident he could well have been arrested, or simply assassinated, but he was protected by his fame. By that time Lu Xun was a household name in China.

Lu Xun's last year of life was painful for two reasons. The disease of tuberculosis that he had suffered from intermittently returned with greater virulence, and the League of Leftwing Writers was closed down amid bitter wrangling. He had invested a great deal of emotional capital in the League, and he resisted its closure, although he had deeply resented the behaviour of the party cadres who ran it. This last act of defiance was typical of his refusal to be subservient to any rule, and it was probably that same independent spirit that earned him the tribute, in a banner draped over his coffin after he finally succumbed to his disease in October 1936, of "The Soul of the Nation." His funeral cortege was joined by thousands.

海；當地的外國租界在當時可算是亂世中的避難所；魯迅就是在當地度過餘生的。

魯迅的小說寫作生涯，隨着他的第二部短篇小說集於1926年出版，也就告一段落。為配合本書的編排，魯迅一生的晚期在下文的介紹可以從簡。當魯迅對國民黨救國的希望幻滅之後，就轉而寄望於共產黨，因為該黨至少有合理的主張。他更為左翼組織擔任代言人，左翼作家聯盟 (1930–1935) 就是他最活躍的左翼組織。這時，雜文一類辯論文章已是魯迅的拿手好戲，而雜文也正是魯迅晚年寫得最多的體裁，內容包括時事以及有關文化的課題。這些雜文最初在雜誌發表時往往冠以不同的筆名，後來結集重印時就都用「魯迅」之名，所以魯迅也就成為一直備受注目的公眾人物。他先後於1929與1932年返回北京探望母親，每次到當地大學演講都座無虛席。身為異見分子而如此大模大樣地出席公開場合，遭逮捕甚至刺殺也有可能。但他的名氣成了他的護身符；當時魯迅在中國已是家喻戶曉的人物。

魯迅生命中的最後一年是痛苦的，原因有二。他所得的肺結核病晚年變本加厲；左翼作家聯盟因成員之間矛盾日深而終於解散。他對左翼作家聯盟費了一番心血，於是公然反對該組織就此結束，雖然他對組織領導的作風深惡痛絕。他一生中最後的這次抗爭行動，貫徹着他不受規條約束的作風；也許正因為他特立獨行的精神，魯迅在1936年10月病逝之後，他的棺木上蓋上「民族魂」的讚語；送殯的人更數以千計。

So ended Lu Xun's personal odyssey from a privileged son of the provincial gentry in the last decades of empire, through the stages of awakened young intellectual, unsuccessful crusader, repressed bureaucrat and literary celebrity, to settle in the final role of scourge of the establishment.

As for his posthumous fate, he was singled out for extravagant praise by Chairman Mao in 1940. Consequently he became an icon in China, for some good and much ill. After the Chinese Communist Party assumed power in 1949 it was a crime even to hint that Lu Xun had any shortcomings, with the result of tainting the whole of his record with the suspicion of falsity. The image projected of him was that of a faithful servant of the cause, ever vigilant, ever righteous. On the other hand, the reading of his actual words kept alive in private minds the spirit of independent thought and distrust of authority. Since the 1980s the mantle of irreproachable modern sage has been lifted, and discussion of Lu Xun's life and work has been relatively free. In reaction to the previous hero worship, there is now some denigration along with continuing, though more realistic, praise. Lu Xun still stands, on his own merits, as the most eminent literary figure in the first half of the twentieth century.

The New-Year Sacrifice and Other Stories

The present selection of stories is taken from the collections *Call to Arms* (1923) and *Wandering* (1926), with the exception of "Forging the Swords," which was completed in 1927 and included in the collection

　　回顧魯迅的過去，從出生於末代皇朝的一個鄉紳之家，逐步蛻變成醒覺的年青知識分子，壯志未酬的鬥士，鬱鬱不得志的官僚，文藝界的明星，到最後成為當權派的剋星，就此終其不平凡的一生。

　　至於魯迅身後，經毛主席在1940年特別點名嘉許之後，魯迅更成為舉國上下的偶像；結果是好的少，壞的多。1949年中國共產黨上台之後，就更不容許任何人批評魯迅；影響所及，反而予人文過飾非的印象。魯迅給塑造成共產主義的忠僕，時刻保持警覺，而又永不犯錯。但另一方面，魯迅的讀者自當心裏明白，魯迅作品的要義，其實正在於獨立的思考和對當權者的不信任。從1980年代起，魯迅其人及其作品，已一改以往神聖不可侵犯的面貌，有關的討論因而變得較為自由。針對過去崇拜英雄的心理，今天已能容納批評的意見；至於溢美之詞，當然也不斷有，但較諸以往則顯得實事求是得多。就其人及其作品而論，魯迅不愧是二十世紀上半葉中國文壇首屈一指的巨匠。

《祝福及其他》

　　本選集中的小說出自《吶喊》(1923)與《彷徨》(1926)兩個集子，只有1927年寫成的《鑄劍》一篇收在《故事新編》(1936)集中。這些小

Old Tales Retold (1936). They do not all correspond to any one ideal conception of "the short story." At the time the earlier ones were written, notions of the difference between short stories, sketches, impressions, and such like, were rather hazy, and Lu Xun personally was not very bothered about genre distinctions. "A Small Incident" and "Village Opera" in particular, especially because they are written in the first person, seem to belong to the category of essay or reminiscence, but they are in fact *embellished* narratives, experience transformed in the mind of the author, and therefore cross the boundary from truth to fiction. "Forging the Swords" is in a class by itself, as it is declaredly the rewriting of a legend, but it is even more obviously an imaginative reconstruction.

The first story in the first collection, "A Madman's Diary," is recognizably a short story in the Russian mode, in that it borrowed its title from Gogol and incorporates structural devices from other Russian authors, but it is untypical of Lu Xun's own stories that followed in that it carries an overt thesis. That was because it was intended as a contribution to the magazine *New Youth*, which was leading a campaign to expose the inhumanity of traditional Chinese culture and replace it with modern humanitarian values. Lu Xun conformably produced a propaganda piece, which nevertheless is disguised with authentic touches of persecution mania.

The keynote of inhumanity in Chinese society resounds in the stories that immediately followed "A Madman's Diary." Kong Yiji, in the story of the same name, is a human wreck thrown up by the classical system of education, derided by the working class into whose ranks he has descended, and denied all understanding and compassion. His life is valued, negatively, by the wine bill he leaves behind: nineteen coppers. And "Medicine" actually takes up an incident cited by the "madman," namely the consumption of fresh human blood in the vain hope of curing tuberculosis. But now the stories are told barely, with

説未必完全符合「短篇小説」的標準。魯迅早期作品寫作之時，何謂短篇小説，何謂短文，何謂隨想，界線仍很模糊；魯迅本人對文學體裁的分類也不大注重。《一件小事》和《社戲》兩篇尤其如此，兩篇都以第一人稱來寫，似乎更接近於散文或回憶錄的體裁，但其中的敘述部分經過一番修飾，而有關經驗部分更在作者心中經過轉化，因此已超越寫實而進入小説虛構的境界。《鑄劍》一篇尤其別具一格，因為名曰故事新編，但實際上卻明明是富於想像力的再創造。

第一個集子的第一篇小説《狂人日記》，篇名出自果戈理同名小説，其中不少結構手法取材於其他俄國作家，顯然以俄國短篇小説為藍本；但其中論題明確，跟集子中其他魯迅作品有所不同。這是由於該小説當初發表於《新青年》，時值該刊發起揭露中國不人道的封建傳統，並提倡以新時代的人道價值觀取而代之；魯迅樂於為文宣傳，但其中卻以逼真的「迫害狂」患者口吻作為掩飾。

集子中的其他小説作品，也貫徹着中國封建社會吃人的主題。《孔乙己》的主角孔乙己，是科舉制度下的犧牲品；淪為低下層卻遭低下層的揶揄，得不到半點同情和諒解；一生的價值只等於最後拖欠的酒錢 —— 十九個錢。《藥》更進一步講述《狂人日記》中提及的一件事，就是以人血醫治癆病。但至此魯迅的故事都變得平鋪直敘，

no themes stated, and so it was to be with all that followed. Though several featured an "I" narrator, this "I" is not to be mistaken for the spokesman of the author. He is almost always an "unreliable narrator."

"Medicine," only the third in the series, already marks Lu Xun's advance to full maturity in the practice of the art of the short story. The absence of stage directions to the four scenes in which the story of the end of a young life is told, or two young lives if we include that of the executed revolutionary, makes the reader actively participate in the enactment of the episodes, and the perspective shifts progressively from the dim consciousness of the poor father in the first scene, to the brightly lit stage of the teahouse in the middle scenes, to culminate in the long view of the desolate graveyard, which finally dissolves in the flight of the crow to the far horizon. The flight of the crow seems to be imbued with more than natural significance, but it is another sign of maturity that its implied symbolism is ambiguous.

A less obvious but important accomplishment of "Medicine" is the creation of minor characters. The regular customers of the teahouse have only bit parts, but the typicality of their one-line remarks makes them spring instantly to life. Such characters come into their own in "Storm in a Teacup." This story is in much lighter vein. It is an amusing treatment of the pigtail theme at village level, occasioned by the actual, though very brief, restoration of the Qing emperor to the throne by the "Pigtail General" Zhang Xun in 1917. Its artistic highpoint is the creation of idiosyncratic manners of speech for each of the characters: dialogue occupies an unusually high proportion of the text. The success of this rural counter-idyll no doubt encouraged Lu Xun to embark on his township counter-idyll, "The True Story of Ah Q," to which a companion volume to this is devoted.

In between these two came "My Old Home," which turns from

不再有明確的主題，其他小說作品亦如是。雖然好幾部作品中有
「我」作為敘述者，但這個「我」卻並不能當做作者的代言人看待；他
畢竟是個「不可靠的敘述者」。

　　《藥》雖然只是集子中的第三部短篇小說，但卻標誌着魯迅短篇
小說技巧已臻圓熟。全篇分四個場景，交代兩個年青人 (若將遭處決
的年青革命黨也計算在內) 生命的隕滅；從描述可憐老父模糊意識狀
態的第一幕，轉移到以茶館為舞台焦點的中段，到後來孤墳的遠景
以至借烏鴉飛向遠處天空作結的最後一幕，其中全不用舞台指示，
讓讀者如同親身參與故事情節的推演。烏鴉高飛一節，似乎已超越
了以自然景物作為襯托的表現手法；但畢竟言有盡而意無窮，也是
作者趨於成熟的又一表現。

　　至於《藥》另一較少引起注意但卻同樣重要的成就，要算是對小
人物的塑造。故事中段的茶館常客雖然只是閑角，但各具特色的對
白卻足以令人物躍然紙上。《風波》中的小人物也別具一格，故事的
調子則輕鬆得多，講的是農村裏的一場辮子風波；故事中還輕描淡
寫，提及1917年「辮子將軍」張勳復辟一事。全篇藝術表現手法最突
出之處，在於小說人物各自有獨特的說話方式；故事中對白部分也
佔有異常高的比例。這個以農村為背景的反面故事大獲成功，對魯
迅後來寫《阿Q正傳》這個以城市為背景的反面故事，無疑產生了鼓
舞的作用；本選集則以姊妹篇的方式跟《阿Q正傳》的英漢對照版一
同面世。

　　《故鄉》是在上述兩篇小說之間推出的作品，但卻不再是對現實

observation of the outside world to introspection of the inner world of a person very like the author, though not identical with him. It is a cleverly composed reflection on memory deceived and dreams dissolved. Socially-conscious criticism has concentrated on the sad fate of the peasant Runtu, the lively boyhood companion of the narrator reduced to numbness in adulthood by life's burdens, but the focus is in fact much wider than that. Disappointment, deterioration and disillusion are felt to be a common fate, and though the story ends on an upbeat note, the hope which comforts the narrator has only a flickering flame.

The five stories starting with "The New-Year Sacrifice" in this selection belong to Lu Xun's second collection of fiction, *Wandering*. The setting of this collection shifts from the country village to the city, and the characters belong mostly to the educated class. "The New-Year Sacrifice" forms a link with the *Call to Arms* stories in that the inset story is of an unfortunate peasant woman, but the narrator is an educated man who seals her unhappiness by confirming what he knows to be her superstitious fears. This well-meaning but weak-minded narrator belongs to the type which is central to this second collection. They are intellectuals who have imbibed lofty ideals with a modern education, but when their hopes are disappointed find themselves disoriented "superfluous men," like many a hero of previous Russian fiction. The Chinese title of the collection, *Panghuang*, more precisely means wavering or vacillating, unable to decide which course to take. So we see in several stories a history of compromise, backsliding, and even betrayal of principles. In "In the Tavern" the central character is of a sensitive and sentimental kind, who likens himself to a fly that flies off when disturbed but only completes a small circle before returning to its starting point. In "The Misanthrope" the central character is still an active radical when first seen, but when driven to the wall he does an abrupt about-face, and ends his days in

世界的客觀描述，而是對個人內心世界的深入剖析；這一個人跟作者本人十分相似，但卻並不完全相同。全篇以巧妙的手法回憶過去，包含着模糊的記憶和破滅的夢境。至於對社會的控訴，則主要在於農民閏土的坎坷命運 —— 故事敘述者的這位童年朋友給現實生活的重擔壓得透不過氣來，但故事重點其實遠不止於此。失望、衰敗、理想的幻滅，在作者看來其實是所有人命運的寫照；雖然故事結尾筆調略見積極，但教敘述者感到欣慰的希望卻其實是渺茫的。

本選集中以《祝福》為首的五篇小說，最初收錄在魯迅的第二部短篇小說集《彷徨》中。這五篇小說的故事背景由農村變為城市，小說人物亦多屬知識分子。《祝福》一篇與上一小說集《吶喊》中作品的共通之處，在於一方面以一農村女子的不幸遭遇為內容，另一方面敘述者則以知識分子的身分，斷定女子出於迷信的恐懼是造成她不幸的罪魁禍首。心地善良卻又意志薄弱，正是魯迅第二部小說集中所有敘述者的特點。這些敘述者都受過新時代的教育，胸懷崇高的理想，但當理想破滅，又都變成了「多餘的人」，與過去不少俄羅斯小說的主角同一命運。小說集名為「彷徨」，其中幾篇作品的人物也往往表現出妥協、反覆、甚至違背原則的行徑。《在酒樓上》一篇，中心人物屬多愁善感之類，更以蒼蠅自況，意即給人嚇飛了，亦不過繞一個小圈子，依舊返回原地。至於《孤獨者》一篇，故事主角起初還是個特立獨行的異類，但後來走投無路卻一反常態，變得虛偽

falsity and dissipation. Both these characters disclose themselves to a friend who is the "I" narrator of the story, while Juansheng in "Regret for the Past" tells his own story. His illusions are in the private sphere of romantic union, and when disillusion sets in he is a less unfortunate victim than the girlfriend whom he persuades to share them, but his conclusion is like that of the others, that he must in future take "oblivion and falsehood" as his guide.

Despite this similarity in theme, these stories are quite different in structure and tone: each is a fresh experiment in the writer's craft. The gloom that they share does not pervade the whole collection, either. For example, the attempt of a struggling writer to produce a story in conformity with market tastes in "A Happy Family" is treated with humorous irony.

The undercurrent of pain and passion in *Call to Arms* is no longer evident in *Wandering*. The latter is more analytical and contemplative. It addressed the life style of the present day rather than the heritage of the past. Subsequently Lu Xun gave up writing fiction altogether in favour of dealing directly with contemporary issues in essays.

David Pollard
Research Centre for Translation
The Chinese University of Hong Kong

起來，更過着放浪形骸的生活。上述兩個故事的主角，都有一個他們相識的「我」來敘述他們的故事；《傷逝》一篇主角涓生的故事，則由主角親自來講，並以主角對愛情的幻想為內容。到後來愛情的理想終告幻滅，受傷害最深的卻並非主角，而是主角的戀人，她當初正因為相信主角才對彼此的愛情存有幻想。最後主角的結論「用遺忘和說謊做我的前導」，亦與本選集中其他故事大同小異。

雖然本選集中故事的主題有共通之處，但結構與調子卻各有不同：每一篇都是作者寫作手法上的新嘗試，而沈鬱的調子雖然在集中頗為普遍，但亦不見得每篇如是。《幸福的家庭》一篇講一個作家努力要寫出迎合市場口味的作品，反諷之餘亦可見作者的幽默。

《吶喊》各故事中所蘊含的一股痛苦與激情的暗流，在《彷徨》中已不復見。《彷徨》的故事較着重內省與分析，描寫的是當時社會上的所見所聞，而不是過去遺傳的人和事。魯迅本人後來也棄寫小說而改寫以當代生活為背景的散文。

香港中文大學翻譯研究中心
卜立德撰、譚柏山譯

《狂人日記》 **"A Madman's Diary"**

他們會吃人，就未必不會吃我。 (插圖：裘沙、王偉君)

They eat human beings, so they may eat me.

(Illustration by Qiu Sha and Wang Weijun)

《孔乙己》"Kong Yiji"

孔乙己爭辯道：「……竊書！……讀書人的事，能算偷麼？」……引得眾人都
哄笑起來……　　　　　　　　　　　　　　　　　　（插圖：裘沙、王偉君）

He protested, "Taking books ... for a scholar ... can't be counted as stealing."...
which soon had everybody roaring with laughter....

（Illustration by Qiu Sha and Wang Weijun）

《藥》"Medicine"

華大媽忙看他兒子和別人的墳……心裏忽然感到一種不足和空虛……

(插圖：裘沙、王偉君)

Little Shuan's mother looked round and found her own son's grave....
Suddenly she had a sense of futility....

(Illustration by Qiu Sha and Wang Weijun)

《祝福》 **"The New-Year Sacrifice"**

柳媽……乾枯的小眼睛一看祥林嫂的額角，又釘住她的眼。

(插圖：裘沙、王偉君)

Amah Liu's ... small beady eyes swept Xianglin's Wife's forehead, then
fastened on her eyes.　　　　　(Illustration by Qiu Sha and Wang Weijun)

狂 人 日 記

A Madman's Diary

A MADMAN'S DIARY

Two brothers, whose names I need not mention here, were both good friends of mine in high school; but after a separation of many years we gradually lost touch. Some time ago I happened to hear that one of them was seriously ill, and since I was going back to my old home I broke my journey to call on them. I saw only one, however, who told me that the invalid was his younger brother.

"I appreciate your coming such a long way to see us," he said, "but my brother recovered some time ago and has gone elsewhere to take up an official post." Then, laughing, he produced two volumes of his brother's diary, saying that from these the nature of his past illness could be seen and there was no harm in showing them to an old friend. I took the diary away, read it through, and found that he had suffered from a form of persecution complex. The writing was most confused and incoherent, and he had made many wild statements; moreover he had omitted to give any dates, so that only by the colour of the ink and the differences in the writing could one tell that it was not all written at one time. Certain sections, however, were not altogether disconnected, and I have copied out a part to serve as a subject for medical research. I have not altered a single illogicality in the diary and have changed only the names, even though the people referred to are all country folk, unknown to the world and of no

狂人日記

　　某君昆仲，今隱其名，皆余昔日在中學校時良友；分隔多年，消息漸闕。日前偶聞其一大病；適歸故鄉，迂道往訪，則僅晤一人，言病者其弟也。勞君遠道來視，然已早癒，赴某地候補矣。因大笑，出示日記二冊，謂可見當日病狀，不妨獻諸舊友。持歸閱一過，知所患蓋「迫害狂」之類。語頗錯雜無倫次，又多荒唐之言；亦不着月日，惟墨色字體不一，知非一時所書。間亦有略具聯絡者，今撮錄一篇，以供醫家研究。記中語誤，一字不易；惟人名雖皆村

consequence. As for the title, it was chosen by the diarist himself after his recovery, and I did not change it.

I

Tonight the moon is very bright.

I have not seen it for over thirty years, so today when I saw it I felt in unusually high spirits. I begin to realize that during the past thirty-odd years I have been in the dark; but now I must be extremely careful. Otherwise why should the Zhaos' dog have looked at me twice?

I have reason for my fear.

II

Tonight there is no moon at all, I know that this is a bad omen. This morning when I went out cautiously, Mr. Zhao had a strange look in his eyes, as if he were afraid of me, as if he wanted to murder me. There were seven or eight others who discussed me in a whisper. And they were afraid of my seeing them. So, indeed, were all the people I passed. The fiercest among them grinned at me; whereupon I shivered from head to foot, knowing that their preparations were complete.

I was not afraid, however, but continued on my way. A group of children in front were also discussing me, and the look in their eyes

人，不為世間所知，無關大體，然亦悉易去。至於書名，則本人癒後所題，不復以改也。七年四月二日識。

今天晚上，很好的月光。

我不見他，已是三十多年；今天見了，精神分外爽快。才知道以前的三十多年，全是發昏；然而須十分小心。不然，那趙家的狗，何以看我兩眼呢？

我怕得有理。

今天全沒月光，我知道不妙。早上小心出門，趙貴翁的眼色便怪：似乎怕我，似乎想害我。還有七八個人，交頭接耳的議論我，又怕我看見。一路上的人，都是如此。其中最兇的一個人，張着嘴，對我笑了一笑；我便從頭直冷到腳跟，曉得他們佈置，都已妥當了。

我可不怕，仍舊走我的路。前面一夥小孩子，也在那裏議論

was just like that in Mr. Zhao's while their faces too were ghastly pale. I wondered what grudge these children could have against me to make them behave like this. I could not help calling out, "Tell me!" But then they ran away.

I wonder what grudge Mr. Zhao has against me, what grudge the people on the road have against me. I can think of nothing except that twenty years ago I trod on Mr. Gu Jiu's old ledgers, and Mr. Gu was most displeased. Although Mr. Zhao does not know him, he must have heard talk of this and decided to avenge him, thus he is conspiring against me with the people on the road. But then what of the children? At that time they were not yet born, so why should they eye me so strangely today, as if they were afraid of me, as if they wanted to murder me? This really frightens me, it is so bewildering and upsetting. I know. They must have learned this from their parents!

III

I can't sleep at night. Everything requires careful consideration if one is to understand it.

Those people, some of whom have been pilloried by the magistrate, slapped in the face by the local gentry, had their wives taken away by bailiffs or their parents driven to suicide by creditors, never looked as frightened and as fierce then as they did yesterday.

The most extraordinary thing was that woman on the street yesterday who was spanking her son. "Little devil!" She cried. "I'm so angry I could eat you!" Yet all the time it was me she was looking at. I

我；眼色也同趙貴翁一樣，臉色也都鐵青。我想我同小孩子有甚麼
仇，他也這樣。忍不住大聲説，「你告訴我！」他們可就跑了。

我想：我同趙貴翁有甚麼仇，同路上的人又有甚麼仇；只有廿
年以前，把古久先生的陳年流水簿子，踹了一腳，古久先生很不高
興。趙貴翁雖然不認識他，一定也聽到風聲，代抱不平；約定路上
的人，同我作冤對。但是小孩子呢？那時候，他們還沒有出世，何
以今天也睜着怪眼睛，似乎怕我，似乎想害我。這真教我怕，教我
納罕而且傷心。

我明白了。這是他們娘老子教的！

晚上總是睡不着。凡事須得研究，才會明白。

他們——也有給知縣打枷過的，也有給紳士掌過嘴的，也有衙
役佔了他妻子的，也有老子娘被債主逼死的；他們那時候的臉色，
全沒有昨天這麼怕，也沒有這麼兇。

最奇怪的是昨天街上的那個女人，打他兒子，嘴裏説道，「老子
呀！我要咬你幾口才出氣！」他眼睛卻看着我。我出了一驚，遮掩不

gave a start, unable to hide my alarm. Then all those longtoothed people with livid faces began to hoot with laughter. Old Chen hurried forward and dragged me home.

He dragged me home. The folk at home all pretended not to know me; they had the same look in their eyes as all the others. When I went into the study, they locked me in as if cooping up a chicken or a duck. This incident left me even more bewildered.

A few days ago a tenant of ours from Wolf Cub Village came to report the failure of the crops and told my elder brother that a notorious character in their village had been beaten to death; then some people had taken out his heart and liver, fried them in oil, and eaten them as a means of increasing their courage. When I interrupted, the tenant and my brother both stared at me. Only today have I realized that they had exactly the same look in their eyes as those people outside.

Just to think of it sets me shivering from the crown of my head to the soles of my feet.

They eat human beings, so they may eat me.

I see that the woman's "eat you," the laughter of those longtoothed people with livid faces, and the tenant's story the other day are obviously secret signs. I realize all the poison in their speech, all the daggers in their laughter. Their teeth are white and glistening: they use these teeth to eat men.

Evidently, although I am not a bad man, ever since I trod on Mr. Gu's ledgers it has been touch-and-go with me. They seem to have secrets which I cannot guess, and once they are angry they will call anyone a bad character. I remember when my elder brother taught me to write compositions, no matter how good a man was, if I produced arguments to the contrary he would mark that passage to show his approval; while if I excused evildoers he would say, "Good for

住；那青面獠牙的一夥人，便都哄笑起來。陳老五趕上前，硬把我拖回家中了。

拖我回家，家裏的人都裝作不認識我；他們的眼色，也全同別人一樣。進了書房，便反扣上門，宛然是關了一隻雞鴨。這一件事，越教我猜不出底細。

前幾天，狼子村的佃戶來告荒，對我大哥說，他們村裏的一個大惡人，給大家打死了；幾個人便挖出他的心肝來，用油煎炒了吃，可以壯壯膽子。我插了一句嘴，佃戶和大哥便都看我幾眼。今天才曉得他們的眼光，全同外面的那夥人一模一樣。

想起來，我從頂上直冷到腳跟。

他們會吃人，就未必不會吃我。

你看那女人「咬你幾口」的話，和一夥青面獠牙人的笑，和前天佃戶的話，明明是暗號。我看出他話中全是毒，笑中全是刀。他們的牙齒，全是白厲厲的排着，這就是吃人的傢伙。

照我自己想，雖然不是惡人，自從踹了古家的簿子，可就難說了。他們似乎別有心思，我全猜不出，況且他們一翻臉，便說人是惡人。我還記得大哥教我做論，無論怎樣好人，翻他幾句，他便打

you, that shows originality." How can I possibly guess their secret thoughts — especially when they are ready to eat people?

Everything requires careful consideration if one is to understand it. In ancient times, as I recollect, people often ate human beings, but I am rather hazy about it. I tried to look this up, but my history has no chronology and scrawled all over each page are the words: "Confucian Virtue and Morality." Since I could not sleep anyway, I read intently half the night until I began to see words between the lines. The whole book was filled with the two words — "Eat people."

All these words written in the book, all the words spoken by our tenant, eye me quizzically with an enigmatic smile.

I too am a man, and they want to eat me!

IV

In the morning I sat quietly for some time. Old Chen brought in lunch: one bowl of vegetables, one bowl of steamed fish. The eyes of the fish were white and hard, and its mouth was open just like those people who want to eat human beings. After a few mouthfuls I could not tell whether the slippery morsels were fish or human flesh, so I brought it all up.

I said, "Old Chen, tell my brother that I feel quite suffocated and want to have a stroll in the garden." Old Chen said nothing but went out, and presently he came back and opened the gate.

I did not move, but watched to see how they would treat me, feeling certain that they would not let me go. Sure enough! My elder

上幾個圈；原諒壞人幾句，他便說「翻天妙手」，與眾不同。我那裏猜得到他們的心思，究竟怎樣，況且是要吃的時候。

凡事總須研究，才會明白。古來時常吃人，我也還記得，可是不甚清楚。我翻開歷史一查，這歷史沒有年代，歪歪斜斜的每葉上都寫着「仁義道德」幾個字。我橫豎睡不着，仔細看了半夜，才從字縫裏看出字來，滿本都寫着兩個字是「吃人」！

書上寫着這許多字，佃戶說了這許多話，卻都笑吟吟的睜着怪眼睛看我。

我也是人，他們想要吃我了！

四

早上，我靜坐了一會。陳老五送進飯來，一碗菜，一碗蒸魚；這魚的眼睛，白而且硬，張着嘴，同那一夥想吃人的人一樣。吃了幾筷，滑溜溜的不知是魚是人，便把他兜肚連腸的吐出。

我說「老五，對大哥說，我悶得慌，想到園裏走走。」老五不答應，走了；停一會，可就來開了門。

我也不動，研究他們如何擺佈我；知道他們一定不肯放鬆。果

brother came slowly out, leading an old man. There was a murderous gleam in his eyes, and fearing that I would see it he lowered his head, stealing side-glances at me from behind his glasses.

"You seem very well today," said my brother.

"Yes," said I.

"I have invited Mr. Ho here today to examine you."

"All right," I replied. Actually I knew quite well that this old man was the executioner in disguise! Feeling my pulse was simply a pretext for him to see how fat I was; for this would entitle him to a share of my flesh. Still I was not afraid. Although I do not eat men my courage is greater than theirs. I held out my two fists to see what he would do. The old man sat down, closed his eyes, fumbled for some time, remained motionless for a while; then opened his shifty eyes and said, "Don't let your imagination run away with you. Rest quietly for a few days, and you will be better."

Don't let your imagination run away with you! Rest quietly for a few days! By fattening me of course they'll have more to eat. But what good will it do me? How can it be "better"? The whole lot of them wanting to eat people yet stealthily trying to keep up appearances, not daring to do it outright, was really enough to make me die of laughter. I couldn't help it, I nearly split my sides, I was so amused. I knew that this laughter voiced courage and integrity. Both the old man and my brother turned pale, awed by my courage and integrity.

But my courage just makes them all the more eager to eat me, to acquire some of my courage for themselves. The old man went out of the gate, but before he had gone far he said to my brother in a low voice. "To be eaten at once!" My brother nodded. So you are in it too! This stupendous discovery, though it came as a shock, is no more than I might expect: the accomplice in eating me is my elder brother!

然！我大哥引了一個老頭子，慢慢走來；他滿眼兇光，怕我看出，只是低頭向着地，從眼鏡橫邊暗暗看我。大哥說，「今天你彷彿很好。」我說「是的。」大哥說，「今天請何先生來，給你診一診。」我說「可以！」其實我豈不知道這老頭子是劊子手扮的！無非借了看脈這名目，揣一揣肥瘠：因這功勞，也分一片肉吃。我也不怕；雖然不吃人，膽子卻比他們還壯。伸出兩個拳頭，看他如何下手。老頭子坐着，閉了眼睛，摸了好一會，呆了好一會；便張開他鬼眼睛說，「不要亂想。靜靜的養幾天，就好了。」

不要亂想，靜靜的養！養肥了，他們是自然可以多吃；我有甚麼好處，怎麼會「好了」？他們這群人，又想吃人，又是鬼鬼祟祟，想法子遮掩，不敢直捷下手，真要令我笑死。我忍不住，便放聲大笑起來，十分快活。自己曉得這笑聲裏面，有的是義勇和正氣。老頭子和大哥，都失了色，被我這勇氣正氣鎮壓住了。

但是我有勇氣，他們便越想吃我，沾光一點這勇氣。老頭子跨出門，走不多遠，便低聲對大哥說道，「趕緊吃罷！」大哥點點頭。原來也有你！這一件大發見，雖似意外，也在意中：合夥吃我的人，便是我的哥哥！

The eater of human flesh is my elder brother!

I am the younger brother of an eater of human flesh!

I, who will be eaten by others, am the younger brother of an eater of human flesh!

V

These few days I have been thinking again: suppose that old man were not an executioner in disguise, but a real doctor; he would be nonetheless an eater of human flesh. That book on herbs by his predecessor Li Shizhen states explicitly that men's flesh can be boiled and eaten; how then can he still deny that he eats men?

As for my elder brother, I have also good reason to suspect him. When he was teaching me, he told me himself, "People exchange their sons to eat." And once in discussing a bad man he said that not only did the fellow deserve to be killed, he should "have his flesh eaten and his hide slept on." I was still young at the time, and for quite a while my heart beat faster. That story our tenant from Wolf Cub Village told the other day about eating a man's heart and liver didn't surprise him at all — he kept nodding his head. He is evidently just as cruel as before. Since it is possible to "exchange sons to eat," then anything can be exchanged, anyone can be eaten. In the past I simply listened to his explanations and let it go at that; now I know that when he gave me these explanations, not only was there human fat at the corner of his lips, but his whole heart was set on eating men.

吃人的是我哥哥！

我是吃人的人的兄弟！

我自己被人吃了，可仍然是吃人的人的兄弟！

五

這幾天是退一步想：假使那老頭子不是劊子手扮的，真是醫生，也仍然是吃人的人。他們的祖師李時珍做的「本草甚麼」上，明明寫着人肉可以煎吃；他還能說自己不吃人麼？

至於我家大哥，也毫不冤枉他。他對我講書的時候，親口說過可以「易子而食」；又一回偶然議論起一個不好的人，他便說不但該殺，還當「食肉寢皮」。我那時年紀還小，心跳了好半天。前天狼子村佃戶來說吃心肝的事，他也毫不奇怪，不住的點頭。可見心思是同從前一樣狠。既然可以「易子而食」，便甚麼都易得，甚麼人都吃得。我從前單聽他講道理，也糊塗過去；現在曉得他講道理的時候，不但唇邊還抹着人油，而且心裏滿裝着吃人的意思。

VI

Pitch dark. I don't know whether it is day or night. The Zhaos' dog had started barking again.

The fierceness of a lion, the timidity of a rabbit, the craftiness of a fox....

VII

I know their way: they are not prepared to kill outright, nor would they dare, for fear of the consequences. Instead they have banded together and set traps everywhere, to force me to kill myself. The behaviour of the men and women in the street a few days ago and my elder brother's attitude these last few days make it quite obvious. What they like best is for a man to take off his belt and hang himself from a beam; for then they can enjoy their hearts' desire without being blamed for murder. Naturally that delights them and sets them roaring with laughter. On the other hand, if a man is frightened or worried to death, though that makes him rather thin, they still nod in approval.

They only eat dead flesh! I remember reading somewhere of a hideous beast with an ugly look in its eye called "hyena," which often eats dead flesh. Even the largest bones it crunches into fragments and swallows; the mere thought of this makes your hair stand on end. Hyenas are related to wolves, wolves belong to the canine species.

六

黑漆漆的，不知是日是夜。趙家的狗又叫起來了。

獅子似的兇心，兔子的怯弱，狐狸的狡猾，……

七

我曉得他們的方法，直捷殺了，是不肯的，而且也不敢，怕有
禍祟。所以他們大家連絡，佈滿了羅網，逼我自戕。試看前幾天街
上男女的樣子，和這幾天我大哥的作為，便足可悟出八九分了。最
好是解下腰帶，掛在樑上，自己緊緊勒死；他們沒有殺人的罪名，
又償了心願，自然都歡天喜地的發出一種嗚嗚咽咽的笑聲。否則驚
嚇憂愁死了，雖則略瘦，也還可以首肯幾下。

他們是只會吃死肉的！──記得甚麼書上說，有一種東西，叫
「海乙那」的，眼光和樣子都很難看；時常吃死肉，連極大的骨頭，
都細細嚼爛，嚥下肚子去，想起來也教人害怕。「海乙那」是狼的親

The other day the Zhaos' dog eyed me several times: it is obviously in the plot too as their accomplice. The old man's eyes were cast down, but that did not deceive me.

The most deplorable is my elder brother. He's a man too, so why isn't he afraid, why is he plotting with others to eat me? Does force of habit blind a man to what's wrong? Or is he so heartless that he will knowingly commit a crime?

In cursing man-eaters, I shall start with my brother. In dissuading man-eaters, I shall start with him too.

VIII

Actually such arguments should have convinced them long ago....

Suddenly someone came in. He was only about twenty years old and I did not see his features very clearly. His face was wreathed in smiles, but when he nodded to me his smile didn't seem genuine. I asked him. "Is it right to eat human beings?"

Still smiling, he replied, "When there is no famine how can one eat human beings?"

I realized at once he was one of them; but still I summoned up courage to repeat my question:

"Is it right?"

"What makes you ask such a thing? You really are ... fond of a joke.... It is very fine today."

眷，狼是狗的本家。前天趙家的狗，看我幾眼，可見他也同謀，早已接洽。老頭子眼看着地，豈能瞞得我過。

最可憐的是我的大哥，他也是人，何以毫不害怕；而且合夥吃我呢？還是歷來慣了，不以為非呢？還是喪了良心，明知故犯呢？

我詛咒吃人的人，先從他起頭；要勸轉吃人的人，也先從他下手。

八

其實這種道理，到了現在，他們也該早已懂得，……

忽然來了一個人；年紀不過二十左右，相貌是不很看得清楚，滿面笑容，對了我點頭，他的笑也不像真笑。我便問他，「吃人的事，對麼？」他仍然笑着說，「不是荒年，怎麼會吃人。」我立刻就曉得，他也是一夥，喜歡吃人的；便自勇氣百倍，偏要問他。

「對麼？」

「這等事問他甚麼。你真會……說笑話。……今天天氣很好。」

"It is fine, and the moon is very bright. But I want to ask you: is it right?"

He looked disconcerted and muttered, "No...."

"No? Then why do they still do it?"

"What are you talking about?"

"What am I talking about? They are eating men now in Wolf Cub Village, and you can see it written all over the books, in fresh red ink."

His expression changed. He grew ghastly pale. "It may be so," he said staring at me. "That's the way it's always been...."

"Does that make it right?"

"I refuse to discuss it with you. Anyway, you shouldn't talk about it. It's wrong for anyone to talk about it."

I leaped up and opened my eyes wide, but the man had vanished. I was soaked with sweat. He was much younger than my elder brother, but even so he was in it. He must have been taught by his parents. And I am afraid he has already taught his son; that is why even the children look at me so fiercely.

IX

Wanting to eat men, at the same time afraid of being eaten themselves, they all eye each other with the deepest suspicion.

How comfortable life would be for them if they could rid themselves of such obsessions and go to work, walk, eat and sleep at ease.

天氣是好，月色也很亮了。可是我要問你，「對麼？」

他不以為然了。含含糊糊的答道，「不……」

「不對？他們何以竟吃？！」

「沒有的事……」

「沒有的事？狼子村現吃；還有書上都寫着，通紅斬新！」

他便變了臉，鐵一般青。睜着眼說，「有許有的，這是從來如此……」

「從來如此，便對麼？」

「我不同你講這些道理；總之你不該說，你說便是你錯！」

我直跳起來，張開眼，這人便不見了。全身出了一大片汗。他的年紀，比我大哥小得遠，居然也是一夥；這一定是他娘老子先教的。還怕已經教給他兒子了；所以連小孩子，也都惡狠狠的看我。

九

自己想吃人，又怕被別人吃了，都用着疑心極深的眼光，面面相覷。……

去了這心思，放心做事走路吃飯睡覺，何等舒服。這只是一條

They have only this one step to take. Yet fathers and sons, husbands and wives, brothers, friends, teachers and students, sworn enemies and even strangers, have all joined in this conspiracy, discouraging and preventing each other from taking this step.

X

Early this morning I went to find my elder brother. He was standing outside the hall door looking at the sky when I walked up behind him, standing between him and the door, and addressed him with exceptional poise and politeness:

"Brother, I have something to say to you."

"Go ahead then." He turned quickly towards me, nodding,

"It's nothing much, but I find it hard to say. Brother, probably all primitive people ate a little human flesh to begin with. Later, because their views altered some of them stopped and tried so hard to do what was right that they changed into men, into real men. But some are still eating people — just like reptiles. Some have changed into fish, birds, monkeys, and finally men; but those who make no effort to do what's right are still reptiles. When those who eat men compare themselves with those who don't, how ashamed they must be. Probably much more ashamed than the reptiles are before monkeys.

"In ancient times Yi Ya boiled his son for Jie and Zhou to eat; that is the old story. But actually since the creation of heaven and earth by Pan Gu men have been eating each other, from the time of Yi Ya's son to the time of Xu Xilin, and from the time of Xu Xilin down to the man caught

門檻，一個關頭。他們可是父子、兄弟、夫婦、朋友、師生、仇敵和各不相識的人，都結成一夥，互相勸勉，互相牽掣，死也不肯跨過這一步。

十

大清早，去尋我大哥；他立在堂門外看天，我便走到他背後，攔住門，格外沉靜，格外和氣的對他說，

「大哥，我有話告訴你。」

「你說就是，」他趕緊回過臉來，點點頭。

「我只有幾句話，可是說不出來。大哥，大約當初野蠻的人，都吃過一點人。後來因為心思不同，有的不吃人了，一味要好，便變了人，變了真的人。有的卻還吃，——也同蟲子一樣，有的變了魚、鳥、猴子，一直變到人。有的不要好，至今還是蟲子。這吃人的人比不吃人的人，何等慚愧。怕比蟲子的慚愧猴子，還差得很遠很遠。

「易牙蒸了他兒子，給桀紂吃了，還是一直從前的事。誰曉得從盤古開闢天地以後，一直吃到易牙的兒了；從易牙的兒子，一直吃

in Wolf Cub Village. Last year they executed a criminal in the city, and a consumptive soaked a piece of bread in his blood and sucked it.

"They want to eat me, and of course you can do nothing about it single-handed; but why must you join them? As maneaters they are capable of anything. If they eat me, they can eat you as well; members of the same group can still eat each other. But if you will just change your ways, change right away, then everyone will have peace. Although this has been going on since time immemorial, today we could make a special effort to do what is right, and say this can't be done! I'm sure you can say that, Brother. The other day when the tenant wanted the rent reduced, you said it couldn't be done."

As first he only smiled cynically, then a murderous gleam came into his eyes, and when I spoke of their secret he turned pale. Outside the gate quite a crowd had gathered, among them Mr. Zhao and his dog, all craning their necks to peer in. I could not see all their faces, some of them seemed to be masked; others were the old lot, long-toothed with livid faces, concealing their laughter. I knew they were one gang, all eaters of human flesh. But I also knew that they did not all think alike by any means. Some of them thought that since it had always been so, men should be eaten. Others knew they shouldn't eat men but still wanted to, and were afraid people might discover their secret; so although what I said made them angry they still smiled their cynical, tight-lipped smiles.

Suddenly my brother's face darkened.

"Clear off, the whole lot of you!" He reared. "What's the point of looking at a madman?"

Then I realized part of their cunning. They would never be willing to change their stand, and their plans were all laid: they had labelled me a madman. In future when I was eaten, not only would there be no

到徐錫林；從徐錫林，又一直吃到狼子村捉住的人。去年城裏殺了
犯人，還有一個生癆病的人，用饅頭蘸血舐。

「他們要吃我，你一個人，原也無法可想；然而又何必去入夥。
吃人的人，甚麼事做不出；他們會吃我，也會吃你，一夥裏面，也
會自吃。但只要轉一步，只要立刻改了，也就人人太平。雖然從來
如此，我們今天也可以格外要好，説是不能！大哥，我相信你能
説，前天佃戶要減租，你説過不能。」

當初，他還只是冷笑，隨後眼光便兇狠起來，一到説破他們的
隱情，那就滿臉都變成青色了。大門外立着一夥人，趙貴翁和他的
狗，也在裏面，都探頭探腦的挨進來。有的是看不出面貌，似乎用
布蒙着；有的是仍舊青面獠牙，抿着嘴笑，我認識他們是一夥，都
是吃人的人。可是也曉得他們心思很不一樣，一種是以為從來如
此，應該吃的；一種是知道不該吃，可是仍然要吃，又怕別人説破
他，所以聽了我的話，越發氣憤不過，可是抿着嘴冷笑。

這時候，大哥也忽然顯出兇相，高聲喝道，

「都出去！瘋子有甚麼好看！」

這時候，我又懂得一件他們的巧妙了。他們豈但不肯改，而且
早已佈置；預備下一個瘋子的名目罩上我。將來吃了，不但太平無

trouble but people would probably be grateful to them. When our tenant spoke of the villagers eating a bad character, it was exactly the same device. This is their old trick.

Old Chen came in too in a towering temper. But they could not stop my mouth, I had to warn those people:

"You should change, change from the bottom of your hearts. You must realize that there will be no place for man-eaters in the world in future.

"If you don't change, you may all be eaten by each other. However many of you there are, you will be wiped out by the real men, just as wolves are killed by hunter — just like reptiles!"

Old Chen drove everybody away. My brother had disappeared, Old Chen advised me to go back to my room. It was pitch dark in there. The beams and rafters shook above my head. After shaking for a while they grew bigger and bigger. They piled on top of me.

The weight was so great, I couldn't move. They meant that I should die. However, knowing that the weight was false I struggled out, dripping with sweat. But I had to warn them:

"You must change at once, change from the bottom of your hearts! You must know that there'll be no place for man-eaters in future...."

XI

The sun has stopped shining, the door is never opened. Just two meals day after day.

事，怕還會有人見情。佃戶說的大家吃了一個惡人，正是這方法。這是他們的老譜！

陳老五也氣憤憤的直走進來。如何按得住我的口，我偏要對這夥人說，

「你們可以改了，從真心改起！要曉得將來容不得吃人的人，活在世上。

「你們要不改，自己也會吃盡。即使生得多，也會給真的人除滅了，同獵人打完狼子一樣！——同蟲子一樣！」

那一夥人，都被陳老五趕走了。大哥也不知那裏去了。陳老五勸我回屋子裏去。屋裏面全是黑沉沉的。橫樑和椽子都在頭上發抖；抖了一會，就大起來，堆在我身上。

萬分沉重，動彈不得；他的意思是要我死。我曉得他的沉重是假的，便掙扎出來，出了一身汗。可是偏要說，

「你們立刻改了，從真心改起！你們要曉得將來是容不得吃人的人，……」

十一

太陽也不出，門也不開，日日是兩頓飯。

Picking up my chopsticks, I thought of my elder brother. I know now how my little sister died: it was all through him. My sister was only five at the time. I can still remember how sweet she looked, poor thing. Mother wept as if she would never stop, but he begged her not to cry, probably because he had eaten our sister himself and so this weeping made him rather ashamed. If he had any sense of shame....

My sister was eaten by my brother, but I don't know whether Mother realized it or not.

I think Mother must have known, but when she wept she didn't say so outright, probably because she also thought it proper. I remember when I was four or five, sitting in the cool of the hall, my brother told me that if a man's parents were ill he should cut off a piece of his flesh and boil it for them, if he wanted to be considered a good son; and Mother didn't contradict him. If one piece could be eaten, obviously so could the whole. And yet just to think of the weeping then still makes my heart bleed; that is the extraordinary thing about it!

XII

I can't bear to think of it.

It has only just dawned on me that all these years I have been living in a place where for four thousand years human flesh has been eaten. My brother had just taken over the charge of the house when our sister died, and he may well have used her flesh in our food, making us eat it unwittingly.

我捏起筷子，便想起我大哥；曉得妹子死掉的緣故，也全在他。那時我妹子才五歲，可愛可憐的樣子，還在眼前。母親哭個不住，他卻勸母親不要哭；大約因為自己吃了，哭起來不免有點過意不去。如果還能過意不去，……

妹子是被大哥吃了，母親知道沒有，我可不得而知。

母親想也知道；不過哭的時候，卻並沒有說明，大約也以為應當的了。記得我四五歲時，坐在堂前乘涼，大哥說爺娘生病，做兒子的須割下一片肉來，煮熟了請他吃，才算好人；母親也沒有說不行。一片吃得，整個的自然也吃得。但是那天的哭法，現在想起來，實在還教人傷心，這真是奇極的事！

十二

不能想了。

四千年來時時吃人的地方，今天才明白，我也在其中混了多年；大哥正管着家務，妹子恰恰死了，他未必不和在飯菜裏，暗暗給我們吃。

I may have eaten several pieces of my sister's flesh unwittingly, and now it is my turn....

How can a man like myself, after four thousand years of man-eating history — even though I knew nothing about it at first — ever hope to face real men?

XIII

Perhaps there are still children who haven't eaten men?

Save the children....

April 1918

我未必無意之中，不吃了我妹子的幾片肉，現在也輪到我自己，……

有了四千年吃人履歷的我，當初雖然不知道，現在明白，難見真的人！

十三

沒有吃過人的孩子，或者還有？

救救孩子……

一九一八年四月。

孔 乙 己

Kong Yiji

KONG YIJI

The layout of Luzhen's taverns is unique. In each, facing you as you enter, is a bar in the shape of a carpenter's square where hot water is kept ready for warming rice wine. When men come off work at midday and in the evening they spend four coppers on a bowl of wine — or so they did twenty years ago; now it costs ten — and drink this warm, standing by the bar, taking it easy. Another copper will buy a plate of salted bamboo shoots or peas flavoured with aniseed to go with the wine, while a dozen will buy a meat dish; but most of the customers here belong to the short-coated class, few of whom can afford this. As for those in long gowns, they go into the inner room to order wine and dishes and sit drinking at their leisure.

At the age of twelve I started work as a pot-boy in Prosperity Tavern at the edge of the town. The boss put me to work in the outer room, saying that I looked too much of a fool to serve long-gowned customers. The short-coated customers there were easier to deal with, it is true, but among them were quite a few pernickety ones who insisted on watching for themselves while the yellow wine was ladled from the keg, looked for water at the bottom of the wine-pot, and personally

孔 乙 己

　　魯鎮的酒店的格局，是和別處不同的：都是當街一個曲尺形的大櫃台，櫃裏面預備着熱水，可以隨時溫酒。做工的人，傍午傍晚散了工，每每花四文銅錢，買一碗酒，——這是二十多年前的事，現在每碗要漲到十文，——靠櫃外站着，熱熱的喝了休息；倘肯多花一文，便可以買一碟鹽煮筍，或者茴香豆，做下酒物了，如果出到十幾文，那就能買一樣葷菜，但這些顧客，多是短衣幫，大抵沒有這樣闊綽。只有穿長衫的，才踱進店面隔壁的房子裏，要酒要菜，慢慢地坐喝。

　　我從十二歲起，便在鎮口的咸亨酒店裏當夥計，掌櫃說，樣子太傻，怕侍候不了長衫主顧，就在外面做點事罷。外面的短衣主顧，雖然容易說話，但嘮嘮叨叨纏夾不清的也很不少。他們往往要親眼看着黃酒從壇子裏舀出，看過壺子底裏有水沒有，又親看將壺

inspected the pot's immersion into the hot water. Under such strict surveillance, diluting the wine was very hard indeed. Thus it did not take my boss many days to decide that this job too was beyond me. Luckily I had been recommended by somebody influential, so he could not sack me. Instead I was transferred to the dull task of simply warming wine.

After that I stood all day behind the bar attending to my duties. Although I gave satisfaction at this post, I found it somewhat boring and monotonous. Our boss was a grim-faced man, nor were the customers much pleasanter, which made the atmosphere a gloomy one. The only times when there was any laughter were when Kong Yiji came to the tavern. That is why I remember him.

Kong Yiji was the only long-gowned customer who used to drink his wine standing. A big, pallid man whose wrinkled face often bore scars, he had a large, unkempt and grizzled beard. And although he wore a long grown it was dirty and tattered. It had not by the look of it been washed or mended for ten years or more. He used so many archaisms in his speech that half of it was barely intelligible. And as his surname was Kong, he was given the nickname Kong Yiji from *kong, yi, ji,* the first three characters in the old-fashioned children's copybook. Whenever he came in, everyone there would look at him and chuckle. And someone was sure to call out:

"Kong Yiji! What are those fresh scars on your face?"

Ignoring this, he would lay nine coppers on the bar and order two bowls of heated wine with a dish of aniseed-peas. Then someone else would bawl:

"You must have been stealing again!"

"Why sully a man's good name for no reason at all?" Kong Yiji would ask, raising his eyebrows.

子放在熱水裏，然後放心：在這嚴重監督之下，屢水也很為難。所以過了幾天，掌櫃又説我幹不了這事。幸虧薦頭的情面大，辭退不得，便改為專管溫酒的一種無聊職務了。

我從此便整天的站在櫃台裏，專管我的職務。雖然沒有甚麼失職，但總覺有些單調，有些無聊。掌櫃是一副凶臉孔，主顧也沒有好聲氣，教人活潑不得；只有孔乙己到店，才可以笑幾聲，所以至今還記得。

孔乙己是站着喝酒而穿長衫的唯一的人。他身體很高大；青白臉色，皺紋間時常夾些傷痕；一部亂蓬蓬的花白的鬍子。穿的雖然是長衫，可是又髒又破，似乎十多年沒有補，也沒有洗。他對人説話，總是滿口之乎者也，教人半懂不懂的。因為他姓孔，別人便從描紅紙上的「上大人孔乙己」這半懂不懂的話裏，替他取下一個綽號，叫作孔乙己。孔乙己一到店，所有喝酒的人便都看着他笑，有的叫道，『孔乙己，你臉上又添上新傷疤了！』他不回答，對櫃裏説，「溫兩碗酒，要一碟茴香豆。」便排出九文大錢。他們又故意的高聲嚷道，「你一定又偷了人家的東西了！」孔乙己睜大眼睛説，「你怎麼這樣憑空污人清白……」「甚麼清白？我前天親眼見你偷了何家

"Good name? Why, the day before yesterday you were trussed up and beaten for stealing books from the Ho family. I saw you!"

At that Kong Yiji would flush, the veins on his forehead standing out as he protested, "Taking books can't be counted as stealing.... Taking books ... for a scholar ... can't be counted as stealing." Then followed such quotations from the classics as "A gentlemen keeps his integrity even in poverty," together with a spate of archaisms which soon had everybody roaring with laughter, enlivening the whole tavern.

From the gossip that I heard, it seemed that Kong Yiji had studied the classics but never passed the official examinations and, not knowing any way to make a living, he had grown steadily poorer until he was almost reduced to beggary. Luckily he was a good calligrapher and could find enough copying work to fill his rice bowl. But unfortunately he had his failings too: laziness and a love of tippling. So after a few days he would disappear, taking with him books, paper, brushes and inkstone. And after this had happened several times, people stopped employing him as a copyist. Then all he could do was resort to occasional pilfering. In our tavern, though, he was a model customer who never failed to pay up. Sometimes, it is true, when he had no ready money, his name would be chalked up on our tally-board; but in less than a month he invariably settled the bill, and the name Kong Yiji would be wiped off the board again.

After Kong Yiji had drunk half a bowl of wine, his flushed cheeks would stop burning. But then someone would ask:

"Kong Yiji, can you really read?"

When he glanced back as if such a question were not worth answering, they would continue, "How is it you never passed even the lowest official examination?"

的書，吊着打。」孔乙己便漲紅了臉，額上的青筋條條綻出，爭辯道：「竊書不能算偷……竊書！……讀書人的事，能算偷麼？」接連便是難懂的話，甚麼「君子固窮」，甚麼「者乎」之類，引得眾人都哄笑起來：店內外充滿了快活的空氣。

聽人家背地裏談論，孔乙己原來也讀過書，但終於沒有進學，又不會營生；於是愈過愈窮，弄到將要討飯了。幸而寫得一筆好字，便替人家鈔鈔書，換一碗飯吃。可惜他又有一樣壞脾氣，便是好喝懶做。坐不到幾天，便連人和書籍紙張筆硯，一齊失蹤。如是幾次，叫他鈔書的人也沒有了。孔乙己沒有法，便免不了偶然做些偷竊的事。但他在我們店裏，品行卻比別人都好，就是從不拖欠；雖然間或沒有現錢，暫時記在粉板上，但不出一月，定然還清，從粉板上拭去了孔乙己的名字。

孔乙己喝過半碗酒，漲紅的臉色漸漸復了原，旁人便又問道，「孔乙己，你當真認識字麼？」孔乙己看着問他的人，顯出不屑置辯的神氣。他們便接着說道，「你怎的連半個秀才也撈不到呢？」

At once a grey tinge would overspread Kong Yiji's dejected, discomfited face, and he would mumble more of those unintelligible archaisms. Then everyone there would laugh heartily again, enlivening the whole tavern.

At such times I could join in the laughter with no danger of a dressing-down from my boss. In fact he always put such questions to Kong Yiji himself, to raise a laugh. Knowing that it was no use talking to the men, Kong Yiji would chat with us boys. Once he asked me:

"Have you had any schooling?"

When I nodded curtly he said, "Well then, I'll test you. How do you write the *hui* in aniseed-peas?"

Who did this beggar think he was, testing me! I turned away and ignored him. After waiting for some time he said earnestly:

"You can't write it, eh? I'll show you. Mind you remember. You ought to remember such characters, because you'll need them to write up your accounts when you have a shop of your own."

It seemed to me that I was still very far from having a shop of my own; in addition to which, our boss never entered aniseed-peas in his account-book. Half amused and half exasperated, I drawled, "I don't need you to show me. Isn't it the *hui* written with the element for grass?"

Kong Yiji's face lit up. Tapping two long finger-nails on the bar, he nodded. "Quite correct!" He said. "There are four different ways of writing *hui*. Do you know them?"

But my patience exhausted, I scowled and moved away. Kong Yiji had dipped his finger in wine to trace the characters on the bar. When he saw my utter indifference his face fell and he sighed.

孔乙己立刻顯出頹唐不安模樣，臉上籠上了一層灰色，嘴裏説些話；這回可是全是之乎者也之類，一些不懂了。在這時候，眾人也都哄笑起來：店內外充滿了快活的空氣。

　　在這些時候，我可以附和着笑，掌櫃是決不責備的。而且掌櫃見了孔乙己，也每每這樣問他，引人發笑。孔乙己自己知道不能和他們談天，便只好向孩子説話。有一回對我説道，「你讀過書麼？」我略略點一點頭。他説，「讀過書，……我便考你一考。茴香豆的茴字，怎樣寫的？」我想，討飯一樣的人，也配考我麼？便回過臉去，不再理會。孔乙己等了許久，很懇切的説道，「不能寫罷？……我教給你，記着！這些字應該記着。將來做掌櫃的時候，寫賬要用。」我暗想我和掌櫃的等級還很遠呢，而且我們掌櫃也從不將茴香豆上賬；又好笑，又不耐煩，懶懶的答他道，「誰要你教，不是草頭底下一個來回的回字麼？」孔乙己顯出極高興的樣子，將兩個指頭的長指甲敲着櫃台，點頭説，「對呀對呀！……回字有四樣寫法，你知道麼？」我愈不耐煩了，努着嘴走遠。孔乙己剛用指甲蘸了酒，想在櫃上寫字，見我毫不熱心，便又嘆一口氣，顯出極惋惜的樣子。

Sometimes children in the neighbourhood, hearing laughter, came in to join in the fun and surrounded Kong Yiji. Then he would give them aniseed-peas, one apiece. After eating the peas the children would still hang round, their eyes fixed on the dish. Growing flustered, he would cover it with his hand and bending forward from the waist would say, "There aren't many left, not many at all." Straightening up to look at the peas again, he would shake his head and reiterate, "Not many, I do assure you. Not many, nay, not many at all." Then the children would scamper off, shouting with laughter.

That was how Kong Yiji contributed to our enjoyment, but we got along all right without him too.

One day, shortly before the Mid-Autumn Festival I think it was, my boss who was slowly making out his accounts took down the tally-board. "Kong Yiji hasn't shown up for a long time," he remarked suddenly. "He still owes nineteen coppers." That made me realize how long it was since we had seen him.

"How could he?" rejoined one of the customers. "His legs were broken in that last beating up."

"Ah!" said my boss.

"He'd been stealing again. This time he was fool enough to steal from Mr. Ding, the provincial-grade scholar. As if anybody could get away with that!"

"So what happened?"

"What happened? First he wrote a confession, then he was beaten. The beating lasted nearly all night, and they broke both his legs."

"And then?"

"Well, his legs were broken."

有幾回，鄰舍孩子聽得笑聲，也趕熱鬧，圍住了孔乙己。他便給他們茴香豆吃，一人一顆。孩子吃完豆，仍然不散，眼睛都望着碟子。孔乙己着了慌，伸開五指將碟子罩住，彎腰下去説道，「不多了，我已經不多了。」直起身又看一看豆，自己搖頭説，「不多不多！多乎哉？不多也。」於是這一群孩子都在笑聲裏走散了。

孔乙己是這樣的使人快活，可是沒有他，別人也便這麼過。

有一天，大約是中秋前的兩三天，掌櫃正在慢慢的結賬，取下粉板，忽然説，「孔乙己長久沒有來了。還欠十九個錢呢！」我才也覺得他的確長久沒有來了。一個喝酒的人説道，「他怎麼會來？……他打折了腿了。」掌櫃説，「哦！」「他總仍舊是偷。這一回，是自己發昏，竟偷到丁舉人家裏去了。他家的東西，偷得的麼？」「後來怎麼樣？」「怎麼樣？先寫服辯，後來是打，打了大半夜，再打折了

"Yes, but after?"

"After? ... Who knows? He may be dead."

My boss asked no further questions but went on slowly making up his accounts.

After the Mid-Autumn Festival the wind grew daily colder as winter approached, and even though I spent all my time by the stove I had to wear a padded jacket. One afternoon, when the tavern was deserted, as I sat with my eyes closed I heard the words:

"Warm a bowl of wine."

It was said in a low but familiar voice. I opened my eyes. There was no one to be seen. I stood up to look out. There below the bar, facing the door, sat Kong Yiji. His face was thin and grimy — he looked a wreck. He had on a ragged lined jacket and was squatting cross-legged on a mat which was attached to his shoulders by a straw rope. When he saw me he repeated:

"Warm a bowl of wine."

At this point my boss leaned over the bar to ask, "Is that Kong Yiji? You still owe nineteen coppers."

"That ... I'll settle next time." He looked up dejectedly. "Here's cash. Give me some good wine."

My boss, just as in the past, chuckled and said:

"Kong Yiji, you've been stealing again!"

But instead of stout denial, the answer simply was:

"Don't joke with me."

"Joke? How did your legs get broken if you hadn't been stealing?"

腿。」「後來呢？」「後來打折了腿了。」「打折了怎樣呢？」「怎樣？……誰曉得？許是死了。」掌櫃也不再問，仍然慢慢的算他的賬。

中秋過後，秋風是一天涼比一天，看看將近初冬；我整天的靠着火，也須穿上棉襖了。一天的下半天，沒有一個顧客，我正合了眼坐着。忽然間聽得一個聲音，「溫一碗酒。」這聲音雖然極低，卻很耳熟。看時又全沒有人。站起來向外一望，那孔乙己便在櫃台下對了門檻坐着。他臉上黑而且瘦，已經不成樣子；穿一件破夾襖，盤着兩腿，下面墊一個蒲包，用草繩在肩上掛住；見了我，又說道，「溫一碗酒。」掌櫃也伸出頭去，一面說，「孔乙己麼？你還欠十九個錢呢！」孔乙己很頹唐的仰面答道，「這……下回還清罷。這一回是現錢，酒要好。」掌櫃仍然同平常一樣，笑着對他說，「孔乙己，你又偷了東西了！」但他這回卻不十分分辯，單說了一句「不要取笑！」「取笑？要是不偷，怎麼會打斷腿？」孔乙己低聲說道，「跌

"I fell," whispered Kong Yiji. "Broke them in a fall." His eyes pleaded with the boss to let the matter drop. By now several people had gathered round, and they all laughed with the boss. I warmed the wine, carried it over, and set it on the threshold. He produced four coppers from his ragged coat pocket, and as he placed them in my hand I saw that his own hands were covered with mud — he must have crawled there on them. Presently he finished the wine and, to the accompaniment of taunts and laughter, slowly pushed himself off with his hands.

A long time went by after that without our seeing Kong Yiji again. At the end of the year, when the boss took down the tally-board he said, "Kong Yiji still owes nineteen coppers." At the Dragon-Boat Festival the next year he said the same thing again. But when the Mid-Autumn Festival arrived he was silent on the subject, and another New Year came round without our seeing any more of Kong Yiji.

Nor have I ever seen him since — no doubt Kong Yiji really is dead.

March 1919

斷，跌，跌……」他的眼色，很像懇求掌櫃，不要再提，此時已經聚
集了幾個人，便和掌櫃都笑了。我溫了酒，端出去，放在門檻上。
他從破衣袋裏摸出四文大錢，放在我手裏，見他滿手是泥，原來他
便用這手走來的。不一會，他喝完酒，便又在旁人的説笑聲中，坐
着用這手慢慢走去了。

　　自此以後，又長久沒有看見孔乙己。到了年關，掌櫃取下粉板
説，「孔乙己還欠十九個錢呢！」到第二年的端午，又説「孔乙己還欠
十九個錢呢！」到中秋可是沒有説，再到年關也沒有看見他。

　　我到現在終於沒有見——大約孔乙己的確死了。

　　　　　　　　　　　　　　　　　　　　一九一九年三月。

藥

Medicine

MEDICINE

I

It was autumn, in the small hours of the morning. The moon had gone down, but the sun had not yet risen, and the sky appeared a sheet of darkling blue. Apart from night-prowlers, all was asleep. Old Shuan suddenly sat up in bed. He struck a match and lit the grease-covered oil-lamp, which shed a ghostly light over the two rooms of the teahouse.

"Are you going now, Dad?" queried an old woman's voice. And from the small inner room a fit of coughing was heard.

"H'm."

Old Shuan listened as he fastened his clothes, then stretching out his hand said, "Let's have it."

After some fumbling under the pillow his wife produced a packet of silver dollars which she handed over. Old Shuan pocketed it nervously, patted his pocket twice, then lighting a paper lantern and blowing out the lamp went into the inner room. A rustling was heard, and then more coughing. When all was quiet again, Old Shuan called softly, "Son!... Don't you get up!... Your mother will see to the shop."

Receiving no answer, Old Shuan assumed his son must be sound

藥

秋天的後半夜，月亮下去了，太陽還沒有出，只剩下一片烏藍的天；除了夜遊的東西，甚麼都睡着。華老栓忽然坐起身，擦着火柴，點上遍身油膩的燈盞，茶館的兩間屋子裏，便彌滿了青白的光。

「小栓的爹，你就去麼？」是一個老女人的聲音。裏邊的小屋子裏，也發出一陣咳嗽。

「唔。」老栓一面聽，一面應，一面扣上衣服；伸手過去說，「你給我罷。」

華大媽在枕頭底下掏了半天，掏出一包洋錢，交給老栓，老栓接了，抖抖的裝入衣袋，又在外面按了兩下；便點上燈籠，吹熄燈盞，走向裏屋子去了。那屋子裏面，正在窸窸窣窣的響，接着便是一通咳嗽。老栓候他平靜下去，才低低的叫道，「小栓……你不要起來。……店麼？你娘會安排的。」

老栓聽得兒子不再說話，料他安心睡了；便出了門，走到街

asleep again; so he went out into the street. In the darkness nothing could be seen but the grey roadway. The lantern light fell on his pacing feet. Here and there he came across dogs, but none of them barked. It was much colder than indoors, yet Old Shuan's spirits rose, as if he had grown suddenly younger and possessed some miraculous life-giving power. He had lengthened his stride. And the road became increasingly clear, the sky increasingly bright.

Absorbed in his walking, Old Shuan was startled when he saw the crossroad lying distinctly ahead of him. He walked back a few steps to stand under the eaves of a shop, in front of its closed door. After some time he began to feel chilly.

"Uh, an old chap."

"Seems rather cheerful...."

Old Shuan started again and, opening his eyes, saw several men passing. One of them even turned back to look at him, and although he could not see him clearly, the man's eyes shone with a lustful light, like a famished person's at the sight of food. Looking at his lantern, Old Shuan saw it had gone out. He patted his pocket — the hard packet was still there. Then he looked round and saw many strange people, in twos and threes, wandering about like lost souls. However, when he gazed steadily at them, he could not see anything else strange about them.

Presently he saw some soldiers strolling around. The large white circles on their uniforms, both in front and behind, were clear even at a distance; and as they drew nearer, the dark red border could be seen too. The next second, with a trampling of feet, a crowd rushed past. Thereupon the small groups which had arrived earlier suddenly converged and surged forward. Just before the crossroad, they came to a sudden stop and grouped themselves in a semi-circle.

上。街上黑沉沉的一無所有，只有一條灰白的路，看得分明。燈光照着他的兩腳，一前一後的走。有時也遇到幾隻狗，可是一隻也沒有叫。天氣比屋子裏冷得多了；老栓倒覺爽快，彷彿一旦變了少年，得了神通，有給人生命的本領似的，跨步格外高遠。而且路也愈走愈分明，天也愈走愈亮了。

老栓正在專心走路，忽然吃了一驚，遠遠裏看見一條丁字街，明明白白橫着。他便退了幾步，尋到一家關着門的舖子，蹩進簷下，靠門立住了。好一會，身上覺得有些發冷。

「哼，老頭子。」

「倒高興……。」

老栓又吃一驚，睜眼看時，幾個人從他面前過去了。一個還回頭看他，樣子不甚分明，但很像久餓的人見了食物一般，眼裏閃出一種攫取的光。老栓看看燈籠，已經熄了。按一按衣袋，硬硬的還在。仰起頭兩面一望，只見許多古怪的人，三三兩兩，鬼似的在那裏徘徊；定睛再看，卻也看不出甚麼別的奇怪。

沒有多久，又見幾個兵，在那邊走動；衣服前後的一個大白圓圈，遠地裏也看得清楚，走過面前的，並且看出號衣上暗紅色的鑲邊。——一陣腳步聲響，一眨眼，已經擁過了一大簇人。那三三兩兩的人，也忽然合作一堆，潮一般向前趕；將到丁字街口，便突然立住，簇成一個半圓。

Old Shuan looked in that direction too, but could only see people's backs. Craning their necks as far as they would go, they looked like so many ducks, held and lifted by some invisible hand. For a moment all was still; then a sound was heard, and a stir swept through the onlookers. There was a rumble as they pushed back, sweeping past Old Shuan and nearly knocking him down.

"Hey! Give me the cash, and I'll give you the goods!" A man clad entirely in black stood before him, his eyes like daggers, making Old Shuan shrink to half his normal size. This man was thrusting one huge extended hand towards him, while in the other he held a roll or steamed bread, from which crimson drops were dripping to the ground.

Hurriedly Old Shuan fumbled for his dollars, and trembling he was about to hand them over, but he dared not take the object. The other grew impatient, and shouted, "What are you afraid of? Why not take it?" When Old Shuan still hesitated, the man in black snatched his lantern and tore off its paper shade to wrap up the roll. This package he thrust into Old Shuan's hand, at the same time seizing the silver and giving it a cursory feel. Then he turned away, muttering, "Old fool...."

"Whose sickness is this for?" Old Shuan seemed to hear someone ask; but he made no reply. His whole mind was on the package, which he carried as carefully as if it were the sole heir to an ancient house. Nothing else mattered now. He was about to transplant this new life to his own home, and reap much happiness. The sun too had risen; lighting up the broad highway before him, which led straight home, and the worn tablet behind him at the crossroad with its faded gold inscription: "Ancient Pavilion."

老栓也向那邊看，卻只見一堆人的後背；頸項都伸得很長，彷彿許多鴨，被無形的手捏住了的，向上提着。靜了一會，似乎有點聲音，便又動搖起來，轟的一聲，都向後退；一直散到老栓立着的地方，幾乎將他擠倒了。

「喂！一手交錢，一手交貨！」一個渾身黑色的人，站在老栓面前，眼光正像兩把刀，刺得老栓縮小了一半。那人一隻大手，向他攤着；一隻手卻撮着一個鮮紅的饅頭，那紅的還是一點一點的往下滴。

老栓慌忙摸出洋錢，抖抖的想交給他，卻又不敢去接他的東西。那人便焦急起來，嚷道，「怕甚麼？怎的不拿！」老栓還躊躇着；黑的人便搶過燈籠，一把扯下紙罩，裹了饅頭，塞與老栓；一手抓過洋錢，捏一捏，轉身去了。嘴裏哼着說，「這老東西……。」

「這給誰治病的呀？」老栓也似乎聽得有人問他，但他並不答應；他的精神，現在只在一個包上，彷彿抱着一個十世單傳的嬰兒，別的事情，都已置之度外了。他現在要將這包裹的新的生命，移植到他家裏，收穫許多幸福。太陽也出來了；在他面前，顯出一條大道，直到他家中，後面也照見丁字街頭破匾上「古口亭口」這四個黯淡的金字。

II

When Old Shuan reached home, the shop had been cleaned, and the rows of tea-tables were shining brightly; but no customers had arrived. Only his son was sitting at a table by the wall, eating. Beads of sweat stood out on his forehead, his lined jacket was sticking to his spine, and his shoulder blades stuck out so sharply, an inverted V seemed stamped there. At this sight, Old Shuan's brow, which had been clear, contracted again. His wife hurried in from the kitchen, with expectant eyes and a tremor to her lips.

"Get it?"

"Yes."

They went together into the kitchen, and conferred for a time. Then the old woman went out, to return shortly with a dried lotus leaf which she spread on the table. Old Shuan unwrapped the crimson-stained roll from the lantern paper and transferred it to the lotus leaf. Little Shuan had finished his meal, but his mother exclaimed hastily:

"Sit still, Little Shuan! Don't come over here."

Mending the fire in the stove, Old Shuan put the green package and the red and white lantern paper into the stove together. A red-black flame flared up, and a strange odour permeated the shop.

"Smells good! What are you eating?" The hunchback had arrived. He was one of those who spend all their time in teahouses, the first to come in the morning and the last to leave. Now he had just stumbled to a corner table facing the street, and sat down. But no one answered his question.

二

　　老栓走到家，店面早經收拾乾淨，一排一排的茶桌，滑溜溜的發光。但是沒有客人；只有小栓坐在裏排的桌前吃飯，大粒的汗，從額上滾下，夾襖也帖住了脊心，兩塊肩胛骨高高凸出，印成一個陽文的「八」字。老栓見這樣子，不免皺一皺展開的眉心。他的女人，從灶下急急走出，睜着眼睛，嘴唇有些發抖。

　　「得了麼？」

　　「得了。」

　　兩個人一齊走進灶下，商量了一會；華大媽便出去了，不多時，拿着一片老荷葉回來，攤在桌上。老栓也打開燈籠罩，用荷葉重新包了那紅的饅頭。小栓也吃完飯，他的母親慌忙說：

　　「小栓——你坐着，不要到這裏來。」

　　一面整頓了灶火，老栓便把一個碧綠的包，一個紅紅白白的破燈籠，一同塞在灶裏；一陣紅黑的火焰過去時，店屋裏散滿了一種奇怪的香味。

　　「好香！你們吃甚麼點心呀？」這是駝背五少爺到了。這人每天總在茶館裏過日，來得最早，去得最遲，此時恰恰蹩到臨街的壁角的桌邊，便坐下問話，然而沒有人答應他。「炒米粥麼？」仍然沒有人應。老栓匆匆走出，給他泡上茶。

"Puffed rice gruel?"

Still no reply. Old Shuan hurried out to brew tea for him.

"Come here, Little Shuan!" His mother called him into the inner room, set a stool in the middle, and sat the child down. Then, bringing him a round black object on a plate, she said gently:

"Eat it up... then you'll be better."

Little Shuan picked up the black object and looked at it. He had the oddest feeling, as if he were holding his own life in his hands. Presently he split it carefully open. From within the charred crust a jet of white vapour escaped, then scattered, leaving only two halves of a white flour steamed roll. Soon it was all eaten, the flavour completely forgotten, only the empty plate left. His father and mother were standing one on each side of him, their eyes apparently pouring something into him and at the same time extracting something. His small heart began to beat faster, and, putting his hands to his chest, he began to cough again.

"Have a sleep; then you'll be all right," said his mother.

Obediently, Little Shuan coughed himself to sleep. The woman waited till his breathing was regular, then covered him lightly with a much patched quilt.

III

The shop was crowded, and Old Shuan was busy, carrying a big copper kettle to make tea for one customer after another. But there were dark circles under his eyes.

「小栓進來罷！」華大媽叫小栓進了裏面的屋子，中間放好一條櫈，小栓坐了。他的母親端過一碟烏黑的圓東西，輕輕說：

「吃下去罷，——病便好了。」

小栓撮起這黑東西，看了一會，似乎拿着自己的性命一般，心裏說不出的奇怪。十分小心的拗開了，焦皮裏面竄出一道白氣，白氣散了，是兩半個白麵的饅頭。——不多工夫，已經全在肚裏了，卻全忘了甚麼味；面前只剩下一張空盤。他的旁邊，一面立着他的父親，一面立着他的母親，兩人的眼光，都彷彿要在他身裏注進甚麼又要取出甚麼似的；便禁不住心跳起來，按着胸膛，又是一陣咳嗽。

「睡一會罷，——便好了。」

小栓依他母親的話，咳着睡了。華大媽候他喘氣平靜，才輕輕的給他蓋上了滿幅補釘的夾被。

三

店裏坐着許多人，老栓也忙了，提着大銅壺，一趟一趟的給客人沖茶；兩個眼眶，都圍着一圈黑線。

"Aren't you well, Old Shuan?... what's wrong with you?" asked one greybeard.

"Nothing."

"Nothing?... No, I suppose from your smile, there couldn't be," the old man corrected himself.

"It's just that Old Shuan's busy," said the hunchback. "If his son...." But before he could finish, a heavy-jowled man burst in. He had over his shoulders a dark brown shirt, unbuttoned and fastened carelessly by a broad dark brown girdle at his waist. As soon as he entered, he shouted to Old Shuan:

"Has he taken it? Any better? Luck's with you, Old Shuan. What luck! If not for my hearing of things so quickly...."

Holding the kettle in one hand, the other straight by his side in an attitude of respect, Old Shuan listened with a smile. In fact, all present were listening respectfully. The old woman, dark circles under her eyes too, came out smiling with a bowl containing tea-leaves and an added olive, over which Old Shuan poured boiling water for the newcomer.

"This is a guaranteed cure! Not like other things!" Declared the heavy-jowled man. "Just think, brought back warm, and eaten warm!"

"Yes indeed, we couldn't have managed it without Uncle Kang's help." The old woman thanked him very warmly.

"A guaranteed cure! Eaten warm like this. A roll dipped in human blood like this can cure any consumption!"

The old woman seemed a little disconcerted by the word "consumption," and turned a shade paler; however, she forced a smile again at once and found some pretext to leave. Meanwhile the

「老栓，你有些不舒服麼？——你生病麼？」一個花白鬍子的人
說。

「沒有。」

「沒有？——我想笑嘻嘻的，原也不像……」花白鬍子便取消了
自己的話。

「老栓只是忙。要是他的兒子……」駝背五少爺話還未完，突然
闖進了一個滿臉橫肉的人，披一件玄色布衫，散着紐釦，用很寬的
玄色腰帶，胡亂捆在腰間。剛進門，便對老栓嚷道：

「吃了麼？好了麼？老栓，就是運氣了你！你運氣，要不是我信
息靈……。」

老栓一手提了茶壺，一手恭恭敬敬的垂着；笑嘻嘻的聽。滿座
的人，也都恭恭敬敬的聽。華大媽也黑着眼眶，笑嘻嘻的送出茶碗
茶葉來，加上一個橄欖，老栓便去沖了水。

「這是包好！這是與眾不同的。你想，趁熱的拿來，趁熱吃
下。」橫肉的人只是嚷。

「真的呢，要沒有康大叔照顧，怎麼會這樣……」華大媽也很感
激的謝他。

「包好，包好！這樣的趁熱吃下。這樣的人血饅頭，甚麼癆病都
包好！」

華大媽聽到「癆病」這兩個字，變了一點臉色，似乎有些不高
興；但又立刻堆上笑，搭赸着走開了。這康大叔卻沒有覺察，仍然

man in brown was indiscreet enough to go on talking at the top of his voice until the child in the inner room was woken and started coughing.

"So you've had such a stroke of luck for your Little Shuan! Of course his sickness will be cured completely. No wonder Old Shuan keeps smiling." As he spoke, the greybeard walked up to the man in brown, and lowered his voice to ask:

"Mr. Kang, I heard the criminal executed today came from the Xia family. Who was it? And why was he executed?"

"Who? Son of Widow Xia, of course! Young rascal!"

Seeing how they were all hanging on his words, Mr. Kang's spirits rose even higher. His jowls quivered, and he made his voice as loud as he could.

"The rogue didn't want to live, simply didn't want to! There was nothing in it for me this time. Even the clothes stripped from him were taken by Red-eye, the jailer. Our Old Shuan was luckiest, and after him Third Uncle Xia. He pocketed the whole reward — twenty-five taels of bright silver — and didn't have to spend a cent!"

Little Shuan walked slowly out of the inner room, his hands to his chest, coughing repeatedly. He went to the kitchen, filled a bowl with cold rice, added hot water to it, and sitting down started to eat. His mother, hovering over him, asked softly:

"Do you feel better, son? Still as hungry as ever."

"A guaranteed cure!" Kang glanced at the child, then turned back to address the company. "Third Uncle Xia is really smart. If he hadn't informed, even his family would have been executed, and their property confiscated. But instead? Silver! That young rogue was a real scoundrel! He even tried to incite the jailer to revolt!"

提高了喉嚨只是嚷，嚷得裏面睡着的小栓也合夥咳嗽起來。

「原來你家小栓碰到了這樣的好運氣了。這病自然一定全好；怪不得老栓整天的笑着呢。」花白鬍子一面說，一面走到康大叔面前，低聲下氣的問道，「康大叔——聽說今天結果的一個犯人，便是夏家的孩子，那是誰的孩子？究竟是甚麼事？」

「誰的？不就是夏四奶奶的兒子麼？那個小傢伙！」康大叔見眾人都聳起耳朵聽他，便格外高興，橫肉塊塊飽綻，越發大聲說，「這小東西不要命，不要就是了。我可是這一回一點沒有得到好處；連剝下來的衣服，都給管牢的紅眼睛阿義拿去了。——第一要算我們栓叔運氣；第二是夏三爺賞了二十五兩雪白的銀子，獨自落腰包，一文不花。」

小栓慢慢的從小屋子走出，兩手按了胸口，不住的咳嗽；走到灶下，盛出一碗冷飯，泡上熱水，坐下便吃。華大媽跟着他走，輕輕的問道，「小栓，你好些麼？——你仍舊只是肚餓？……」

「包好，包好！」康大叔瞥了小栓一眼，仍然回過臉，對眾人說，「夏三爺真是乖角兒，要是他不先告官，連他滿門抄斬。現在怎樣？銀子！——這小東西也真不成東西！關在牢裏，還要勸牢頭造反。」

"No! The idea of it!" A man in his twenties, sitting in the back row, expressed indignation.

"You know, Red-eye went to sound him out, but he started chatting with him. He said the great Qing empire belongs to us. Just think: Is that kind of talk rational? Red-eye knew he had only an old mother at home, but had never imagined he was so poor. He couldn't squeeze anything out of him; he was already good and angry, and then the young fool would 'scratch the tiger's head', so he gave him a couple of slaps."

"Red-eye is a good boxer. Those slaps must have hurt!" The hunchback in the corner by the wall exulted.

"The rotter was not afraid of being beaten. He even said how sorry he was."

"Nothing to be sorry about in beating a wretch like that," said Greybeard.

Kang looked at him superciliously and said disdainfully, "You misunderstood. The way he said it, he was sorry for Red-eye."

His listeners' eyes took on a glazed look, and no one spoke. Little Shuan had finished his rice and was perspiring profusely, his head steaming.

"Sorry for Red-eye — crazy! He must have been crazy!" said Greybeard, as if suddenly he saw light.

"He must have been crazy!" echoed the man in his twenties.

Once more the customers began to show animation, and conversation was resumed. Under cover of the noise, the child was seized by a paroxysm of coughing. Kang went up to him, clapped him on the shoulder, and said:

「阿呀，那還了得。」坐在後排的一個二十多歲的人，很現出氣憤模樣。

「你要曉得紅眼睛阿義是去盤盤底細的，他卻和他攀談了。他說：這大清的天下是我們大家的。你想：這是人話麼？紅眼睛原知道他家裏只有一個老娘，可是沒有料到他竟會那麼窮，榨不出一點油水，已經氣破肚皮了。他還要老虎頭上搔癢，便給他兩個嘴巴！」

「義哥是一手好拳棒，這兩下，一定夠他受用了。」壁角的駝背忽然高興起來。

「他這賤骨頭打不怕，還要説可憐可憐哩。」

花白鬍子的人説，「打了這種東西，有甚麼可憐呢？」

康大叔顯出看他不上的樣子，冷笑着説，「你沒有聽清我的話；看他神氣，是説阿義可憐哩！」

聽着的人的眼光，忽然有些板滯；話也停頓了。小栓已經吃完飯，吃得滿身流汗，頭上都冒出蒸氣來。

「阿義可憐——瘋話，簡直是發了瘋了。」花白鬍子恍然大悟似的説。

「發了瘋了。」二十多歲的人也恍然大悟的説。

店裏的坐客，便又現出活氣，談笑起來。小栓也趁着熱鬧，拚命咳嗽；康大叔走上前，拍他肩膀説：

"A guaranteed cure! Don't cough like that, Little Shuan! A guaranteed cure!"

"Crazy!" agreed the hunchback, nodding his head.

IV

Originally, the land adjacent to the city wall outside the West Gate had been public land. The zigzag path slanting across it, trodden out by passers-by seeking a short cut, had become a natural boundary line. Left of the path, executed criminals or those who had died of neglect in prison were buried. Right of the path were paupers' graves. The serried ranks of grave mounds on both sides looked like the rolls laid out for a rich man's birthday.

The Qing Ming Festival that year was unusually cold. Willows were only beginning to put forth shoots no larger than grains. Shortly after daybreak, Old Shuan's wife brought four dishes and a bowl of rice to set before a new grave in the right section, and wailed before it. When she had burned paper money she sat on the ground in a stupor as if waiting for something; but for what, she herself did not know. A breeze sprang up and stirred her short hair, which was certainly whiter than in the previous year.

Another woman came down the path, grey-haired and in rags. She was carrying an old, round, red-lacquered basket, with a string of paper money hanging from it; and she walked haltingly. When she saw Old Shuan's wife sitting on the ground watching her, she hesitated, and a flush of shame spread over her pale face. However, she sum-

「包好！小栓——你不要這麼咳。包好！」

「瘋了。」駝背五少爺點着頭說。

四

西關外靠着城根的地面，本是一塊官地；中間歪歪斜斜一條細路，是貪走便道的人，用鞋底造成的，但卻成了自然的界限。路的左邊，都埋着死刑和瘐斃的人，右邊是窮人的叢塚。兩面都已埋到層層疊疊，宛然闊人家裏祝壽時候的饅頭。

這一年的清明，分外寒冷；楊柳才吐出半粒米大的新芽。天明未久，華大媽已在右邊的一坐新墳前面，排出四碟菜，一碗飯，哭了一場。化過紙，呆呆的坐在地上；彷彿等候甚麼似的，但自己也說不出等候甚麼。微風起來，吹動他短髮，確乎比去年白得多了。

小路上又來了一個女人，也是半白頭髮，襤褸的衣裙；提一個破舊的朱漆圓籃，外掛一串紙錠，三步一歇的走。忽然見華大媽坐在地上看他，便有些躊躇，慘白的臉上，現出些羞愧的顏色；但終

moned up courage to cross over to a grave in the left section, where she set down her basket.

That grave was directly opposite Little Shuan's, separated only by the path. As Old Shuan's wife watched the other woman set out four dishes and a bowl of rice, then stand up to wail and burn paper money, she thought, "It must be her son in that grave too." The older woman took a few aimless steps and stared vacantly around, then suddenly she began to tremble and stagger backward: she felt giddy.

Fearing sorrow might send her out of her mind, Old Shuan's wife got up and stepped across the path, to say quietly, "Don't grieve, let's go home."

The other nodded, but her eyes were still fixed, and she muttered, "Look! What's that?"

Looking where she pointed, Old Shuan's wife saw that the grave in front had not yet been overgrown with grass. Ugly patches of soil still showed. But when she looked carefully, she was surprised to see at the top of the mound a wreath of red and white flowers.

Both of them suffered from failing eyesight, yet they could see these red and white flowers clearly. There were not many, but they were placed in a circle; and although not very fresh, were neatly set out. Little Shuan's mother looked round and found her own son's grave, like most of the rest, dotted with only a few little, pale flowers shivering in the cold. Suddenly she had a sense of futility and stopped feeling curious about the wreath.

Meantime the old woman had gone up to the grave to look more closely. "They have no roots," she said to herself. "They can't have grown here. Who could have been here? Children don't come here to

於硬着頭皮，走到左邊的一坐墳前，放下了籃子。

那墳與小栓的墳，一字兒排着，中間只隔一條小路。華大媽看他排好四碟菜，一碗飯，立着哭了一通，化過紙錠；心裏暗暗地想，「這墳裏的也是兒子了。」那老女人徘徊觀望了一回，忽然手腳有些發抖，蹌蹌踉踉退下幾步，瞪着眼只是發怔。

華大媽見這樣子，生怕他傷心到快要發狂了；便忍不住立起身，跨過小路，低聲對他說，「你這位老奶奶不要傷心了，──我們還是回去罷。」

那人點一點頭，眼睛仍然向上瞪着；也低聲吃吃的說道，「你看，──看這是甚麼呢？」

華大媽跟了他指頭看去，眼光便到了前面的墳，這墳上草根還沒有全合，露出一塊一塊的黃土，煞是難看。再往上仔細看時，卻不覺也吃一驚；──分明有一圈紅白的花，圍着那尖圓的墳頂。

他們的眼睛都已老花多年了，但望這紅白的花，卻還能明白看見。花也不很多，圓圓的排成一個圈，不很精神，倒也整齊。華大媽忙看他兒子和別人的墳，卻只有不怕冷的幾點青白小花，零星開着；便覺得心裏忽然感到一種不足和空虛，不願意根究。那老女人又走近幾步，細看了一遍，自言自語的說，「這沒有根，不像自己開

play, and none of our relatives have ever been. What could have happened?" She puzzled over it, until suddenly her tears began to fall, and she cried aloud:

"Son, they all wronged you, and you do not forget. Is your grief still so great that today you worked this wonder to let me know?"

She looked all around, but could see only a crow perched on a leafless bough. "I know," she continued. "They murdered you. But a day of reckoning will come, Heaven will see to it. Close your eyes in peace.... If you are really here, and can hear me, make that crow fly on to your grave as a sign."

The breeze had long since dropped, and the dry grass stood stiff and straight as copper wires. A faint, tremulous sound vibrated in the air, then faded and died away. All around was deathly still. They stood in the dry grass, looking up at the crow; and the crow, on the rigid bough of the tree, its head drawn in, stood immobile as iron.

Time passed. More people, young and old, came to visit the graves.

Old Shuan's wife felt somehow as if a load had been lifted from her mind and, wanting to leave, she urged the other:

"Let's go."

The old woman sighed, and listlessly picked up the rice and dishes. After a moment's hesitation she started slowly off, still muttering to herself:

"What could it mean?"

They had not gone thirty paces when they heard a loud caw behind them. Startled, they looked round and saw the crow stretch its

的。──這地方有誰來呢？孩子不會來玩；──親戚本家早不來了。──這是怎麼一回事呢？」她想了又想，忽又流下淚來，大聲説道：

「瑜兒，他們都冤枉了你，你還是忘不了，傷心不過，今天特意顯點靈，要我知道麼？」他四面一看，只見一隻烏鴉，站在一株沒有葉的樹上，便接着説，「我知道了。──瑜兒，可憐他們坑了你，他們將來總有報應，天都知道；你閉了眼睛就是了。──你如果真在這裏，聽到我的話，──便教這烏鴉飛上你的墳頂，給我看罷。」

微風早經停息了；枯草支支直立，有如銅絲。一絲發抖的聲音，在空氣中愈顫愈細，細到沒有，周圍便都是死一般靜。兩人站在枯草叢裏，仰面看那烏鴉；那烏鴉也在筆直的樹枝間，縮着頭，鐵鑄一般站着。

許多的工夫過去了；上墳的人漸漸增多，幾個老的小的，在土墳間出沒。

華大媽不知怎的，似乎卸下了一挑重擔，便想到要走；一面勸着説，「我們還是回去罷。」

那老女人嘆一口氣，無精打采的收起飯菜；又遲疑了一刻，終於慢慢地走了。嘴裏自言自語的説，「這是怎麼一回事呢？……」

他們走不上二三十步遠，忽聽得背後「啞──」的一聲大叫；兩

wings, brace itself to take off, then fly like an arrow towards the far horizon.

April 1919

個人都竦然的回過頭，只見那烏鴉張開兩翅，一挫身，直向着遠處
的天空，箭也似的飛去了。

　　　　　　　　　　　　　　　　一九一九年四月。

一件小事

A Small Incident

A SMALL INCIDENT

Six years have slipped by since I came from the country to the capital. During that time the number of so-called affairs of state I have witnessed or heard about is far from small, but none of them made much impression. If asked to define their influence on me, I can only say they taught me to take a poorer view of people every day.

One small incident, however, which struck me as significant and jolted me out of my irritability, remains fixed even now in my memory.

It was the winter of 1917, a strong north wind was blustering, but the exigencies of earning my living forced me to be up and out early. I met scarcely a soul on the road, but eventually managed to hire a rickshaw to take me to S— Gate. Presently the wind dropped a little, having blown away the drifts of dust on the road to leave a clean broad highway, and the rickshaw man quickened his pace. We were just approaching S— Gate when we knocked into someone who slowly toppled over.

It was a grey-haired woman in ragged clothes. She had stepped out abruptly from the roadside in front of us, and although the rickshaw man had swerved, her tattered padded waistcoat, unbuttoned and billowing in the wind, had caught on the shaft. Luckily the rickshaw

一件小事

　　我從鄉下跑到京城裏，一轉眼已經六年了。其間耳聞目睹的所謂國家大事，算起來也很不少；但在我心裏，都不留甚麼痕跡，倘要我尋出這些事的影響來說，便只是增長了我的壞脾氣，——老實說，便是教我一天比一天的看不起人。

　　但有一件小事，卻於我有意義，將我從壞脾氣裏拖開，使我至今忘記不得。

　　這是民國六年的冬天，大北風颳得正猛，我因為生計關係，不得不一早在路上走。一路幾乎遇不見人，好容易才僱定了一輛人力車，教他拉到S門去。不一會，北風小了，路上浮塵早已颳淨，剩下一條潔白的大道來，車伕也跑得更快。剛近S門，忽而車把上帶着一個人，慢慢地倒了。

　　跌倒的是一個女人，花白頭髮，衣服都很破爛。伊從馬路邊上突然向車前橫截過來；車伕已經讓開道，但伊的破棉背心沒有上扣，微風吹着，向外展開，所以終於兜着車把。幸而車伕早有點停

man had slowed down, otherwise she would certainly have had a bad fall and it might have been a serious accident.

She huddled there on the ground, and the rickshaw man stopped. As I did not believe the old woman was hurt and as no one else had seen us, I thought this halt of his uncalled for, liable to land him in trouble and hold me up.

"It's all right," I said. "Go on."

He paid no attention — he may not have heard — but set down the shafts, took the old woman's arm and gently helped her up.

"Are you all right?" He asked.

"I hurt myself falling."

I thought: I saw how slowly you fell, how could you be hurt? Putting on an act like this is simply disgusting. The rickshaw man asked for trouble, and now he's got it. He'll have to find his own way out.

But the rickshaw man did not hesitate for a minute after hearing the old woman's answer. Still holding her arm, he helped her slowly forward. Rather puzzled by this I looked ahead and saw a police-station. Because of the high wind, there was no one outside. It was there that the rickshaw man was taking the old woman.

Suddenly I had the strange sensation that his dusty retreating figure had in that instant grown larger. Indeed, the further he walked the larger he loomed, until I had to look up to him. At the same time he seemed gradually to be exerting a pressure on me which threatened to overpower the small self hidden under my fur-lined gown.

Almost paralysed at that juncture I sat there motionless, my mind a blank, until a policeman came out. Then I got down from the rickshaw.

步，否則伊定要栽一個大觔斗，跌到頭破血出了。

伊伏在地上；車伕便也立住腳。我料定這老女人並沒有傷，又沒有別人看見，便很怪他多事，要自己惹出是非，也誤了我的路。

我便對他說，「沒有甚麼的。走你的罷！」

車伕毫不理會，——或者並沒有聽到，——卻放下車子，扶那老女人慢慢起來，攙着臂膊立定，問伊說：

「你怎麼啦？」

「我摔壞了。」

我想，我眼見你慢慢倒地，怎麼會摔壞呢，裝腔作勢罷了，這真可憎惡。車伕多事，也正是自討苦吃，現在你自己想法去。

車伕聽了這老女人的話，卻毫不躊躇，仍然攙着伊的臂膊，便一步一步的向前走。我有些詫異，忙看前面，是一所巡警分駐所，大風之後，外面也不見人。這車伕扶着那老女人，便正是向那大門走去。

我這時突然感到一種異樣的感覺，覺得他滿身灰塵的後影，剎時高大了，而且愈走愈大，須仰視才見。而且他對於我，漸漸的又幾乎變成一種威壓，甚而至於要榨出皮袍下面藏着的「小」來。

我的活力這時大約有些凝滯了，坐着沒動，也沒有想，直到看見分駐所裏走出一個巡警，才下了車。

The policeman came up to me and said, "Get another rickshaw. He can't take you any further."

On the spur of the moment I pulled a handful of coppers from my coat pocket and handed them to the policeman. "Please give him this," I said.

The wind had dropped completely, but the road was still quiet. As I walked along thinking, I hardly dared to think about myself. Quite apart from what had happened earlier, what had I meant by that handful of coppers? Was it a reward? Who was I to judge the rickshaw man? I could give myself no answer.

Even now, this incident keeps coming back to me. It keeps distressing me and makes me try to think about myself. The politics and the fighting of those years have slipped my mind as completely as the classics I read as a child. Yet this small incident keeps coming back to me, often more vivid than in actual life, teaching me shame, spurring me on to reform, and imbuing me with fresh courage and fresh hope.

July 1920

巡警走近我說，「你自己僱車罷，他不能拉你了。」

我沒有思索的從外套袋裏抓出一大把銅元，交給巡警，說，「請你給他……」

風全住了，路上還很靜。我走着，一面想，幾乎怕敢想到我自己。以前的事姑且擱起，這一大把銅元又是甚麼意思？獎他麼？我還能裁判車伕麼？我不能回答自己。

這事到了現在，還是時時記起。我因此也時時熬了苦痛，努力的要想到我自己。幾年來的文治武力，在我早如幼小時候所讀過的「子曰詩云」一般，背不上半句了。獨有這一件小事，卻總是浮在我眼前，有時反更分明，教我慚愧，催我自新，並且增長我的勇氣和希望。

一九二零年七月。

風 波

Storm in a Teacup

STORM IN A TEACUP

On the mud flat by the river, the sun's bright yellow rays were gradually fading. The parched leaves of the tallow trees beside the river were at last able to take breath, while below them a few striped mosquitoes danced and droned. The smoke from the peasants' kitchen chimneys along the riverside dwindled, as the women and children sprinkled the ground before their doors with water and set out little tables and low stools. Everyone knew it was time for the evening meal.

The old folk and the men sat on the low stools, fanning themselves with plantain-leaf fans as they chatted. The children raced about or squatted under the tallow trees playing with pebbles. The women brought out steamed black dried rape and yellow rice, piping hot. Some literati passing in a pleasure boat waxed quite lyrical at the sight.

"Such carefree tranquillity!" They exclaimed. "How idyllic!"

However, these literati were wide of the mark, not having heard what Old Mrs. Ninepounder was saying. Old Mrs. Ninepounder was in a towering temper, whacking the legs of her stool with a tattered plantain fan.

"Seventy-nine years I've lived, that's enough," she declared. "I'm

風　　波

　　臨河的土場上，太陽漸漸的收了他通黃的光線了。場邊靠河的烏桕樹葉，乾巴巴的才喘過氣來，幾個花腳蚊子在下面哼着飛舞。面河的農家的煙突裏，逐漸減少了炊煙，女人孩子們都在自己門口的土場上潑些水，放下小桌子和矮凳；人知道，這已經是晚飯時候了。

　　老人男人坐在矮凳上，搖着大芭蕉扇閒談，孩子飛也似的跑，或者蹲在烏桕樹下賭玩石子。女人端出烏黑的蒸乾菜和松花黃的米飯，熱蓬蓬冒煙。河裏駛過文人的酒船，文豪見了，大發詩興，說，「無思無慮，這真是田家樂呵！」

　　但文豪的話有些不合事實，就因為他們沒有聽到九斤老太的話。這時候，九斤老太正在大怒，拿破芭蕉扇敲着凳腳說：

　　「我活到七十九歲了，活夠了，不願意眼見這些敗家相，——還

sick of watching this family go to the dogs.... Better die and be done with it. Just one minute to supper time, yet still eating roast beans — do you want to eat us out of house and home?"

Her great-granddaughter Sixpounder was just running towards her with a handful of beans, but seeing the situation she flew straight to the river bank and hid herself behind a tallow tree. Sticking out her small head with its twin tufts, she hooted, "Old Won't-die!"

Old Mrs. Ninepounder for all her great age was not deaf. She did not, however, catch what the child had called and went on muttering to herself, "Yes, indeed. Each generation is worse than the last."

It was the somewhat unusual custom in this village for mothers to weigh their children at birth and to call them the number of pounds they happened to weigh. Since Old Mrs. Ninepounder's celebration of her fiftieth birthday she had gradually become a fault-finder, for ever complaining that in her young days the summer had not been so hot nor the beans so tough as now. In a word, there was something wrong with the present-day world. Why else had Sixpounder weighed three pounds less than her great-grandfather and one pound less than her father, Sevenpounder? Surely this was irrefutable evidence. So she reiterated emphatically, "Yes, indeed. Each generation is worse than the last."

Her granddaughter-in-law, Mrs. Sevenpounder, had just brought out a basket of rice. Planking this down on the table, she said crossly, "There you go again, granny! Sixpounder weighed six pounds five ounces at birth, didn't she? Your family scales weigh light: eighteen ounces to the pound. With proper sixteen-ounce scales, Sixpounder would have weighed over seven pounds. I don't believe grandfather and father really weighed a full nine or eight pounds either. I daresay they were weighed with fourteen-ounce scales...."

是死的好。立刻就要吃飯了，還吃炒豆子，吃窮了一家子！」

伊的曾孫女兒六斤捏着一把豆，正從對面跑來，見這情形，便直奔河邊，藏在烏桕樹後，伸出雙丫角的小頭，大聲説，「這老不死的！」

九斤老太雖然高壽，耳朵卻還不很聾，但也沒有聽到孩子的話，仍舊自己説，「這真是一代不如一代！」

這村莊的習慣有點特別，女人生下孩子，多喜歡用秤稱了輕重，便用斤數當作小名。九斤老太自從慶祝了五十大壽以後，便漸漸的變了不平家，常説伊年青的時候，天氣沒有現在這般熱，豆子也沒有現在這般硬：總之現在的時世是不對了。何況六斤比伊的曾祖，少了三斤，比伊父親七斤，又少了一斤，這真是一條顛撲不破的實例，所以伊又用勁説，「這真是一代不如一代！」

伊的兒媳七斤嫂子正捧着飯籃走到桌邊，便將飯籃在桌上一摔，憤憤的説，「你老人家又這麽説了。六斤生下來的時候，不是六斤五兩麽？你家的秤又是私秤，加重稱，十八兩秤；用了準十六，我們的六斤該有七斤多哩。我想便是太公和公公，也不見得正是九斤八斤十足，用的秤也許是十四兩……」

"Each generation is worse than the last."

Before Mrs. Sevenpounder could answer, she saw her husband emerge from the top of the lane and rounded on him instead.

"Why so late back, you zombie? I thought you must be dead, keeping us waiting all this time for supper!"

Although a villager, Sevenpounder had always wanted to better himself. For three generations — grandfather, father and son — not a man in his family had handled a hoe. Like his father before him he worked on a boat which left Luzhen every morning for the town, returning to Luzhen in the evening. As a result he knew pretty well all that was going on; where, for instance, the thunder god had blasted a centipede spirit, or where a virgin had given birth to a demon. In the village he was quite a personage. Still he stuck to the country custom of not lighting a lamp for supper in the summer, so if he came home late he rated a scolding.

In one hand Sevenpounder held a speckled bamboo pipe over six feet long with an ivory mounthpiece and a pewter bowl. He walked slowly over, his head bent, and sat on one of the low stools. Sixpounder seized this chance to slip out and sit down beside him, calling "Dad!" But her father made no answer.

"Each generation is worse than the last," repeated Old Mrs. Ninepounder.

Sevenpounder slowly raised his head and sighed. "There's an emperor again on the Dragon Throne."

Mrs. Sevenpounder looked blank for a moment. Suddenly taking in the news she cried, "Good! That means another general amnesty, doesn't it?"

Sevenpounder sighed again. "I've no queue."

「一代不如一代！」

七斤嫂還沒有答話，忽然看見七斤從小巷口轉出，便移了方向，對他嚷道，「你這死屍怎麼這時候才回來，死到那裏去了！不管人家等着你開飯！」

七斤雖然住在農村，卻早有些飛黃騰達的意思。從他的祖父到他，三代不捏鋤頭柄了；他也照例的幫人撐着航船，每日一回，早晨從魯鎮進城，傍晚又回到魯鎮，因此很知道些時事：例如甚麼地方，雷公劈死了蜈蚣精；甚麼地方，閨女生了一個夜叉之類。他在村人裏面，的確已經是一名出場人物了。但夏天吃飯不點燈，卻還守着農家習慣，所以回家太遲，是該罵的。

七斤一手捏着象牙嘴白銅斗六尺多長的湘妃竹煙管，低着頭，慢慢地走來，坐在矮櫈上。六斤也趁勢溜出，坐在他身邊，叫他爹爹。七斤沒有應。

「一代不如一代！」九斤老太説。

七斤慢慢地抬起頭來，嘆一口氣説，「皇帝坐了龍庭了。」

七斤嫂呆了一刻，忽而恍然大悟的道，「這可好了，這不是又要皇恩大赦了麼！」

七斤又嘆一口氣，説，「我沒有辮子。」

"Does the emperor insist on queues?"

"He does."

"How do you know?" she demanded in dismay.

"Everybody in Prosperity Tavern says so."

At that Mrs. Sevenpounder realized instinctively that things were in a bad way, because Prosperity Tavern was a place where you could pick up all the news. She threw a glance at Sevenpounder's shaved head, unable to hold back her anger, blaming him, hating him, resenting him. Then, abruptly reduced to despair, she filled a bowl with rice and slapped it down before him. "Hurry up and eat. Pulling a long face won't grow a queue for you, will it?"

The sun had withdrawn its last rays, the darkling water was cooling off again. From the mud flat rose a clatter of bowls and chopsticks, and the backs of all the diners were beaded with sweat. Mrs. Sevenpounder had finished three bowls of rice when she happened to look up. At once her heart started pounding. Through the tallow leaves she could see the short plump figure of Seventh Master Zhao approaching from the one-plank bridge. And he was wearing his long sapphire-blue glazed cotton gown.

Seventh Master Zhao was the owner of Abundance Tavern in the next village, the only notable within a radius of thirty *li* who also had some learning. And because of this learning there was about him a whiff of the musty odour of a departed age. He owned a dozen volumes of the *Romance of the Three Kingdoms* annotated by Jin Shengtan, which he would sit poring over character by character. Not only could he tell you the names of the Five Tiger Generals, he even knew that Huang Zhong was also known as Hansheng, and Ma Chao as Mengqi. After the Revolution he had coiled his queue on the top of his head like a Taoist priest, and he often remarked with a sigh that if only

「皇帝要辮子麼？」

「皇帝要辮子。」

「你怎麼知道呢？」七斤嫂有些着急，趕忙的問。

「咸亨酒店裏的人，都説要的。」

七斤嫂這時從直覺上覺得事情似乎有些不妙了，因為咸亨酒店是消息靈通的所在。伊一轉眼瞥見七斤的光頭，便忍不住動怒，怪他恨他怨他；忽然又絕望起來，裝好一碗飯，搡在七斤的面前道，「還是趕快吃你的飯罷！哭喪着臉，就會長出辮子來麼？」

太陽收盡了他最末的光線了，水面暗暗地回復過涼氣來；土場上一片碗筷聲響，人人的脊樑上又都吐出汗粒。七斤嫂吃完三碗飯，偶然抬起頭，心坎裏便禁不住突突地發跳。伊透過烏桕葉，看見又矮又胖的趙七爺正從獨木橋上走來，而且穿着寶藍色竹布的長衫。

趙七爺是鄰村茂源酒店的主人，又是這三十里方圓以內的唯一的出色人物兼學問家；因為有學問，所以又有些遺老的臭味。他有十多本金聖嘆批評的《三國志》，時常坐着一個字一個字的讀；他不但能説出五虎將姓名，甚而至於還知道黃忠表字漢升和馬超表字孟起。革命以後，他便將辮子盤在頂上，像道士一般；常常嘆息説，

Zhao Yun were still alive the empire would not be in such a bad way.

Mrs. Sevenpounder's eyesight was good. She had noticed at once that Seventh Master Zhao no longer looked like a Taoist. He had shaved the front of his head and let his queue down. From this she knew beyond a doubt that an emperor had ascended the throne, that queues were required again, and that Sevenpounder must be in great danger. For Seventh Master Zhao did not wear his long glazed cotton gown for nothing. During the last three years he had only worn it twice: once when his enemy Pock-marked Asi fell ill, once when First Master Lu who had wrecked his wineshop died. This was the third time, and it undoubtedly meant that something had happened to rejoice his heart and bode ill for his enemies.

Two years ago, Mrs. Sevenpounder remembered, her husband in a fit of drunkenness had cursed Seventh Master Zhao as a "bastard." Hence she at once realized instinctively the danger her husband was in, and her heart started pounding.

As Seventh Master Zhao passed them, all those sitting eating stood up and, pointing their chopsticks at their rice bowls, invited him to join them. He nodded greetings to them all, urging them to go on with their meal, while he made straight for Sevenpounder's table. Sevenpounder's family got up at once to greet him. Seventh Master Zhao urged them with a smile, "Go on with your meal, please!" At the same time he took a good look at the food on the table.

"That dried rape smells good — have you heard the news?" Seventh Master Zhao was standing behind Sevenpounder opposite Mrs. Sevenpounder.

"There's an emperor again on the Dragon Throne," said Sevenpounder.

倘若趙子龍在世，天下便不會亂到這地步了。七斤嫂眼睛好，早望
見今天的趙七爺已經不是道士，卻變成光滑頭皮，烏黑髮頂；伊便
知道這一定是皇帝坐了龍庭，而且一定須有辮子，而且七斤一定是
非常危險。因為趙七爺的這件竹布長衫，輕易是不常穿的，三年以
來，只穿過兩次：一次是和他嘔氣的麻子阿四病了的時候，一次是
曾經砸爛他酒店的魯大爺死了的時候；現在是第三次了，這一定又
是於他有慶，於他的仇家有殃了。

　　七斤嫂記得，兩年前七斤喝醉了酒，曾經罵過趙七爺是「賤
胎」，所以這時便立刻直覺到七斤的危險，心坎裏突突地發起跳來。

　　趙七爺一路走來，坐着吃飯的人都站起身，拿筷子點着自己的
飯碗說，「七爺，請在我們這裏用飯！」七爺也一路點頭，說道「請
請」，卻一徑走到七斤家的桌旁。七斤們連忙招呼，七爺也微笑着說
「請請」，一面細細的研究他們的飯菜。

　　「好香的乾菜，——聽到了風聲了麼？」趙七爺站在七斤的後面
七斤嫂的對面說。

　　「皇帝坐了龍庭了。」七斤說。

Watching Seventh Master's expression, Mrs. Sevenpounder forced a smile. "Now that there's an emperor on the throne, when will there be a general amnesty?" She asked.

"A general amnesty?... All in good time." Suddenly Seventh Master spoke more sternly, "But what about Sevenpounder's queue, eh? That's the important thing. You know how it was in the time of the Long Hairs: keep your hair and lose your head; keep your head and lose your hair."

Sevenpounder and his wife had never read any books, so this classical lore was lost on them; but this statement from a learned man like Seventh Master convinced them that the situation must be desperate, past saving. It was as if they had received their death sentence. Their ears buzzed, and they were unable to utter another word.

"Each generation is worse than the last." Old Mrs. Ninepounder, feeling put out, seized this chance to speak to Seventh Master Zhao. "The Long Hairs nowadays just cut off men's queues, leaving them looking neither Buddhist nor Taoist. The old Long Hairs never did that. Seventy-nine years I've lived and that's enough. The old Long Hairs wore red satin turbans with one end hanging down, right down to their heels. The prince wore a yellow satin turban with one end hanging down ... yellow satin. Red satin, yellow satin ... I've lived long enough ... seventy-nine."

"What's to be done?" Muttered Mrs. Sevenpounder, standing up. "Such a big family, old and young, and all dependent on him...."

"There's nothing you can do." Seventh Master Zhao shook his head. "The punishment for having no queue is written down clearly in a book, sentence by sentence. The size of a man's family makes no difference."

When Mrs. Sevenpounder heard that it was written in a book, she

七斤嫂看着七爺的臉，竭力陪笑道，「皇帝已經坐了龍庭，幾時皇恩大赦呢？」

「皇恩大赦？——大赦是慢慢的總要大赦罷。」七爺說到這裏，聲色忽然嚴厲起來，「但是你家七斤的辮子呢，辮子？這倒是要緊的事。你們知道：長毛時候，留髮不留頭，留頭不留髮，……」

七斤和他的女人沒有讀過書，不很懂得這古典的奧妙，但覺得有學問的七爺這麼說，事情自然非常重大，無可挽回，便彷彿受了死刑宣告似的，耳朵裏嗡的一聲，再也說不出一句話。

「一代不如一代，——」九斤老太正在不平，趁這機會，便對趙七爺說，「現在的長毛，只是剪人家的辮子，僧不僧，道不道的。從前的長毛，這樣的麼？我活到七十九歲了，活夠了。從前的長毛是——整匹的紅緞子裹頭，拖下去，拖下去，一直拖到腳跟；王爺是黃緞子，拖下去，黃緞子；紅緞子，黃緞子，——我活夠了，七十九歲了。」

七斤嫂站起身，自言自語的說，「這怎麼好呢？這樣的一班老小，都靠他養活的人，……」

趙七爺搖頭道，「那也沒法。沒有辮子，該當何罪，書上都一條一條明明白白寫着的。不管他家裏有些甚麼人。」

七斤嫂聽到書上寫着，可真是完全絕望了；自己急得沒法，便

really gave way to despair. Beside herself with anxiety, she felt a sudden fresh hatred for Sevenpounder. Pointing her chopsticks at the tip of his nose, she cried. "As you make your bed, so you must lie on it! Didn't I say at the time of the revolt: Don't go out with the boat, don't go to town. But go he would. Off he rolled, and in town they cut off his queue, his glossy black queue. Now he looks neither Buddhist nor Taoist. He's made his own bed, he'll have to lie on it. But what right has the wretch to drag us into it? Jail-bird zombie...."

Seventh Master Zhao's arrival in the village made all the villagers finish their supper quickly and gather round Sevenpounder's table. Sevenpounder knew how unseemly it was for a prominent citizen to be cursed in public like this by his wife. So he raised his head to retort slowly:

"You've plenty to say today, but at the time...."

"Jail-bird zombie!..."

Widow Ba Yi had the kindest heart of all the onlookers there. Carrying her two-year-old, born after her husband's death, she was watching the fun at Mrs. Sevenpounder's side. Now she felt things had gone too far and hurriedly tried to make peace.

"Never mind, Mrs. Sevenpounder. People aren't spirits — who can foretell the future? Didn't you yourself say at the time there was nothing to be ashamed of in having no queue? Besides, no order's come down yet from the big mandarin in the yamen...."

Before she had finished, Mrs. Sevenpounder's ears were scarlet. She turned her chopsticks to point at the widow's nose. "*Aiya*, what a thing to say, Mrs. Ba Yi! I'm still a human being, ain't I — how could I have said anything so ridiculous? Why, at the time I cried for three whole days. Ask anyone you like. Even this little devil Sixpounder cried...." Sixpounder had just finished a big bowl of rice and was

忽然又恨到七斤。伊用筷子指着他的鼻尖説，「這死屍自作自受！造反的時候，我本來説，不要撐船了，不要上城了。他偏要死進城去，滾進城去，進城便被人剪去了辮子。從前是絹光烏黑的辮子，現在弄得僧不僧道不道的。這囚徒自作自受，帶累了我們又怎麼説呢？這活死屍的囚徒……」

村人看見趙七爺到村，都趕緊吃完飯，聚在七斤家飯桌的周圍。七斤自己知道是出場人物，被女人當大眾這樣辱罵，很不雅觀，便只得抬起頭，慢慢地説道：

「你今天説現成話，那時你……」

「你這活死屍的囚徒……」

看客中間，八一嫂是心腸最好的人，抱着伊的兩週歲的遺腹子，正在七斤嫂身邊看熱鬧；這時過意不去，連忙解勸説，「七斤嫂，算了罷。人不是神仙，誰知道未來事呢？便是七斤嫂，那時不也説，沒有辮子倒也沒有甚麼醜麼？況且衙門裏的大老爺也還沒有告示，……」

七斤嫂沒有聽完，兩個耳朵早通紅了；便將筷子轉過向來，指着八一嫂的鼻子，説，「阿呀，這是甚麼話呵！八一嫂，我自己看來倒還是一個人，會説出這樣昏誕糊塗話麼？那時我是，整整哭了三天，誰都看見；連六斤這小鬼也都哭，……」六斤剛吃完一大碗飯，

holding out her empty bowl clamouring to have it refilled. Mrs. Sevenpounder, being in a temper, smacked her chopsticks down between the twin tufts on the child's head. "Who wants you to barge in?" She yelled. "Little slut!"

Crack! The empty bowl in Sixpounder's hand thudded to the ground striking the corner of a brick so that a big piece broke off. Sevenpounder jumped to his feet and picked up the broken bowl. Having fitted the pieces together he examined it, swearing, "Mother's!" He gave Sixpounder a slap that knocked her over. Sixpounder lay there crying until Old Mrs. Ninepounder took her hand and led her away repeating, "Each generation is worse than the last."

Now it was Widow Ba Yi's turn to be angry. "How can you hit out at random like that, Mrs. Sevenpounder!" She shouted.

Seventh Master Zhao had been looking on with a smile, but after Widow Ba Yi's statement that no order had come down from "the big mandarin in the yamen" he began to lose his temper. Coming right up to the table, he declared, "Hitting out at random doesn't matter. The Imperial Army will be here any time now. I'd have you know the new Protector is General Zhang, who's descended from Zhang Fei of the former state of Yan. With his huge lance eighteen feet long, he dares take on ten thousand men. Who can stand against him?" Raising both hands as if grasping a huge invisible lance, he took a few swift paces towards Widow Ba Yi. "Are you a match for him?"

Widow Ba Yi was trembling with rage as she held her child. But the sudden sight of Seventh Master Zhao bearing down on her with glaring eyes, his whole face oozing sweat, gave her the fright of her life. Not daring to say more, she turned and fled. Then Seventh Master Zhao left too. The villagers as they made way for him deplored Widow Ba Yi's interference, while a few men who had cut their queues and started growing them again hid hastily behind the rest for fear

拿了空碗，伸手去嚷着要添。七斤嫂正沒好氣，便用筷子在伊的雙丫角中間，直扎下去，大喝道：「誰要你來多嘴！你這偷漢的小寡婦！」

撲的一聲，六斤手裏的空碗落在地上了，恰巧又碰着一塊磚角，立刻破成一個很大的缺口。七斤直跳起來，撿起破碗，合上了檢查一回，也喝道，「入娘的！」一巴掌打倒了六斤。六斤躺着哭，九斤老太拉了伊的手，連說着「一代不如一代」，一同走了。

八一嫂也發怒，大聲説，「七斤嫂，你『恨棒打人』……」

趙七爺本來是笑着旁觀的；但自從八一嫂説了「衙門裏的大老爺沒有告示」這話以後，卻有些生氣了。這時他已經繞出桌旁，接道説，「『恨棒打人』，算甚麼呢。大兵是就要到的。你可知道，這回保駕的是張大帥，張大帥就是燕人張翼德的後代，他一支丈八蛇矛，就有萬夫不當之勇，誰能抵擋他，」他兩手同時捏起空拳，彷彿握着無形的蛇矛模樣，向八一嫂搶進幾步道，「你能抵擋他麼！」

八一嫂正氣得抱着孩子發抖，忽然見趙七爺滿臉油汗，瞪着眼，準對伊衝過來，便十分害怕，不敢説完話，回身走了。趙七爺也跟着走去，眾人一面怪八一嫂多事，一面讓開路，幾個剪過辮子重新留起的便趕快躲在人叢後面，怕他看見。趙七爺也不細心察

Seventh Master should see them. However, without making a careful inspection Seventh Master passed through the group, dived behind the tallow trees and with a parting "Think you're a match for him!" strode on to the one-plank bridge and swaggered off.

The villagers stood there blankly, turning things over in their minds. All felt they were indeed no match for Zhang Fei, hence Sevenpounder's life was as good as lost. And since Sevenpounder had broken the imperial law he should not, they felt, have adopted that lordly air, smoking that long pipe of his, when he told them the news from town. So the thought that he had broken the law gave them a certain pleasure. They would have liked to air their views, but did not know what to say. Buzzing mosquitoes, brushing past their bare arms, zoomed back to swarm beneath the tallow trees; and the villagers too slowly scattered to their homes, shut their doors and went to bed. Grumbling to herself, Mrs. Sevenpounder also cleared away the dishes and took in the table and stools, then closed the door and went to bed.

Sevenpounder took the broken bowl inside, then sat on the doorstep smoking. He was so worried, however, that he forgot to inhale, and the light in the pewter bowl of his six-foot speckled bamboo pipe with the ivory mouthpiece gradually turned black. It struck him that matters had reached a most dangerous pass, and he tried to think of a way out, some plan of action. But his thoughts were in too much of a whirl for him to straighten them out. "Queues, eh, queues? An eighteen foot lance. Each generation is worse than the last! An emperor is on the Dragon Throne. The broken bowl will have to be taken to town to be riveted. Who's a match for him? It's written in a book. Mother's!..."

Early the next day, as usual, Sevenpounder went with the boat to town, coming back to Luzhen towards evening with his six-foot speckled bamboo pipe and the rice bowl. At supper he told Old Mrs. Ninepounder that he had had the bowl riveted in town. Because it

訪，通過人叢，忽然轉入烏柏樹後，說道「你能抵擋他麼！」跨上獨木橋，揚長去了。

村人們呆呆站着，心裏計算，都覺得自己確乎抵不住張翼德，因此也決定七斤便要沒有性命。七斤既然犯了皇法，想起他往常對人談論城中的新聞的時候，就不該含着長煙管顯出那般驕傲模樣，所以對於七斤的犯法，也覺得有些暢快。他們也彷彿想發些議論，卻又覺得沒有甚麼議論可發。嗡嗡的一陣亂嚷，蚊子都撞過赤膊身子，闖到烏柏樹下去做市；他們也就慢慢地走散回家，關上門去睡覺。七斤嫂咕嘻着，也收了傢伙和桌子矮橙回家，關上門睡覺了。

七斤將破碗拿回家裏，坐在門檻上吸煙；但非常憂愁，忘卻了吸煙，象牙嘴六尺多長湘妃竹煙管的白銅斗裏的火光，漸漸發黑了。他心裏但覺得事情似乎十分危急，也想想些方法，想些計劃，但總是非常模糊，貫穿不得：「辮子呢辮子？丈八蛇矛。一代不如一代！皇帝坐龍庭。破的碗須得上城去釘好。誰能抵擋他？書上一條一條寫着。入娘的！……」

第二日清晨，七斤依舊從魯鎮撐航船進城，傍晚回到魯鎮，又拿着六尺多長的湘妃竹煙管和一個飯碗回村。他在晚飯席上，對九斤老太說，這碗是在城內釘合的，因為缺口大，所以要十六個銅

was such a large break, sixteen copper clamps had been needed, each costing three cash, making the total cost forty-eight cash.

"Each generation is worse than the last," said Old Mrs. Ninepounder crossly. "I've lived long enough. Three cash for a clamp. Clamps didn't cost so much in the old days. The clamps we had.... Seventy-nine years I've lived...."

After this, though Sevenpounder continued making his daily trip to town, his house seemed to be under a cloud. Most of the villagers kept out of his way, no longer coming to ask him the news from town. Mrs. Sevenpounder was in a bad temper too, constantly addressing him as "Jail-bird."

A fortnight or so later, on his return from town Sevenpounder found his wife in a rare good humour. "Heard anything in town?" She asked him.

"No, nothing."

"Is there an emperor on the Dragon Throne?"

"They didn't say."

"Did no one in Prosperity Tavern say anything?"

"No, nothing."

"I don't believe there's an emperor again. I passed Seventh Master Zhao's wineshop today and he was sitting there reading, with his queue coiled on top of his head again. He wasn't wearing his long gown either."

"..."

"Do you think there's no emperor after all?"

"I think probably not."

釘，三文一個，一總用了四十八文小錢。

九斤老太很不高興的説，「一代不如一代，我是活夠了。三文錢一個釘；從前的釘，這樣的麼？從前的釘是……我活了七十九歲了，——」

此後七斤雖然是照例日日進城，但家景總有些黯淡，村人大抵迴避着，不再來聽他從城內得來的新聞。七斤嫂也沒有好聲氣，還時常叫他「囚徒」。

過了十多日，七斤從城內回家，看見他的女人非常高興，問他説，「你在城裏可聽到些甚麼？」

「沒有聽到些甚麼。」

「皇帝坐了龍庭沒有呢？」

「他們沒有説。」

「咸亨酒店裏也沒有人説麼？」

「也沒人説。」

「我想皇帝一定是不坐龍庭了。我今天走過趙七爺的店前，看見他又坐着唸書了，辮子又盤在頂上了，也沒有穿長衫。」

「……」

「你想，不坐龍庭了罷？」

「我想，不坐了罷。」

Today Sevenpounder is once more respected and well treated by his wife and the villagers. In the summer his family still have their meals on the mud flat outside their door, and everyone greets them with smiles. Old Mrs. Ninepounder celebrated her eightieth birthday some time ago and is as full of complaints, as hale and hearty as ever. Sixpounder's twin tufts of hair have changed into a thick braid. Although recently they started binding her feet, she can still help Mrs. Sevenpounder with odd jobs. She hobbles to and fro on the mud flat carrying the rice bowl with sixteen copper rivets.

October 1920

　　現在的七斤，是七斤嫂和村人又都早給他相當的尊敬，相當的
待遇了。到夏天，他們仍舊在自家門口的土場上吃飯；大家見了，
都笑嘻嘻的招呼。九斤老太早已做過八十大壽，仍然不平而且康
健。六斤的雙丫角，已經變成一支大辮子了；伊雖然新近裹腳，卻
還能幫同七斤嫂做事，捧着十八個銅釘的飯碗，在土場上一瘸一拐
的往來。

　　　　　　　　　　　　　　　　一九二零年十月。

故 郷

My Old Home

MY OLD HOME

Braving the bitter cold, I travelled more than two thousand *li* back to the old home I had left over twenty years ago.

It was late winter. As we drew near my former home the day became overcast and a cold wind blew into the cabin of our boat, while all one could see through the chinks in our bamboo awning were a few desolate villages, void of any sign of life, scattered far and near under the sombre yellow sky. I could not help feeling depressed.

Ah! Surely this was not the old home I had been remembering for the past twenty years?

The old home I remembered was not in the least like this. My old home was much better. But if you asked me to recall its peculiar charm or describe its beauties, I had no clear impression, no words to describe it. And now it seemed this was all there was to it. Then I rationalized the matter to myself, saying: Home was always like this, and although it had not improved, still it is not so depressing as I imagine; it is only my mood that has changed, because I am coming back to the country this time with no illusions.

This time I had come with the sole object of saying goodbye. The old house our clan had lived in for so many years had already been sold to another family, and was to change hands before the end of the

故　　鄉

我冒了嚴寒，回到相隔二千餘里，別了二十餘年的故鄉去。

時候既然是深冬；漸近故鄉時，天氣又陰晦了，冷風吹進船艙中，嗚嗚的響，從縫隙向外一望，蒼黃的天底下，遠近橫着幾個蕭索的荒村，沒有一些活氣。我的心禁不住悲涼起來了。

阿！這不是我二十年來時時記得的故鄉？

我所記得的故鄉全不如此。我的故鄉好得多了。但要我記起他的美麗，說出他的佳處來，卻又沒有影像，沒有言辭了。彷彿也就如此。於是我自己解釋說：故鄉本也如此，——雖然沒有進步，也未必有如我所感的悲涼，這只是我自己心情的改變罷了，因為我這次回鄉，本沒有甚麼好心緒。

我這次是專為了別他而來的。我們多年聚族而居的老屋，已經公同賣給別姓了，交屋的期限，只在本年，所以必須趕在正月初一

year. I had to hurry there before New Year's Day to say goodbye for ever to the familiar old house, and to move my family to another place where I was working, far from my old home town.

At dawn on the second day I reached the gateway of my home. Broken stems of withered grass on the roof, trembling in the wind, made very clear the reason why this old house could not avoid changing hands. Several branches of our clan had probably already moved away, so it was unusually quiet. By the time I reached the house my mother was already at the door to welcome me, and my eight-year-old nephew, Hong'er rushed out after her.

Though Mother was delighted, she was also trying to hide a certain feeling of sadness. She told me to sit down and rest and have some tea, letting the removal wait for the time being. Hong'er, who had never seen me before, stood watching me at a distance.

But finally we had to talk about the removal. I said that rooms had already been rented elsewhere, and I had bought a little furniture; in addition it would be necessary to sell all the furniture in the house in order to buy more things. Mother agreed, saying that the luggage was nearly all packed, and about half the furniture that could not be easily moved had already been sold. Only it was difficult to get people to pay up.

"You can rest for a day or two, and call on our relatives, and then we can go," said Mother.

"Yes."

"Then there is Runtu. Each time he comes here he always asks after you, and wants very much to see you again. I told him the probable date of your return home, and he may be coming any time."

At this point a strange picture suddenly flashed into my mind: a

以前，永別了熟識的老屋，而且遠離了熟識的故鄉，搬家到我在謀食的異地去。

　　第二日清早晨我到了我家的門口了。瓦楞上許多枯草的斷莖當風抖着，正在說明這老屋難免易主的原因。幾房的本家大約已經搬走了，所以很寂靜。我到了自家的房外，我的母親早已迎着出來了，接着便飛出了八歲的侄兒宏兒。

　　我的母親很高興，但也藏着許多淒涼的神情，教我坐下，歇息，喝茶，且不談搬家的事。宏兒沒有見過我，遠遠的對面站着只是看。

　　但我們終於談到搬家的事。我說外間的寓所已經租定了，又買了幾件傢俱，此外須將家裏所有的木器賣去，再去增添。母親也說好，而且行李也略已齊集，木器不便搬運的，也小半賣去了，只是收不起錢來。

　　「你休息一兩天，去拜望親戚本家一回，我們便可以走了。」母親說。

　　「是的。」

　　「還有閏土，他每到我家來時，總問起你，很想見你一回面。我已經將你到家的大約日期通知他，他也許就要來了。」

　　這時候，我的腦裏忽然閃出一幅神異的圖畫來：深藍的天空中

golden moon suspended in a deep blue sky and beneath it the seashore, planted as far as the eye could see with jadegreen watermelons, while in their midst a boy of eleven or twelve, wearing a silver necklet and grasping a steel pitchfork in his hand, was thrusting with all his might at a *zha* which dodged the blow and escaped through his legs.

This boy was Runtu. When I first met him he was little more than ten — that was thirty years ago, and at that time my father was still alive and the family well off, so I was really a spoilt child. That year it was our family's turn to take charge of a big ancestral sacrifice, which came round only once in thirty years, and hence was an important one. In the first month the ancestral images were presented and offerings made, and since the sacrificial vessels were very fine and there was such a crowd of worshippers, it was necessary to guard against theft. Our family had only one part-time servant. (In our district we divide servants into three classes: those who work all the year for one family are called full-timers; those who are hired by the day are called dailies; and those who farm their own land and only work for one family at New Year, during festivals or when rents are being collected are called part-timers.) And since there was so much to be done, he told my father that he would send for his son Runtu to look after the sacrificial vessels.

When my father gave his consent I was overjoyed, because I had long since heard of Runtu and knew that he was about my own age, born in the intercalary month, and when his horoscope was told it was found that of the five elements that of earth was lacking, so his father called him Runtu (Intercalary Earth). He could set traps and catch small birds.

I looked forward every day to New Year, for New Year would bring Runtu. At last the end of the year came, and one day Mother told me that Runtu had come, and I flew to see him. He was standing in the

掛着一輪金黃的圓月，下面是海邊的沙地，都種着一望無際的碧綠的西瓜，其間有一個十一二歲的少年，項帶銀圈，手捏一柄鋼叉，向一匹猹盡力的刺去，那猹卻將身一扭，反從他的胯下逃走了。

這少年便是閏土。我認識他時，也不過十多歲，離現在將有三十年了；那時我的父親還在世，家景也好，我正是一個少爺。那一年，我家是一件大祭祀的值年。這祭祀，説是三十多年才能輪到一回，所以很鄭重；正月裏供祖像，供品很多，祭器很講究，拜的人也很多，祭器也很要防偷去。我家只有一個忙月（我們這裏給人做工的分三種：整年給一定人家做工的叫長年；按日給人做工的叫短工；自己也種地，只在過年過節以及收租時候來給一定的人家做工的稱忙月），忙不過來，他便對父親説，可以叫他的兒子閏土來管祭器的。

我的父親允許了；我也很高興，因為我早聽到閏土這名字，而且知道他和我彷彿年紀，閏月生的，五行缺土，所以他的父親叫他閏土。他是能裝弶捉小鳥雀的。

我於是日日盼望新年，新年到，閏土也就到了。好容易到了年末，有一日，母親告訴我，閏土來了，我便飛跑的去看。他正在廚

kitchen. He had a round, crimson face and wore a small felt cap on his head and a gleaming silver necklet on his neck, showing that his father doted on him and, fearing he might die, had made a pledge with the gods and Buddhas, using the necklet as a talisman. He was very shy, and I was the only person he was not afraid of. When there was no one else there, he would talk with me, so in a few hours we were fast friends.

I don't know what we talked of then, but I remember that Runtu was in high spirits, saying that since he had come to town he had seen many new things.

The next day I wanted him to catch birds.

"Can't be done," he said. "It's only possible after a heavy snowfall. On our sands, after it snows, I sweep clear a patch of ground, prop up a big threshing basket with a short stick, and scatter husks of grain beneath; then when I see the birds coming to eat, from a distance I give a tug to the string tied to the stick, and the birds are caught in the basket. There are all kinds: wild pheasants, woodcocks, woodpigeons, bluebacks...."

Accordingly I looked forward very eagerly to snow.

"Just now it is too cold," said Runtu another time, "but you must come to our place in summer. In the daytime we will go to the seashore to look for shells, there are green ones and red ones, besides 'scare-devil' shells and 'Buddha's hands.' In the evening when Dad and I go to see to the watermelons, you shall come too."

"Is it to look out for thieves?"

"No. If passers-by are thirsty and pick a watermelon, folk down our way don't consider it as stealing. What we have to look out for are stoats, hedgehogs and *zha*. When you hear a crunching sound under

房裏，紫色的圓臉，頭戴一頂小氈帽，頸上套一個明晃晃的銀項圈，這可見他的父親十分愛他，怕他死去，所以在神佛面前許下願心，用圈子將他套住了。他見人很怕羞，只是不怕我，沒有旁人的時候，便和我說話，於是不到半日，我們便熟識了。

我們那時候不知道談些甚麼，只記得閏土很高興，說是上城之後，見了許多沒有見過的東西。

第二日，我便要他捕鳥。他說：

「這不能。須大雪下了才好。我們沙地上，下了雪，我掃出一塊空地來，用短棒支起一個大竹匾，撒下粃穀，看鳥雀來吃時，我遠遠地將縛在棒上的繩子只一拉，那鳥雀就罩在竹匾下了。甚麼都有：稻雞、角雞、鵓鴣、藍背……」

我於是又很盼望下雪。

閏土又對我說：

「現在太冷，你夏天到我們這裏來。我們日裏到海邊檢貝殼去，紅的綠的都有，鬼見怕也有，觀音手也有。晚上我和爹管西瓜去，你也去。」

「管賊麼？」

「不是。走路的人口渴了摘一個瓜吃，我們這裏是不算偷的。要管的是獾豬、刺蝟、猹。月亮地下，你聽，啦啦的響了，猹在咬瓜

the moonlight, made by the biting the melons, then you take your pitchfork and creep stealthily over...."

I had no idea then what this thing called *zha* was — and I am not much clearer now, for that matter — but somehow I felt it was something like a small dog, and very fierce.

"Don't they bite people?"

"You have a pitchfork. You go across, and when you see it you strike. It's a very cunning creature and will rush towards you and get away between you legs. Its fur is as slippery as oil...."

I had never known that all these strange things existed: at the seashore were shells all the colours of the rainbow; watermelons had such a dangerous history, yet all I had known of them before was that they were sold in the greengrocer's.

"On our shore, when the tide comes in, there are lots of jumping fish, each with two legs like a frog...."

Runtu's mind was a treasure-house of such strange lore, all of it outside the ken of my former friends. They were ignorant of all these things and, while Runtu lived by the sea, they like me could see only the four corners of the sky above the high courtyard wall.

Unfortunately, a month after New Year Runtu had to go home. I burst into tears and he took refuge in the kitchen, crying and refusing to come out, until finally he was carried off by his father. Later he sent me by his father a packet of shells and a few very beautiful feathers, and I sent him presents once or twice, but we never saw each other again.

Now that my mother mentioned him, this childhood memory sprang into life like a flash of lightning, and I seemed to see my beautiful old home. So I answered:

了。你便捏了胡叉，輕輕地走去……」

我那時並不知道這所謂猹的是怎麼一件東西——便是現在也沒有知道——只是無端的覺得狀如小狗而很兇猛。

「他不咬人麼？」

「有胡叉呢。走到了，看見猹了，你便刺。這畜生很伶俐，倒向你奔來，反從胯下竄了。他的皮毛是油一般的滑……」

我素不知道天下有這許多新鮮事：海邊有如許五色的貝殼；西瓜有這樣危險的經歷，我先前單知道他在水果店裏出賣罷了。

「我們沙地裏，潮汛要來的時候，就有許多跳魚兒只是跳，都有青蛙似的兩個腳……」

阿！閏土的心裏有無窮無盡的希奇的事，都是我往常的朋友所不知道的。他們不知道一些事，閏土在海邊時，他們都和我一樣只看見院子裏高牆上的四角的天空。

可惜正月過去了，閏土須回家裏去，我急得大哭，他也躲到廚房裏，哭着不肯出門，但終於被他父親帶走了。他後來還託他的父親帶給我一包貝殼和幾支很好看的鳥毛，我也曾送他一兩次東西，但從此沒有再見面。

現在我的母親提起了他，我這兒時的記憶，忽而全都閃電似的蘇生過來，似乎看到了我的美麗的故鄉了。我應聲說：

"Fine! And he — how is he?"

"He?... He's not at all well off either," said Mother. And then, looking out of the door: "Here come those people again. They say they want to buy our furniture; but actually they just want to see what they can pick up. I must go and watch them."

Mother stood up and went out. Several women's voices could be heard outside. I called Hong'er to me and started talking to him, asking him whether he could write, and whether he was glad to be leaving.

"Shall we be going by train?"

"Yes, we shall go by train."

"And boat?"

"We shall take a boat first."

"Oh! Like this! With such a long moustache!" A strange shrill voice suddenly rang out.

I looked up with a start, and saw a woman of about fifty with prominent cheekbones and thin lips standing in front of me, her hands on her hips, not wearing a skirt but with trousered legs apart, just like the compass in a box of geometrical instruments.

I was flabbergasted.

"Don't you know me? And I have held you in my arms!"

I felt even more flabbergasted. Fortunately my mother came in just then and said, "He has been away so long, you must excuse him for forgetting."

"You should remember," she said to me, "this is Mrs. Yang from across the road.... She has a beancurd shop."

「這好極！他，——怎樣？……」

「他？……他景況也很不如意……」母親說着，便向房外看，「這些人又來了。說是買木器，順手也就隨便拿走的，我得去看看。」

母親站起身，出去了。門外有幾個女人的聲音。我便招宏兒走近面前，和他閒話：問他可會寫字，可願意出門。

「我們坐火車去麼？」

「我們坐火車去。」

「船呢？」

「先坐船，……」

「哈！這模樣了！鬍子這麼長了！」一種尖利的怪聲突然大叫起來。

我吃了一嚇，趕忙抬起頭，卻見一個凸顴骨，薄嘴唇，五十歲上下的女人站在我面前，兩手搭在髀間，沒有繫裙，張着兩腳，正像一個畫圖儀器裏細腳伶仃的圓規。

我愕然了。

「不認識了麼？我還抱過你咧！」

我愈加愕然了。幸而我的母親也就進來，從旁說：

「他多年出門，統忘卻了。你該記得罷，」便向着我說，「這是斜對門的楊二嫂，……開豆腐店的。」

Then, to be sure, I remembered. When I was a child there was a Mrs. Yang who used to sit nearly all day long in the beancurd shop across the road, and everybody used to call her Beancurd Beauty. But she used to powder herself, and her cheekbones were not so prominent then nor her lips so thin; moreover she remained seated all the time, so that I had never noticed this resemblance to a compass. In those days people said that, thanks to her, that beancurd shop did very good business. But, probably on account of my age, she had made no impression on me, so that later I forgot her entirely. However, the Compass was extremely indignant and looked at me most contemptuously, just as one might look at a Frenchman who had never heard of Napoleon or an American who had never heard of Washington, and smiling sarcastically she said:

"You had forgotten? But naturally I must be beneath your notice...."

"Certainly not ... I ..." I answered nervously, getting to my feet.

"Then you listen to me, Master Xun. You have grown rich, and they are too heavy to move, so you can't possibly want these old pieces of furniture any more. You had better let me take them away. Poor people like us can do with them."

"I haven't grown rich. I must sell these in order to buy...."

"Oh, come now, you have been made the intendant of a circuit, and do you still say you're not rich? You have three concubines now, and whenever you go out it is in a big sedan-chair with eight bearers, and do you still say you're not rich? Hah! You can't hide anything from me."

Knowing there was nothing I could say, I remained silent.

"Come now, really, the more money people have the more miserly

　　哦，我記得了。我孩子時候，在斜對門的豆腐店裏確乎終日坐着一個楊二嫂，人都叫伊「豆腐西施」。但是擦着白粉，顴骨沒有這麼高，嘴唇也沒有這麼薄，而且終日坐着，我也從沒有見過這圓規式的姿勢。那時人説：因為伊，這豆腐店的買賣非常好。但這大約因為年齡的關係，我卻並未蒙着一毫感化，所以竟完全忘卻了。然而圓規很不平，顯出鄙夷的神色，彷彿嗤笑法國人不知道拿破侖，美國人不知道華盛頓似的，冷笑説：

　　「忘了？這真是貴人眼高……」

　　「那有這事……我……」我惶恐着，站起來説。

　　「那麼，我對你説。迅哥兒，你闊了，搬動又笨重，你還要甚麼這些破爛木器，讓我拿去罷。我們小戶人家，用得着。」

　　「我並沒有闊哩。我須賣了這些，再去……」

　　「阿呀呀，你放了道台了，還説不闊？你現在有三房姨太太；出門便是八抬的大轎，還説不闊？嚇，甚麼都瞞不過我。」

　　我知道無話可説了，便閉了口，默默的站着。

　　「阿呀阿呀，真是愈有錢，便愈是一毫不肯放鬆，愈是一毫不肯

they get, and the more miserly they are the more money they get,"
said the Compass, turning indignantly away and walking slowly off,
casually picking up a pair of Mother's gloves and stuffing them into
her pocket as she went out.

After this a number of relatives in the neighbourhood came to call.
In the intervals between entertaining them I did some packing, and so
three or four days passed.

One very cold afternoon, I was sitting drinking tea after lunch when
I was aware of someone coming in, and turned my head to see who it
was. At the first glance I gave an involuntary start, and hastily stood
up and went over to welcome him.

The newcomer was Runtu. But although I knew at a glance that
this was Runtu, it was not the Runtu I remembered. He had grown to
twice his former size. His round face, crimson before, had become
sallow and acquired deep lines and wrinkles; his eyes too had become
like his father's with rims swollen and red, a feature common to most
of the peasants who work by the sea and are exposed all day to the
wind from the ocean. He wore a shabby felt cap and just one very thin
padded jacket, with the result that he was shivering from head to foot.
He was carrying a paper package and a long pipe, nor was his hand
the plump red hand I remembered, but coarse and clumsy and
chapped, like the bark of a pine tree.

Delighted as I was, I did not know how to express myself, and
could only say:

"Oh! Runtu — so it's you?..."

After this there were so many things I wanted to talk about, they
should have poured out like a string of beads: woodcocks, jumping
fish, shells, *zha*.... But I was tongue-tied, unable to put all I was thinking into words.

放鬆，便愈有錢⋯⋯」圓規一面憤憤的回轉身，一面絮絮的説，慢慢向外走，順便將我母親的一副手套塞在褲腰裏，出去了。

此後又有近處的本家和親戚來訪問我。我一面應酬，偷空便收拾些行李，這樣的過了三四天。

一日是天氣很冷的午後，我吃過午飯，坐着喝茶，覺得外面有人進來了，便回頭去看。我看時，不由的非常出驚，慌忙站起身，迎着走去。

這來的便是閏土。雖然我一見便知道是閏土，但又不是我這記憶上的閏土了。他身材增加了一倍；先前的紫色的圓臉，已經變作灰黃，而且加上了很深的皺紋；眼睛也像他父親一樣，周圍都腫得通紅，這我知道，在海邊種地的人，終日吹着海風，大抵是這樣的。他頭上是一頂破氈帽，身上只一件極薄的棉衣，渾身瑟索着；手裏提着一個紙包和一支長煙管，那手也不是我所記得的紅活圓實的手，卻又粗又笨而且開裂，像是松樹皮了。

我這時很興奮，但不知道怎麼説才好，只是説：

「阿！閏土哥，──你來了？⋯⋯」

我接着便有許多話，想要連珠一般湧出：角雞、跳魚兒、貝殼、猹，⋯⋯但又總覺得被甚麼擋着似的，單在腦裏面迴旋，吐不出口外去。

He stood there, mixed joy and sadness showing on his face. His lips moved, but not a sound did he utter. Finally, assuming a respectful attitude, he said clearly:

"Master! ..."

I felt a shiver run through me; for I knew then what a lamentably thick wall had grown up between us. Yet I could not say anything.

He turned his head to call:

"Shuisheng, bow to the master." Then he pulled forward a boy who had been hiding behind his back, and this was just the Runtu of twenty years before, only a little paler and thinner, and he had no silver necklet on his neck.

"This is my fifth." he said. "He has not seen any society, so he is shy and awkward."

Mother came downstairs with Hong'er, probably after hearing out voices.

"I got the letter some time ago, madam," said Runtu. "I was really so pleased to know that the master was coming back...."

"Now, why ever are you so polite? Weren't you playmates together in the past?" said Mother gaily. "You had better still call him Brother Xun as before."

"Oh, you are really too.... What bad manners that would be. I was a child then and didn't understand." As he was speaking Runtu motioned Shuisheng to come and bow, but the child was shy, and only stood stock-still behind his father.

"So he is Shuisheng? Your fifth?" asked Mother. "We are all strangers, you can't blame him for feeling shy. Hong'er had better take him to play."

他站住了，臉上現出歡喜和淒涼的神情；動着嘴唇，卻沒有作聲。他的態度終於恭敬起來了，分明的叫道：

「老爺！……」

我似乎打了一個寒噤；我就知道，我們之間已經隔了一層可悲的厚障壁了，我也說不出話。

他回過頭去說，「水生，給老爺磕頭。」便拖出躲在背後的孩子來，這正是一個廿年前的閏土，只是黃瘦些，頸子上沒有銀圈罷了。「這是第五個孩子，沒有見過世面，躲躲閃閃……」

母親和宏兒下樓來了，他們大約也聽到了聲音。

「老太太。信是早收到了。我實在喜歡的了不得，知道老爺回來……」閏土說。

「阿，你怎的這樣客氣起來。你們先前不是哥弟稱呼麼？還是照舊：迅哥兒。」母親高興的說。

「阿呀，老太太真是……這成甚麼規矩。那時是孩子，不懂事……」閏土說着，又叫水生上來打拱，那孩子卻害羞，緊緊的只貼在他背後。

「他就是水生？第五個？都是生人，怕生也難怪的；還是宏兒和他去走走。」母親說。

When Hong'er heard this he went over to Shuisheng, and Shuisheng went out with him, entirely at his ease. Mother asked Runtu to sit down, and after a little hesitation he did so; then leaning his long pipe against the table he handed over the paper package, saying:

"In winter there is nothing worth bringing; but these few beans we dried ourselves there, if you will excuse the liberty, sir."

When I asked him how things were with him, he just shook his head.

"In a very bad way. Even my sixth can do a little work, but still we haven't enough to eat ... and then there is no security.... All sorts of people want money, and there is no fixed rule ... and the harvests are bad. You grow things, and when you take them to sell you always have to pay several taxes and lose money, while if you don't try to sell, the things may go bad.... "

He kept shaking his head; yet, although his face was lined with wrinkles, not one of them moved, just as if he were a stone statue. No doubt he felt intensely bitter, but could not express himself. After a pause he took up his pipe and began to smoke in silence.

From her chat with him, Mother learned that he was busy at home and had to go back the next day; and since he had had no lunch, she told him to go to the kitchen and fry some rice for himself.

After he had gone out, Mother and I both shook our heads over his hard life: many children, famines, taxes, soldiers, bandits, officials and landed gentry, all had squeezed him as dry as a mummy. Mother said that we should offer him all the things we were not going to take away, letting him choose for himself.

That afternoon he picked out a number of things: two long tables, four chairs, an incense-burner and candlesticks, and one balance. He

宏兒聽得這話，便來招水生，水生卻鬆鬆爽爽同他一路出去了。母親叫閏土坐，他遲疑了一回，終於就了坐，將長煙管靠在桌旁，遞過紙包來，說：

「冬天沒有甚麼東西了。這一點乾青豆倒是自家曬在那裏的，請老爺……」

我問問他的景況。他只是搖頭。

「非常難。第六個孩子也會幫忙了，卻總是吃不夠……又不太平……甚麼地方都要錢，沒有定規……收成又壞。種出東西來，挑去賣，總要捐幾回錢，折了本；不去賣，又只能爛掉……」

他只是搖頭；臉上雖然刻着許多皺紋，卻全然不動，彷彿石像一般。他大約只是覺得苦，卻又形容不出，沉默了片時，便拿起煙管來默默的吸煙了。

母親問他，知道他的家裏事務忙，明天便得回去；又沒有吃過午飯，便叫他自己到廚下炒飯吃去。

他出去了；母親和我都嘆息他的景況：多子、饑荒、苛稅、兵、匪、官、紳，都苦得他像一個木偶人了。母親對我說，凡是不必搬走的東西，盡可以送他，可以聽他自己去揀擇。

下午，他揀好了幾件東西：兩條長桌，四個椅子，一副香爐和燭台，一桿抬秤。他又要所有的草灰（我們這裏煮飯是燒稻草的，那

also asked for all the ashes from the stove (in our part we cook over straw, and the ashes can be used to fertilize sandy soil), saying that when we left he would come to take them away by boat.

That night we talked again, but not of anything serious; and the next morning he went away with Shuisheng.

After another nine days it was time for us to leave. Runtu came in the morning. Shuisheng had not come with him — he had just brought a little girl of five to watch the boat. We were very busy all day, and had no time to talk. We also had quite a number of visitors, some to see us off, some to fetch things, and some to do both. It was nearly evening when we got on the boat, and by that time everything in the house, however old or shabby, large or small, fine or coarse, had been cleared away.

As we set off, the green mountains on either side of the river became deep blue in the dusk, receding towards the stern of the boat.

Hong'er and I, leaning against the cabin window, were looking out together at the indistinct scene outside, when suddenly he asked:

"Uncle, when shall we go back?"

"Go back? Do you mean that before you've left you want to go back?"

"Well, Shuisheng has invited me to his home...." He opened wide his black eyes in anxious thought.

Mother and I both felt rather sad, and so Runtu's name came up again. Mother said that ever since our family started packing up, Mrs. Yang from the beancurd shop had come over every day, and the day before in the ash-heap she had unearthed a dozen bowls and plates, which after some discussion she insisted must have been buried there by Runtu, so that when he came to remove the ashes he could take

灰，可以做沙地的肥料），待我們啟程的時候，他用船來載去。

夜間，我們又談些閒天，都是無關緊要的話；第二天早晨，他就領了水生回去了。

又過了九日，是我們啟程的日期。閏土早晨便到了，水生沒有同來，卻只帶着一個五歲的女兒管船隻。我們終日很忙碌，再沒有談天的工夫。來客也不少，有送行的，有拿東西的，有送行兼拿東西的。待到傍晚我們上船的時候，這老屋裏的所有破舊大小粗細東西，已經一掃而空了。

我們的船向前走，兩岸的青山在黃昏中，都裝成了深黛顏色，連着退向船後梢去。

宏兒和我靠着船窗，同看外面模糊的風景，他忽然問道：

「大伯！我們甚麼時候回來？」

「回來？你怎麼還沒有走就想回來了。」

「可是，水生約我到他家玩去咧……」他睜着大的黑眼睛，痴痴的想。

我和母親也都有些惘然，於是又提起閏土來。母親說，那豆腐西施的楊二嫂，自從我家收拾行李以來，本是每日必到的，前天伊在灰堆裏，掏出十多個碗碟來，議論之後，便定說是閏土埋着的，

them home at the same time. After making this discovery Mrs. Yang was very pleased with herself, and flew off taking the dog-teaser with her. (The dog-teaser is used by poultry keepers in our part. It is a wooden cage inside which food is put, so that hens can stretch their necks in to eat but dogs can only look on furiously.) And it was a marvel, considering the size of her feet, how fast she could run.

I was leaving the old house farther and farther behind, while the hills and rivers of my old home were also receding gradually ever farther in the distance. But I felt no regret. I only felt that all round me was an invisible high wall, cutting me off from my fellow, and this depressed me thoroughly. The vision of that small hero with the silver necklet among the watermelons had formerly been as clear as day, but now it had suddenly blurred, adding to depression.

Mother and Hong'er fell asleep.

I lay down, listening to the water rippling beneath the boat, and knew that I was going my way. I thought: although there is such a barrier between Runtu and myself, our children still have much in common, for wasn't Hong'er thinking of Shuisheng just now? I hope they will not be like us, that they will not allow a barrier to grow up between them. But again I would not like them, because they want to be one, to have a treadmill existence like mine, nor to suffer like Runtu until they become stupefied, nor yet, like others, to devote all their energies to dissipation. They should have a new life, a life we have never experienced.

The access of hope made me suddenly afraid. When Runtu had asked for the incense-burner and candlesticks I had laughed up my sleeve at him, to think that he was still worshipping idols and would never put them out of his mind. Yet what I now called hope was no more than an idol I had created myself. The only difference was that

他可以在運灰的時候，一齊搬回家裏去；楊二嫂發見了這件事，自己很以為功，便拿了那狗氣殺（這是我們這裏養雞的器具，木盤上面有着柵欄，內盛食料，雞可以伸進頸子去啄，狗卻不能，只能看着氣死），飛也似的跑了，虧伊裝着這麼高底的小腳，竟跑得這樣快。

老屋離我愈遠了；故鄉的山水也都漸漸遠離了我，但我卻並不感到怎樣的留戀。我只覺得我四面有看不見的高牆，將我隔成孤身，使我非常氣悶；那西瓜地上的銀項圈的小英雄的影像，我本來十分清楚，現在卻忽地模糊了，又使我非常的悲哀。

母親和宏兒都睡着了。

我躺着，聽船底潺潺的水聲，知道我在走我的路。我想：我竟與閏土隔絕到這地步了，但我們的後輩還是一氣，宏兒不是正在想念水生麼。我希望他們不再像我，又大家隔膜起來……然而我又不願意他們因為要一氣，都如我的辛苦輾轉而生活，也不願意他們都如閏土的辛苦麻木而生活，也不願意都如別人的辛苦恣睢而生活。他們應該有新的生活，為我們所未經生活過的。

我想到希望，忽然害怕起來了。閏土要香爐和燭台的時候，我還暗地裏笑他，以為他總是崇拜偶像，甚麼時候都不忘卻。現在我

what he desired was close at hand, while what I desired was less easily realized.

As I dozed, a stretch of jade-green seashore spread itself before my eyes, and above a round golden moon hung from a deep blue sky. I thought: hope cannot be said to exist, nor can it be said not to exist. It is just like roads across the earth. For actually the earth had no roads to begin with, but when many men pass one way, a road is made.

January 1921

所謂希望，不也是我自己手製的偶像麼？只是他的願望切近，我的
願望茫遠罷了。

　　我在朦朧中，眼前展開一片海邊碧綠的沙地來，上面深藍的天
空中掛着一輪金黃的圓月。我想：希望是本無所謂有，無所謂無
的。這正如地上的路；其實地上本沒有路，走的人多了，也便成了
路。

　　　　　　　　　　　　　　　　　　一九二一年一月。

社 戲

Village Opera

VILLAGE OPERA

In the past twenty years only twice have I been to see Chinese opera. During the first ten years I saw none, lacking both the wish and the opportunity. The two occasions on which I went were in the last ten years, but each time I left without seeing anything in it.

The first time was in 1912 when I was new to Beijing. A friend told me Beijing had the best opera and that seeing it was an experience not to be missed. I thought it might be interesting to see an opera, especially in Beijing, and hurried in high spirits to some theatre, the name of which escapes me. The performance had already started. Even outside I could hear the beat of the drums. As we squeezed in, gaudy colours flashed into view, then I saw many heads in the auditorium; but when I collected myself to look around there were still a few empty seats in the middle. As I squeezed my way in to sit down, someone addressed me. Already there was such a buzzing in my ears that I had to listen hard to catch what he was saying — "Sorry, these seats are taken!"

We withdrew to the back, but then a man with a glossy queue led us to one side and indicated an unoccupied place. This was a bench only a quarter the width of my thighs, but with legs two-thirds longer than mine. To begin with I hadn't the courage to get up there. Then,

社　　戲

　　我在倒數上去的二十年中，只看過兩回中國戲，前十年是絕不看，因為沒有看戲的意思和機會，那兩回全在後十年，然而都沒有看出甚麼來就走了。

　　第一回是民國元年我初到北京的時候，當時一個朋友對我說，北京戲最好，你不去見見世面麼？我想，看戲是有味的，而況在北京呢。於是都興致勃勃的跑到甚麼園，戲文已經開場了，在外面也早聽到冬冬地響。我們挨進門，幾個紅的綠的在我的眼前一閃爍，便又看見戲台下滿是許多頭，再定神四面看，卻見中間也還有幾個空座，擠過去要坐時，又有人對我發議論，我因為耳朵已經喤喤的響着了，用了心，才聽到他是說「有人，不行！」

　　我們退到後面，一個辮子很光的卻來領我們到了側面，指出一個地位來。這所謂地位者，原來是一條長櫈，然而他那坐板比我的上腿要狹到四分之三，他的腳比我的下腿要長達三分之二。我先是

being reminded of some instrument of torture, with an involuntary shudder I fled.

I had gone some way when suddenly I heard my friend's voice asking, "Well, what's the matter?" Looking over my shoulder I saw he had followed me out. "Why are you marching along without a word?" he inquired in great surprise.

"I'm sorry," I told him. "There's such a ding-dong skirling in my ears, I didn't hear you."

Whenever I thought back to this it struck me as most strange and I supposed that the opera had been a very poor one — or else a theatre was no place for me.

I forget in what year I made the second venture, but funds were being raised for flood victims in Hubei and Tan Xinpei was still alive. By paying two dollars for a ticket, you contributed money and could go to the Number One Theatre to see an opera with a cast made up for the most part of famous actors, one being Tan Xinpei himself. I bought a ticket primarily to satisfy the collector, but then some busybody seized the chance to tell me why Tan Xinpei simply had to be seen. At that, I forgot the disastrous ding-dong skirling of a few years before and went to the theatre — probably half because that precious ticket had cost so much that I would feel uncomfortable unless I used it. I learned that Tan Xinpei made his appearance late in the evening, and the Number One Theatre was a modern one where you did not have to fight for your seat. That reassured me, and I waited till nine o'clock before setting out. To my surprise, just as before, it was full. There was hardly any standing-room and I had to squeeze into the crowd at the rear to watch an actor singing an old woman's part. He had a paper spill burning at each corner of his mouth and there was a devil-soldier beside him. After racking my brains I guessed that this might be Maudgalyayana's mother, because the next to come on was a monk.

沒有爬上去的勇氣，接着便聯想到私刑拷打的刑具，不由的毛骨悚然的走出了。

走了許多路，忽聽到我的朋友的聲音道，「究竟怎的？」我回過臉去，原來他也被我帶出去了。他很詫異的說，「怎麼總是走，不答應？」我說，「朋友，對不起，我耳朵只在蓬蓬喤喤的響，並沒有聽到你的話。」

後來我每一想到，便很以為奇怪，似乎這戲太不好，——否則便是我近來在戲台下不適於生存了。

第二回忘記了那一年，總之是募集湖北水災捐而譚叫天還沒有死。捐法是兩元錢買一張戲票，可以到第一舞台去看戲，扮演的多是名角，其一就是小叫天。我買了一張票，本是對於勸募人聊以塞責的，然而似乎又有好事家乘機對我說了些叫天不可不看的大法要了。我於是忘了前幾年的蓬蓬喤喤之災，竟到第一舞台去了，但大約一半也因為重價購來的寶票，總得使用了才舒服。我打聽得叫天出台是遲的，而第一舞台卻是新式構造，用不着爭座位，便放了心，延宕到九點鐘才出去，誰料照例，人都滿了，連立足也難，我只得擠在遠處的人叢中看一個老旦在台上唱。那老旦嘴邊插着兩個點火的紙捻子，旁邊有一個鬼卒，我費盡思量，才疑心他或者是目連的母親，因為後來又出來了一個和尚。然而我又不知道那名角是

Not recognizing the actor, I asked a fat gentleman squeezed in on my left who he was. "Gong Yunfu!" he said, throwing me a withering sidelong glance. My face burned with shame over my ignorant blunder, and I mentally resolved at all costs to ask no more questions. Then I watched a heroine and her maid sing, next an old man and some other characters I could not identify. After that, I watched a whole group fight a free-for-all, and after that two or three people fighting together — from after nine till ten, from ten till eleven, from eleven till eleven-thirty, from eleven-thirty till twelve — but still there was no sign of Tan Xinpei.

Never in my life have I waited so patiently for anything. But the wheezes of the fat gentleman next to me, the ding-dong skirling, gonging and drumming on the stage, the whirling of gaudy colours, combined with the lateness of the hour, suddenly made me realize that this was no place for me. Mechanically turning round, I tried with might and main to shove my way out and felt the place behind me fill up at once — no doubt the elastic fat gentleman had expanded his right side into the space I vacated. With my retreat cut off, naturally there was nothing to do but push and push till at last I was out of the door. Apart from the rickshaws waiting for playgoers, there were practically no pedestrians in the street; but there were still a dozen or so people by the gate looking up at the programme, and another group not looking at anything who must, I thought, be waiting to watch the women come out after the show ended. And still no sign of Tan Xinpei....

But the night air was so crisp, it really "seeped into my heart." This seemed to be the first time I had known such good air in Beijing.

I said goodbye to Chinese opera that night, never thinking about it again, and if by any chance I passed a theatre it meant nothing to me for in spirit we were long since poles apart.

A few days ago, however, I happened to read a Japanese book —

誰，就去問擠小在我左邊的一位胖紳士。他很看不起似的斜瞥了我一眼，説道，「龔雲甫！」我深愧淺陋而且粗疏，臉上一熱，同時腦裏也製出了決不再問的定章，於是看小旦唱，看花旦唱，看老生唱，看不知甚麼角色唱，看一大班人亂打，看兩三個人互打，從九點多到十點，從十點到十一點，從十一點到十一點半，從十一點半到十二點，——然而叫天竟還沒有來。

我向來沒有這樣忍耐的等候過甚麼事物，而況這身邊的胖紳士的吁吁的喘氣，這台上的鼕鼕喤喤的敲打，紅紅綠綠的晃盪，加之以十二點，忽而使我省悟到在這裏不適於生存了。我同時便機械的擰轉身子，用力往外只一擠，覺得背後便已滿滿的，大約那彈性的胖紳士早在我的空處胖開了他的右半身了。我後無回路，自然擠而又擠，終於出了大門。街上除了專等看客的車輛之外，幾乎沒有甚麼行人了，大門口卻還有十幾個人昂着頭看戲目，別有一堆人站着並不看甚麼，我想：他們大概是看散戲之後出來的女人們的，而叫天卻還沒有來……

然而夜氣很清爽，真所謂「沁人心脾」，我在北京遇着這樣的好空氣，彷彿這是第一遭了。

這一夜，就是我對於中國戲告了別的一夜，此後再沒有想到他，即使偶而經過戲園，我們也漠不相關，精神上早已一在天之南一在地之北了。

但是前幾天，我忽在無意之中看到一本日本文的書，可惜忘記

unfortunately I have forgotten the title and author, but it was about Chinese opera. One chapter made the point that Chinese opera is so full of gongs and cymbals, shouting and leaping, that it makes the spectators' heads swim and is quite unsuited for a theatre; if performed in the open and watched from a distance, it has its charm. I felt that this put into words what had remained unformulated in my mind, because as a matter of fact I clearly remembered seeing a really good opera in the country and it was under its influence, perhaps, that after coming to Beijing I went twice to the theatre. It is a pity that, somehow or other, the name of that book escapes me.

As to when I saw that good opera, it was really "long, long ago," when I could not have been much more than eleven or twelve. It was the custom in Luzhen where we lived for married women not yet in charge of the household to go back to their parents' home for the summer. Although my father's mother was then still quite strong, my mother had quite a few domestic duties which made it impossible for her to spend many days at her old home during the summer. All she could spare was a few days after visiting the ancestral graves, and at such times I always went with her to stay in her parents' house. That was in Pingqiao Village not far from the sea, a very remote little village on a river with less than thirty households of peasants and fishermen, and just one tiny grocery. To me, however, it was heaven, for not only was I treated as a guest of honour but here I could skip reading the *Book of Songs*.

There were many children for me to play with. For with the arrival of a visitor from such a distance they got leave from their parents to do less work in order to play with me. In a small village, the guest of one family is virtually the guest of the whole community. We were all about the same age, but when it came to determining seniority many were at least my uncles or granduncles, since everybody in the village had the same family name and belonged to one clan. But we were all good friends, and if by some chance we fell out and I hit one of my

了書名和著者，總之是關於中國戲的。其中有一篇，大意彷彿說，中國戲是大敲，大叫，大跳，使看客頭昏腦眩，很不適於劇場，但若在野外散漫的所在，遠遠的看起來，也自有他的風致。我當時覺着這正是說了在我意中而未曾想到的話，因為我確記得在野外看過很好的好戲，到北京以後的連進兩回戲園去，也許還是受了那時的影響哩。可惜我不知道怎麼一來，竟將書名忘卻了。

至於我看那好戲的時候，卻實在已經是「遠哉遙遙」的了，其時恐怕我還不過十一二歲。我們魯鎮的習慣，本來是凡有出嫁的女兒，倘自己還未當家，夏間便大抵回到母家去消夏。那時我的祖母雖然還康健，但母親也已分擔了些家務，所以夏期便不能多日的歸省了，只得在掃墓完畢之後，抽空去住幾天，這時我便每年跟了我的母親住在外祖母的家裏。那地方叫平橋村，是一個離海邊不遠，極偏僻的，臨河的小村莊；住戶不滿三十家，都種田，打魚，只有一家很小的雜貨店。但在我是樂土：因為我在這裏不但得到優待，又可以免唸「秩秩斯干幽幽南山」了。

和我一同玩的是許多小朋友，因為有了遠客，他們也都從父母那裏得了減少工作的許可，伴我來遊戲。在小村裏，一家的客，幾乎也就是公共的。我們年紀都相仿，但論起行輩來，卻至少是叔子，有幾個還是太公，因為他們合村都同姓，是本家。然而我們是

granduncles, it never occurred to any child or grown-up in the village to call me "insubordinate." Ninety-nine out of a hundred of them could neither read not write.

We spent most of our days digging up earthworms, putting them on little hooks made of copper wire, and lying on the river bank to catch prawns. The silliest of water creatures, prawns willingly use their own pincers to push the point of the hook into their mouths; so in a few hours we could catch a big bowlful. It was the custom to give these prawns to me. Another thing we did was to graze buffaloes together. But, maybe because they are animals of a higher order, oxen and buffaloes are hostile to strangers, and they treated me with such contempt that I never dared get too close. I could only follow at a distance and stand there. At such times my small friends, no longer impressed by my ability to recite classical poetry, would all start hooting with laughter.

What I looked forward to most was going to Zhaozhuang to see the opera. Zhaozhuang was a slightly larger village five *li* away. Since Pingqiao was too small to afford to put on operas, every year it chipped in towards a performance at Zhaozhuang. At the time, it never occurred to me to wonder why they should put on operas every year. Thinking back to it now, I dare say it may have been a ritual drama for the late spring festival.

The year that I was eleven or twelve, this longawaited day came round again. But as ill luck would have it, there was no boat for hire that morning. Pingqiao Village had only one big ferry-boat, which put out in the morning and came back in the evening, and it was out of the question to use this. All the other boats were unsuitable, being too small. And the neighbouring villages, when people were sent to ask, had no boats either — they had all been hired already. My grandmother, very vexed, blamed the family for not hiring one earlier and

朋友，即使偶而吵鬧起來，打了太公，一村的老老小小，也決沒有一個會想出「犯上」這兩個字來，而他們也百分之九十九不識字。

我們每天的事情大概是掘蚯蚓，掘來穿在銅絲的小鉤上，伏在河沿上去釣蝦。蝦是水世界裏的呆子，決不憚用了自己的兩個鉗捧着鉤尖送到嘴裏去的，所以不半天便可以釣到一大碗。這蝦照例是歸我吃的。其次便是一同去放牛，但或者因為高等動物了的緣故罷，黃牛水牛都欺生，敢於欺侮我，因此我也總不敢走近身，只好遠遠地跟着，站着。這時候，小朋友們便不再原諒我會讀「秩秩斯干」，卻全都嘲笑起來了。

至於我在那裏所第一盼望的，卻在到趙莊去看戲。趙莊是離平橋村五里的較大的村莊；平橋村太小，自己演不起戲，每年總付給趙莊多少錢，算作合做的。當時我並不想到他們為甚麼年年要演戲。現在想，那或者是春賽，是社戲了。

就在我十一二歲時候的這一年，這日期也看看等到了。不料這一年真可惜，在早上就叫不到船。平橋村只有一隻早出晚歸的航船是大船，決沒有留用的道理。其餘的都是小船，不合用；央人到鄰村去問，也沒有，早都給別人定下了。外祖母很氣惱，怪家裏的人不早定，絮叨起來。母親便寬慰伊，説我們魯鎮的戲比小村裏的好

started nagging. To console her, Mother said that our operas at Luzhen were much better than in these little villages, and as we saw several a year there was no need to go today. But I was nearly in tears from chagrin, and Mother did her best to impress on me on no account to make a scene, because it would upset my grandmother; nor must I go with other people either, or Grandmother might worry.

In a word, it had fallen through. In the afternoon, when all my friends had left and the opera had started, I imagined I could hear the sound of gongs and drums and knew they were in front of the stage buying soyabean milk to drink.

I caught no prawns that day, did not eat much either. Mother was very upset but could not think what to do. By supper time Grandmother too had finally caught on and she said I was right to be cross, they had been too remiss, and never before had guests been treated so badly. After the meal, youngsters back from the opera gathered round and gaily described it to us. I was the only one silent. They all sighed and said how sorry they were for me. Suddenly one of the brightest, Shuangxi, had an inspiration and asked, "A big boat? Hasn't Eighth Granduncle's ferry-boat come back?" A dozen other boys cottoned on and at once started agitating to take the boat and go with me. I cheered up. But Grandmother was nervous, thinking we were all children and undependable. And Mother said it would not be fair to ask grown-ups to stay up all night and go with us, as they all had to work the next day. While our fate hung in the balance, Shuangxi went to the root of the problem, declaring loudly, "I guarantee it'll be all right! It's a big boat, Brother Xun never jumps around, and all of us can swim!"

It was true. Not a boy in the dozen but could swim, and two or three of them were first-rate swimmers in the sea.

Grandmother and Mother, convinced, raised no further objections. Both smiled. We immediately rushed out.

得多，一年看幾回，今天就算了。只有我急得要哭，母親卻竭力的
囑咐我，說萬不能裝模裝樣，怕又招外祖母生氣，又不准和別人一
同去，說是怕外祖母要擔心。

　　總之，是完了。到下午，我的朋友都去了，戲已經開場了，我
似乎聽到鑼鼓的聲音，而且知道他們在戲台下買豆漿喝。

　　這一天我不釣蝦，東西也少吃。母親很為難，沒有法子想。到
晚飯時候，外祖母也終於覺察了，並且說我應當不高興，他們太怠
慢，是待客的禮數裏從來所沒有的。吃飯之後，看過戲的少年們也
都聚攏來了，高高興興的來講戲。只有我不開口；他們都嘆息而且
表同情。忽然間，一個最聰明的雙喜大悟似的提議了，他說，「大
船？八叔的航船不是回來了麼？」十幾個別的少年也大悟，立刻攛掇
起來，說可以坐了這航船和我一同去。我高興了。然而外祖母又怕
都是孩子們，不可靠；母親又說是若叫大人一去，他們白天全有工
作，要他熬夜，是不合情理的。在這遲疑之中，雙喜可又看出底細
來了，便又大聲的說道，「我寫包票！船又大；迅哥兒向來不亂跑；
我們又都是識水性的！」

　　誠然！這十多個少年，委實沒有一個不會鳧水的，而且兩三個
還是弄潮的好手。

　　外祖母和母親也相信，便不再駁回，都微笑了。我們立刻一哄
的出了門。

My heart after being so heavy was suddenly light, and I felt as though floating on air. Once outside, I saw in the moonlight a ferry-boat with a white awning moored at the bridge. We all jumped aboard, Shuangxi seizing the front pole and Afa the back one, while the younger boys sat down with me in the middle and those a little older went to the stern. By the time Mother followed us out to warn "Be careful!" we had already cast off. We pushed off from the bridge, floated back a few feet, then moved forward under the bridge, floated back a few feet, then moved forward under the bridge. Two oars were set up, each manned by two boys who changed shifts every *li*. Chatter, laughter and shouts mingled with the lapping of water against our bow; to our right and left stretched emerald green fields of beans and wheat, as we flew forward towards Zhaozhuang.

The scent of beans, wheat and river-weeds wafted towards us through the mist, and the moonlight shone faintly through it. Distant grey hills, undulating like the backs of some leaping iron beasts, seemed to be racing past the stern of our boat; but I still felt our progress was slow. When the oarsmen had changed shifts, four times, we began to make out the faint outline of Zhaozhuang and to catch the sound of singing and music. There were several lights too, which we guessed must be on the stage unless they were fishermen's lights.

The music was probably fluting. Eddying round and round and up and down, it soothed me and set me dreaming at the same time, till I felt as though I was about to drift far away with it through the night air heavy with the scent of beans, wheat and river-weeds.

As we approached the lights, they proved to be fishermen's lights and I realized it was not Zhaozhuang that I had been looking at. Directly ahead of us was a pine-wood where I had played the year before and seen a broken stone horse, fallen on its side, as well as a stone sheep couched in the grass. Once past the wood, our

我的很重的心忽而輕鬆了，身體也似乎舒展到說不出的大。一出門，便望見月下的平橋內泊着一隻白篷的航船，大家跳下船，雙喜拔前篙，阿發拔後篙，年幼的都陪我坐在艙中，較大的聚在船尾。母親送出來吩咐「要小心」的時候，我們已經點開船，在橋石上一磕，退後幾尺，即又上前出了橋。於是架起兩支櫓，一支兩人，一里一換，有說笑的，有嚷的，夾着潺潺的船頭激水的聲音，在左右都是碧綠的豆麥田地的河流中，飛一般徑向趙莊前進了。

兩岸的豆麥和河底的水草所發散出來的清香，夾雜在水氣中撲面的吹來；月色便朦朧在這水氣裏。淡黑的起伏的連山，彷彿是踴躍的鐵的獸脊似的，都遠遠地向船尾跑去了，但我卻還以為船慢。他們換了四回手，漸望見依稀的趙莊，而且似乎聽到歌吹了，還有幾點火，料想便是戲台，但或者也許是漁火。

那聲音大概是橫笛，宛轉，悠揚，使我的心也沉靜，然而又自失起來，覺得要和他瀰散在含着豆麥蘊藻之香的夜氣裏。

那火接近了，果然是漁火；我才記得先前望見的也不是趙莊。那是正對船頭的一叢松柏林，我去年也曾經去遊玩過，還看見破的石馬倒在地下，一個石羊蹲在草裏呢。過了那林，船便彎進了叉

boat rounded a bend into a cove, and Zhaozhuang was really before us.

Our eyes were drawn to the stage standing in a plot of empty ground by the river outside the village, hazy in the distant moonlight, barely distinguishable from its surroundings. It seemed that the fairy-land I had seen in pictures had come alive here. The boat was moving faster now, and presently we could make out figures on the stage and a blaze of gaudy colours. The river close to the stage was black with the boat awnings of the spectators.

"There's no room near the stage, let's watch from a distance," suggested Afa.

The boat had slowed down now, and soon we arrived. True enough, it was impossible to get close to the stage. We had to make fast even further away from it than the shrine opposite. But, in any case, we did not want our boat with its white awning to mix with those black ones and, besides, there was no room....

While we hastily moored, there appeared on the stage a man with a long black beard and four pennons fixed to his back. With a spear he fought a whole group of bare-armed men. Shuangxi told us this was a famous acrobat who could turn eighty-four somersaults one after the other. He had counted for himself earlier in the day.

We all crowded to the bow to watch the fighting, but the acrobat did not turn any somersaults. Only a few of the bare-armed men turned over heels a few times, then trooped off. Then a girl came out and sang in a shrill falsetto. "There aren't many watching in the evening," said Shuangxi, "and the acrobat's taking it easy. Who wants to show off to an empty house?" That made sense to me, because by then there were not many spectators. The country folk, having work to do the next day, could not stay up all night and had gone home to bed. Standing

港，於是趙莊便真在眼前了。

最惹眼的是屹立在莊外臨河的空地上的一座戲台，模糊在遠外的月夜中，和空間幾乎分不出界限，我疑心畫上見過的仙境，就在這裏出現了。這時船走得更快，不多時，在台上顯出人物來，紅紅綠綠的動，近台的河裏一望烏黑的是看戲的人家的船篷。

「近台沒有甚麼空了，我們遠遠的看罷。」阿發説。

這時船慢了，不久就到，果然近不得台旁，大家只能下了篙，比那正對戲台的神棚還要遠。其實我們這白篷的航船，本也不願意和烏篷的船在一處，而況並沒有空地呢……

在停船的匆忙中，看見台上有一個黑的長鬍子的背上插着四張旗，捏着長槍，和一群赤膊的人正打仗。雙喜説，那就是有名的鐵頭老生，能連翻八十四個筋斗，他日裏親自數過的。

我們便都擠在船頭上看打仗，但那鐵頭老生卻又並不翻筋斗，只有幾個赤膊的人翻，翻了一陣，都進去了，接着走出一個小旦來，咿咿呀呀的唱。雙喜説，「晚上看客少，鐵頭老生也懈了，誰肯顯本領給白地看呢？」我相信這話對，因為其時台下已經不很有人，鄉下人為了明天的工作，熬不得夜，早都睡覺去了，疏疏朗朗的站

there still were just a scattering of a few dozen idlers from Zhaozhuang and the villages around. The families of the local rich remained in the boats with black awnings, but they were not really interested in the opera. Most of them had come to the opera to eat cakes, fruit or melon-seeds. So it could really be reckoned an empty house.

As a matter of fact, I was not too keen on somersaults either. What I wanted most to see was a snake spirit swathed in white, its two hands clasping above it a wand-like snake's head, and next a leaping tiger dressed in yellow. But I waited a long time in vain. As soon as the girl left, out came a very old man acting the part of a young one. Feeling tired, I asked Guisheng to buy me some soyabean milk. He came back presently to say, "There isn't any. The deaf man who sells it has gone. There was some in the daytime, I drank two bowls then. I'll get you a dipperful of water to drink."

Instead of drinking the water, I stuck it out as best I could. I cannot say what I saw, but by degrees something strange seemed to happen to the faces of the players, whose features blurred as if melting into one flattened surface. Most of the younger boys yawned, while the older ones chatted among themselves. It was only when a clown in a red shirt was fastened to a pillar on the stage, and a greybeard started horsewhipping him, that we roused ourselves to watch again and laughed. I really think that was the best scene of the evening.

But then the old woman came out. This was the character I dreaded most, especially when she sat down to sing. Now I saw by everybody's disappointment that they felt just as I did. To start with, the old woman simply walked to and fro singing, then she sat on a chair in the middle of the stage. I felt most dismayed, and Shuangxi and the rest started swearing. I waited patiently till, after a long time, the old woman raised her hand. I thought she was going to stand up. But dashing my hopes

着的不過是幾十個本村和鄰村的閒漢。烏篷船裏的那些土財主的家
眷固然在，然而他們也不在乎看戲，多半是專到戲台下來吃糕餅水
果和瓜子的。所以簡直可以算白地。

　　然而我的意思卻也並不在乎看翻筋斗。我最願意看的是一個人
蒙了白布，兩手在頭上捧着一支棒似的蛇頭的蛇精，其次是套了黃
布衣跳老虎。但是等了許多時都不見，小旦雖然進去了，立刻又出
來了一個很老的小生。我有些疲倦了，託桂生買豆漿去。他去了一
刻，回來說，「沒有。賣豆漿的聾子也回去了。日裏倒有，我還喝了
兩碗呢。現在去舀一瓢水來給你罷。」

　　我不喝水，支撐着仍然看，也說不出見了些甚麼，只覺得戲子
的臉都漸漸的有些稀奇了，那五官漸不明顯，似乎融成一片的再沒
有甚麼高低。年紀小的幾個多打呵欠了，大的也各管自己談話。忽
而一個紅衫的小丑被綁在台柱子上，給一個花白鬍子的用馬鞭打起
來了，大家才又振作精神的笑着看。在這一夜裏，我以為這實在要
算是最好的一折。

　　然而老旦終於出台了。老旦本來是我所最怕的東西，尤其是怕
他坐下了唱。這時候，看見大家也都很掃興，才知道他們的意見是
和我一致的。那老旦當初還只是踱來踱去的唱，後來竟在中間的一
把交椅上坐下了。我很擔心；雙喜他們卻就破口喃喃的罵。我忍耐
的等着，許多工夫，只見那老旦將手一抬，我以為就要站起來了，

she lowered her hand slowly again just as before, and went on singing. Some of the boys in the boat could not help groaning; the rest began to yawn again. Finally Shuangxi, when he could stand it no longer, said he was afraid she might go on singing till dawn and we had better leave. We all promptly agreed, becoming as eager as when we had set out. Three or four boys ran to the stern, seized the poles to punt back several yards, then headed the boat around. Cursing the old woman, they set up the oars and started back for the pine-wood.

Judging by the position of the moon we had not been watching very long, and once we left Zhaozhuang the moonlight seemed unusually bright. When we turned back to look at the lanternlit stage, it appeared just as it had been when we came, hazy as a fairy pavilion, covered in a rosy mist. Once again the flutes sounded melodiously in our ears. I suspected that the old woman must have finished, but could hardly suggest going back again to see.

Soon the pine-wood was behind us. Our boat was moving fairly fast, but there was such thick darkness all around you could tell it was very late. As they discussed the players, laughing and swearing, the rowers pulled harder on the players, laughing and swearing, the rowers pulled harder on the oars. Now the plash of water against our bow was even more distinct. The ferry-boat seemed like a great white fish carrying a freight of children through the foam. Some old fishermen who fished all night stopped their punts to cheer at the sight.

We were still about one *li* from Pingqiao when our boat slowed down, the oarsmen saying that they were tired after rowing so hard, with nothing to eat for hours. It was Guisheng who had a bright idea this time. He said the broad beans were just ripe, and there was fuel on the boat — we could filch some beans and cook them. Everybody approving, we promptly drew alongside the bank and stopped. The pitch-black fields were filled with plump broad beans.

不料他卻又慢慢的放下在原地方，仍舊唱。全船裏幾個人不住的吁氣，其餘的也打起呵欠來。雙喜終於熬不住了，說道，怕他會唱到天明還不完，還是我們走的好罷。大家立刻都贊成，和開船時候一樣踴躍，三四人徑奔船尾，拔了篙，點退幾丈，回轉船頭，架起櫓，罵着老旦，又向那松柏林前進了。

月還沒有落，彷彿看戲也並不很久似的，而一離趙莊，月光又顯得格外的皎潔。回望戲台在燈火光中，卻又如初來未到時候一般，又漂渺得像一座仙山樓閣，滿被紅霞罩着了。吹到耳邊來的又是橫笛，很悠揚；我疑心老旦已經進去了，但也不好意思說再回去看。

不多久，松柏林早在船後了，船行也並不慢，但周圍的黑暗只是濃，可知已經到了深夜。他們一面議論着戲子，或罵，或笑，一面加緊的搖船。這一次船頭的激水聲更其響亮了，那航船，就像一條大白魚背着一群孩子在浪花裏躥，連夜漁的幾個老漁父，也停了艇子看着喝采起來。

離平橋村還有一里模樣，船行卻慢了，搖船的都說很疲乏，因為太用力，而且許久沒有東西吃。這回想出來的是桂生，說是羅漢豆正旺相，柴火又現成，我們可以偷一點來煮吃的。大家都贊成，立刻近岸停了船；岸上的田裏，烏油油的便都是結實的羅漢豆。

"Hey, Afa! They're your family's over here, and Old Liu Yi's over there. Which shall we take?" Shuangxi, the first to leap ashore, called from the bank.

As we all jumped ashore too Afa said, "Wait a bit and I'll have a look." He walked up and down feeling the beans, then straightened up to say, "Take ours, they're much bigger." With a shout we scattered through his family's bean field, each picking a big handful of beans and throwing them into the boat. Shuangxi thought that if we took any more and Afa's mother found out, she would make a scene, so we all went to Old Liu Yi's field to pick another handful each.

Then a few of the older boys started rowing slowly again, while others lit a fire in the stern and the younger boys and I shelled the beans. Soon they were cooked, and them with our fingers. When the beans were finished we went on again, washing the pot and throwing the pods into the river, to destroy all traces. What worried Shuangxi now was that we had used the salt and firewood on Eighth Granduncle's boat, and being a canny old man he was sure to find out and berate us. But after some discussion we decided that we had nothing to fear. If he swore at us, we would ask him to return the tallow branch he had taken the previous year from the river bank, and to his face call him "Old Scabby."

"We're all back! How could anything go wrong? Didn't I guarantee that?" Shuangxi's voice suddenly rang out from the bow.

Looking past him, I saw we were already at Pingqiao and someone was standing at the foot of the bridge — it was my mother to whom Shuangxi had called. As I walked up to the bow the boat passed under the bridge, then stopped, and we all went ashore. Mother was rather angry. She asked why we had come back so late — it was after midnight. But she was pleased to see us too and smilingly invited everyone to go and have some puffed rice.

「阿阿，阿發，這邊是你家的，這邊是老六一家的，我們偷那一邊的呢？」雙喜先跳下去了，在岸上說。

我們也都跳上岸。阿發一面跳，一面說道，「且慢，讓我來看一看罷，」他於是往來的摸了一回，直起身來說道，「偷我們的罷，我們的大得多呢。」一聲答應，大家便散開在阿發家的豆田裏，各摘了一大捧，拋入船艙中。雙喜以為再多偷，倘給阿發的娘知道是要哭罵的，於是各人便到六一公公的田裏又各自偷了一大捧。

我們中間幾個年長的仍然慢慢的搖着船，幾個到後艙去生火，年幼的和我都剝豆。不久豆熟了，便任憑航船浮在水面上，都圍起來用手撮着吃。吃完豆，又開船，一面洗器具，豆莢豆殼全拋在河水裏，甚麼痕跡也沒有了。雙喜所慮的是用了八公公船上的鹽和柴，這老頭子很細心，一定要知道，會罵的。然而大家議論之後，歸結是不怕。他如果罵，我們便要他歸還去年在岸邊拾去的一枝枯柏樹，而且當面叫他「八癩子」。

「都回來了！那裏會錯。我原說過寫包票的！」雙喜在船頭上忽而大聲的說。

我向船頭一望，前面已經是平橋。橋腳上站着一個人，卻是我的母親，雙喜便是對伊說着話。我走出前艙去，船也就進了平橋了，停了船，我們紛紛都上岸。母親頗有些生氣，說是過了三更了，怎麼回來得這樣遲，但也就高興了，笑着邀大家去吃炒米。

They told her we had all had a snack to eat and were sleepy, so we had better get to bed at once, and off we all went to our different homes.

I did not get up till noon the next day, and there was no word of any trouble with Eighth Granduncle over the salt or firewood. That afternoon we went to catch prawns as usual.

"Shuangxi, you little devils stole my beans yesterday! And instead of picking them properly you trampled down quite a few." I looked up and saw Old Liu Yi on a punt, coming back from selling beans. There was still a heap of left-over beans at the bottom of the punt.

"Yes, we were treating a visitor. We didn't mean to take yours to begin with," said Shuangxi. "Look! You've frightened away my prawn!"

When the old man saw me, he stopped punting and chuckled. "Treating a visitor? So you should." Then he asked me, "Was yesterday's opera good, Brother Xun?"

I nodded. "Yes, it was."

"Did you enjoy the beans?"

I nodded again. "Very much."

To my surprise, that gratified Old Liu Yi enormously. Sticking up one thumb he said complacently, "People from big towns who have studied really know what's good! I select my bean seeds one by one, yet country folk who can't tell good from bad say my beans aren't up to other people's. I'll give some to your mother today for her to try...." With that he punted off.

When Mother called me home for supper, on the table there was a large bowl of boiled beans which Old Liu Yi had brought for the two of us. And I heard he had praised me highly to Mother, saying, "He's

　　大家都說已經吃了點心，又渴睡，不如及早睡的好，各自回去了。

　　第二天，我向午才起來，並沒有聽到甚麼關係八公公鹽柴事件的糾葛，下午仍然去釣蝦。

　　「雙喜，你們這班小鬼，昨天偷了我的豆了罷？又不肯好好的摘，踏壞了不少。」我抬頭看時，是六一公公棹着小船，賣了豆回來了，船肚裏還有剩下的一堆豆。

　　「是的。我們請客。我們當初還不要你的呢。你看，你把我的蝦嚇跑了！」雙喜說。

　　六一公公看見我，便停了楫，笑道，「請客？——這是應該的。」於是對我說，「迅哥兒，昨天的戲可好麼？」

　　我點一點頭，說道，「好。」

　　「豆可中吃呢？」

　　我又點一點頭，說道，「很好。」

　　不料六一公公竟非常感激起來，將大拇指一翹，得意的說道，「這真是大市鎮裏出來的讀過書的人才識貨！我的豆種是粒粒挑選過的，鄉下人不識好歹，還說我的豆比不上別人的呢。我今天也要送些給我們的姑奶奶嚐嚐去……」他於是打着楫子過去了。

　　待到母親叫我回去吃晚飯的時候，桌上便有一大碗煮熟了的羅漢豆，就是六一公公送給母親和我吃的。聽說他還對母親極口誇獎

so young, yet he knows what's what. He's sure to come first in the o
fficial examinations in future. Your fortune's as good as made, ma'am."
But when I ate the beans, they did not taste as those of the night before.

It is a fact, right up till now, I have really never eaten such good
beans or seen such a good opera as I did that night.

October 1922

我，説「小小年紀便有見識，將來一定要中狀元。姑奶奶，你的福氣是可以寫包票的了。」但我吃了豆，卻並沒有昨夜的豆那麼好。

　　真的，一直到現在，我實在再沒有吃到那夜似的好豆，——也不再看到那夜似的好戲了。

　　　　　　　　　　　　　　　一九二二年十月。

祝 福

The New-Year Sacrifice

THE NEW-YEAR SACRIFICE

The end of the year by the old calendar does really seem a more natural end to the year for, to say nothing of the villages and towns, the very sky seems to proclaim the New Year's approach. Intermittent flashes from pallid, lowering evening clouds are followed by the rumble of crackers bidding farewell to the Hearth God and, before the deafening reports of the bigger bangs close at hand have died away, the air is filled with faint whiffs of gunpowder. On one such night I returned to Luzhen, my home town. I call it my home town, but as I had not made my home there for some time I put up at the house of a Fourth Uncle since he belongs to the generation before mine in our clan. A former Imperial Academy licentiate who believes in Neo-Confucianism, he seemed very little changed, just slightly older, but without any beard as yet. Having exchanged some polite remarks upon meeting he observed that I was fatter, and having observed that I was fatter launched into a violent attack on the reformists. I did not take this personally, however, as the object of his attack was Kang Youwei. Still, conversation proved so difficult that I shortly found myself alone in the study.

I rose late the next day and went out after lunch to see relatives and friends, spending the following day in the same way. They were all very little changed, just slightly older; but every family was busy preparing for the New-Year sacrifice. This is the great end-of-year ceremony in Luzhen, during which a reverent and splendid welcome

祝　　福

　　舊曆的年底畢竟最像年底，村鎮上不必說，就在天空中也顯出將到新年的氣象來。灰白色的沉重的晚雲中間時時發出閃光，接着一聲鈍響，是送灶的爆竹；近處燃放的可就更強烈了，震耳的大音還沒有息，空氣裏已經散滿了幽微的火藥香。我是正在這一夜回到我的故鄉魯鎮的。雖說故鄉，然而已沒有家，所以只得暫寓在魯四老爺的宅子裏。他是我的本家，比我長一輩，應該稱之曰「四叔」，是一個講理學的老監生。他比先前並沒有甚麼大改變，單是老了些，但也還未留鬍子；一見面是寒暄，寒暄之後說我「胖了，」說我「胖了」之後即大罵其新黨。但我知道，這並非借題在罵我：因為他所罵的還是康有為。但是，談話是總不投機的了，於是不多久，我便一個人剩在書房裏。

　　第二天我起得很遲，午飯之後，出去看了幾個本家和朋友；第三天也照樣。他們也都沒有甚麼大改變，單是老了些；家中卻一律忙，都在準備着「祝福」。這是魯鎮年終的大典，致敬盡禮，迎接福

is given to the God of Fortune so that he will send good luck for the coming year. Chickens and geese are killed, pork is bought, and everything is scrubbed and scoured until all the women's arms — some still in twisted silver bracelets — turn red in the water. After the meat is cooked chopsticks are thrust into it at random, and when this "offering" is set out at dawn, incense and candles are lit and the God of Fortune is respectfully invited to come and partake of it. The worshippers are confined to men and, of course, after worshipping they go on letting off firecrackers as before. This is done every year, in every household — and naturally this year was no exception.

The sky became overcast and in the afternoon it was filled with a flurry of snowflakes, some as large as plum-blossom petals, which merged with the smoke and the bustling atmosphere to make the small town a welter of confusion. By the time I had returned to my uncle's study, the roof of the house was already white with snow which made the room brighter than usual, highlighting the red stone rubbing that hung on the wall of the big character "Longevity" as written by the Taoist saint Chen Tuan. One of the pair of scrolls flanking it had fallen down and was lying loosely rolled up on the long table. The other, still in its place, bore the inscription "Understanding of principles brings peace of mind." Idly, I strolled over to the desk beneath the window to turn over the pile of books on it, but only found an apparently incomplete set of *The Kang Xi Dictionary,* the *Selected Writings of Neo-Confucian Philosophers,* and *Commentaries on the Four Books.* At all events I must leave the next day, I decided.

Besides, the thought of my meeting with Xianglin's Wife the previous day was preying on my mind. It had happened in the afternoon. On my way back from calling on a friend in the eastern part of the town, I had met her by the river and knew from the fixed look in her eyes that she was going to accost me. Of all the people I had seen during this visit to Luzhen, none had changed so much as she had.

神，拜求來年一年中的好運氣的。殺雞，宰鵝，買豬肉；用心細細的洗，女人的臂膊都在水裏浸得通紅，有的還帶着絞絲銀鐲子。煮熟之後，橫七豎八插些筷子在這類東西上，可就稱為「福禮」了，五更天陳列起來，並且點上香燭，恭請福神們來享用；拜的卻只限於男人，拜完自然仍然是放爆竹。年年如此，家家如此，只要買得起福禮和爆竹之類的，——今年自然也如此。天色愈陰暗了，下午竟下起雪來，雪花大的有梅花那麼大，滿天飛舞，夾着煙靄和忙碌的氣色，將魯鎮亂成一團糟。我回到四叔的書房裏時，瓦楞上已經雪白，房裏也映得較光明，極分明的顯出壁上掛着的朱拓的大「壽」字，陳摶老祖寫的；一邊的對聯已經脫落，鬆鬆的卷了放在長桌上，一邊的還在，道是「事理通達心氣和平」。我又無聊賴的到窗下的案頭去一翻，只見一堆似乎未必完全的《康熙字典》，一部《近思錄集注》和一部《四書襯》。無論如何，我明天決計要走了。

　　況且，一想到昨天遇見祥林嫂的事，也就使我不能安住。那是下午，我到鎮的東頭訪過一個朋友，走出來，就在河邊遇見她；而且見她瞪着的眼睛的視線，就知道明明是向我走來的。我這回在魯鎮所見的人們中，改變之大，可以說無過於她的了：五年前的花白

Her hair, streaked with grey five years before, was now completely white, making her appear much older than one around forty. Her sallow, dark-tinged face that looked as if it had been carved out of wood was fearfully wasted and had lost the grief-stricken expression it had borne before. The only sign of life about her was the occasional flicker of her eyes. In one hand she had a bamboo basket containing a chipped, empty bowl; in the other, a bamboo pole, taller than herself, that was split at the bottom. She had clearly become a beggar pure and simple.

I stopped, waiting for her to come and ask for money.

"So you're back?" were her first words.

"Yes."

"That's good. You are a scholar who's travelled and seen the world. There's something I want to ask you." A sudden gleam lit up her lacklustre eyes.

This was so unexpected that surprise rooted me to the spot.

"It's this." She drew two paces nearer and lowered her voice, as if letting me into a secret. "Do dead people turn into ghosts or not?"

My flesh crept. The way she had fixed me with her eyes made a shiver run down my spine, and I felt far more nervous than when a surprise test is sprung on you at school and the teacher insists on standing over you. Personally, I had never bothered myself in the least about whether spirits existed or not; but what was the best answer to give her now? I hesitated for a moment, reflecting that the people here still believed in spirits, but she seemed to have her doubts, or rather hopes — she hoped for life after death and dreaded it at the same time. Why increase the sufferings of someone with a wretched life? For her sake, I thought, I'd better say there was.

的頭髮，即今已經全白，全不像四十上下的人；臉上瘦削不堪，黃中帶黑，而且消盡了先前悲哀的神色，彷彿是木刻似的；只有那眼珠間或一輪，還可以表示她是一個活物。她一手提着竹籃，內中一個破碗，空的；一手拄着一支比她更長的竹竿，下端開了裂：她分明已經純乎是一個乞丐了。

我就站住，預備她來討錢。

「你回來了？」她先這樣問。

「是的。」

「這正好。你是識字的，又是出門人，見識得多。我正要問你一件事——」她那沒有精采的眼睛忽然發光了。

我萬料不到她卻說出這樣的話來，詫異的站着。

「就是——」她走近兩步，放低了聲音，極秘密似的切切的說，「一個人死了之後，究竟有沒有魂靈的？」

我很悚然，一見她的眼釘着我的，背上也就遭了芒刺一般，比在學校裏遇到不及預防的臨時考，教師又偏是站在身旁的時候，惶急得多了。對於魂靈的有無，我自己是向來毫不介意的；但在此刻，怎樣回答她好呢？我在極短期的躊躇中，想，這裏的人照例相信鬼，然而她，卻疑惑了，——或者不如說希望：希望其有，又希望其無……。人何必增添末路的人的苦惱，為她起見，不如說有罷。

"Quite possibly, I'd say," I told her falteringly.

"That means there must be a hell too?"

"What, hell?" I faltered, very taken aback. "Hell? Logically speaking, there should be too — but not necessarily. Who cares anyway?"

"Then will all the members of a family meet again after death?"

"Well, as to whether they'll meet again or not ..." I realized now what an utter fool I was. All my hesitation and manoeuvring had been no match for her three questions. Promptly taking fright, I decided to recant. "In that case ... actually, I'm not sure.... In fact, I'm not sure whether there are ghosts or not either."

To avoid being pressed by any further questions I walked off, then beat a hasty retreat to my uncle's house, feeling thoroughly disconcerted. I may have given her a dangerous answer, I was thinking. Of course, she may just be feeling lonely because everybody else is celebrating now, but could she have had something else in mind? Some premonition? If she had had some other idea, and something happens as a result. Then my answer should indeed be partly responsible.... Then I laughed at myself for brooding so much over a chance meeting when it could have no serious significance. No wonder certain educationists called me neurotic. Besides, I had distinctly declared, "I'm not sure," contradicting the whole of my answer. This meant that even if something did happen, it would have nothing at all to do with me.

"I'm not sure" is a most useful phrase.

Bold inexperienced youngsters often take it upon themselves to solve problems or choose doctors for other people, and if by any chance things turn out badly they may well be held to blame; but by concluding

「也許有罷，──我想。」我於是吞吞吐吐的說。

「那麼，也就有地獄了？」

「阿！地獄？」我很吃驚，只得支吾着，「地獄？──論理，就該也有。──然而也未必，……誰來管這等事……。」

「那麼，死掉的一家的人，都能見面的？」

「唉唉，見面不見面呢？……」這時我已知道自己也還是完全一個愚人，甚麼躊躇，甚麼計劃，都擋不住三句問。我即刻膽怯起來了，便想全翻過先前的話來，「那是，……實在。我說不清……。其實，究竟有沒有魂靈，我也說不清。」

我乘她不再緊接的問，邁開步便走，匆匆的逃回四叔的家中，心裏很覺得不安逸。自己想，我這答話怕於她有些危險。她大約因為在別人的祝福時候，感到自身的寂寞了，然而會不會含有別的甚麼意思的呢？──或者是有了甚麼預感了？倘有別的意思，又因此發生別的事，則我的答話委實該負若干的責任……。但隨後也就自笑，覺得偶爾的事，本沒有甚麼深意義，而我偏要細細推敲，正無怪教育家要說是生着神經病；而況明明說過「說不清」，已經推翻了答話的全局，即使發生甚麼事，於我也毫無關係了。

「說不清」是一句極有用的話。不更事的勇敢的少年，往往敢於給人解決疑問，選定醫生，萬一結果不佳，大抵反成了怨府，然而

their advice with this evasive expression they achieve blissful immunity from reproach. The necessity for such a phrase was brought home to me still more forcibly now, since it was indispensable even in speaking with a beggar woman.

However, I remained uneasy, and even after a night's rest my mind dwelt on it with a certain sense of foreboding. The oppressive snowy weather and the gloomy study increased my uneasiness. I had better leave the next day and go back to the city. A large dish of plain shark's fin stew at the Fu Xing Restaurant used to cost only a dollar. I wondered if this cheap delicacy had risen in price or not. Though my good companions of the old days had scattered, that shark's fin must still be sampled even if I were on my own. Whatever happened I would leave the next day, I decided.

Since, in my experience, things I hoped would not happen and felt should not happen invariably did occur all the same, I was much afraid this would prove another such case. And, sure enough, the situation soon took a strange turn. Towards evening I heard what sounded like a discussion in the inner room, but the conversation ended before long and my uncle walked away observing loudly, "What a moment to choose! Now of all times! Isn't that proof enough she was a bad lot?"

My initial astonishment gave way to a deep uneasiness; I felt that this had something to do with me. I looked out of the door, but no one was there. I waited impatiently till their servant came in before dinner to brew tea. Then at last I had a chance to make some inquiries.

"Who was Mr. Lu so angry with just now?" I asked.

"Why, Xianglin's Wife, of course," was the curt reply.

"Xianglin's Wife? Why?" I pressed.

"She's gone."

一用這説不清來作結束，便事事逍遙自在了。我在這時，更感到這一句話的必要，即使和討飯的女人説話，也是萬不可省的。

但是我總覺得不安，過了一夜，也仍然時時記憶起來，彷彿懷着甚麼不祥的預感；在陰沉的雪天裏，在無聊的書房裏，這不安愈加強烈了。不如走罷，明天進城去。福興樓的清燉魚翅，一元一大盤，價廉物美，現在不知增價了否？往日同遊的朋友，雖然已經雲散，然而魚翅是不可不吃的，即使只有我一個……。無論如何，我明天決計要走了。

我因為常見些但願不如所料，以為未必竟如所料的事，卻每每恰如所料的起來，所以很恐怕這事也一律。果然，特別的情形開始了。傍晚，我竟聽到有些人聚在內室裏談話，彷彿議論甚麼事似的；但不一會，説話聲也就止了，只有四叔且走而且高聲的説：

「不早不遲，偏偏要在這時候，——這就可見是一個謬種！」

我先是詫異，接着是很不安，似乎這話於我有關係。試望門外，誰也沒有。好容易待到晚飯前他們的短工來沖茶，我才得了打聽消息的機會。

「剛才，四老爺和誰生氣呢？」我問。

「還不是和祥林嫂？」那短工簡捷的説。

「祥林嫂？怎麼了？」我又趕緊的問。

「老了。」

"Dead?" My heart missed a beat. I started and must have changed colour. But since the servant kept his head lowered, all this escaped him. I pulled myself together enough to ask.

"When did she die?"

"When? Last night or today — I'm not sure."

"How did she die?"

"How? Of poverty of course." After this stolid answer he withdrew, still without having raised his head to look at me.

My agitation was only short-lived, however. For now that my premonition had come to pass, I no longer had to seek comfort in my own "I'm not sure," or his "dying of poverty," and my heart was growing lighter. Only from time to time did I still feel a little guilty. Dinner was served, and my uncle impressively kept me company. Tempted as I was to ask about Xianglin's Wife, I knew that, although he had read that "ghosts and spirits are manifestations of the dual forces of Nature," he was still so superstitious that on the eve of the New-Year sacrifice it would be unthinkable to mention anything like death or illness. In case of necessity one should use veiled allusions. But since this was unfortunately beyond me I had to bite back the questions which kept rising to the tip of my tongue. And my uncle's solemn expression suddenly made me suspect that he looked on me too as a bad lot who had chosen this moment, now of all times, to come and trouble him. To set his mind at rest as quickly as I could, I told him at once of my plan to leave Luzhen the next day and go back to the city. He did not press me to stay, and at last the uncomfortably quiet meal came to an end.

Winter days are short, and because it was snowing darkness had already enveloped the whole town. All was stir and commotion in the

「死了？」我的心突然緊縮，幾乎跳起來，臉上大約也變了色。但他始終沒有抬頭，所以全不覺。我也就鎮定了自己，接着問：

「甚麼時候死的？」

「甚麼時候？——昨天夜裏，或者就是今天罷。——我說不清。」

「怎麼死的？」

「怎麼死的？——還不是窮死的？」他淡然的回答，仍然沒有抬頭向我看，出去了。

然而我的驚惶卻不過暫時的事，隨着就覺得要來的事，已經過去，並不必仰仗我自己的「說不清」和他之所謂「窮死的」的寬慰，心地已經漸漸輕鬆，不過偶然之間，還似乎有些負疚。晚飯擺出來了，四叔儼然的陪着。我也還想打聽些關於祥林嫂的消息，但知道他雖然讀過「鬼神者二氣之良能也」，而忌諱仍然極多，當臨近祝福時候，是萬不可提起死亡疾病之類的話的；倘不得已，就該用一種替代的隱語，可惜我又不知道，因此屢次想問，而終於中止了。我從他儼然的臉色上，又忽而疑他正以為我不早不遲，偏要在這時候來打攪他，也是一個謬種，便立刻告訴他明天要離開魯鎮，進城去，趁早放寬了他的心。他也不很留。這樣悶悶的吃完了一餐飯。

冬季日短，又是雪天，夜色早已籠罩了全市鎮。人們都在燈下

lighted houses, but outside was remarkably quiet. And the snowflakes hissing down on the thick snowdrifts intensified one's sense of loneliness. Seated alone in the amber light of the vegetable-oil lamp I reflected that this wretched and forlorn woman, abandoned in the dust like a worn-out toy of which its owners have tired, had once left her own imprint in the dust, and those who enjoyed life must have wondered at her for wishing to live on; but now at last she had been swept away by death. Whether spirits existed or not I did not know; but in this world of ours the end of a futile existence, the removal of someone whom others are tired of seeing, was just as well both for them and for the individual concerned. Occupied with these reflections, I listened quietly to the hissing of the snow outside, until little by little I felt more relaxed.

But the fragments of her life that I had seen or heard about before combined now to form a whole.

She was not from Luzhen. Early one winter, when my uncle's family wanted a new maid, Old Mrs. Wei the go-between brought her along. She had a white mourning band round her hair and was wearing a black skirt, blue jacket, and pale green bodice. Her age was about twenty-six, and though her face was sallow her cheeks were red. Old Mrs. Wei introduced her as Xianglin's Wife, a neighbour of her mother's family, who wanted to go out to work now that her husband had died. My uncle frowned at this, and my aunt knew that he disapproved of taking on a widow. She looked just the person for them, though, with her big strong hands and feet; and, judging by her downcast eyes and silence, she was a good worker who would know her place. So my aunt ignored my uncle's frown and kept her. During her trial period she worked from morning till night as if she found resting irksome, and proved strong enough to do the work of a man; so on the third day she was taken on for five hundred cash a month.

匆忙，但窗外很寂靜。雪花落在積得厚厚的雪褥上面，聽去似乎瑟瑟有聲，使人更加感得沉寂。我獨坐在發出黃光的菜油燈下，想，這百無聊賴的祥林嫂，被人們棄在塵芥堆中的，看得厭倦了的陳舊的玩物，先前還將形骸露在塵芥裏，從活得有趣的人們看來，恐怕要怪訝她何以還要存在，現在總算被無常打掃得乾乾淨淨了。魂靈的有無，我不知道；然而在現世，則無聊生者不生，即使厭見者不見：為人為己也還都不錯。我靜聽着窗外似乎瑟瑟作響的雪花聲，一面想，反而漸漸的舒暢起來。

然而先前所見所聞的她的半生事跡的斷片，至此也聯成一片了。

她不是魯鎮人。有一年的冬初，四叔家裏要換女工，做中人的衛老婆子帶她進來了，頭上紮着白頭繩，烏裙，藍夾襖，月白背心，年紀大約二十六七，臉色青黃，但兩頰卻還是紅的。

衛老婆子叫她祥林嫂，說是自己母家的鄰舍，死了當家人，所以出來做工了。四叔皺了皺眉，四嬸已經知道了他的意思，是在討厭她是一個寡婦。但看她模樣還周正，手腳都壯大，又只是順着眼，不開一句口，很像一個安分耐勞的人，便不管四叔的皺眉，將她留下了。試工期內，她整天的做，似乎閒着就無聊，又有力，簡直抵得過一個男子，所以第三天就定局，每月工錢五百文。

Everybody called her Xianglin's Wife and no one asked her own name, but since she had been introduced by someone from Wei Village as a neighbour, her surname was presumably also Wei. She said little, only answering briefly when asked a question. Thus it took them a dozen days or so to find out bit by bit that she had a strict mother-in-law at home and a brother-in-law of ten or so, old enough to cut wood. Her husband, who had died that spring, had been a woodcutter too, and had been ten years younger than she was. This little was all they could learn.

Time passed quickly. She went on working as hard as ever, not caring what she ate, never sparing herself. It was generally agreed that the Lu family's maid actually got through more work than a hard-working man. At the end of the year, she swept and mopped the floors, killed the chickens and geese, and sat up to boil the sacrificial meat, all single-handed, so that they did not need to hire extra help. And she for her part was quite contented. Little by little the trace of a smile appeared at the corners of her mouth, while her face became whiter and plumper.

Just after the New Year she came back from washing rice by the river most upset because in the distance she had seen a man, pacing up and down on the opposite bank, who looked like her husband's elder cousin — very likely he had come in search of her. When my aunt in alarm pressed her for more information, she said nothing. As soon as my uncle knew of this he frowned.

"That bad," he observed. "She must have run away."

Before very long this inference was confirmed.

About a fortnight later, just as this incident was beginning to be forgotten, Old Mrs. Wei suddenly brought along a woman in her thirties whom she introduced as Xianglin's mother. Although this woman

　　大家都叫她祥林嫂；沒問她姓甚麼，但中人是衛家山人，既說是鄰居，那大概也就姓衛了。她不很愛說話，別人問了才回答，答的也不多。直到十幾天之後，這才陸續的知道她家裏還有嚴厲的婆婆；一個小叔子，十多歲，能打柴了；她是春天沒了丈夫的；他本來也打柴為生，比她小十歲：大家所知道的就只是這一點。

　　日子很快的過去了，她的做工卻毫沒有懈，食物不論，力氣是不惜的。人們都說魯四老爺家裏僱着了女工，實在比勤快的男人還勤快。到年底，掃塵，洗地，殺雞，宰鵝，徹夜的煮福禮，全是一人擔當，竟沒有添短工。然而她反滿足，口角邊漸漸的有了笑影，臉上也白胖了。

　　新年才過，她從河邊淘米回來時，忽而失了色，說剛才遠遠地看見一個男人在對岸徘徊，很像夫家的堂伯，恐怕是正為尋她而來的。四嬸很驚疑，打聽底細，她又不說。四叔一知道，就皺一皺眉，道：

　　「這不好。恐怕她是逃出來的。」

　　她誠然是逃出來的，不多久，這推想就證實了。

　　此後大約十幾天，大家正已漸漸忘卻了先前的事，衛老婆子忽而帶了一個三十多歲的女人進來了，說那是祥林嫂的婆婆。那女人

looked like the hill-dweller she was, she behaved with great self-possession and has a ready tongue in her head. After the usual civilities she apologized for coming to take her daughter-in-law back, explaining that early spring was a busy time and they were short-handed at home with only old people and children around.

"If her mother-in-law wants her back, there's nothing more to be said," was my uncle's comment.

Thereupon her wages were reckoned up. They came to 1,750 cash, all of which she had left in the keeping of her mistress without spending any of it. My aunt gave the entire sum to Xianglin's mother, who took her daughter-in-law's clothes as well, expressed her thanks, and left. By this time it was noon.

"Oh, the rice! Didn't Xianglin's Wife go to wash the rice?" exclaimed my aunt some time later. It was probably hunger that reminded her of lunch.

A general search started then for the rice-washing basket. My aunt searched the kitchen, then the hall, then the bedroom; but not a sign of the basket was to be seen. My uncle could not find it outside either, until he went right down to the river-side. Then he saw it set down fair and square on the bank, some vegetables beside it.

Some people on the bank told him that a boat with a white awning had moored there that morning but, since the awning covered the boat completely, they had no idea who was inside and had paid no special attention to begin with. But when Xianglin's Wife had arrived and was kneeling down to wash rice, two men who looked as if they came from the hills had jumped off the boat and seized her. Between them they dragged her on board. She wept and shouted at first but soon fell silent, probably because she was gagged. Then along came two women, a stranger and Old Mrs. Wei. It was difficult to see clearly into the

雖是山裏人模樣，然而應酬很從容，説話也能幹，寒暄之後，就賠
罪，説她特來叫她的兒媳回家去，因為開春事務忙，而家中只有老
的和小的，人手不夠了。

「既是她的婆婆要她回去，那有甚麼話可説呢。」四叔説。

於是算清了工錢，一共一千七百五十文，她全存在主人家，一
文也還沒有用，便都交給她的婆婆。那女人又取了衣服，道過謝，
出去了。其時已經是正午。

「阿呀，米呢？祥林嫂不是去淘米的麼？……」好一會，四嬸這
才驚叫起來。她大約有些餓，記得午飯了。

於是大家分頭尋淘籮。她先到廚下，次到堂前，後到臥房，全
不見淘籮的影子。四叔踱出門外，也不見，直到河邊，才見平平正
正的放在岸上，旁邊還有一株菜。

看見的人報告説，河裏面上午就泊了一隻白篷船，篷是全蓋起
來的，不知道甚麼人在裏面，但事前也沒有人去理會他。待到祥林
嫂出來淘米，剛剛要跪下去，那船裏便突然跳出兩個男人來，像是
山裏人，一個抱住她，一個幫着，拖進船去了。祥林嫂還哭喊了幾
聲，此後便再沒有甚麼聲息，大約給用甚麼堵住了罷。接着就走上
兩個女人來，一個不認識，一個就是衛婆子。窺探艙裏，不很分

boat, but the victim seemed to be lying, tied up, on the planking.

"Disgraceful! Still ..." said my uncle.

That day my aunt cooked the midday meal herself, and their son Aniu lit the fire.

After lunch Old Mrs. Wei came back. "Disgraceful!" said my uncle.

"What's the meaning of this? How dare you show your face here again?" My aunt, who was washing up, started fuming as soon as she saw her. "First you recommended her, then help them carry her off, causing such a shocking commotion. What will people think? Are you trying to make fools of our family ?"

"*Aiya*, I was completely taken in! I've come specially to clear this up. How was I to know she'd left home without permission from her mother-in-law when she asked me to find her work? I'm sorry, Mr. Lu. I'm sorry, Mrs. Lu. I'm growing so stupid and careless in my old age, I've let my patrons down. It's lucky for me you're such kind, generous people, never hard on those below you. I promise to make it up to you by finding someone good this time."

"Still ..."said my uncle.

That concluded the affair of Xianglin's Wife, and before long it was forgotten.

My aunt was the only one who still spoke of Xianglin's Wife. This was because most of the maids taken on afterwards turned out to be lazy or greedy, or both, none of them giving satisfaction. At such times she would invariably say to herself, "I wonder what's become of her now ?" — implying that she would like to have her back. But by the next New Year she too had given up hope.

The first month was nearing its end when Old Mrs. Wei called on

明，她像是捆了躺在船板上。

「可惡！然而……。」四叔說。

這一天是四嫂自己煮午飯；他們的兒子阿牛燒火。

午飯之後，衛老婆子又來了。

「可惡！」四叔說。

「你是甚麼意思？虧你還會再來見我們。」四嬸洗着碗，一見面就憤憤的說，「你自己薦她來，又合夥劫她去，鬧得沸反盈天的，大家看了成個甚麼樣子？你拿我們家裏開玩笑麼？」

「阿呀阿呀，我真上當。我這回，就是為此特地來說說清楚的。她來求我薦地方，我那裏料得到是瞞着她的婆婆的呢。對不起，四老爺，四太太。總是我老發昏不小心，對不起主顧。幸而府上是向來寬洪大量，不肯和小人計較的。這回我一定薦一個好的來折罪……。」

「然而……。」四叔說。

於是祥林嫂事件便告終結，不久也就忘卻了。

只有四嬸，因為後來僱用的女工，大抵非懶即饞，或者饞而且懶，左右不如意，所以也還提起祥林嫂。每當這些時候，她往往自言自語的說，「她現在不知道怎麼樣了？」意思是希望她再來。但到第二年的新正，她也就絕了望。

新正將盡，衛老婆子來拜年了，已經喝得醉醺醺的，自說因為

my aunt to wish her a happy New Year. Already tipsy, she explained that the reason for her coming so late was that she had been visiting her family in Wei Village in the hills for a few days. The conversation, naturally, soon touched on Xianglin's Wife.

"Xianglin's Wife?" cried Old Mrs. Wei cheerfully. "She's in luck now. When her mother-in-law dragged her home, she'd promised her to the sixth son of the He family in He Glen. So a few days after her return they put her in the bridal chair and sent her off."

"Gracious! What a mother-in-law!" exclaimed my aunt.

"Ah, madam, you really talk like a great lady! This is nothing to poor folk like us who live up in the hills. That young brother-in-law of hers still had no wife. If they didn't marry her off, where would the money have come from to get him one? Her mother-in-law is a clever, capable woman, a fine manager; so she married her off into the mountains. If she'd betrothed her to a family in the same village, she wouldn't have made so much; but as very few girls are willing to take a husband deep in the mountains at the back of beyond, she got eighty thousand cash. Now the second son has a wife, who cost only fifty thousand; and after paying the wedding expenses she's still over ten thousand in hand. Wouldn't you call her a fine manager?"

"But was Xianglin's Wife willing?"

"It wasn't a question of willing or not. Of course any woman would make a row about it. All they had to do was tie her up, shove her into the chair, carry her to the man's house, force on her the two of them into their room — and that was that. But Xianglin's Wife is quite a character. I heard that she made a terrible scene. It was working for a scholar's family, everyone said, that made her different from other people. We go-betweens see life, madam. Some widows sob and shout

回了一趟衛家山的娘家，住下幾天，所以來得遲了。她們問答之間，自然就談到祥林嫂。

「她麼？」衛老婆子高興的說，「現在是交了好運了。她婆婆來抓她回去的時候，是早已許給了賀家墺的賀老六的，所以回家之後不幾天，也就裝在花轎裏抬去了。」

「阿呀，這樣的婆婆！……」四嬸驚奇的說。

「阿呀，我的太太！你真是大戶人家的太太的話。我們山裏人，小戶人家，這算得甚麼？她有小叔子，也得娶老婆。不嫁了她，那有這一注錢來做聘禮？她的婆婆倒是精明強幹的女人呵，很有打算，所以就將她嫁到裏山去。倘許給本村人，財禮就不多；惟獨肯嫁進深山野墺裏去的女人少，所以她就到手了八十千。現在第二個兒子的媳婦也娶進了，財禮只花了五十，除去辦喜事的費用，還剩十多千。嚇，你看，這多麼好打算？……」

「祥林嫂竟肯依？……」

「這有甚麼依不依。——鬧是誰也總要鬧一鬧的；只要用繩子一捆，塞在花轎裏，抬到男家，捺上花冠，拜堂，關上房門，就完事了。可是祥林嫂真出格，聽說那時實在鬧得利害，大家還都說大約因為在唸書人家做過事，所以與眾不同呢。太太，我們見得多了：

when they remarry; some threaten to kill themselves; some refuse to go through the cermony of bowing to heaven and earth after they've been carried to man's house; some even smash the wedding candlesticks. But Xianglin's Wife was really extraordinary. They said she screamed and cursed all the way to He Glen, so that she was completely hoarse by the time they got there. When they dragged her out the chair, no matter how the two chair-bearers and her brother-in-law held her, they couldn't make her go through the ceremony. The moment they were off guard and had loosened their grip — gracious Buddha! — she bashed her head on a corner of the altar, gashing it so badly that blood spurted out. Even though they smeared on two handfuls of incense ashes and toed it up with two pieces of red cloth, they couldn't stop the bleeding. It took quite a few of them to shut her up finally with the man in the bridal chamber, but even then she went on cursing. Oh, it was really...." Shaking her head, she lowered her eyes and fell silent.

"And what then?" asked my aunt.

"They said that the next day she didn't get up." Old Mrs. Wei raised her eyes.

"And after?"

"After? She got up. At the end of the year she had a baby, a boy, who was reckoned as two this New Year. These few days when I was at home, some people back from a visit to He Glen said they'd seen her and her son, and both mother and child are plump. There's no mother-in-law over her, her man is a strong fellow who can earn a living, and the house belongs to them. Oh, yes she's in luck all right."

After this event my aunt gave up talking of Xianglin's Wife.

But one autumn, after two New Years had passed since this good news of Xianglin's Wife, she once more crossed the threshold of my

回頭人出嫁，哭喊的也有，說要尋死覓活的也有，抬到男家鬧得拜不成天地的也有，連花燭都砸了的也有。祥林嫂可是異乎尋常，他們說她一路只是嚎，罵，抬到賀家墺，喉嚨已經全啞了，拉出轎來，兩個男人和她的小叔子使勁的擒住她也還拜不成天地。他們一不小心，一鬆手，阿呀，阿彌陀佛，她就一頭撞在香案角上，頭上碰了一個大窟窿，鮮血直流，用了兩把香灰，包上兩塊紅布還止不住血呢。直到七手八腳的將她和男人反關在新房裏，還是罵，阿呀呀，這真是……」她搖一搖頭，順下眼睛，不說了。

「後來怎麼樣呢？」四嬸還問。

「聽說第二天也沒有起來。」她抬起眼來說。

「後來呢？」

「後來？——起來了。她到年底就生了一個孩子，男的，新年就兩歲了。我在娘家這幾天，就有人到賀家墺去，回來說看見他們娘兒倆，母親也胖，兒子也胖；上頭又沒有婆婆；男人所有的是力氣，會做活；房子是自家的。——唉唉，她真是交了好運了。」

從此之後，四嬸也就不再提起祥林嫂。

但有一年的秋季，大約是得到祥林嫂好運的消息之後的又過了

uncle's house, placing her round bulb-shaped basket on the table and her small bedding-roll under the eaves. As before, she had a white mourning band round her hair and was wearing a black skirt, blue jacket, and pale green bodice. Her face was sallow, her cheeks no longer red; and her downcast eyes, stained with tears, had lost their brightness. Just as before, it was Old Mrs. Wei who brought her to my aunt.

"It was really a bolt from the blue," she explained compassionately. "Her husband was a strong young fellow; who'd have thought that typhoid fever would carry him off? He'd taken a turn for the better, but then he ate some cold rice and got worse again. Luckily she had the boy and she can work — she's able to gather firewood, pick tea, or raise silkworms — so she could have managed on her own. But who'd have thought that the child, too, would be carried off by a wolf? It was nearly the end of spring, yet a wolf came to the glen — who could have guessed that? Now she's all on her own. Her husband's elder brother has taken over the house and turned her out. So she's no way to turn for help except to her former mistress. Luckily this time there's nobody to stop her and you happen to be needing someone, madam. That's why I've brought her here. I think someone used to your ways is much better than a new hand.... "

"I was really too stupid, really ..." put in Xianglin's Wife, raising her lacklustre eyes. "All I knew was that when it snowed and wild beasts up in the hills had nothing to eat, they might come to the villages. I didn't know that in spring they might come too. I got up at dawn and opened the door, filled a small basket with beans and told our Amao to sit on the doorstep and shell them. He was such a good boy; he always did as he was told, and out he went. Then I went to the back to chop wood and wash the rice, and when the rice was in the pan I wanted to steam the beans. I called Amao, but there was no answer. When I went out to look there were beans all over the ground but no Amao. He never went to the neighbours' houses to play; and, sure

兩個新年，她竟又站在四叔家的堂前了。桌上放著一個荸薺式的圓籃，簷下一個小鋪蓋。她仍然頭上紮着白頭繩，烏裙；藍夾襖，月白背心，臉色青黃，只是兩頰上已經消失了血色，順着眼，眼角上帶些淚痕，眼光也沒有先前那樣精神了。而且仍然是衛老婆子領着，顯出慈悲模樣，絮絮的對四嬸說：

「……這實在是叫作『天有不測風雲』，她的男人是堅實人，誰知道年紀青青，就會斷送在傷寒上？本來已經好了的，吃了一碗冷飯，復發了。幸虧有兒子；她又能做，打柴摘茶養蠶都來得，本來還可以守着，誰知道那孩子又會給狼銜去的呢？春天快完了，村上倒反來了狼，誰料到？現在她只剩了一個光身了。大伯來收屋，又趕她。她真是走投無路了，只好來求老主人。好在她現在已經再沒有甚麼牽掛，太太家裏又湊巧要換人，所以我就領她來。——我想，熟門熟路，比生手實在好得多。……」

「我真傻，真的，」祥林嫂抬起她沒有神采的眼睛來，接着說。「我單知道下雪的時候野獸在山墺裏沒有食吃，會到村裏來；我不知道春天也會有。我一清早起來就開了門。拿小籃盛了一籃豆，叫我們的阿毛坐在門檻上剝豆去。他是很聽話的，我的話句句聽；他出去了。我就在屋後劈柴，淘米，米下了鍋，要蒸豆。我叫阿毛，沒有應，出去一看；只見豆撒得一地，沒有我們的阿毛了。他是不到

enough, though I asked everywhere he wasn't there. I got so worried, I begged people to help me find him. Not until that afternoon, after searching high and low, did they try the gully. There they saw one of his little shoes caught on a bramble. 'That's bad,' they said. 'A wolf must have got him.' And sure enough, further on, there he was lying in the wolf's den, all his innards eaten away, still clutching that little basket tight in his hand....'' At this point she broke down and could not go on.

My aunt had been undecided at first, but the rims of her eyes were rather red by the time Xianglin's Wife broke off. After a moment's thought she told her to take her things to the servant's quarters. Old Mrs. Wei heaved a sigh, as if a great weight had been lifted from her mind; and Xianglin's Wife, looking more relaxed than when first she came, went off quietly to put away her bedding without having to be told the way. So she started work again as a maid in Luzhen.

She was still known as Xianglin's Wife.

But now she was a very different woman. She had not worked there more than two or three days before her mistress realized that she was not as quick as before. Her memory was much worse too, while her face, like a death-mask, never showed the least trace of a smile. Already my aunt was expressing herself as not too satisfied. Though my uncle had frowned as before when she first arrived, they always had such trouble finding servants that he raised no serious objections, simply warning his wife on the quiet that while such people might seem very pathetic they exerted a bad moral influence. She could work for them but must have nothing to do with ancestral sacrifices. They would have to prepare all the dishes themselves. Otherwise they would be unclean and the ancestors would not accept them.

別家去玩的；各處去一問，果然沒有。我急了，央人出去尋。直到下半天，尋來尋去尋到山墺裏，看見刺柴上掛着一隻他的小鞋。大家都說，糟了，怕是遭了狼了。再進去；他果然躺在草窠裏，肚裏的五臟已經都給吃空了，手上還緊緊的捏着那隻小籃呢。……」她接着但是嗚咽，說不出成句的話來。

四嬸起初還躊躕，待到聽完她自己的話，眼圈就有些紅了。她想了一想，便教拿圓籃和鋪蓋到下房去。衛老婆子彷彿卸了一肩重擔似的噓一口氣；祥林嫂比初來時候神氣舒暢些，不待指引，自己馴熟的安放了鋪蓋，她從此又在魯鎮做女工了。

大家仍然叫她祥林嫂。

然而這一回，她的境遇卻改變得非常大。上工之後的兩三天，主人們就覺得她手腳已沒有先前一樣靈活，記性也壞得多，死屍似的臉上又整日沒有笑影，四嬸的口氣上，已頗有些不滿了。當她初到的時候，四叔雖然照例皺過眉，但鑑於向來僱用女工之難，也就並不大反對，只是暗暗地告誡四嬸說，這種人雖然似乎很可憐，但是敗壞風俗的，用她幫忙還可以，祭祀時候可用不着她沾手，一切飯菜，只好自己做，否則，不乾不淨，祖宗是不吃的。

The most important events in my uncle's household were ancestral sacrifices, and formerly these had kept Xianglin's Wife especially busy, but now she had virtually nothing to do. As soon as the table had been placed in the centre of the hall and a front curtain fastened around its legs, she started setting out the winecups and chopsticks in the way she still remembered.

"Put those down, Xianglin's Wife," cried my aunt hastily. "Leave that to me."

She drew back sheepishly then and went for the candlesticks.

"Put those down, Xianglin's Wife," cries my aunt again in haste. "I'll fetch them."

After walking round in the hall several times without finding anything to do, she moved doubtfully away. All she could do that day was to sit by the stove and feed the fire.

The townspeople still called her Xianglin's Wife, but in quite a different tone from before; and although they still talked to her, their manner was colder. Quite impervious to this, staring straight in front of her, she would tell everybody the story which night or day was never out of her mind.

"I was really too stupid, really," she would say. "All I knew was that when it snowed and the wild beasts up in the hills had nothing to eat, they might come to the villages. I got up at dawn and opened the door, filled a small basket with beans and told our Amao to sit on the doorstep and shell them. He was such a good boy; he always did as he was told, and out he went. Then I went to the back to chop wood and wash the rice, and when the rice was in the pan I wanted to steam the beans. I called Amao, but there was no answer. When I went out to look, there were beans all over the ground but no Amao. He never went to the neighbours' houses to play; and, sure enough, though I

　　四叔家裏最重大的事件是祭祀，祥林嫂先前最忙的時候也就是祭祀，這回她卻清閒了。桌子放在堂中央，繫上桌幃，她還記得照舊的去分配酒杯和筷子。

　　「祥林嫂，你放着罷！我來擺。」四嬸慌忙的説。

　　她訕訕的縮了手，又去取燭台。

　　「祥林嫂，你放着罷！我來拿。」四嬸又慌忙的説。

　　她轉了幾個圓圈，終於沒有事情做，只得疑惑的走開。她在這一天可做的事是不過坐在灶下燒火。

　　鎮上的人們也仍然叫她祥林嫂，但音調和先前很不同；也還和她講話，但笑容卻冷冷的了。她全不理會那些事，只是直着眼睛，和大家講她自己日夜不忘的故事：

　　「我真傻，真的，」她説。「我單知道雪天是野獸在深山裏沒有食吃，會到村裏來；我不知道春天也會有。我一大早起來就開了門，拿小籃盛了一籃豆，叫我們的阿毛坐在門檻上剝豆去。他是很聽話的孩子，我的話句句聽；他就出去了。我就在屋後劈柴，淘米，米下了鍋，打算蒸豆。我叫，『阿毛！』沒有應。出去一看，只見豆撒得滿地，沒有我們的阿毛了。各處去一問，都沒有。我急了，央人

asked everywhere he wasn't there. I got so worried, I begged people to help me find him. Not until that afternoon, after searching high and low, did they try the gully. There they saw one of his little shoes caught on a bramble. 'That's bad,' they said. 'A wolf must have got him.' And sure enough, further on, there he was lying in the wolf's den, all his innards eaten away, still clutching that little basket tight in his hand...." At this point her voice would be choked with tears.

This story was so effective that men hearing it often stopped smiling and walked blankly away, while the women not only seemed to forgive her but wiped the contemptuous expression off their faces and added their tears to hers. Indeed, some old women who had not heard her in the street sought her out specially to hear her sad tale. And when she broke down, they too shed the tears which had gathered in their eyes, after which they sighed and went away satisfied, exchanging eager comments.

As for her, she asked nothing better than to tell her sad story over and over again, often gathering three or four hearers around her. But before long everybody knew it so well that no trace of a tear could be seen even in the eyes of the most kindly, Buddha-invoking old ladies. In the end, practically the whole town could recite it by heart and were bored and exasperated to hear it repeated.

"I was really too stupid, really," she would begin.

"Yes. All you knew was that in snowy weather, when the wild beasts in the mountains had nothing to eat, they might come down to the villages." Cutting short her recital abruptly, they walked away.

She would stand there open-mouthed, staring after them stupidly, and then wander off as if she too were bored by the story. But she still tried hopefully to lead up from other topics such as small baskets, and other people's children to the story of her Amao. At the sight of a child

去尋去。直到下半天，幾個人尋到山墺裏，看見刺柴上掛着一隻他的小鞋，大家都説，完了，怕是遭了狼了。再進去；果然，他躺在草窠裏，肚裏的五臟已經都給吃空了，可憐他手裏還緊緊的捏着那隻小籃呢。……」她於是淌下眼淚來，聲音也嗚咽了。

這故事倒頗有效，男人聽到這裏，往往斂起笑容，沒趣的走了開去；女人們卻不獨寬恕了她似的，臉上立刻改換了鄙薄的神氣，還要陪出許多眼淚來。有些老女人沒有在街頭聽到她的話，便特意尋來，要聽她這一段悲慘的故事。直到她説到嗚咽，她們也就一齊流下那停在眼角上的眼淚，嘆息一番，滿足的去了，一面還紛紛的評論着。

她就只是反覆的向人説她悲慘的故事，常常引住了三五個人來聽她。但不久，大家也都聽得純熟了，便是最慈悲的唸佛的老太太們，眼裏也再不見有一點淚的痕跡。後來全鎮的人們幾乎都能背誦她的話，一聽到就煩厭得頭痛。

「我真傻，真的，」她開首説。

「是的，你是單知道雪天野獸在深山裏沒有食吃，才會到村裏來的。」他們立即打斷她的話，走開去了。

她張着口怔怔的站着，直着眼睛看他們，接着也就走了，似乎自己也覺得沒趣。但她還妄想，希圖從別的事，如小籃，豆，別人

of two or three she would say, "Ah, if my Amao were alive he'd be just that size...."

Children would take fright at the look in her eyes and clutch the hem of their mothers' clothes to tug them away. Left by herself again, she would eventually walk away. In the end everybody knew what she was like. If a child were present they would ask with a spurious smile, "If your Amao were alive, Xianglin's Wife, wouldn't he be just that size?"

She may not have realized that her tragedy, after being generally savoured for so many days, had long since grown so stale that it now aroused only revulsion and disgust. But she seemed to sense the cold mockery in their smiles, and the fact that there was no need for her to say any more. So she would simply look at them in silence.

New-Year preparations always start in Luzhen on the twentieth day of the twelfth lunar month. That year my uncle's household had to take on a temporary manservant. And since there was more than he could do they asked Amah Liu to help by killing the chickens and geese; but being a devout vegetarian who would not kill living creatures, she would only wash the sacrificial vessels. Xianglin's Wife, with nothing to do but feed the fire, sat there at a loose end watching Amah Liu as she worked. A light snow began to fall.

"Ah, I was really too stupid," said Xianglin's Wife as if to herself, looking at the sky and sighing.

"There you go again, Xianglin's Wife." Amah Liu glanced with irritation at her face. "Tell me, wasn't that when you got that scar on your forehead?"

All the reply she received was a vague murmur.

"Tell me this: What made you willing after all?"

的孩子上，引出她的阿毛的故事來。倘一看見兩三歲的小孩子，她
就說：

「唉唉，我們的阿毛如果還在，也就有這麼大了……」

孩子看見她的眼光就吃驚，牽着母親的衣襟催她走。於是又只
剩下她一個，終於沒趣的也走了。後來大家又都知道了她的脾氣，
只要有孩子在眼前，便似笑非笑的先問她，道：

「祥林嫂，你們的阿毛如果還在，不是也就有這麼大了麼？」

她未必知道她的悲哀經大家咀嚼賞鑑了許多天，早已成為渣
滓，只值得煩厭和唾棄；但從人們的笑影上，也彷彿覺得這又冷又
尖，自己再沒有開口的必要了。她單是一瞥他們，並不回答一句
話。

魯鎮永遠是過新年，臘月二十以後就忙起來了。四叔家裏這回
須僱男短工，還是忙不過來，另叫柳媽做幫手，殺雞，宰鵝；然而
柳媽是善女人，吃素，不殺生的，只肯洗器皿。祥林嫂除燒火之
外，沒有別的事，卻閒着了，坐着只看柳媽洗器皿。微雪點點的下
來了。

「唉唉，我真傻，」祥林嫂看了天空，嘆息着，獨語似的說。「祥
林嫂，你又來了。」柳媽不耐煩的看着她的臉，說。「我問你：你額
角上的傷疤，不就是那時撞壞的麼？」

「唔唔。」她含糊的回答。

「我問你：你那時怎麼後來竟依了呢？」

"Willing?"

"Yes. Seems to me you must have been willing. Otherwise...."

"Oh, you don't know how strong he was."

"I don't believe it. I don't believe he was so strong that you with your strength couldn't have kept him off. You must have ended up willing. That talk of his being so strong is just an excuse."

"Why ... just try for yourself and see." She smiled. Amah Liu's lined face broken into a smile too, wrinkling up like a walnut-shell. Her small beady eyes swept the other woman's forehead, then fastened on her eyes. At once Xianglin's Wife stopped smiling, as if embarrassed, and turned her eyes away to watch the snow.

"That was really a bad bargain you struck, Xianglin's Wife," said Amah Liu mysteriously. "If you'd held out longer or knocked yourself to death outright, that would have been better. As it is, you're guilty of a great sin though you lived less than two years with your second husband. Just think: when you go down to the lower world, the ghosts of both men will start fighting over you. Which ought to have you? The King of Hell will have to saw you into two and divide you between them. I feel it really is...."

Xianglin's Wife's face registered terror then. This was something no one had told her up in the mountains.

"Better guard against that in good time, I say. Go to the Temple of the Tutelary God and buy a threshold to be trampled on instead of you by thousands of people. If you atone for your sins in this life you'll escape torment after death."

Xianglin's Wife said nothing at the time, but she must have taken this advice to heart, for when she got up the next morning there were dark rims round her eyes. After breakfast she went to the Temple of the

「我麼？……」

「你呀。我想：這總是你自己願意了，不然……。」

「阿阿，你不知道他力氣多麼大呀。」

「我不信。我不信你這麼大的力氣，真會拗他不過。你後來一定是自己肯了，倒推説他力氣大。」

「阿阿，你……你倒自己試試看。」她笑了。

柳媽的打皺的臉也笑起來，使她蹙縮得像一個核桃；乾枯的小眼睛一看祥林嫂的額角，又釘住她的眼。祥林嫂似乎很侷促了，立刻斂了笑容，旋轉眼光，自去看雪花。

「祥林嫂，你實在不合算。」柳媽詭秘的説。「再一強，或者索性撞一個死，就好了。現在呢，你和你的第二個男人過活不到兩年，倒落了一件大罪名。你想，你將來到陰司去，那兩個死鬼的男人還要爭，你給了誰好呢？閻羅大王只好把你鋸開來，分給他們。我想，這真是……。」

她臉上就顯出恐怖的神色來，這是在山村裏所未曾知道的。

「我想，你不如及早抵當。你到土地廟裏去捐一條門檻，當做你的替身，給千人踏，萬人跨，贖了這一世的罪名，免得死了去受苦。」

她當時並不回答甚麼話，但大約非常苦悶了，第二天早上起來的時候，兩眼上便都圍着大黑圈。早飯之後，她便到鎮的西頭的土

Tutelary God at the west end of the town and asked to buy a threshold as an offering. At first the priest refused, only giving a grudging consent after she was reduced to tears of desperation. The price charged was twelve thousand cash.

She had long since given up talking to people after their contemptuous reception of Amao's story; but as word of her conversation with Amah Liu spread, many of the townsfolk took a fresh interest in her and came once more to provoke her into talking. The topic, of course, had changed to the scar on her forehead.

"Tell me, Xianglin's Wife, what made you willing in the end?" one would ask.

"What a waste, to have bashed yourself like that for nothing," another would chime in, looking at her scar.

She must have known from their smiles and tone of voice that they were mocking her, for she simply stared at them without a word and finally did not even turn her head. All day long she kept her lips tightly closed, bearing on her head the scar considered by everyone as a badge of shame, while she shopped, swept the floor, washed the vegetables, and prepared the rice in silence. Nearly a year went by before she took her accumulated wages from my aunt, changed them for twelve silver dollars, and asked for leave to go to the west end of the town. In less time than it takes for a meal she was back again, looking much comforted. With an unaccustomed light in her eyes, she told my aunt contentedly that she had now offered up a threshold in the Temple of the Tutelary God.

When the time came for the ancestral sacrifice at the winter solstice she worked harder than ever, and as soon as my aunt took out the sacrificial vessels and helped Aniu to carry the table into the middle of the hall, she went confidently to fetch the winecups and chopsticks.

地廟裏去求捐門檻。廟祝起初執意不允許，直到她急得流淚，才勉強答應了。價目是大錢十二千。

她久已不和人們交口，因為阿毛的故事是早被大家厭棄了的；但自從和柳媽談了天，似乎又即傳揚開去，許多人都發生了新趣味，又來逗她說話了。至於題目，那自然是換了一個新樣，專在她額上的傷疤。

「祥林嫂，我問你：你那時怎麼竟肯了？」一個說。

「唉，可惜，白撞了這一下。」一個看着她的疤，應和道。

她大約從他們的笑容和聲調上，也知道是在嘲笑她，所以總是瞪着眼睛，不說一句話，後來連頭也不回了。她整日緊閉了嘴唇，頭上帶着大家以為恥辱的記號的那傷痕，默默的跑街，掃地，洗菜，淘米。快夠一年，她才從四嬸手裏支取了歷來積存的工錢，換算了十二元鷹洋請假到鎮的西頭去。但不到一頓飯時候；她便回來，神氣很舒暢，眼光也分外有神，高興似的對四嬸說，自己已經在土地廟捐了門檻了。

冬至的祭祖時節，她做得更出力，看四嬸裝好祭品，和阿牛將桌子抬到堂屋中央，她便坦然的去拿酒杯和筷子。

"Put those down, Xianglin's Wife!" my aunt called hastily.

She withdrew her hand as if scorched, her face turned ashen grey, and instead of fetching the candlesticks she just stood there in a daze until my uncle came in to burn some incense and told her to go away. This time the change in her was phenomenal: the next day her eyes were sunken, her spirit seemed broken. She took fright very easily too, afraid not only of the dark and of shadows, but of meeting anyone. Even the sight of her own master or mistress set her trembling like a mouse that had strayed out of its hole in broad daylight. The rest of the time she would sit stupidly as if carved out of wood. In less than half a year her hair had turned grey, and her memory had deteriorated so much that she often forgot to go and wash the rice.

"What come over Xianglin's Wife? We should never have taken her on again," my aunt would sometimes say in front of her, as if to warn her.

But there was no change in her, no sign that she would ever recover her wits. So they decided to get rid of her and tell her to go back to Old Mrs. Wei. That was what they were saying, at least, while I was there; and judging by subsequent developments, this is evidently what they must have done. But whether she started begging as soon as she left my uncle's house, or whether she went first to Old Mrs. Wei and later became a beggar, I do not know.

I was woken up by the noisy explosion of crackers close at hand and, from the faint glow shed by the yellow oil lamp and the bangs of fireworks as my uncle's household celebrated the sacrifice, I knew that it must be nearly dawn. Listening drowsily I heard vaguely the ceaseless explosion of crackers in the distance. It seemed to me that the whole town was enveloped by the dense cloud of noise in the sky, mingling with the whirling snowflakes. Enveloped in this medley of sound I relaxed; the doubt which had preyed on my mind from dawn

「你放着罷，祥林嫂！」四嬸慌忙大聲説。

　她像是受了炮烙似的縮手，臉色同時變作灰黑，也不再去取燭台，只是失神的站着。直到四叔上香的時候，教她走開，她才走開。這一回她的變化非常大，第二天，不但眼睛窈陷下去，連精神也更不濟了。而且很膽怯，不獨怕暗夜，怕黑影，即使看見人，雖是自己的主人，也總惴惴的，有如在白天出穴遊行的小鼠；否則呆坐着，直是一個木偶人。不半年，頭髮也花白起來了，記性尤其壞，甚而至於常常忘卻了去淘米。

　「祥林嫂怎麼這樣了？倒不如那時不留她。」四嬸有時當面就這樣説，似乎是警告她。

　然而她總如此，全不見有伶俐起來的希望。他們於是想打發她走了，教她回到衛老婆子那裏去。但當我還在魯鎮的時候，不過單是這樣説；看現在的情狀，可見後來終於實行了。然而她是從四叔家出去就成了乞丐的呢，還是先到衛老婆子家然後再成乞丐的呢？那我可不知道。

　我給那些因為在近旁而極響的爆竹聲驚醒，看見豆一般大的黃色的燈火光，接着又聽得畢畢剝剝的鞭炮，是四叔家正在「祝福」了；知道已是五更將近時候。我在朦朧中，又隱約聽到遠處的爆竹聲聯綿不斷，似乎合成一天音響的濃雲，夾着團團飛舞的雪花，擁抱了全市鎮。我在這繁響的擁抱中，也懶散而且舒適，從白天以至

till night was swept clean away by the festive atmosphere, and I felt only that the saints of heaven and earth had accepted the sacrifice and incense and were reeling with intoxication in the sky, preparing to give Luzhen's people boundless good fortune.

February 7, 1924

初夜的疑慮，全給祝福的空氣一掃而空了，只覺得天地聖眾歆享了
牲醴和香煙，都醉醺醺的在空中蹣跚，預備給魯鎮的人們以無限的
幸福。

一九二四年二月七日。

在酒樓上

In the Tavern

IN THE TAVERN

During my travels from the north to the southeast I made a detour to my home and then went on to S— . This town, only thirty *li* from my native place, can be reached in less than half a day by a small boat. I had taught for a year in a school here. In the depth of winter after snow the landscape was bleak; but a combination of indolence and nostalgia made me put up briefly in the Luo Si Hotel, a new hotel since my time. The town was small. I looked for several old colleagues I thought I might find, but not one of them was there. They had long since gone their different ways. And when I passed the gate of the school that too had changed its name and appearance, making me feel quite a stranger. In less than two hours my enthusiasm had waned and I rather reproached myself for coming.

The hotel I was in let rooms but did not serve meals, which had to be ordered from outside, but these were about as unpalatable as mud. Outside the window was only a stained and spotted wall, covered with withered moss. Above was the leaden sky, a colourless dead white; moreover a flurry of snow had begun to fall. Since my lunch had been poor and I had nothing to do to while away the time, my thoughts turned quite naturally to a small tavern I had known well in the past called One Barrel House, which I reckoned could not be far from the hotel. I immediately locked my door and set out to find it.

在酒樓上

　　我從北地向東南旅行，繞道訪了我的家鄉，就到S城。這城離我的故鄉不過三十里，坐了小船，小半天可到，我曾在這裏的學校裏當過一年的教員。深冬雪後，風景淒清，懶散和懷舊的心緒聯結起來，我竟暫寓在S城的洛思旅館裏了；這旅館是先前所沒有的。城圈本不大，尋訪了幾個以為可以會見的舊同事，一個也不在，早不知散到那裏去了；經過學校的門口，也改換了名稱和模樣，於我很生疏。不到兩個時辰，我的意興早已索然，頗悔此來為多事了。

　　我所住的旅館是租房不賣飯的，飯菜必須另外叫來，但又無味，入口如嚼泥土。窗外只有漬痕斑駁的牆壁，帖着枯死的莓苔；上面是鉛色的天，白皚皚的絕無精采，而且微雪又飛舞起來了。我午餐本沒有飽，又沒有可以消遣的事情，便很自然的想到先前有一家很熟識的小酒樓，叫一石居的，算來離旅館並不遠。我於是立即

Actually, all I wanted was to escape the boredom of my stay, not to do any serious drinking. One Barrel House was still there, its narrow mouldering front and dilapidated signboard unchanged. But from the landlord down to the waiters there was not a soul I knew — in One Barrel House too I had become a complete strange. Still I climbed the familiar stairway in the corner to the little upper storey. The five small wooden tables up here were unchanged; only the window at the back, originally latticed, had been fitted with glass panes.

"A catty of yellow wine. To go with it? Ten pieces of fried beancurd with plenty of paprika sauce."

As I gave this order to the waiter who had come up with me I went and sat down at the table by the back window. The fact that the place was empty enabled me to pick the best seat, one with a view of the deserted garden below. Most likely this did not belong to the tavern. I had looked out at it many times in the past, sometimes too in snowy weather. But now, to eyes accustomed to the north, the sight was sufficiently striking. Several old plum trees in full bloom were braving the snow as if oblivious of the depth of winter; while among the thick dark green foliage of a camellia beside the crumbling pavilion a dozen crimson blossoms blazed bright as flame in the snow, indignant and arrogant, as if despising the wanderer's wanderlust. At this I suddenly remembered the moistness of the heaped snow here, clinging, glistening and shining, quite unlike the dry northern snow which when a high wind blows will fly up to fill the sky like mist....

"Your wine, sir ..." said the waiter carelessly, putting down my cup, chopsticks, wine-pot and dish. The wine had come. I turned to the table, set everything straight and filled my cup. I felt that the north was certainly not my home, yet when I came south I could only count as a stranger. The powdery dry snow which whirled through the air

鎖了房門，出街向那酒樓去。其實也無非想姑且逃避客中的無聊，並不專為買醉。一石居是在的，狹小陰濕的店面和破舊的招牌都依舊；但從掌櫃以至堂倌卻已沒有一個熟人，我在這一石居中也完全成了生客。然而我終於跨上那走熟的屋角的扶梯去了，由此徑到小樓上。上面也依然是五張小板桌；獨有原是木櫺的後窗卻換嵌了玻璃。

「一斤紹酒。——菜？十個油豆腐，辣醬要多！」

我一面說給跟我上來的堂倌聽，一面向後窗走，就在靠窗的一張桌旁坐下了。樓上「空空如也」，任我揀得最好的坐位：可以眺望樓下的廢園。這園大概是不屬於酒家的，我先前也曾眺望過許多回，有時也在雪天裏。但現在從慣於北方的眼睛看來，卻很值得驚異了：幾株老梅竟鬥雪開着滿樹的繁花，彷彿毫不以深冬為意；倒塌的亭子邊還有一株山茶樹，從暗綠的密葉裏顯出十幾朵紅花來，赫赫的在雪中明得如火，憤怒而且傲慢，如蔑視遊人的甘心於遠行。我這時又忽地想到這裏積雪的滋潤，著物不去，晶瑩有光，不比朔雪的粉一般乾，大風一吹，便飛得滿空如煙霧。……

「客人，酒。……」

堂倌懶懶的說着，放下杯，筷，酒壺和碗碟，酒到了。我轉臉向了板桌，排好器具，斟出酒來。覺得北方固不是我的舊鄉，但南來又只能算一個客子，無論那邊的乾雪怎樣紛飛，這裏的柔雪又怎

up there and the clinging soft snow here were equally alien to me. In a slightly melancholy mood I took a leisurely sip of wine. The wine tasted pure and the fried beancurd was excellently cooked, only the paprika sauce was not hot enough; but then the people of S— had never understood pungent flavours.

Probably because it was the afternoon, the place had none of the atmosphere of a tavern. By the time I had drunk three cups, the four other tables were still unoccupied. A sense of loneliness stole over me as I stared at the deserted garden, yet I did not want other customers to come up. Thus I could not help being irritated by the occasional footsteps on the stairs, and was relieved to find it was only the waiter. And so I drank another two cups of wine.

"This time it must be a customer," I thought, at the sound of footsteps much slower than those of the waiter. When I judged that he must be at the top of the stairs, I raised my head rather apprehensively to look at this extraneous company and stood up with a start. It had never occurred to me that I might run into a friend here — if such he would still let me call him. The newcomer was an old classmate who had been my colleague when I knew him at a glance. Only he had become very slow in his movements, quite unlike the spry dynamic Lü Weifu of the old days.

"Well, Weifu, is it you? Fancy meeting you here!"

"Well, well, is it you? Just fancy...."

I invited him to join me, but he seemed to hesitate before doing so. This struck me as strange, then felt rather hurt and annoyed. A closer look revealed that Lü had still the same unkempt hair and beard, but his pale lantern-jawed face was thin and wasted. He appeared very quiet if not dispirited, and his eyes beneath their thick black brows had lost their alertness; but while looking slowly around, at sight of

樣的依戀，於我都沒有甚麼關係了。我略帶些哀愁，然而很舒服的呷一口酒。酒味很純正；油豆腐也煮得十分好；可惜辣醬太淡薄，本來S城人是不懂得吃辣的。

大概是因為正在下午的緣故罷，這雖說是酒樓，卻毫無酒樓氣，我已經喝下三杯酒去了，而我以外還是四張空板桌。我看着廢園，漸漸的感到孤獨，但又不願有別的酒客上來。偶然聽得樓梯上腳步響，便不由的有些懊惱，待到看見是堂倌，才又安心了，這樣的又喝了兩杯酒。

我想，這回定是酒客了，因為聽得那腳步聲比堂倌的要緩得多。約略料他走完了樓梯的時候，我便害怕似的抬頭去看這無干的同伴，同時也就吃驚的站起來。我竟不料在這裏意外的遇見朋友了，——假如他現在還許我稱他為朋友。那上來的分明是我的舊同窗，也是做教員時代的舊同事，面貌雖然頗有些改變，但一見也就認識，獨有行動卻變得格外迂緩，很不像當年敏捷精悍的呂緯甫了。

「阿，——緯甫，是你麼？我萬想不到會在這裏遇見你。」

「阿阿，是你？我也萬想不到……」

我就邀他同坐，但他似乎略略躊躕之後，方才坐下來。我起先很以為奇，接着便有些悲傷，而且不快了。細看他相貌，也還是亂蓬蓬的鬚髮；蒼白的長方臉，然而衰瘦了。精神很沉靜，或者卻是頹唐；又濃又黑的眉毛底下的眼睛也失了精采，但當他緩緩的四顧

the deserted garden they suddenly flashed with the same piercing light I had seen so often at school.

"Well," I said cheerfully but very awkwardly, "it must be ten years since last we saw each other. I heard long ago that you were at Jinan, but I was so wretchedly lazy I never wrote...."

"It was the same with me. I've been at Taiyuan for more than two years now with my mother. When I came back to fetch her I learned that you had already left, left for good and all."

"What are you doing at Taiyuan?" I asked.

"Teaching in the family of a fellow-provincial."

"And before that?"

"Before that?" He took a cigarette from his pocket, lit it and put it to his lips, then watching the smoke he puffed out said reflectively, "Just futile work, amounting to nothing at all."

He in turn asked what I had been doing all these years. I gave him a rough idea, at the same time calling the waiter to bring a cup and chopsticks in order that Lü could share my wine while we had another two catties heated. We also ordered dishes. In the past we had never stood on ceremony, but now we began deferring to each other so that finally we fixed on four dishes suggested by the waiter: peas spiced with aniseed, jellied pork, fried beancurd and salted mackerel.

"As soon as I came back I knew I was a fool." Holding his cigarette in one hand and the winecup in the other, he spoke with a bitter smile. "When I was young, I saw the way bees or flies stuck to one spot. If something frightened them they would buzz off, but after flying in a small circle they would come back to stop in the same place; and I thought this really ridiculous as well as pathetic. Little did I think I'd be flying back myself too after only describing a small circle.

的時候，卻對廢園忽地閃出我在學校時代常常看見的射人的光來。

「我們，」我高興的，然而頗不自然的說，「我們這一別，怕有十年了罷。我早知道你在濟南、可是實在懶得太難，終於沒有寫一封信。……」

「彼此都一樣。可是現在我在太原了，已經兩年多，和我的母親。我回來接她的時候，知道你早搬走了，搬得很乾淨。」

「你在太原做甚麼呢？」我問。

「教書，在一個同鄉的家裏。」

「這以前呢？」

「這以前麼？」他從衣袋裏掏出一枝煙卷來，點了火銜在嘴裏，看着噴出的煙霧，沉思似的說，「無非做了些無聊的事情，等於甚麼也沒有做。」

他也問我別後的景況；我一面告訴他一個大概，一面叫堂倌先取杯筷來，使他先喝着我的酒，然後再去添二斤。其間還點菜，我們先前原是毫不客氣的，但此刻卻推讓起來了，終於說不清那一樣是誰點的，就從堂倌的口頭報告上指定了四樣菜：茴香豆，凍肉，油豆腐，青魚乾。

「我一回來，就想到我可笑。」他一手擎着煙卷，一隻手扶着酒杯，似笑非笑的向我說。「我在少年時，看見蜂子或蠅子停在一個地方，給甚麼來一嚇，即刻飛去了，但是飛了一個小圈子，便又回來停在原地點，便以為這實在很可笑，也可憐。可不料現在我自己也

And I didn't think you'd come back either. Couldn't you have flown a little further?"

"That's difficult to say. Probably I too have simply described a small circle." I also spoke with a rather bitter smile. "But why did you fly back?"

"For something quite futile." In one gulp he emptied his cup, then took several pulls at his cigarette and his eyes widened a little. "Futile — but you may as well hear about it."

The waiter brought up the freshly heated wine and dishes and set them on the table. The smoke and the fragrance of fried beancurd seemed to make the upstairs room more cheerful, while outside the snow fell still more thickly.

"Perhaps you knew," he went on, "that I had a little brother who died when he was three and was buried in the country here. I can't even remember clearly what he looked like, but I've heard my mother say he was a very lovable child and very fond of me. Even now it brings tears to her eyes to speak of him. This spring an elder cousin wrote to tell us that the ground beside his grave was gradually being swamped, and he was afraid before long it would slip into the river: we should go at once and do something about it. This upset my mother so much that she couldn't sleep for several nights — she can read letters herself, you know. But what could I do? I had no money, no time: there was nothing that could be done.

"Now at last, because I'm on holiday over New Year, I've been able to come south to move his grave." He tossed off another cup of wine and looking out of the window exclaimed, "Could you find anything like this up north? Blossom in thick snow, and the soil beneath the snow not frozen. So the day before yesterday I bought a small coffin in town — because I reckoned that the one under the ground

飛回來了，不過繞了一點小圈子。又不料你也回來了。你不能飛得
更遠些麼？」

「這難說，大約也不外乎繞點小圈子罷。」我也似笑非笑的說。
「但是你為甚麼飛回來的呢？」

「也還是為了無聊的事。」他一口喝乾了一杯酒，吸幾口煙，眼
睛略為張大了。「無聊的。——但是我們就談談罷。」

堂倌搬上新添的酒菜來，排滿了一桌，樓上又添了煙氣和油豆
腐的熱氣，彷彿熱鬧起來了；樓外的雪也越加紛紛的下。

「你也許本來知道，」他接着說，「我曾經有一個小兄弟，是三歲
上死掉的，就葬在這鄉下。我連他的模樣都記不清楚了，但聽母親
說，是一個很可愛念的孩子，和我也很相投，至今她提起來還似乎
要下淚。今年春天，一個堂兄就來了一封信，說他的墳邊已經漸漸
的浸了水，不久怕要陷入河裏去了，須得趕緊去設法。母親一知道
就很着急，幾乎幾夜睡不着，——她又自己能看信的。然而我能有
甚麼法子呢？沒有錢，沒有工夫：當時甚麼法也沒有。

「一直挨到現在，趁着年假的閒空，我才得回南給他來遷葬。」
他又喝乾一杯酒，看着窗外，說，「這在那邊那裏能如此呢？積雪裏
會有花，雪地下會不凍。就在前天，我在城裏買了一口小棺材，
——因為我預料那地下的應該早已朽爛了，——帶着棉絮和被褥，

must have rotted long ago — took cotton and bedding, hired four workmen, and went into the country to move his grave, I suddenly felt most elated, eager to dig up the grave, eager to see the bones of the little brother who had been so fond of me: this was a new experience for me. When we reached the grave, sure enough, the river was encroaching on it and the water was less than two feet away. The poor grave not having had any earth added to it for two years was subsiding. Standing there in the snow, I pointed to it firmly and ordered the workmen, 'Dig it up.'

"I really am a commonplace fellow. I felt that my voice at this juncture was rather unnatural, and that this order was the greatest I had given in all my life. But the workmen didn't find it strange in the least, and set to work to dig. When they reached the enclosure I had a look, and sure enough the coffin had rotted almost completely away: there was nothing left but a heap of splinters and chips of wood. My heart beat faster as I set these aside myself, very carefully, wanting to see my little brother. However, I was in for a surprise. Bedding, clothes, skeleton, all had gone!"

"I thought, 'These have all disappeared, but hair, I have always heard, is the last thing to rot. There may still be some hair.' So I bent down and search carefully in the mud where the pillow should have been, but there was none. Not a trace remained."

I suddenly noticed that the rims of his eyes were rather red, but immediately attributed this to the effect of the wine. He had scarcely touched the dishes but had been drinking incessantly and must have drunk more than a catty; his looks and gestures had become more animated, more like the Lü Weifu whom I had known. I called the waiter to heat two more catties of wine, them turned back to face my companion, my cup in my hand, as I listened to him in silence.

"Actually there was really no need to move it: I had only to level

僱了四個土工，下鄉遷葬去。我當時忽而很高興，願意掘一回墳，願意一見我那曾經和我很親睦的小兄弟的骨殖：這些事我生平都沒有經歷過。到得墳地，果然，河水只是咬進來，離墳已不到二尺遠。可憐的墳，兩年沒有培土，也平下去了。我站在雪中，決然的指着他對土工説，『掘開來！』我實在是一個庸人，我這時覺得我的聲音有些希奇，這命令也是一個在我一生中最為偉大的命令。但土工們卻毫不駭怪，就動手掘下去了。待到掘着壙穴，我便過去看，果然，棺木已經快要爛盡了，只剩下一堆木絲和小木片。我的心顫動着，自去撥開這些，很小心的，要看一看我的小兄弟。然而出乎意外！被褥，衣服，骨骼，甚麼也沒有。我想，這些都消盡了，向來聽説最難爛的是頭髮，也許還有罷。我便伏下去，在該是枕頭所在的泥土裏仔仔細細的看，也沒有。蹤影全無！」

　　我忽而看見他眼圈微紅了，但立即知道是有了酒意。他總不很吃菜，單是把酒不停的喝，早喝了一斤多，神情和舉動都活潑起來，漸近於先前所見的呂緯甫。我叫堂倌再添二斤酒，然後回轉身，也拿着酒杯，正對面默默的聽着。

　　「其實，這本已可以不必再遷，只要平了土，賣掉棺材，就此完

the ground, sell the coffin and make an end of the business. Although it might have seemed odd my going to sell the coffin, if the price were low enough the shop from which I bought it would have taken it, and I could at least have recouped a few cents for wine. But I didn't. I still spread out the bedding, wrapped up in cotton some of the clay where his body had been, covered it up, put it in the new coffin, moved it to my father's grave and buried it beside him. And having a brick vault built kept me busy most of yesterday too, supervising the work. But in this way I can count the affair ended, at least enough to deceive my mother and set her mind at rest. Well, well, the look you're giving me shows you are wondering why I've changed so much. Yes, I still remember the time when we went together to the tutelary god's temple to pull off the idols' beards, and how for days on end we used to discuss methods of reforming China until we even came to blows. But this is how I am now, willing to let things slide and to compromise. Sometimes I think, if my old friends were to see me now, probably they would no longer acknowledge me as a friend. But this is what I am like now."

He took out another cigarette, put it to his lips and lit it.

"Judging by your expression, you still expect something of me. Naturally I am much more obtuse than before, but I'm not completely blind yet. This makes me grateful to you, at the same time rather uneasy. I'm afraid I've let down the old friends who even now still wish me well...." He stopped and took several puffs at his cigarette before going on slowly, "Only today, just before coming to this One Barrel House, I did something futile yet something I was glad to do. My former neighbour on the east side was called Changfu. He was a boatman and had a daughter named Ashun. When you came to my house in those days you may have seen her but you certainly wouldn't have paid any attention to her, because she was still small then. She didn't grow up to be pretty either, having just an ordinary thin oval

事了的。我去賣棺材雖然有些離奇，但只要價錢極便宜，原舖子就許要，至少總可以撈回幾文酒錢來。但我不這樣，我仍然鋪好被褥，用棉花裹了些他先前身體所在的地方的泥土，包起來，裝在新棺材裏，運到我父親埋着的墳地上，在他墳旁埋掉了。因為外面用磚墩，昨天又忙了我大半天：監工。但這樣總算完結了一件事，足夠去騙騙我的母親，使她安心些。——阿阿，你這樣的看我，你怪我何以和先前太不相同了麼？是的，我也還記得我們同到城隍廟裏去拔掉神像的鬍子的時候，連日議論些改革中國的方法以至於打起來的時候。但我現在就是這樣了，敷敷衍衍，模模糊糊。我有時自己也想到，倘若先前的朋友看見我，怕會不認我做朋友了。——然而我現在就是這樣。」

他又掏出一枝煙卷來，銜在嘴裏，點了火。

「看你的神情，你似乎還有些期望我，——我現在自然麻木得多了，但是有些事也還看得出。這使我很感激，然而也使我很不安：怕我終於辜負了至今還對我懷着好意的老朋友。……」他忽而停住了，吸幾口煙，才又慢慢的說，「正在今天，剛在我到這一石居來之前，也就做了一件無聊事，然而也是我自己願意做的。我先前的東邊的鄰居叫長富，是一個船戶。他有一個女兒叫阿順，你那時到我家裏來，也許見過的，但你一定沒有留心，因為那時她還小。後來她也長得並不好看，不過是平常的瘦瘦的瓜子臉，黃臉皮；獨有眼

face and pale skin. Only her eyes were unusually large with very long lashes and whites as clear as a cloudless night sky — I mean the cloudless sky of the north on a windless day; here it is not so clear. She was very capable. She lost her mother while in her teens, and had to look after a small brother and sister besides waiting on her father; and all this she did very competently. She was so economical too that the family gradually grew better off. There was scarcely a neighbour who didn't praise her, and even Changfu often expressed his appreciation. When I was setting off on my journey this time, my mother remembered her — old people's memories are so long. She recalled that once Ashun saw someone wearing red velvet flowers in her hair, and wanted a spray for herself. When she couldn't get one she cried nearly all night, so that her father beat her and her eyes remained red and swollen for two or three days. These red flowers came from another province and couldn't be bought even in S—, so how could she ever hope to have any? Since I was coming south this time, my mother told me to buy two sprays for her.

"Far from feeling vexed at this commission, I was actually delighted, really glad of the chance to do something for Ashun. The year before last I came back to fetch my mother, and one day when Changfu was at home I dropped in for some reason to chat with him. By way of refreshment he offered me some buckwheat mush, remarking that they added white sugar to it. As you can see, a boatman who could afford white sugar was obviously not poor and must eat pretty well. I let myself be persuaded but begged them to give me only a small bowl. He quite understood and instructed Ashun, 'These scholars have no appetite. Give him a small bowl, but add more sugar.' However, when she had prepared the concoction and brought it in it gave me quite a turn, because it was a large bowl, as much as I could eat in a whole day. Though compared with Changfu's bowl, admittedly, it was small. This was the first time I had eaten buckwheat

睛非常大，睫毛也很長，眼白又青得如夜的晴天，而且是北方的無風的晴天，這裏的就沒有那麼明淨了。她很能幹，十多歲沒了母親，招呼兩個小弟妹都靠她；又得服侍父親，事事都周到；也經濟，家計倒漸漸的穩當起來了。鄰居幾乎沒有一個不誇獎她，連長富也時常說些感激的話。這一次我動身回來的時候，我的母親又記得她了，老年人記性真長久。她說她曾經知道順姑因為看見誰的頭上戴着紅的剪絨花，自己也想有一朵，弄不到，哭了，哭了小半夜，就挨了她父親的一頓打，後來眼眶還紅腫了兩三天。這種剪絨花是外省的東西，S城裏尚且買不出，她那裏想得到手呢？趁我這一次回南的便，便叫我買兩朵去送她。

「我對於這差使倒並不以為煩厭，反而很喜歡；為阿順，我實在還有些願意出力的意思的。前年，我回來接我母親的時候，有一天，長富正在家，不知怎的我和他閒談起來了。他便要請我吃點心，蕎麥粉，並且告訴我所加的是白糖。你想，家裏能有白糖的船戶，可見決不是一個窮船戶了，所以他也吃得很闊綽。我被勸不過，答應了，但要求只要用小碗。他也很識世故，便囑咐阿順說，『他們文人，是不會吃東西的。你就用小碗，多加糖！』然而等到調好端來的時候，仍然使我吃一嚇，是一大碗，足夠我吃一天。但是和長富吃的一碗比起來，我的也確乎算小碗。我生平沒有吃過蕎麥

mush, and I just could not stomach it though it was so sweet. I gulped down a few mouthfuls and decided to leave the rest when I happened to notice Ashun standing some distance away in one corner of the room, and I simply hadn't the heart to put down my chopsticks. In her face I saw both hope and fear — fear presumably that she had prepared it badly, and hope that we would find it to our liking. I knew that if I left most of my bowl she would feel very disappointed and sorry. I made up my mind to it and shovelled the stuff down, eating almost as fast as Changfu. That taught me how painful it is forcing oneself to eat; and I remembered experiencing the same difficulty as a child when I had to finish a bowl of worm-medicine mixed with brown sugar. I didn't hold it against her though, because her half-suppressed smile of satisfaction when she came to take away our empty bowls more than repaid me for all my discomfort. So that night, although indigestion kept me from sleeping well and I had a series of nightmares, I still wished her a lifetime of happiness and hoped that for her sake the world would change for the better. But such thoughts were only the residue of my old dreams. The next instant I laughed at myself, and promptly forgot them.

"I hadn't known before that she had been beaten on account of a spray of velvet flowers, but when my mother spoke of it I remembered the buckwheat mush incident and became unaccountably diligent. First I made a search in Taiyuan, but none of the shops had them. It was only when I went to Jinan.... "

There was a rustle outside the window as a pile of snow slithered off the camellia which had been bending beneath its weight; then the branches of the tree straightened themselves, flaunting their thick dark foliage and blood-red flowers even more clearly. The sky had grown even more leaden. Sparrows were twittering, no doubt because dusk was falling and finding nothing to eat on the snow-covered ground they were going back early to their nests to sleep.

粉,這回一嚐,實在不可口,卻是非常甜。我漫然的吃了幾口,就想不吃了,然而無意中,忽然間看見阿順遠遠的站在屋角裏,就使我立刻消失了放下碗筷的勇氣。我看她的神情,是害怕而且希望,大約怕自己調得不好,願我們吃得有味。我知道如果剩下大半碗來,一定要使她很失望,而且很抱歉。我於是同時決心,放開喉嚨灌下去了,幾乎吃得和長富一樣快。我由此才知道硬吃的苦痛,我只記得還做孩子時候的吃盡一碗拌着驅除蛔蟲藥粉的沙糖才有這樣難。然而我毫不抱怨,因為她過來收拾空碗時候的忍着的得意的笑容,已盡夠賠償我的苦痛而有餘了。所以我這一夜雖然飽脹得睡不穩,又做了一大串惡夢,也還是祝讚她一生幸福,願世界為她變好。然而這些意思也不過是我的那些舊日的夢的痕跡,即刻就自笑,接着也就忘卻了。

「我先前並不知道她曾經為了一朵剪絨花挨打,但因為母親一説起,便也記得了蕎麥粉的事,意外的勤快起來了。我先在太原城裏搜求了一遍,都沒有;一直到濟南……」

窗外沙沙的一陣聲響,許多積雪從被他壓彎了的一枝山茶樹上滑下去了,樹枝筆挺的伸直,更顯出烏油油的肥葉和血紅的花來。天空的鉛色來得更濃;小鳥雀啾唧的叫着,大概黃昏將近,地面又全罩了雪,尋不出甚麼食糧,都趕早回巢來休息了。

"It was only when I went to Jinan...." He glanced out of the window, then turned back, drained a cup of wine, took several puffs at his cigarette and went on, "Only then did I buy the artificial flowers. I didn't know whether they were the same as those she had been beaten for, but at least they were made of velvet. And not knowing whether she liked deep or light colours, I bought one spray of red, one spray of pink, and brought them both here.

"This afternoon straight after lunch I went to see Changfu, having stayed on an extra day just for this. Though his house was still there it seemed to me rather gloomy, but perhaps that was simply my imagination. His son and second daughter Azhao were standing at the gate. Both of them had grown. Azhao is quite unlike her sister, she looks simply ghastly; but at my approach she rushed into the house. I learned from the boy that Changfu was not at home. 'And your elder sister?' I asked. At that he glared at me and demanded what my business with her was. He looked fierce enough to fling himself at me and bite me. I dithered, then walked away. Nowadays I just let things slide....

"You can have no idea how I dread calling on people, much more so than in the old days. Because I know what a nuisance I am, I am even sick of myself; so, knowing this, why inflict myself on others? But since this commission had to be carried out, after some reflection I went back to the firewood shop almost opposite their house. The proprietor's mother old Mrs. Fa was still there and, what's more, still recognized me. She actually asked me into the shop to sit down. After the usual polite preliminaries I told her why I had come back to S— and was looking for Changfu. I was taken aback when she sighed:

"'What a pity Ashun hadn't the luck to wear these velvet flowers.'"

"Then she told me the whole story. 'It was probably last spring that Ashun began to look pale and thin. Later she had fits of crying,

「一直到了濟南，」他向窗外看了一回，轉身喝乾一杯酒，又吸幾口煙，接着説。「我才買到剪絨花。我也不知道使她挨打的是不是這一種，總之是絨做的罷了。我也不知道她喜歡深色還是淺色，就買了一朵大紅的，一朵粉紅的，都帶到這裏來。

「就是今天午後我一吃完飯，便去看長富，我為此特地躭擱了一天。他的家倒還在，只是看去很有些晦氣色了，但這恐怕不過是我自己的感覺。他的兒子和第二個女兒——阿昭，都站在門口，大了。阿昭長得全不像她姊姊，簡直像一個鬼，但是看見我走向她家，便飛奔的逃進屋裏去。我就問那小子，知道長富不在家。『你的大姊呢？』他立刻瞪起眼睛，連聲問我尋她甚麼事，而且惡狠狠的似乎就要撲過來，咬我。我支吾着退走了，我現在是敷敷衍衍……

「你不知道，我可是比先前更怕去訪人了。因為我已經深知道自己之討厭，連自己也討厭，又何必明知故犯的去使人暗暗地不快呢？然而這回的差使是不能不辦妥的，所以想了一想，終於回到就在斜對門的柴店裏。店主的母親，老發奶奶，倒也還在，而且也還認識我，居然將我邀進店裏坐去了。我們寒暄幾句之後，我就說明了回到S城和尋長富的緣故。不料她嘆息說：

「『可惜順姑沒有福氣戴這剪絨花了。』

「她於是詳細的告訴我，説是『大約從去年春天以來，她就見得

but if asked why she wouldn't say. Sometimes she even cried all night until Changfu couldn't help losing his temper and swearing at her for carrying on like a crazy old maid. But when autumn came she caught a chill, then she took to her bed and never got up again. Only a few days before she died she confessed to Changfu that she had long ago started spitting blood and perspiring at night like her mother. But she hadn't told him for fear of worrying him. One evening her uncle Changgeng came to demand a loan — he was always sponging on them — and when she wouldn't give him any money he sneered, "Don't give yourself airs; your man isn't even up to me!" That upset her, but she was too shy to ask any questions and could only cry. As soon as Changfu knew this, he told her what a decent fellow the man chosen for her was; but it was too late. Besides, she didn't believe him. "It's a good thing I'm already this way," she said. "Now nothing matters any more."'

"Old Mrs. Fa also said, 'If her man really hadn't been up to Changgeng, that would have been truly frightful. Not up to a chicken thief — what sort of creature would that be? But I saw him with my own eyes at the funeral: dressed in clean clothes and quite presentable. And he said with tears in his eyes that he'd worked hard all those years on the boat to save up money to marry, but now the girl was dead. Obviously he was really a good sort, and Changgeng had been lying. It was too bad that Ashun believed such a rascally liar and died for nothing. Still, we can't blame anyone else: this was Ashun's fate.'

"Since that was the case, my business was finished too. But what about the two sprays of artificial flowers I had brought with me? Well, I asked her to give them to Azhao. This Azhao had fled at the sight of me as if I were a wolf or monster; I really didn't want to give them to her. However, give them I did, and I have only to tell my mother that Ashun was delighted with them and that will be that. Who cares about

黃瘦，後來忽而常常下淚了，問她緣故又不說；有時還整夜的哭，哭得長富也忍不住生氣，罵她年紀大了，發了瘋。可是一到秋初，起先不過小傷風；終於躺倒了，從此就起不來。直到咽氣的前幾天才肯對長富說，她早就像她母親一樣，不時的吐紅和流夜汗。但是瞞着，怕他因此要擔心。有一夜，她的伯伯長庚又來硬借錢，——這是常有的事，——她不給，長庚就冷笑着說：你不要驕氣，你的男人比我還不如！她從此就發了愁，又怕羞，不好問，只好哭，長富趕緊將她的男人怎樣的掙氣的話說給她聽，那裏還來得及？況且她也不信，反而說；好在我已經這樣，甚麼也不要緊了。』

「她還說，『如果她的男人真比長庚不如，那就真可怕呵！比不上一個偷雞賊，那是甚麼東西呢？然而他來送殮的時候，我是親眼看見他的，衣服很乾淨，人也體面；還眼淚汪汪的說，自己撐了半世小船，苦熬苦省的積起錢來聘了一個女人，偏偏又死掉了。可見他實在是一個好人，長庚說的全是誑。只可惜順姑竟會相信那樣的賊骨頭的誑話，白送了性命。——但這也不能去怪誰，只能怪順姑自己沒有這一份好福氣。』

「那倒也罷，我的事情又完了。但是帶在身邊的兩朵剪絨花怎麼辦呢？好，我就託她送了阿昭。這阿昭一見我就飛跑，大約將我當做一隻狼或是甚麼，我實在不願意去送她。——但是我也就送她了，對母親只要說阿順見了喜歡的了不得就是。這些無聊的事算甚

such futile affairs anyway? One only wants to muddle through them somehow. When I have muddled through New Year I shall go back to teaching the Confucian classics."

"Is that what you're teaching?" I asked in astonishment.

"Of course. Did you think I was teaching English? First I had two pupils, one studying the *Book of Songs*, the other *Mencius*. Recently I have got another, a girl, who is studying the *Canon for Girls*. I don't even teach mathematics; not that I wouldn't teach it, but they don't want it taught."

"I could really never have guessed that you would be teaching such books."

"Their father wants them to study these. I'm an outsider, it's all the same to me. Who cares about such futile affairs anyway? There's no need to take them seriously...."

His whole face was scarlet as if he were quite drunk, but the gleam in his eyes had died down. I gave a slight sigh, not knowing what to say. There was a clatter on the stairs as several customers came up. The first was short, with a round bloated face; the second was tall, with a conspicuous red nose. Behind them followed others, and as they walked up the small upper floor shook. I turned to Lü Weifu who was trying to catch my eye, then called for the bill.

"Is your salary enough to live on?" I asked as we prepared to leave.

"I have twenty dollars a month, not quite enough to manage on."

"What are your future plans then?"

"Future plans?" I don't know. Just think: Has any single thing turned out as we hoped of all we planned in the past? I'm not sure of

麼？只要模模糊糊。模模糊糊的過了新年，仍舊教我的『子曰詩云』去。」

「你教的是『子曰詩云』麼？」我覺得奇異，便問。

「自然。你還以為教的是ABCD麼？我先是兩個學生，一個讀《詩經》，一個讀《孟子》。新近又添了一個，女的，讀《女兒經》。連算學也不教，不是我不教，他們不要教。」

「我實在料不到你倒去教這類的書，……」

「他們的老子要他們讀這些；我是別人，無乎不可的。這些無聊的事算甚麼？只要隨隨便便，……」

他滿臉已經通紅，似乎很有些醉，但眼光卻又消沉下去了。我微微的嘆息，一時沒有話可說。樓梯上一陣亂響，擁上幾個酒客來，當頭的是矮子，臃腫的圓臉；第二個是長的，在臉上很惹眼的顯出一個紅鼻子；此後還有人，一疊連的走得小樓都發抖。我轉眼去看呂緯甫，他也正轉眼來看我，我就叫堂倌算酒賬。

「你借此還可以支持生活麼？」我一面準備走，一面問。

「是的。——我每月有二十元，也不大能夠敷衍。」

「那麼，你以後預備怎麼辦呢？」

「以後？——我不知道。你看我們那時預想的事可有一件如意？

anything now, not even of what tomorrow will bring, not even of the next minute...."

The waiter brought up the bill and handed it to me. Lü Weifu had abandoned his earlier formality. He just glanced at me, went on smoking, and allowed me to pay.

We left the tavern together, parting at the door because our hotels lay in opposite directions. As I walked back alone to my hotel, the cold wind buffeted my face with snowflakes, but I found this thoroughly refreshing. I saw that the sky, already dark, had interwoven with the houses and streets in the white, shifting web of thick snow.

February 16, 1924

我現在甚麼也不知道，連明天怎樣也不知道，連後一分……」

　　堂倌送上賬來，交給我；他也不像初到時候的謙虛了，只向我看了一眼，便吸煙，聽憑我付了賬。

　　我們一同走出店門，他所住的旅館和我的方向正相反，就在門口分別了。我獨自向着自己的旅館走，寒風和雪片撲在臉上，倒覺得很爽快。見天色已是黃昏，和屋宇和街道都織在密雪的純白而不定的羅網裏。

　　　　　　　　　　　　　　一九二四年二月一六日。

幸福的家庭

A Happy Family

A HAPPY FAMILY

After the style of Xu Qinwen

"... One writes simply as one feels: such a work is like sunlight, radiating from a source of infinite brightness, not like a spark from a flint struck on iron or stone. This alone is true art. And such a writer alone is true artist.... But I ... what do I rank as?"

Having thought so far he suddenly jumped out of bed. It had occurred to him that he must make some money by writing to support his family, and he had already decided to send his manuscripts to the *Happy Monthly* publishers, because the remuneration appeared to be comparatively generous. But in that case the choice of subjects would be limited, otherwise the work would probably not be accepted. All right, let it be limited. What were the chief problems occupying the minds of the younger generation?... Undoubtedly there must be not a few, perhaps a great many, concerning love, marriage, the family.... Yes, there were certainly many people perplexed by such questions, even now discussing them. In that case, write about the family! But how to write?... Otherwise it would probably not be accepted. Why predict anything unlucky? Still....

Jumping out of bed, in four or five steps he reached the desk, sat down, took out a piece of paper with green lines, and promptly yet resignedly wrote the title: A Happy Family.

His pen immediately came to a standstill. He raised his head, his

幸福的家庭

——擬許欽文

　　「……做不做全由自己的便；那作品，像太陽的光一樣，從無量的光源中湧出來，不像石火，用鐵和石敲出來，這才是真藝術。那作者，也才是真的藝術家。——而我，……這算是甚麼？……」他想到這裏，忽然從床上跳起來了。以先他早已想過，須得撈幾文稿費維持生活了；投稿的地方，先定為幸福月報社，因為潤筆似乎比較的豐。但作品就須有範圍，否則，恐怕要不收的。範圍就範圍，……現在的青年的腦裏的大問題是？……大概很不少，或者有許多是戀愛，婚姻，家庭之類的罷。……是的，他們確有許多人煩悶着，正在討論這些事。那麼，就來做家庭。然而怎麼做呢？……否則，恐怕要不收的，何必說些背時的話，然而……。他跳下臥床之後，四五步就走到書桌面前，坐下去，抽出一張綠格紙，毫不遲疑，但又自暴自棄似的寫下一行題目道：《幸福的家庭》。

　　他的筆立刻停滯了；他仰了頭，兩眼瞪着房頂，正在安排那安

two eyes fixed on the ceiling, trying to decide on an environment for this Happy Family.

"Beijing?" he thought. "That won't do; it's too dead, even the atmosphere is dead. Even if a high wall were built round this family, still the air could scarcely be kept separate. No, that would never do! Jiangsu and Zhejiang may start fighting any day, and Fujian is even more out of the question. Sichuan? Guangdong? They are in the midst of fighting. What about Shandong or Henan?... No, one of them might be kidnapped, and if that happened the happy family would become an unhappy one. The rents in the foreign concessions in Shanghai and Tianjin are too high.... Somewhere abroad? Ridiculous. I don't know what Yunnan and Guizhou are like, but communications are too poor...."

He racked his brains but, unable to think of a good place, decided to fix tentatively on A— . Then, however, he thought, "Nowadays many people object to the use of the Western alphabet to represent the names of people and places, saying it lessens the readers' interest. Probably I had better not use it in my story this time, to be on the safe side. In that case what would be a good place? There is fighting in Hunan too; the rents in Dalian have gone up again. In Chahar, Jilin and Heilongjiang I have heard there are brigands, so they won't do either!...

Again he racked his brains to think of a good place, but in vain; so finally he made up his mind to fix tentatively on A— as the name of the place where his Happy Family should be.

"After all this Happy Family will have to be at A— . There can't be any question about that. The family naturally consists of a husband and wife — the master and mistress — who married for love. Their marriage contract contains over forty terms going into great detail, so that they have extraordinary equality and absolute freedom. Moreover they have both had a higher education and belong to the cultured elite.... Japanese-returned students are no longer the fashion,

置這「幸福的家庭」的地方。他想：「北京？不行，死氣沉沉，連空氣也是死的。假如在這家的周圍築一道高牆，難道空氣也就隔斷了麼？簡直不行！江蘇、浙江天天防要開仗；福建更無須說。四川、廣東？都正在打。山東、河南之類？——阿阿，要綁票的，倘使綁去一個，那就成為不幸的家庭了。上海、天津的租界上房租貴；……假如在外國，笑話。雲南、貴州不知道怎樣，但交通也太不便……。」他想來想去，想不出好地方，便要假定為A了，但又想，「現有不少的人是反對用西洋字母來代人地名的，說是要減少讀者的興味。我這回的投稿，似乎也不如不用，安全些。那麼，在那裏好呢？——湖南也打仗；大連仍然房租貴；察哈爾、吉林、黑龍江罷，——聽說有馬賊，也不行！……」他又想來想去，又想不出好地方，於是終於決心，假定這「幸福的家庭」所在的地方叫作A。

「總之，這幸福的家庭一定須在A，無可磋商。家庭中自然是兩夫婦，就是主人和主婦，自由結婚的。他們訂有四十多條條約，非常詳細，所以非常平等，十分自由。而且受過高等教育，優美高尚……。東洋留學生已經不通行，——那麼，假定為西洋留學生

so let them be Western-returned students. The master of the house always wears a foreign suit, his collar is always snowy white. His wife's hair is always curled up like a sparrow's nest in front, her pearly white teeth are always peeping out, but she wears Chinese dress...."

"That won't do, that won't do! Twenty-five catties!"

Hearing a man's voice outside the window he involuntarily turned his head to look. The sun shone through the curtains hanging by the window, dazzling his eyes, while he heard a sound like small bundles of wood being thrown down. "It doesn't matter," he thought, turning back again. "'Twenty-five catties' of what?... They are the cultured elite, devoted to the arts. But because they have both grown up in happy surroundings, they don't like Russian novels. Most Russian novels describe the lower classes, so they are really quite out of keeping with such a family. 'Twenty-five catties'? Never mind. In that case, what books do they read?... Byron's poetry? Keats? That won't do, neither of them are safe.... Ah, I have it: they both like reading *An Ideal Husband*. Although I haven't read the book myself, even university professors praise it so highly that I am sure this couple must enjoy it too. You read it, I read it — they have a copy each, two copies altogether in the family...."

Becoming aware of a hollow feeling in his stomach, he put down the pen and rested his head on his hands, like a globe supported by two axles.

"... The two of them are just having lunch," he thought. "The table is spread with a snowy white table cloth, and the cook brings in the dishes — Chinese food. 'Twenty-five catties.' Of what? Never mind. Why should it be Chinese food? Westerners say Chinese cooking is the most progressive, the best to eat, the most hygienic; so they eat Chinese food. The first dish is brought in, but what is this first dish?..."

罷。主人始終穿洋服，硬領始終雪白；主婦是前頭的頭髮始終燙得蓬蓬鬆鬆像一個麻雀窠，牙齒是始終雪白的露着，但衣服卻是中國裝，……」

「不行不行，那不行！二十五斤！」

他聽得窗外一個男人的聲音，不由的回過頭去看，窗幔垂着，日光照着，明得眩目，他的眼睛昏花了；接着是小木片撒在地上的聲響。「不相干，」他又回過頭來想，「甚麼『二十五斤』？——他們是優美高尚，很愛文藝的。但因為都從小生長在幸福裏，所以不愛俄國的小説……。俄國小説多描寫下等人，實在和這樣的家庭也不合。『二十五斤』？不管他。那麼，他們看看甚麼書呢？——裴倫的詩？吉支的？不行，都不穩當。——哦，有了，他們都愛看《理想之良人》。我雖然沒有見過這部書，但既然連大學教授也那麼稱讚他，想來他們也一定都愛看，你也看，我也看，——他們一人一本，這家庭裏一共有兩本，……」他覺得胃裏有點空虛了，放下筆，用兩隻手支着頭，教自己的頭像地球儀似的在兩個柱子間掛着。

「……他們兩人正在用午餐，」他想，「桌上鋪了雪白的布；廚子送上菜來，——中國菜。甚麼『二十五斤』？不管他。為甚麼倒是中國菜？西洋人説，中國菜最進步，最好吃，最合於衛生：所以他們採用中國菜。送來的是第一碗，但這第一碗是甚麼呢？……」

"Firewood...."

He turned his head with a start, to see standing on his left the mistress of his own family, her two gloomy eyes fastened on his face.

"What?" He spoke rather indignantly, feeling that her coming disturbed his work.

"The firewood is all used up, so today I have bought some more. Last time it was still two hundred and forty cash for ten catties, but today he wants two hundred and sixty. Suppose I give him two hundred and fifty?"

"All right, two hundred and fifty, let it be."

"He has weighted it very unfairly. He insists that there are twenty-four and a half catties, but suppose I count it as twenty-three and a half?"

"All right. Count it as twenty-three and a half catties."

"Then, five fives are twenty-five, three fives are fifteen...."

"Oh, five fives are twenty-five, three fives are fifteen...." He could get no further either, but after stopping for a moment suddenly took up his pen and started working out a sum on the lined paper on which he had written "A Happy Family." After working at it for some time he raised his head to say:

"Five hundred and eighty cash."

"In that case I haven't got enough here; I am still eighty or ninety short...."

He pulled open the drawer of the desk, took out all the money in it — somewhere between twenty and thirty coppers — and put it in her outstretched hand. Then he watched her go out, and finally turned

「劈柴，……」

他吃驚的回過頭去看，靠左肩，便立着他自己家裏的主婦，兩隻陰淒淒的眼睛恰恰釘住他的臉。

「甚麼？」他以為她來攪擾了他的創作，頗有些憤怒了。

「劈柴，都用完了，今天買些。前一回還是十斤兩吊四，今天就要兩吊六。我想給他兩吊五，好不好？」

「好好，就是兩吊五。」

「稱得太吃虧了。他一定只肯算二十四斤半；我想就算他二十三斤半，好不好？」

「好好，就算他二十三斤半。」

「那麼，五五二十五，三五一十五，……」

「唔唔，五五二十五，三五一十五，……」他也説不下去了，停了一會，忽而奮然的抓起筆來，就在寫着一行「幸福的家庭」的綠格紙上起算草，起了好久，這才仰起頭來説道：

「五吊八！」

「那是，我這裏不夠了，還差八九個……。」

他抽開書桌的抽屜，一把抓起所有的銅元，不下二三十，放在她攤開的手掌上，看她出了房，才又回過頭來向書桌。他覺得頭裏

back to the desk. His head seemed to be bursting as if filled to the brim with sharp faggots. Five fives are twenty-five — scattered Arabic numerals were still imprinted on his brain. He gave a long sigh and breathed out again deeply, as if by this means he might expel the firewood, the "five fives are twenty-five," and the Arabic numerals which had stuck in his head. Sure enough, after breathing out his heart seemed much lighter, whereupon he started thinking vaguely again:

"What dish? It doesn't matter, so long as it is something out of the way. Fried pork or prawns' roe and sea-slugs are really too common. I must have them eating 'Dragon and Tiger.' But what is that exactly? Some people say it's made of snakes and cats, and is an upper-class Guangdong dish, only eaten at big feasts. But I've seen the name on the menu in a Jiangsu restaurant; still, Jiangsu people aren't supposed to eat snakes or cats, so it must be, as someone else said, made of frogs and eels. Now what part of the country shall this couple be from? Never mind. After all, people from any part of the country can eat a dish of snake and cat (or frog and eel), without injuring their Happy Family. At any rate, this first dish is to be 'Dragon and Tiger'; there can be no question about that.

"Now that this bowl of 'Dragon and Tiger' is placed in the middle of the table, they take up their chopsticks simultaneously, point to the dish, smile sweetly at each other and say, in a foreign tongue:

"'Chérie, s'il vous plaît!'

"'Voulez-vous commencer, chéri!'

"'Mais non, après vous!'

"Then they reach out their chopsticks simultaneously, and simultaneously take a morsel of snake — no, no, snake's flesh really sounds too peculiar; it would be better after all to say a morsel of eel. It is settled then that: 'Dragon and Tiger' is made of frogs and eels. They

面很脹滿，似乎橛橛叉叉的全被木柴填滿了，五五二十五，腦皮質上還印着許多散亂的阿剌伯數目字。他很深的吸一口氣，又用力的呼出，彷彿要借此趕出腦裏的劈柴，五五二十五和阿剌伯數字來。果然，吁氣之後；心地也就輕鬆不少了，於是仍復恍恍忽忽的想——

「甚麼菜？菜倒不妨奇特點。滑溜里脊，蝦子海參，實在太凡庸。我偏要說他們吃的是『龍虎鬥』。但『龍虎鬥』又是甚麼呢？有人說是蛇和貓，是廣東的貴重菜，非大宴會不吃的。但我在江蘇飯館的菜單上就見過這名目，江蘇人似乎不吃蛇和貓，恐怕就如誰所說，是蛙和鱔魚了。現在假定這主人和主婦為那裏人呢？——不管他。總而言之，無論那裏人吃一碗蛇和貓或者蛙和鱔魚，於幸福的家庭是決不會有損傷的。總之這第一碗一定是『龍虎鬥』，無可磋商。

「於是一碗『龍虎鬥』擺在桌子中央了，他們兩人同時捏起筷子，指着碗沿，笑迷迷的你看我，我看你……。

「『My dear, please.』

「『Please you eat first, my dear.』

「『Oh no, please you！』

「於是他們同時伸下筷子去，同時夾出一塊蛇肉來，——不不，蛇肉究竟太奇怪，還不如說是鱔魚罷。那麼，這碗『龍虎鬥』是蛙和

pick out two morsels of eel simultaneously, exactly the same size. Five fives are twenty-five, three fives.... Never mind. And simultaneously put them in their mouths...." Against his will he wanted to turn round, because he was conscious of a good deal of excitement behind him, and considerable coming and going. But he persevered, and pursued his train of thought distractedly:

"This seems rather sentimental; no family would behave like this. Whatever makes me so woolly-minded? I'm afraid this good subject will never be written up.... Or perhaps there is no need to have returned students; people who have received higher education in China would do just as well. They are both university graduates, the cultured elite, the elite ... The man is a writer; the woman is also a writer, or else a lover of literature. Or else the woman is a poetess; the man is a lover of poetry, a respecter of womanhood. Or else...."

Finally he could contain himself no longer, and turned round.

Beside the bookcase behind him had appeared a mound of cabbages, three at the bottom, two above, and one at the top, confronting him like a large letter A.

"Oh!" He started and gave a sigh, feeling his cheeks burn, while prickles ran up and down his spine. "Ah!" He took a very deep breath to get rid of the prickly feeling in his spine, then went on thinking, "The house of the Happy Family must have plenty of rooms. There is a store-room where things like cabbages are put. The master's study is apart, its walls lined with bookshelves; there are naturally no cabbages there. The shelves are filled with Chinese books and foreign books, including of course *An Ideal Husband* — two copies altogether. There is a separate bedroom, a brass bedstead, or something simpler like one of the elmwood beds made by the convicts of Number One Prison would do equally well. Beneath the bed is very clean...." He glanced beneath his own bed; the firewood had all been used up, and

鳎魚所做的了。他們同時夾出一塊鳎魚來，一樣大小，五五二十五，三五……不管他，同時放進嘴裏去，……」他不能自制的只想回過頭去看，因為他覺得背後很熱鬧，有人來來往往的走了兩三回。但他還熬着，亂嘈嘈的接着想，「這似乎有點肉麻，那有這樣的家庭？唉唉，我的思路怎麼會這樣亂，這好題目怕是做不完篇的了。——或者不必定用留學生，就在國內受了高等教育的也可以。他們都是大學畢業的，高尚優美，高尚……。男的是文學家；女的也是文學家，或者文學崇拜家。或者女的是詩人；男的是詩人崇拜者，女性尊重者。或者……」他終於忍耐不住，回過頭去了。

就在他背後的書架的旁邊，已經出現了一座白菜堆，下層三株，中層兩株，頂上一株，向他疊成一個很大的A字。

「唉唉！」他吃驚的嘆息，同時覺得臉上驟然發熱了，脊樑上還有許多針輕輕的刺着。「吁……。」他很長的噓一口氣，先斥退了脊樑上的針，仍然想，「幸福的家庭的房子要寬綽。有一間堆積房，白菜之類都到那邊去。主人的書房另一間，靠壁滿排着書架，那旁邊自然決沒有甚麼白菜堆；架上滿是中國書，外國書，《理想之良人》自然也在內，——一共有兩部。臥室又一間；黃銅床，或者質樸點，第一監獄工場做的榆木床也就夠，床底下很乾淨，……」他當即

there was only a piece of straw rope left, still coiling there like a dead snake.

"Twenty-three and a half catties...." He felt that the firewood was just about to pour in in a never-ending stream under his bed, and his head ached again, so he got up quickly and went to the door to close it. But he had scarcely put his hand on the door when he felt that this was overhasty and let it go instead, dropping the door curtain that was thick with dust. At the same time he thought, "This method avoids the severity of shutting oneself in, as well as the discomfort of keeping the door open; it is quite in keeping with the *Doctrine of the Mean*.

"... So the master's study door is always closed." He walked back, sat down and thought, "Anyone with business must first knock at the door, and have his permission to come in; that is really the only thing to be done. Now suppose the master is sitting in his study and the mistress comes to discuss literature, she knocks too.... At least of this one can be assured — she will not bring in any cabbages."

"'Entrez, chérie, s'il vous plaît!'"

"But what happens when the master has no time to discuss literature? Does he ignore her, hearing her stand outside tapping gently on the door? That probably wouldn't do. Maybe it is all described in *An Ideal Husband* — that must really be an excellent novel. If I get paid for this article I must buy a copy to read!"

Slap!

His back stiffened, because he knew from experience that this slapping sound was made by his wife's hand striking their three-year-old daughter's head.

"In a Happy Family ..." he thought, his back still rigid, hearing

一瞥自己的床下，劈柴已經用完了，只有一條稻草繩，卻還死蛇似的懶懶的躺着。

「二十三斤半，……」他覺得劈柴就要向床下「川流不息」的進來，頭裏面又有些椏椏叉叉了，便急忙起立，走向門口去想關門。但兩手剛觸着門，卻又覺得未免太暴躁了，就歇了手，只放下那積着許多灰塵的門幕。他一面想，這既無閉關自守之操切，也沒有開放門戶之不安：是很合於「中庸之道」的。

「……所以主人的書房門永遠是關起來的。」他走回來，坐下，想，「有事要商量先敲門，得了許可才能進來，這辦法實在對。現在假如主人坐在自己的書房裏，主婦來談文藝了，也就先敲門。——這可以放心，她必不至於捧着白菜的。

「『Come in, please, my dear.』

「然而主人沒有工夫談文藝的時候怎麼辦呢？那麼，不理她，聽她站在外面老是剝剝的敲？這大約不行罷。或者《理想之良人》裏面都寫着，——那恐怕確是一部好小說，我如果有了稿費，也得去買他一部來看看……。」

拍！

他腰骨筆直了，因為他根據經驗，知道這一聲「拍」是主婦的手掌打在他們的三歲的女兒的頭上的聲音。

「幸福的家庭，……」他聽到孩子的嗚咽了，但還是腰骨筆直的

the child sobbing, "children are born late, yes, born late. Or perhaps it would be better to have none at all, just two people without any ties.... Or it might be better to stay in a hotel and let them look after everything, a single man without...." Hearing the sound of sobbing increasing in volume, he stood up and brushed past the curtain, thinking, "Karl Marx wrote his *Das Kapital* while his children were crying around him. He must really have been a great man...." He walked out, opened the outer door, and was assailed by a strong smell of kerosene. The child was lying to the right of the door, face downwards. As soon as she saw him she started crying aloud.

"There, there, all right! Don't cry, don't cry! There's a good girl." He bent down to pick her up. Having picked her up he turned round to see his wife standing furiously to the left of the door, also with a rigid back, her hands on her hips as if she were preparing to start physical exercises.

"Even you have to come and bully me! You can't help, you only make trouble — even the kerosene lamp had to turn over. What shall we light this evening?..."

"There, there, all right! Don't cry, don't cry!" Ignoring his wife's trembling tones, he carried the child into the house, and stroked her head. "There's a good girl," he repeated. Then he put her down, pulled out a chair and sat down. Setting her between his knees, he raised his hand. "Don't cry, there's a good girl," he said. "Daddy will do 'Pussy Washing' for you." At the same time he craned his neck, licked his palms from a distance twice, then with them traced circles towards his face.

"Aha! Pussy!" She started laughing.

"That's right, that's right. Pussy." He traced several more circles, and then stopped, seeing her smiling at him with tears still in her eyes.

想，「孩子是生得遲的，生得遲。或者不如沒有，兩個人乾乾淨淨。
——或者不如住在客店裏，甚麼都包給他們，一個人幹幹……」他聽
得嗚咽聲高了起來，也就站了起來，鑽過門幕，想着，「馬克思在兒
女的啼哭聲中還會做《資本論》，所以他是偉人，……」走出外間，開
了風門，聞得一陣煤油氣。孩子就躺倒在門的右邊，臉向着地，一
見他，便「哇」的哭出來了。

「阿阿，好好，莫哭莫哭，我的好孩子。」他彎下腰去抱她。

他抱了她回轉身，看見門左邊還站着主婦，也是腰骨筆直，然
而兩手插腰，怒氣沖沖的似乎預備開始練體操。

「連你也來欺侮我！不會幫忙，只會搗亂，——連油燈也要翻了
他。晚上點甚麼？……」

「阿阿，好好，莫哭莫哭，」他把那些發抖的聲音放在腦後，抱
她進房，摩着她的頭，說，「我的好孩子。」於是放下她，拖開椅
子，坐下去，使她站在兩膝的中間，擎起手來道，「莫哭了呵，好孩
子。爹爹做『貓洗臉』給你看。」他同時伸長頸子，伸出舌頭，遠遠的
對着手掌舔了兩舔，就用這手掌向了自己的臉上畫圓圈。

「呵呵呵，花兒。」她就笑起來了。

「是的是的，花兒。」他又連畫上幾個圓圈，這才歇了手，只見

It struck him suddenly that her sweet, innocent face was just like her mother's five years ago, especially her bright red lips, although the general outline was smaller. That had been another bright winter's day when she heard his decision to overcome all obstacles and sacrifice everything for her; when she too looked at him in the same way, smiling, with tears in her eyes. He sat down disconsolately, as if a little drunk.

"Ah, sweet lips," he thought.

The door curtain was suddenly fastened back and the firewood brought in.

Then, suddenly coming to himself again, he saw that the child, still with tears in her eyes, was looking at him with her bright red lips parted. "Lips...." He glanced sidewards to where the firewood was being brought in. "... Probably it will be nothing but five fives are twenty-five, nine nines are eighty-one, all over again! ... And two gloomy eyes...." So thinking he snatched up the green-lined paper with the heading and the figures written on it, crumpled it up and then unfolded it again to wipe her eyes and nose. "Good girl, run along and play by yourself." He pushed her away as he spoke, at the same time throwing the ball of paper into the waste-paper basket.

But at once he felt rather sorry for the child, and, turning his head, followed her with his eyes as she walked forlornly away, while his ears were filled with the sound of firewood. Determined to concentrate, he turned back again and closed his eyes to put a stop to all distracting thoughts, sitting there quietly and peacefully.

He saw passing before him a flat, round, black-freckled flower with an orange centre, which floated from the left of his left eye right over to the opposite side where it disappeared; then a bright green flower,

她還是笑迷迷的掛着眼淚對他看。他忽而覺得,她那可愛的天真的臉,正像五年前的她的母親,通紅的嘴唇尤其像,不過縮小了輪廓。那時也是晴朗的冬天,她聽得他説決計反抗一切阻礙,為她犧牲的時候,也就這樣笑迷迷的掛着眼淚對他看。他惘然的坐着,彷彿有些醉了。

「阿阿,可愛的嘴唇……」他想。

門幕忽然掛起。劈柴運進來了。

他也忽然驚醒,一定睛,只見孩子還是掛着眼淚,而且張開了通紅的嘴唇對他看。「嘴唇……」他向旁邊一瞥,劈柴正在進來,「……恐怕將來也就是五五二十五,九九八十一!……而且兩隻眼睛陰淒淒的……。」他想着,隨即粗暴的抓起那寫着一行題目和一堆算草的綠格紙來,揉了幾揉,又展開來給她拭去了眼淚和鼻涕。「好孩子,自己玩去罷。」他一面推開她,説;一面就將紙團用力的擲在紙簍裏。

但他又立刻覺得對於孩子有些抱歉了,重複回頭,目送着她獨自褮褮的出去;耳朵裏聽得木片聲。他想要定一定神,便又回轉頭,閉了眼睛,息了雜念,平心靜氣的坐着。他看見眼前浮出一朵扁圓的烏花,橙黃心,從左眼的左角漂到右,消失了;接着一朵明

with a dark green centre; and finally a pipe of six cabbages which formed themselves before him into an enormous letter A.

February 18, 1924

綠花，墨綠色的心；接着一座六株的白菜堆，屹然的向他疊成一個
很大的A字。

一九二四年二月一八日。

孤 獨 者

The Misanthrope

THE MISANTHROPE

I

My friendship with Wei Lianshu, now that I come to think of it, was certainly a strange one. It began and ended with a funeral.

When I lived in S—, I often heard him mentioned as an odd fellow: after studying zoology, he had become a history teacher in a middle school; he treated others in cavalier fashion, yet liked to concern himself with their affairs; and while maintaining that the family system should be abolished, he would remit his salary to his grandmother the same day that he drew it. He had many other strange ways, enough to set tongues wagging in the town. One autumn I stayed at Hanshishan with some relatives also named Wei, who were distantly related to him. However, they understood him even less, looking on him as if he were a foreigner. "He's not like us!" they said.

This was not strange, for although China had had modern schools for some twenty years, there was not even a primary school in Hanshishan. He was the only one to have left that mountain village to study; hence in the villagers' eyes he was an undoubted freak. They also envied him though, saying he had made a lot of money.

Towards the end of autumn, there was an epidemic of dysentery in the village, and in alarm I thought of returning to the town. I heard his grandmother had contracted the disease too, and because of her

孤　獨　者

　　我和魏連殳相識一場，回想起來倒也別致，竟是以送殮始，以送殮終。

　　那時我在S城，就時時聽到人們提起他的名字，都說他很有些古怪：所學的是動物學，卻到中學堂去做歷史教員；對人總是愛理不理的，卻常喜歡管別人的閒事；常說家庭應該破壞，一領薪水卻一定立即寄給他的祖母，一日也不拖延。此外還有許多零碎的話柄；總之，在S城裏也算是一個給人當做談助的人。有一年的秋天，我在寒石山的一個親戚家裏閒住；他們就姓魏，是連殳的本家。但他們卻更不明白他，彷彿將他當做一個外國人看待，說是「同我們都異樣的」。

　　這也不足為奇，中國的興學雖說已經二十年了，寒石山卻連小學也沒有。全山村中，只有連殳是出外遊學的學生，所以從村人看來，他確是一個異類；但也很妒羨，說他掙得許多錢。

　　到秋末，山村中痢疾流行了；我也自危，就想回到城中去。那時聽說連殳的祖母就染了病，因為是老年，所以很沉重；山中又沒

age her case was serious. Moreover there was not a single doctor in the village. Wei had no other relative but this grandmother, who led a simple life with a maidservant. As he had lost both parents in his childhood, she had brought him up. She was said to have known much hardship earlier, but was now leading a comfortable life. Since he had neither wife nor children, however, his family was very quiet, and this presumably was one of the things considered freakish about him.

The village was a hundred *li* from the town by land, and seventy *li* by water; so that it would take four days to fetch Wei back. In this out-of-the-way village such matters were considered momentous news, eagerly canvassed by all. The next day the old woman was reported to be in a critical state, and the messenger on his way. However, before dawn she died, her last words being:

"Why won't you let me see my grandson?"

Elders of the clan, close relatives, members of his grandmother's family and others crowded the room anticipating Wei's return, which would be in time for the funeral. The coffin and shroud had long been ready, but the immediate problem was how to cope with this grandson, for they expected he would insist on changes in the funeral rites. After a conference they decided on three terms which he must accept. First, he must wear deep mourning; secondly, he must kowtow to the coffin; and, thirdly, he must let Buddhist monks and Taoist priests say mass. In short, all must be done in the traditional manner.

This decision once reached, they decided to gather there in full force when Wei arrived home, to assist each other in this negotiation which could admit of no compromise. Licking their lips, the villagers eagerly awaited developments. Wei, as a "modern," "a follower of foreign creeds," had always proved unreasonable. A struggle would certainly ensue, which might even result in some novel spectacle.

有一個醫生。所謂他的家屬者，其實就只有一個這祖母，僱一名女工簡單地過活；他幼小失了父母，就由這祖母撫養成人的。聽說她先前也曾經吃過許多苦，現在可是安樂了。但因為他沒有家小，家中究竟非常寂寞，這大概也就是大家所謂異樣之一端罷。

寒石山離城是旱道一百里，水道七十里，專使人叫連殳去，往返至少就得四天。山村僻陋，這些事便算大家都要打聽的大新聞，第二天便轟傳她病勢已經極重，專差也出發了；可是到四更天竟咽了氣，最後的話，是：「為甚麼不肯給我會一會連殳的呢？……」

族長，近房，他的祖母的母家的親丁，閒人，聚集了一屋子，預計連殳的到來，應該已是入殮的時候了。壽材壽衣早已做成，都無須籌畫；他們的第一大問題是在怎樣對付這「承重孫」，因為逆料他關於一切喪葬儀式，是一定要改變新花樣的。聚議之後，大概商定了三大條件，要他必行。一是穿白，二是跪拜，三是請和尚道士做法事。總而言之：是全都照舊。

他們既經議妥，便約定在連殳到家的那一天，一同聚在廳前，排成陣勢，互相策應，並力作一回極嚴厲的談判。村人們都咽着唾沫，新奇地聽候消息；他們知道連殳是「吃洋教」的「新黨」，向來就不講甚麼道理，兩面的爭鬥，大約總要開始的。或者還會釀成一種出人意外的奇觀。

He arrived home, I heard, in the afternoon, and only bowed to his grandmother's shrine as he entered. The elders proceeded at once according to plan. They summoned him to the hall, and after a lengthy preamble led up to the subject. Then, speaking in unison and at length, they gave him no chance to argue. At last, however, they dried up, and a deep silence fell in the hall. All eyes fastened fearfully on his lips. But without changing countenance, he answered simply: "All right."

This was totally unexpected. A weight had been lifted from their minds, yet their hearts felt heavier than ever, for this was so "freakish" as to give rise to anxiety. The villagers looking for news were also disappointed and said to each other, "Strange. He said, 'All right.' Let's go and watch." Wei's "all right " meant that all would be in accordance with tradition, in which case it was not worth watching; still, they wanted to look on, and after dusk the hall filled with light-hearted spectators.

I was one of those who went, having first sent along my gift of incense and candles. As I arrived he was already putting the shroud on the dead. He was a thin man with an angular face, hidden to a certain extent by his dishevelled hair, dark eyebrows and moustache. His eyes gleamed darkly. He laid out the body very well, as deftly as an expert, so that the spectators were impressed. According to the local custom, at a married woman's funeral members of the dead woman's family found fault even if all was well done; however he remained silent, complying with their wishes with a face devoid of all expression. A grey-haired old woman standing before me gave a sigh of envy and respect.

Then people kowtowed; then they wailed, all the women chanting as they wailed. When the body was put in the coffin, all kowtowed again, then wailed again, until the lid of the coffin was nailed down. Silence reigned for a moment, and then there was stir of surprise

傳說連殳的到家是下午，一進門，向他祖母的靈前只是彎了一彎腰。族長們便立刻照預定計劃進行，將他叫到大廳上，先說過一大篇冒頭，然後引入本題，而且大家此唱彼和，七嘴八舌，使他得不到辯駁的機會。但終於話都說完了，沉默充滿了全廳，人們全數悚然地緊看着他的嘴。只見連殳神色也不動，簡單地回答道：

「都可以的。」

這又很出於他們的意外，大家的心的重擔都放下了，但又似乎反加重，覺得太「異樣」，倒很有些可慮似的。打聽新聞的村人們也很失望，口口相傳道，「奇怪！他說『都可以』哩！我們看去罷！」都可以就是照舊，本來是無足觀了，但他們也還要看，黃昏之後，便欣欣然聚滿了一堂前。

我也是去看的一個，先送了一份香燭；待到走到他家，已見連殳在給死者穿衣服了。原來他是一個短小瘦削的人，長方臉，蓬鬆的頭髮和濃黑的鬚眉佔了一臉的小半，只見兩眼在黑氣裏發光。那穿衣也穿得真好，井井有條，彷彿是一個大殮的專家，使旁觀者不覺嘆服。寒石山老例，當這些時候，無論如何，母家的親丁是總要挑剔的；他卻只是默默地，遇見怎麼挑剔便怎麼改，神色也不動；站在我前面的一個花白頭髮的老太太，便發出羨慕感嘆的聲音。

其次是拜；其次是哭，凡女人們都唸唸有詞。其次入棺；其次又是拜；又是哭，直到釘好了棺蓋。沉靜了一瞬間，大家忽而擾動

and dissatisfaction. I too suddenly realized that Wei had not shed a single tear from beginning to end. He was simply sitting on the mourner's mat, his two eyes gleaming darkly.

In this atmosphere of surprise and dissatisfaction, the ceremony ended. The disgruntled mourners seemed about to leave, but Wei was still sitting on the mat, lost in thought. Suddenly, tears fell from his eyes, then he burst into a long wail like a wounded wolf howling in the wilderness at the dead of night, anger and sorrow mingled with his agony. This was not in accordance with tradition and, taken by surprise, we were at a loss. After a little hesitation, some went to try to persuade him to stop, and these were joined by more and more people until finally there was a crowd round him. But he sat there wailing, motionless as an iron statue.

With a sense of anti-climax, the crowd dispersed. Wei continued to cry for about half an hour, then suddenly stopped, and without a word to the mourners went straight inside. Later it was reported by spies that he had gone into his grandmother's room, lain down on the bed and, to all appearances, fallen sound asleep.

Two days later, on the eve of my return to town, I heard the villagers discussing eagerly, as if they were possessed, how Wei intended to burn most of his dead grandmother's furniture and possessions, giving the rest to the maidservant who had served her during her life and attended her on her deathbed. Even the house was to be lent to the maid for an indefinite period. Wei's relatives argued themselves hoarse, but he was adamant.

Largely out of curiosity, perhaps, on my way back I passed his house and went in to express condolence. He received me wearing a hemless white mourning dress, and his expression was as cold as ever. I urged him not to take it so to heart, but apart from grunting non-committally all he said was:

了，很有驚異和不滿的形勢。我也不由的突然覺到：連殳就始終沒有落過一滴淚，只坐在草薦上，兩眼在黑氣裏閃閃地發光。

大殮便在這驚異和不滿的空氣裏面完畢。大家都怏怏地，似乎想走散。但連殳卻還坐在草薦上沉思。忽然，他流下淚來了，接着就失聲，立刻又變成長嚎，像一匹受傷的狼，當深夜在曠野中嗥叫，慘傷裏夾雜着憤怒和悲哀。這模樣，是老例上所沒有的，先前也未曾預防到，大家都手足無措了，遲疑了一會，就有幾個人上前去勸止他，愈去愈多，終於擠成一大堆。

但他卻只是兀坐着號咷，鐵塔似的動也不動。

大家又只得無趣地散開；他哭着，哭着，約有半點鐘，這才突然停了下來，也不向吊客招呼，徑自往家裏走。接着就有前去窺探的人來報告：他走進他祖母的房裏，躺在床上，而且，似乎就睡熟了。

隔了兩日，是我要動身回城的前一天，便聽到村人都遭了魔似的發議論，說連殳要將所有的器具大半燒給他祖母，餘下的便分贈生時侍奉，死時送終的女工，並且連房屋也要無期地借給她居住了。親戚本家都說到舌敝唇焦，也終於阻當不住。

恐怕大半也還是因為好奇心，我歸途中經過他家的門口，便又順便去弔慰。他穿了毛邊的白衣出見，神色也還是那樣，冷冷的。我很勸慰了一番；他卻除了唯唯諾諾之外，只回答了一句話，是：

"Thanks for your concern."

II

Early that winter we met for the third time. It was in a bookshop in S—, where we nodded simultaneously, showing at least that we were acquainted. But it was at the end of that year, after I lost my job, that we became friends. Thenceforward I paid Wei many visits. In the first place, of course, I had nothing to do; in the second place he was said to sympathize with lame dogs, despite his habitual reserve. However, fortune being fickle, lame dogs do not remain lame for ever, hence he had few steady friends. Report proved true, for as soon as I sent in my card, he received me. His sitting-room consisted of two rooms thrown into one, quite bare of ornament, with nothing in it apart from table and chairs but some bookcases. Although he was reputed to be terribly "modern," there were few modern books on the shelves. He knew that I had lost my job; but after the usual polite remarks had been exchanged, host and guest sat silent, with nothing to say to each other. I noticed he very quickly finished his cigarette, only dropping it to the ground when it nearly burnt his fingers.

"Have a cigarette," he said suddenly, reaching for another.

So I took one and, between puffs, spoke of teaching and books, still finding very little to say. I was just thinking of leaving when shouts and footsteps were heard outside the door, and four children rushed in. The eldest was about eight or nine, the smallest four or five. The hands, faces and clothes were very dirty, and they were thoroughly

「多謝你的好意。」

二

　　我們第三次相見就在這年的冬初，S城的一個書舖子裏，大家同時點了一點頭，總算是認識了。但使我們接近起來的，是在這年底我失了職業之後。從此，我便常常訪問連殳去。一則，自然是因為無聊賴；二則，因為聽人說，他倒很親近失意的人的，雖然素性這麼冷。但是世事升沉無定，失意人也不會長是失意人，所以他也就很少長久的朋友。這傳說果然不虛，我一投名片，他便接見了。兩間連通的客廳，並無甚麼陳設，不過是桌椅之外，排列些書架，大家雖說他是一個可怕的「新黨」，架上卻不很有新書。他已經知道我失了職業；但套話一說就完，主客便只好默默地相對，逐漸沉悶起來。我只見他很快地吸完一枝煙，煙蒂要燒着手指了，才拋在地面上。

　　「吸煙罷。」他伸手取第二枝煙時，忽然說。

　　我便也取了一枝，吸着，講些關於教書和書籍的，但也還覺得沉悶。我正想走時，門外一陣喧嚷和腳步聲，四個男女孩子闖進來了。大的八九歲，小的四五歲，手臉和衣服都很髒，而且醜得可

unprepossessing; yet Wei's face lit up with pleasure, and getting up at once he walked to the other room, saying:

"Come, Daliang, Erliang, all of you! I have bought the mouth-organs you wanted yesterday."

The children rushed in after him, to return immediately with a mouth-organ apiece; but once outside they started fighting, and one of them cried.

"There's one each; they're exactly the same. Don't squabble!" he said as he followed them.

"Whose children are they?" I asked.

"The landlord's. They have no mother, only a grandmother."

"Your landlord is a widower?"

"Yes. His wife died three or four years ago, and he has not remarried. Otherwise, he would not rent his spare rooms to a bachelor like me." He said this with a cold smile.

I wanted very much to ask why he had remained single so long, but I did not know him well enough.

Once you knew him well, he was a good talker. He was full of ideas, many of them quite remarkable. What exasperated me were some of his guests. As a result, probably, of reading Yu Dafu's romantic stories, they constantly referred to themselves as "the young unfortunate" or "the outcast"; and, sprawling on the big chairs like lazy and arrogant crabs, they would sigh, smoke and frown all at the same time.

Then there were the landlord's children, who were always fighting among themselves, knocking over bowls and plates, begging for cakes, keeping up an ear-splitting din. Yet the sight of them invariably

以。但是連殳的眼裏卻即刻發出歡喜的光來了，連忙站起，向客廳間壁的房裏走，一面説道：

「大良，二良，都來！你們昨天要的口琴，我已經買來了。」

孩子們便跟着一齊擁進去，立刻又各人吹着一個口琴一擁而出，一出客廳門，不知怎的便打將起來。有一個哭了。

「一人一個，都一樣的。不要爭呵！」他還跟在後面囑咐。

「這麼多的一群孩子都是誰呢？」我問。

「是房主人的。他們都沒有母親，只有一個祖母。」

「房東只一個人麼？」

「是的。他的妻子大概死了三四年了罷，沒有續娶。——否則，便要不肯將餘屋租給我似的單身人。」他説着，冷冷地微笑了。

我很想問他何以至今還是單身，但因為不很熟，終於不好開口。

只要和連殳一熟識，是很可以談談的。他議論非常多，而且往往頗奇警。使人不耐的倒是他的有些來客，大抵是讀過《沉淪》的罷，時常自命為「不幸的青年」或是「零餘者」，螃蟹一般懶散而驕傲地堆在大椅子上，一面唉聲嘆氣，一面皺着眉頭吸煙。還有那房主的孩子們，總是互相爭吵，打翻碗碟，硬討點心，亂得人頭昏。但

dispelled Wei's customary coldness, and they seemed to be the most precious thing in his life. Once the third child was said to have measles. He was so worried that his dark face took on an even darker hue. The attack proved a light one, however, and thereafter the children's grandmother made a joke of his anxiety.

"Children are always good. They are all so innocent ..." he seized an opening to say one day, having, apparently, sensed my impatience.

"Not always," I answered casually.

"Always. Children have none of the faults of grown-ups. If they turn out badly later, as you contend, it is because they have been moulded by their environment. Originally they are not bad, but innocent.... I think China's only hope lies in this."

"I don't agree. Without the root of evil, how could they bear evil fruit in later life? Take a seed, for example. It is because it contains the embryo leaves, flowers and fruits, that it can grow later into these things. There must be a cause...." Since my unemployment, just like those great officials who resigned from office and took up Buddhism, I had been reading the Buddhist sutras. I did not understand Buddhist philosophy though, and was just talking at random.

However, Wei was annoyed. He gave me a look, then said no more. I could not tell whether he had more to say, or whether he felt it not worth arguing with me. But he looked cold again, as he had not done for a long time, and smoked two cigarettes one after the other in silence. By the time he reached for the third cigarette, I had to beat a retreat.

Our estrangement lasted three months. Then, owing in part to forgetfulness, in part to the fact that he fell out with those "innocent" children, he came to consider my slighting remarks about children as excusable. Or so I surmised. This happened in my house after drinking

連殳一見他們，卻再不像平時那樣的冷冷的了，看得比自己的性命還寶貴。聽說有一回，三良發了紅斑痧，竟急得他臉上的黑氣愈見其黑了；不料那病是輕的，於是後來便被孩子們的祖母傳作笑柄。

「孩子總是好的。他們全是天真……。」他似乎也覺得我有些不耐煩了，有一天特地乘機對我說。

「那也不盡然。」我只是隨便回答他。

「不。大人的壞脾氣，在孩子們是沒有的。後來的壞，如你平日所攻擊的壞，那是環境教壞的。原來卻並不壞，天真……。我以為中國的可以希望，只在這一點。」

「不。如果孩子中沒有壞根苗，大起來怎麼會有壞花果？譬如一粒種子，正因為內中本含有枝葉花果的胚，長大時才能夠發出這些東西來。何嘗是無端……。」我因為閒着無事，便也如大人先生們一下野，就要吃素談禪一樣，正在看佛經。佛理自然是並不懂得的，但竟也不自檢點，一味任意地說。

然而連殳氣忿了，只看了我一眼，不再開口。我也猜不出他是無話可說呢，還是不屑辯。但見他又顯出許久不見的冷冷的態度來，默默地連吸了兩枝煙；待到他再取第三枝時，我便只好逃走了。

這仇恨是歷了三月之久才消釋的。原因大概是一半因為忘卻，一半則他自己竟也被「天真」的孩子所仇視了，於是覺得我對於孩子的冒瀆的話倒也情有可原。但這不過是我的推測。其時是在我的寓

one day, when, with a rather melancholy look, he cocked his head, and said:

"Come to think of it, it's really curious. On my way here I met a small child with a reed in his hand, which he pointed at me, shouting, 'Kill!' He was just a toddler...."

"He must have been moulded by his environment."

As soon as I had said this, I wanted to take it back. However, he did not seem to care, just went on drinking heavily, smoking furiously in between.

"I meant to ask you," I said, trying to change the subject. "You don't usually call on people, what made you come out today? I've known you for more than a year, yet this is the first time you've been here."

"I was just going to tell you: don't call on me for the time being. There are a father and son in my place who are perfect pests. They are scarcely human!"

"Father and son? Who are they?" I was surprised.

"My cousin and his son. Well, the son resembles the father."

"I suppose they came to town to see you and have a good time?"

"No. They came to talk me into adopting the boy."

"What, to adopt the boy?" I exclaimed in amazement. "But you are not married."

"They know I won't marry. But that's nothing to them. Actually they want to inherit that tumble-down house of mine in the village. I have no other property, you know; as soon as I get money I spend it. I've only that house. Their purpose in life is to drive out the old

裏的酒後，他似乎微露悲哀模樣，半仰着頭道：

「想起來真覺得有些奇怪。我到你這裏來時，街上看見一個很小的小孩，拿了一片蘆葉指着我道：殺！他還不很能走路……。」

「這是環境教壞的。」

我即刻很後悔我的話。但他卻似乎並不介意，只竭力地喝酒，其間又竭力地吸煙。

「我倒忘了，還沒有問你，」我使用別的話來支吾，「你是不大訪問人的，怎麼今天有這興致來走走呢？我們相識有一年多了，你到我這裏來卻還是第一回。」

「我正要告訴你呢：你這幾天切莫到我寓裏來看我了。我的寓裏正有很討厭的一大一小在那裏，都不像人！」

「一大一小？這是誰呢？」我有些詫異。

「是我的堂兄和他的小兒子。哈哈，兒子正如老子一般。」

「是上城來看你。帶便玩玩的罷？」

「不。說是來和我商量，就要將這孩子過繼給我的。」

「呵！過繼給你？」我不禁驚叫了，「你不是還沒有娶親麼？」

「他們知道我不娶的了。但這都沒有甚麼關係。他們其實是要過繼給我那一間寒石山的破屋子。我此外一無所有，你是知道的；錢一到手就化完。只有這一間破屋子。他們父子的一生的事業是在逐

maidservant who is living in the place for the time being."

The cynicism of his remark took me aback. However I tried to soothe him, by saying:

"I don't think your relatives can be so bad. They are only rather old-fashioned. For instance, that year when you cried bitterly, they came forward eagerly to plead with you...."

"When I was a child and my father died, I cried bitterly because they wanted to take the house from me and make me put my mark on the document, and they came forward eagerly *then* to plead with me...." He looked up, as if searching the air for that bygone scene.

"The crux of the matter is — you have no children. Why don't you get married?" I had found a way to change the subject, and this was something I had been wanting to ask for a long time. It seemed an excellent opportunity.

He looked at me in surprise, then dropped his gaze to his knees, and started smoking. I received no answer to my question.

III

Yet, even this inane existence he was not allowed to enjoy in peace. Gradually there appeared anonymous attacks in the less reputable papers, and in the schools rumours spread concerning him. This was not the simple gossip of the old days, but deliberately damaging. I knew this was the outcome of articles he had taken to writing for the magazines, so I paid no attention. The citizens of S— disliked nothing more than fearless argument, and anyone guilty of it would indubitably

出那一個借住着的老女工。」

他那詞氣的冷峭，實在又使我悚然。但我還慰解他說：

「我看你的本家也還不至於此。他們不過思想略舊一點罷了。譬如，你那年大哭的時候，他們就都熱心地圍着使勁來勸你……。」

「我父親死去之後，因為奪我屋子，要我在筆據上畫花押，我大哭着的時候，他們也是這樣熱心地圍着使勁來勸我……。」他兩眼向上凝視，彷彿要在空中尋出那時的情景來。

「總而言之：關鍵就全在你沒有孩子。你究竟為甚麼老不結婚的呢？」我忽而尋到了轉舵的話，也是久已想問的話，覺得這時是最好的機會了。

他詫異地看看我，過了一會，眼光便移到他自己的膝髁上去了，於是就吸煙，沒有回答。

　　但是，雖在這一種百無聊賴的境地中，也還不給連殳安住。漸漸地，小報上有匿名人來攻擊他，學界上也常有關於他的流言，可是這已經並非先前似的單是話柄，大概是於他有損的了。我知道這是他近來喜歡發表文章的結果，倒也並不介意。S城人最不願意有人發些沒有顧忌的議論，一有，一定要暗暗地來叮他，這是向來如此

become the object of secret attacks. This was the rule, and Wei knew it too. However, in spring, when I heard he had been asked to resign by the school authorities, I confessed it surprised me. Of course, this was only to be expected, and it surprised me simply because I had hoped my friend could escape. The citizens of S— were not proving more vicious than usual.

I was occupied then with my own problems, negotiating to go to a school in Shanyang that autumn, so I had no time to call on him. Some three months passed before I was at leisure, and even then it had not occurred to me to visit him. One day, passing the main street, I happened to pause before a second-hand bookstall, where I was started to see displayed an early edition of the *Commentaries on the "Records of the Historian,"* from Wei's collection. He was no connoisseur, but he loved books, and I knew he prized this particular book. He must be very hard pressed to have sold it. It seemed scarcely possible he could have become so poor only two or three months after losing his job; yet he spent money as soon as he had it, and had never saved. So I decided to call on him. On the same street I bought a bottle of liquor, two packages of peanuts and two smoked fish-heads.

His door was closed. I called out twice, but there was no reply. Thinking he was asleep, I called louder, hammering on the door at the same time.

"He's probably out." The children's grandmother, a fat woman with small eyes, thrust her grey head out from the opposite window, and spoke impatiently.

"Where has he gone?" I asked.

"Where? Who knows — where could he go? You can wait, he will be back soon."

So I pushed open the door and went into his sitting-room. It was

的，連殳自己也知道。但到春天，忽然聽説他已被校長辭退了。這卻使我覺得有些兀突；其實，這也是向來如此的，不過因為我希望着自己認識的人能夠幸免，所以就以為兀突罷了，S城人倒並非這一回特別惡。

其時我正忙着自己的生計，一面又在接洽本年秋天到山陽去當教員的事，竟沒有工夫去訪問他，待到有些餘暇的時候，離他被辭退那時大約快有三個月了，可是還沒有發生訪問連殳的意思。有一天，我路過大街，偶然在舊書攤前停留，卻不禁使我覺到震悚，因為在那裏陳列着的一部汲古閣初印本《史記索隱》，正是連殳的書。他喜歡書，但不是藏書家，這種本子，在他是算作貴重的善本，非萬不得已，不肯輕易變賣的。難道他失業剛才兩三月，就一貧至此麼？雖然他向來一有錢即隨手散去，沒有甚麼貯蓄。於是我便決意訪問連殳去，順便在街上買了一瓶燒酒，兩包花生米，兩個熏魚頭。

他的房門關閉着，叫了兩聲，不見答應。我疑心他睡着了，更加大聲地叫，並且伸手拍着房門。

「出去了罷！」大良們的祖母，那三角眼的胖女人，從對面的窗口探出她花白的頭來了，也大聲説，不耐煩似的。

「那裏去了呢？」我問。

「那裏去了？誰知道呢？——他能到那裏去呢，你等着就是，一會兒總會回來的。」

我便推開門走進他的客廳去。真是「一日不見，如隔三秋」，滿

greatly changed, looking desolate in its emptiness. There was little furniture left, while all that remained of his library were those foreign books which could not be sold. The middle of the room was still occupied by the table round which those woeful and gallant young men, unrecognized geniuses, and dirty, noisy children had formerly gathered. Now it all seemed very quiet, and there was a thin layer of dust on the table. I put the bottle and packages down, pulled over a chair, and sat down by the table facing the door.

Very soon, sure enough, the door opened, and someone stepped in as silently as a shadow. It was Wei. It might have been the twilight that made his face look dark; but his expression was unchanged.

"Ah, it's you? How long have you been here?" He seemed pleased.

"Not very long," I said. "Where have you been?"

"Nowhere in particular. Just taking a stroll."

He pulled up a chair too and sat by the table. We started drinking, and spoke of his losing his job. However, he did not care to talk much about it, considering it as only to be expected. He had come across many similar cases. It was not strange at all, and not worth discussing. As usual, he drank heavily, and discoursed on society and the study of history. Something made me glance at the empty bookshelves and, remembering the *Commentaries on the "Records of the Historian,"* I was conscious of a slight loneliness and sadness.

"Your sitting-room has a deserted look.... Have you had fewer visitors recently?"

"None at all. They don't find it much fun when I'm not in a good mood. A bad mood certainly makes people uncomfortable. Just as no one goes to the park in winter...."

He took two sips of liquor in succession, then fell silent. Suddenly,

眼是淒涼和空空洞洞，不但器具所餘無幾了；連書籍也只剩了在S城
決沒有人會要的幾本洋裝書。屋中間的圓桌還在，先前曾經常常圍
繞着憂鬱慷慨的青年，懷才不遇的奇士和腌臢吵鬧的孩子們，現在
卻見得很閒靜，只在面上蒙着一層薄薄的灰塵。我就在桌上放了酒
瓶和紙包，拖過一把椅子來，靠桌旁對着房門坐下。

　　的確不過是「一會兒」，房門一開，一個人悄悄地陰影似的進來
了，正是連殳。也許是傍晚之故罷，看去彷彿比先前黑，但神情卻
還是那樣。

　　「阿！你在這裏？來得多久了？」他似乎有些喜歡。

　　「並沒有多久。」我說，「你到那裏去了？」

　　「並沒有到那裏去，不過隨便走走。」

　　他也拖過椅子來，在桌旁坐下；我們便開始喝燒酒，一面談些
關於他的失業的事。但他卻不願意多談這些；他以為這是意料中的
事，也是自己時常遇到的事，無足怪，而且無可談的。他照例只是
一意喝燒酒，並且依然發些關於社會和歷史的議論。不知怎地我此
時看見空空的書架，也記起汲古閣初印本的《史記索隱》，忽而感到
一種淡漠的孤寂和悲哀。

　　「你的客廳這麼荒涼……。近來客人不多了麼？」

　　「沒有了。他們以為我心境不佳，來也無意味。心境不佳，實在
是可以給人們不舒服的。冬天的公園，就沒有人去……。」他連喝兩

looking up, he asked, "I suppose you have had no luck either in finding work?"

Although I knew he was only venting his feelings as a result of
drinking, I felt indignant at the way people treated him. Just as I was
about to say something, he pricked up his ears, then, scooping up
some peanuts, went out. Outside, the laughter and shouts of the children could be heard.

But as soon as he went out, the children became quiet. It sounded
as if they had left. He went after them, and said something, but I could
hear no reply. Then he came back, as silent as a shadow, and put the
handful of peanuts back in the package.

"They don't even want to eat anything I give them," he said
sarcastically, in a low voice.

"Old Wei," I said, forcing a smile, although I was sick at heart, "I
think you are tormenting yourself unnecessarily. Why think so poorly
of your fellow men?"

He only smiled cynically.

"I haven't finished yet. I suppose you consider that people like
me, who come here occasionally, do so in order to kill time or amuse
themselves at your expense?"

"No, I don't. Well, sometimes I do. Perhaps they come to find something to talk about."

"Then you are wrong. People are not like that. You are really wrap-
ping yourself up in a cocoon. You should take a more cheerful view."
I sighed.

"Maybe. But tell me, where does the thread for the cocoon come
from? Of course, there are plenty of people like that; take my

口酒，默默地想着，突然，仰起臉來看着我問道，「你在圖謀的職業也還是毫無把握罷？……」

我雖然明知他已經有些酒意，但也不禁憤然，正想發話，只見他側耳一聽，便抓起一把花生米，出去了。門外是大良們笑嚷的聲音。

但他一出去，孩子們的聲音便寂然，而且似乎都走了。他還追上去，說些話，卻不聽得有回答。他也就陰影似的悄悄地回來，仍將一把花生米放在紙包裏。

「連我的東西也不要吃了。」他低聲，嘲笑似的說。

「連殳，」我很覺得悲涼，卻強裝着微笑，說，「我以為你太自尋苦惱了。你看得人間太壞……。」

他冷冷的笑了一笑。

「我的話還沒有完哩。你對於我們，偶而來訪問你的我們，也以為因為閒着無事，所以來你這裏，將你當做消遣的資料的罷？」

「並不。但有時也這樣想。或者尋些談資。」

「那你可錯誤了。人們其實並不這樣。你實在親手造了獨頭繭，將自己裹在裏面了。你應該將世間看得光明些。」我嘆惜着說。

「也許如此罷。但是，你說：那絲是怎麼來的？——自然，世上也盡有這樣的人，譬如，我的祖母就是。我雖然沒有分得她的血

grandmother, for example. Although I have none of her blood in my veins, I may inherit her fate. But that doesn't matter, I have already bewailed my fate together with hers."

"I still don't understand why you cried so bitterly," I said bluntly.

"You mean at my grandmother's funeral? No, you wouldn't." He lit the lamp. "I suppose it was because of that that we became friends," he said quietly. "You know, this grandmother was my grandfather's second wife. My father's own mother died when he was three." Growing thoughtful, he drank silently, and finished a smoked fish-head.

"I didn't know it to begin with. Only, from my childhood I was puzzled. At that time my father was still alive, and our family was well off. During the lunar New Year we would hang up the ancestral images and hold a grand sacrifice. It was one of my rare pleasures to look at those splendidly dressed images. At that time a maidservant would always carry me to an image, and point at it, saying, 'This is your own grandmother. Bow to her so that she will protect you and make you grown up strong and healthy.' I could not understand how I came to have another grandmother, in addition to the one beside me. But I liked this grandmother who was 'my own.' She was not as old as the granny at home. Young and beautiful, wearing a red costume with golden embroidery and a headdress decked with pearls, she resembled my mother. When I looked at her, her eyes seemed to gaze down on me, and a faint smile appeared on her lips. I knew she was very fond of me too.

"But I like the granny at home too, who sat all day under the window slowly plying her needle. However, no matter how merrily I laughed and played in front of her, or called to her, I could not make her laugh; and that made me feel she was cold, unlike other children's grandmothers. Still, I liked her. Later on, though, I gradually cooled towards her, not because I had grown older and learned she was not

液，卻也許會繼承她的運命。然而這也沒有甚麼要緊，我早已預先一起哭過了……。」

我即刻記起他祖母大殮時候的情景來，如在眼前一樣。

「我總不解你那時的大哭……。」於是鶻突地問了。

「我的祖母入殮的時候罷？是的，你不解的。」他一面點燈，一面冷靜地說，「你的和我交往，我想，還正因為那時的哭哩。你不知道，這祖母，是我父親的繼母；他的生母，他三歲時候就死去了。」他想着，默默地喝酒，吃完了一個熏魚頭。

「那些往事，我原是不知道的。只是我從小時候就覺得不可解。那時我的父親還在，家景也還好，正月間一定要懸掛祖像，盛大地供養起來。看着這許多盛裝的畫像，在我那時似乎是不可多得的眼福。但那時，抱着我的一個女工總指了一幅像說『這是你自己的祖母。拜拜罷，保祐你生龍活虎似的大得快。』我真不懂得我明明有着一個祖母，怎麼又會有甚麼『自己的祖母』來。可是我愛這『自己的祖母』，她不比家裏的祖母一般老；她年青，好看，穿着描金的紅衣服，戴着珠冠，和我母親的像差不多。我看她時，她的眼睛也注視我，而且口角上漸漸增多了笑影：我知道她一定也是極其愛我的。

「然而我也愛那家裏的，終日坐在窗下慢慢地做針線的祖母。雖然無論我怎樣高興地在她面前玩笑，叫她，也不能引她歡笑，常使我覺得冷冷地，和別人的祖母們有些不同。但我還愛她。可是到後來，我逐漸疏遠她了；這也並非因為年紀大了，已經知道她不是我

my own grandmother, but rather because I was exasperated by the way she kept on sewing mechanically, day in day out. She was unchanged, however. She sewed, looked after me, loved and protected me as befoe; and though she seldom smiled, she never scolded me. It was the same after my father died. Later on, we lived almost entirely on her sewing, so it was still the same, until I went to school...."

The light flickered as the kerosene gave out, and he stood up to refill the lamp from a small tin kettle under the bookcase.

"The price of kerosene has gone up twice this month," he said slowly, after turning up the wick. "Life will become harder every day. She remained the same until I graduated from school and got a job, when our life became more secure. She didn't change, I suppose, until she was sick and couldn't carry on, but had to take to her bed....

"Since her later days, I think, were not too unhappy on the whole, and she lived to a great age, I need not have mourned. Besides, weren't there a lot of others there eager to wail? Even those who had tried their hardest to rob her wailed, or appeared bowed down with grief." He laughed. "However, at that moment her whole life rose to my mind — the life of one who created loneliness for herself and tasted its bitterness. And I felt there were many people like that. I wanted to weep for them; but perhaps it was largely because I was too sentimental....

"Your present advice to me is what I felt with regard to her. But actually my ideas at that time were wrong. As for myself, since I grew up my feelings for her cooled...."

He paused, with a cigarette between his fingers and bending his head lost himself in thought. The lamp-light flickered.

"Well, it is hard to live so that no one will mourn for your death," he said, as if to himself. After a pause he looked up at me, and asked,

父親的生母的緣故，倒是看久了終日終年的做針線，機器似的，自然免不了要發煩。但她卻還是先前一樣，做針線；管理我，也愛護我，雖然少見笑容，卻也不加呵斥。直到我父親去世，還是這樣；後來呢，我們幾乎全靠她做針線過活了，自然更這樣，直到我進學堂……。」

燈火銷沉下去了，煤油已經將涸，他便站起，從書架下摸出一個小小的洋鐵壺來添煤油。

「只這一月裏，煤油已經漲價兩次了……。」他旋好了燈頭，慢慢地說。「生活要日見其困難起來。——她後來還是這樣，直到我畢業，有了事做，生活比先前安定些；恐怕還直到她生病，實在打熬不住了，只得躺下的時候罷………。」

「她的晚年，據我想，是總算不很辛苦的，享壽也不小了，正無須我來下淚。況且哭的人不是多著麼？連先前竭力欺凌她的人們也哭，至少是臉上很慘然，哈哈！……可是我那時不知怎地，將她的一生縮在眼前了，親手造成孤獨，又放在嘴裏去咀嚼的人的一生。而且覺得這樣的人還很多哩。這些人們，就使我要痛哭，但大半也還是因為我那時太過於感情用事……。」

「你現在對於我的意見，就是我先前對於她的意見。然而我的那時的意見，其實也不對的。便是我自己，從略知世事起，就的確逐漸和她疏遠起來了……。」

他沉默了，指間夾著煙卷，低了頭，想著。燈火在微微地發抖。

「呵，人要使死後沒有一個人為他哭，是不容易的事呵。」他自言自語似的說；略略一停，便仰起臉來向我道，「想來你也無法可

"I suppose you can't help? I shall have to find something to do very soon."

"Have you no other friends you could ask?" I was in no position to help myself then, let alone others.

"I have a few, but they are all in the same boat...."

When I left him, the full moon was high in the sky and the night was very still.

IV

The teaching profession in Shanyang was no bed of roses. I taught for two months without receiving a cent of salary, until I had to cut down on cigarettes. But the school staff, even those earning only fifteen or sixteen dollars a month, were easily contented. They all had iron constitutions steeled by hardship, and, although lean and haggard, would work from morning till night; while if interrupted at work by their superiors, they would stand up respectfully. Thus they all practised plain living and high thinking. This reminded me, somehow, of Wei's parting words. He was then even more hard up, and often looked embarrassed, having apparently lost his former cynicism. When he heard that I was leaving, he had come late at night to see me off, and, after hesitating for some time, had stuttered:

"Would there be anything for me there? Even copying work, at twenty to thirty dollars a month, would do. I...."

I was surprised. I had not thought he would consider anything so low, and did not know how to answer.

想。我也還得趕緊尋點事情做……。」

「你再沒有可託的朋友了麼?」我這時正是無法可想,連自己。

「那倒大概還有幾個的,可是他們的境遇都和我差不多……。」

我辭別連殳出門的時候,圓月已經升在中天了,是極靜的夜。

四

山陽的教育事業的狀況很不佳。我到校兩月,得不到一文薪水,只得連煙卷也節省起來。但是學校裏的人們,雖是月薪十五、六元的小職員,也沒有一個不是樂天知命的,仗着逐漸打熬成功的銅筋鐵骨,面黃肌瘦地從早辦公一直到夜,其間看見名位較高的人物,還得恭恭敬敬地站起,實在都是不必「衣食足而知禮節」的人民。我每看見這情狀,不知怎的總記起連殳臨別託付我的話來。他那時生計更其不堪了,窘相時時顯露,看去似乎已沒有往時的深沉,知道我就要動身,深夜來訪,遲疑了許久,才吞吞吐吐地說道:

「不知道那邊可有法子想?——便是鈔寫,一月二、三十塊錢的也可以的。我……。」

我很詫異了,還不料他竟肯這樣的遷就,一時說不出話來。

"I ... I have to live a little longer...."

"I'll look out when I get there. I'll do my best."

This was what I had promised at the time, and the words often rang in my ears later, as if Wei were before me, stuttering, "I have to live a little longer." I tried to interest various people in his case, but to no avail. There were few vacancies, and many unemployed; they always ended by apologizing for being unable to help, and I would write him an apologetic letter. By the end of the term, things had gone from bad to worse. The magazine *Reason*, edited by some of the local gentry, began to attack me. Naturally no names were mentioned, but it cleverly insinuated that I was stirring up trouble in the school, even my recommendation of Wei being interpreted as a manoeuvre to gather a clique about me.

So I had to keep quiet. Apart from attending class, I lay low in my room, sometimes even fearing I might be considered as stirring up trouble when cigarette smoke escaped from my window. For Wei, naturally, I could do nothing. This state of affairs prevailed till midwinter.

It had been snowing all day, and the snow had not stopped by evening. Outside was so still, you could almost hear the sound of stillness. I closed my eyes and sat there in the dim lamplight, doing nothing, imagining the snowflakes falling to augment the boundless drifts of snow. It would be nearly New Year at home too, and everybody would be busy. I saw myself a child again, making a snowman with a group of children on the level ground in the back yard. The eyes of the snowman, made of jet-black fragments of coal, suddenly turned into Wei's eyes.

"I have to live a little longer." The same voice again.

"What for?" I asked inadvertently, aware immediately of the ineptitude of my remark.

「我……，我還得活幾天……。」

「那邊去看一看，一定竭力去設法罷。」

這是我當日一口承當的答話，後來常常自己聽見，眼前也同時浮出連殳的相貌，而且吞吞吐吐地說道「我還得活幾天。」到這些時，我便設法向各處推薦一番；但有甚麼效驗呢，事少人多，結果是別人給我幾句抱歉的話，我就給他幾句抱歉的信。到一學期將完的時候，那情形就更加壞了起來。那地方的幾個紳士所辦的《學理周報》上，竟開始攻擊我了，自然是決不指名的，但措辭很巧妙，使人一見就覺得我是在挑剔學潮，連推薦連殳的事，也算是呼朋引類。

我只好一動不動，除上課之外，便關起門來躲着，有時連煙卷的煙鑽出窗隙去，也怕犯了挑剔學潮的嫌疑。連殳的事，自然更是無從說起了。這樣地一直到深冬。

下了一天雪，到夜還沒有止，屋外一切靜極，靜到要聽出靜的聲音來。我在小小的燈火光中，閉目枯坐，如見雪花片片飄墜，來增補這一望無際的雪堆；故鄉也準備過年了，人們忙得很；我自己還是一個兒童，在後園的平坦處和一伙小朋友塑雪羅漢。雪羅漢的眼睛是用兩塊小炭嵌出來的，顏色很黑，這一閃動，便變了連殳的眼睛。

「我還得活幾天！」仍是這樣的聲音。

「為甚麼呢？」我無端地這樣問，立刻連自己也覺得可笑了。

It was this reply that woke me up. I sat up, lit a cigarette and opened the window, only to find the snow falling even faster. Then I heard a knock at the door, and a moment later it opened to admit the servant, whose step I knew. He handed me a big envelope, more than six inches in length. The address was scrawled, but I saw Wei's name on it.

This is the first letter he had written me since I left S—. Knowing he was a bad correspondent, I had not wondered at his silence, only sometimes I had felt he should have given me some news of himself. So the receipt of this letter was quite a surprise. I tore it open. The letter had been hastily scrawled, and said:

... Shenfei,

How should I address you? I am leaving a blank for you to fill in as you please. It will be all the same to me.

I have altogether received three letters from you. I did not reply for one simple reason: I had no money even to buy stamps.

Perhaps you would like to know what has happened to me. To put it simply: I have failed. I thought I had failed before, but I was wrong then; now, however, I am really a failure. Formerly there was someone who wanted me to live a little longer, and I wished it too, but found it difficult. Now, there is no need, yet I must go on living....

Shall I then live on?

The one who wanted me to live a little longer could not live himself. He was trapped and killed by the enemy. Who killed him? No one knows.

Changes take place so swiftly! During the last half year I have virtually been a beggar; it's true, I could be considered a beggar. However, I had my purpose: I was willing to beg for the cause, to

這可笑的問題使我清醒，坐直了身子，點起一枝煙卷來；推窗一望，雪果然下得更大了。聽得有人叩門；不一會，一個人走進來，但是聽熟的客寓雜役的腳步。他推開我的房門，交給我一封六寸多長的信，字跡很潦草，然而一瞥便認出「魏緘」兩個字，是連生寄來的。

這是從我離開S城以後他給我的第一封信。我知道他疏懶，本不以杳無消息為奇，但有時也頗怨他不給一點消息。待到接了這信，可又無端地覺得奇怪了，慌忙拆開來。裏面也用了一樣潦草的字體；寫着這樣的話：

「申飛……。

「我稱你甚麼呢？我空着。你自己願意稱甚麼，你自己添上去罷。我都可以的。

「別後共得三信，沒有覆。這原因很簡單：我連買郵票的錢也沒有。

「你或者願意知道些我的消息，現在簡直告訴你罷：我失敗了。先前，我自以為是失敗者，現在知道那並不，現在才真是失敗者了。先前，還有人願意我活幾天，我自己也還想活幾天的時候，活不下去；現在，大可以無須了，然而要活下去……。

「然而就活下去麼？

「願意我活幾天的，自己就活不下去。這人已被敵人誘殺了。誰殺的呢？誰也不知道。

「人生的變化多麼迅速呵！這半年來，我幾乎求乞了，實際，也可以算得已經求乞。然而我還有所為，我願意為此求

go cold and hungry for it, to be lonely for it, to suffer hardship for it. But I did not want to destroy myself. So you see, the fact that one person wanted me to live on proved extremely potent. But now there is no one, not one. At the same time I feel I do not deserve to live, nor do some other people either, in my opinion. Yet, I am conscious of wanting to live on to spite those who wish me dead; for at least there is no one left who wants me to live decently, and so no one can be hurt. I don't want to hurt such people. But now there is no one, not one. What a joy! Wonderful! I am now doing what I formerly detested and opposed. I am now giving up all I formerly believed in and upheld. I have really failed — but I have won.

Do you think I am mad? Do you think I have become a hero or a great man? No, it is not that, it is very simple; I have become adviser to General Du, hence I have eighty dollars salary a month.

... Shenfei,

What will you think of me? You decide; it is the same to me.

Perhaps you still remember my former sitting-room, the one in which we had our first and last talks. I am still using it. There are new guests, new bribes, new flattery, new seeking for promotion, new kowtows and bows, new mahjong and drinking games, new haughtiness and disgust, new sleeplessness and vomiting of blood....

You said in your last letter that your teaching was not going well. Would you like to be an adviser? Say the word, and I will arrange it for you. Actually, work in the gatehouse would be the same. There would be the same guests, bribes and flattery....

It is snowing heavily here. How is it where you are? It is now midnight, and having just vomited some blood has sobered me. I

乞，為此凍餒，為此寂寞，為此辛苦。但滅亡是不願意的。你看，有一個願意我活幾天的，那力量就這麼大。然而現在是沒有了，連這一個也沒有了。同時，我自己也覺得不配活下去；別人呢？也不配的。同時，我自己又覺得偏要為不願意我活下去的人們而活下去；好在願意我好好地活下去的已經沒有了，再沒有誰痛心。使這樣的人痛心，我是不願意的。然而現在是沒有了，連這一個也沒有了。快活極了，舒服極了；我已經躬行我先前所憎惡，所反對的一切，拒斥我先前所崇仰，所主張的一切了。我已經真的失敗，——然而我勝利了。

「你以為我發了瘋麼？你以為我成了英雄或偉人了麼？不，不的。這事情很簡單，我近來已經做了杜師長的顧問，每月的薪水就有現洋八十元了。

「申飛……。

「你將以我為甚麼東西呢，你自己定就是，我都可以的。

「你大約還記得我舊時的客廳罷，我們在城中初見和將別時候的客廳。現在我還用着這客廳。這裏有新的賓客，新的饋贈，新的頌揚，新的鑽營，新的磕頭和打拱，新的打牌和猜拳，新的冷眼和惡心，新的失眠和吐血……。

「你前信說你教書很不如意。你願意也做顧問麼？可以告訴我，我給你辦。其實是做門房也不妨，一樣地有新的賓客和新的饋贈，新的頌揚……。

「我這裏下大雪了。你那裏怎樣？現在已是深夜，吐了兩

recall that you have actually written three times in succession to me since autumn — amazing! So I must give you some news of myself, hoping you will not be shocked.

I probably shall not write again; you know my ways of old. When will you be back? If you come soon, we may meet again. Still, I suppose we have taken different roads, so you had better forget me. I thank you from the bottom of my heart for trying to find work for me. But now please forget me; I am doing "well."

Wei Lianshu

December 14th

Though this letter did not "shock " me, when, after a hasty perusal, I read it carefully again, I felt both uneasy and relieved. At least his livelihood was secure, and I need not worry any more. At any rate, I could do nothing here. I thought of writing to him, but felt there was nothing to say.

In fact, I was gradually forgetting him. His face no longer sprang so often to my mind's eye. However, less than ten days after hearing from him the office of the *S— Weekly* started sending me its paper. I did not read such papers as a rule, but since it was sent to me I glanced at some of the contents. And this reminded me of Wei, for the paper frequently carried poems and essays about him, such as "Calling on the Scholar Wei at Night During a Snowstorm," "A Poetic Gathering at the Scholarly Abode of Adviser Wei," and so forth. Once, indeed, under the heading "Table Talk," they retailed with gusto certain stories which had previously been considered material for ridicule, but which had now become "Tables of an Eccentric Genius." Only an exceptional man, it was implied, could have done such unusual things.

Although this recalled him to me, my impression of him was

口血，使我清醒起來。記得你竟從秋天以來陸續給了我三封信，這是怎樣的可以驚異的事呵。我必須寄給你一點消息，你或者不至於倒抽一口冷氣罷。

「此後，我大約不再寫信的了，我這習慣是你早已知道的。何時回來呢？倘早，當能相見。——但我想，我們大概究竟不是一路的；那麼，請你忘記我罷。我從我的真心感謝你先前常替我籌劃生計；但是現在忘記我罷；我現在已經『好』了。

連殳。

十二月十四日。」

這雖然並不使我「倒抽一口冷氣」，但草草一看之後，又細看了一遍，卻總有些不舒服，而同時可又夾雜些快意和高興；又想，他的生計總算已經不成問題，我的擔子也可以放下了，雖然在我這一面始終不過是無法可想。忽而又想寫一封信回答他，但又覺得沒有話說，於是這意思也立即消失了。

我的確漸漸地在忘卻他。在我的記憶中，他的面貌也不再時常出現。但得信之後不到十天，S城的學理七日報社忽然接續着郵寄他們的《學理七日報》來了。我是不大看這些東西的，不過既經寄到，也就隨手翻翻。這卻使我記起連殳來，因為裏面常有關於他的詩文，如《雪夜謁連殳先生》，《連殳顧問高齋雅集》等等；有一回，《學理閒譚》裏還津津地敘述他先前所被傳為笑柄的事，稱作「逸聞」，言外大有「且夫非常之人，必能行非常之事」的意思。

不知怎地雖然因此記起，但他的面貌卻總是逐漸模糊；然而又

growing fainter. Yet all the time he seemed to be gaining a closer hold on me, which often gave me an inexplicable sense of uneasiness and cast a shadow of apprehension. However, by autumn the newspaper stopped coming, while the Shanyang magazine began to publish the first instalment of a long essay called "The Element of Truth in Rumours," which asserted that rumours about certain gentlemen had reached the ears of the mighty. My name was among those attacked. I had then to be very careful. I had to take care that my cigarette smoke did not get in other people's way. All these precautions took so much time I could attend to nothing else, and naturally had no leisure to think of Wei. I had actually forgotten him.

However, I could not hold my job till summer. By the end of May I had left Shanyang.

V

I wandered between Shanyang, Licheng and Taigu for more than half a year, but could find no work, so I decided to go back to S— . I arrived one afternoon in early spring. It was a cloudy day with everything wrapped in mist. Since there were vacant rooms in my old hostel, I stayed there. On the road I had started thinking of Wei, and after my arrival I made up my mind to call on him after dinner. Taking two packages of the well-known Wenxi cakes, I threaded my way through several damp streets, stepping cautiously past many sleeping dogs, until I reached his door. It seemed very bright inside. I thought even his rooms were better lit since he had become an adviser, and smiled to myself. However, when I looked up, I saw a strip of white paper stuck on the door. It occurred to me, as I stepped inside, that the

似乎和我日加密切起來，往往無端感到一種連自己也莫明其妙的不安和極輕微的震顫。幸而到了秋季，這《學理七日報》就不寄來了；山陽的《學理周刊》上卻又按期登起一篇長論文：《流言即事實論》。裏面還說，關於某君們的流言，已在公正士紳間盛傳了。這是專指幾個人的，有我在內；我只好極小心，照例連吸煙卷的煙也謹防飛散。小心是一種忙的苦痛，因此會百事俱廢，自然也無暇記得連殳。總之：我其實已經將他忘卻了。

但我也終於敷衍不到暑假，五月底，便離開了山陽。

五

從山陽到歷城，又到太谷，一總轉了大半年，終於尋不出甚麼事情做，我便又決計回S城去了。到時是春初的下午，天氣欲雨不雨，一切都罩在灰色中；舊寓裏還有空房，仍然住下。

在道上，就想起連殳的了，到後，便決定晚飯後去看他。我提着兩包聞喜名產的煮餅，走了許多潮濕的路，讓道給許多攔路高臥的狗，這才總算到了連殳的門前。裏面彷彿特別明亮似的。我想，一做顧問，連寓裏也格外光亮起來了，不覺在暗中一笑。但仰面一看，門旁卻白白的，分明帖着一張斜角紙。我又想，大良們的祖母

children's grandmother might be dead; but I went straight in.

In the dimly lit courtyard there was a coffin, by which some soldier or orderly in uniform was standing, talking to the children's grandmother. A few workers in short coats were loitering there too. My heart began to beat faster. Just then she turned to look at me.

"Ah, you're back? Why didn't you come earlier?" she suddenly exclaimed.

"Who ... who has passed away?" actually by now I knew, but yet I asked.

"Adviser Wei died the day before yesterday."

I looked around. The sitting-room was dimly lit, probably by one lamp only; the front room, however, was decked with white funeral curtains, and the woman's grandchildren had gathered outside that room.

"His body is there," she said, coming forward and pointing to the front room. "After Mr. Wei was promoted, I let him my front room too; that is where he is now."

There was no writing on the funeral curtain. In front stood a long table, then a square table, spread with some dozen dishes. As I went in, two men in long white gowns suddenly appeared to bar the way, their eyes, like those of a dead fish, fixed in surprise and mistrust on my face. I hastily explained my relation with Wei, and the landlady came up to confirm my statement. Then their hands and eyes dropped, and they allowed me to go forward to bow to the dead.

As I bowed, a wail sounded beside me from the floor. Looking down I saw a child of about ten, kneeling on a mat, also dressed in white. His hair had been cut short, and had some hemp attached to it.

死了罷；同時也跨進門，一直向裏面走。

微光所照的院子裏，放着一具棺材，旁邊站一個穿軍衣的兵或是馬弁，還有一個和他談話的，看時卻是大良的祖母；另外還閒站着幾個短衣的粗人。我的心即刻跳起來了。她也轉過臉來凝視我。

「阿呀！您回來了？何不早幾天……。」她忽而大叫起來。

「誰……誰沒有了？」我其實是已經大概知道的了，但還是問。

「魏大人，前天沒有的。」

我四顧，客廳裏暗沉沉的，大約只有一盞燈；正屋裏卻掛着白的孝幃，幾個孩子聚在屋外，就是大良、二良們。

「他停在那裏，」大良的祖母走向前，指着說，「魏大人恭喜之後，我把正屋也租給他了；他現在就停在那裏。」

孝幃上沒有別的，前面是一張條桌，一張方桌；方桌上擺着十來碗飯菜。我剛跨進門，當面忽然現出兩個穿白長衫的來攔住了，瞪了死魚似的眼睛，從中發出驚疑的光來，釘住了我的臉。我慌忙說明我和連殳的關係，大良的祖母也來從旁證實；他們的手和眼光這才逐漸弛緩下去，默許我近前去鞠躬。

我一鞠躬，地下忽然有人嗚嗚的哭起來了，定神看時，一個十多歲的孩子伏在草薦上，也是白衣服，頭髮剪得很光的頭上還絡着一大綹苧麻絲。

Later I found out that one of these men was Wei's cousin, his nearest in kin, while the other was a distant nephew. I asked to be allowed to see Wei, but they tried their best to dissuade me, saying I was too "polite." Finally they gave in, and lifted the curtain.

This time I saw Wei in death. But, strangely enough, though he was wearing a crumpled shirt, stained in front with blood, and his face was very lean, his expression was unchanged. He was sleeping so placidly, with closed mouth and eyes, that I was tempted to put my finger before his nostrils to see if he were still breathing.

Everything was deathly still, both the living and the dead. As I withdrew, his cousin accosted me to state that Wei's untimely death, just when he was in the prime of life and had a great future before him was not only a calamity for his humble family but a cause of sorrow for his friends. He seemed to be apologizing for Wei for dying. Such eloquence is rare among villagers. However, after that he fell silent again, and everything was deathly still, both the living and the dead.

Feeling cheerless, but by no means sad, I withdrew to the courtyard to chat with the old woman. She told me the funeral would soon take place; they were waiting for the shroud. And when the coffin was nailed down, people born under certain stars should not be near. She rattled on, her words pouring out like a flood. She spoke of Wei's illness, incidents during his life, and even voiced certain criticisms.

"You know, after Mr. Wei came into luck, he was a different man. He held his head high and looked very haughty. He stopped treating people in his old pedantic way. Did you know, he used to act like an idiot, and call me madam? Later on," she chuckled, "he called me 'old bitch'; it was too funny for words. When people sent him rare herbs like atractylis, instead of eating them himself, he would throw them into the courtyard, just here, and call out, 'You take this, old bitch!' After he came into luck, he had scores of visitors; so I vacated my

我和他們寒暄後，知道一個是連殳的從堂兄弟，要算最親的了；一個是遠房侄子。我請求看一看故人，他們卻竭力攔阻，說是「不敢當」的。然而終於被我説服了，將孝幃揭起。

這回我會見了死的連殳。但是奇怪！雖然穿一套皺的短衫褲，大襟上還有血跡，臉上也瘦削得不堪，然而面目卻還是先前那樣的面目，寧靜地閉着嘴，合着眼，睡着似的，幾乎要使我伸手到他鼻子前面，去試探他可是其實還在呼吸着。

一切是死一般靜，死的人和活的人。我退開了，他的從堂兄弟卻又來周旋，説「舍弟」正在年富力強，前程無限的時候，竟遽爾「作古」了，這不但是「衰宗」不幸，也太使朋友傷心。言外頗有替連殳道歉之意；這樣地能説，在山鄉中人是少有的。但此後也就沉默了，一切是死一般靜，死的人和活的人。

我覺得很無聊，怎樣的悲哀倒沒有，便退到院子裏，和大良們的祖母閒談起來。知道入殮的時候是臨近了，只待壽衣送到；釘棺材釘時，「子午卯酉」四生肖是必須躲避的。她談得高興了，説話滔滔地泉流似的湧出，說到他的病狀，説到他生時的情景，也帶些關於他的批評。

「你可知道魏大人自從交運之後，人就和先前兩樣了，臉也抬高起來，氣昂昂的。對人也不再先前那麼迂。你知道，他先前不是像一個啞子，見我是叫老太太的麼？後來就叫『老傢伙』。唉唉，真是有趣。人送他仙居术，他自己是不吃的，就摔在院子裏，——就是這地方，——叫道，『老傢伙，你吃去罷。』他交運之後，人來人

front room for him and moved into a side one. As we have always said jokingly, he became a different man after his good luck. If you had come one month earlier, you could have seen all the fun here: drinking games practically every day, talking, laughing, singing, poetry writing and mahjong games....

"He used to be more afraid of children than they are of their own father, practically grovelling to them. But recently that changed too, and he was a good one for jokes. My grandchildren liked to play with him, and would go to his rooms whenever they could. He would think up all sorts of practical jokes. For instance, when they wanted him to buy things for them, he would make them bark like dogs or make a thumping kowtow. Ah, that was fun. Two months ago, my second grandchild asked him to buy him a pair of shoes, and had to make three thumping kowtows. He's still wearing them; they aren't worn out yet."

When one of the men in white came out, she stopped talking. I asked about Wei's illness, but there was little she could tell me. She knew only that he had been losing weight for a long time, but they had thought nothing of it because he always looked so cheerful. About a month before, they heard he had been coughing blood, but it seemed he had not seen a doctor. Then he had to stay in bed, and three days before he died he seemed to have lost the power of speech. His cousin had come all the way from the village to ask him if he had any savings, but he said not a word. His cousin thought he was shamming, but some people had said those dying of consumption did lose the power of speech....

"But Mr. Wei was a queer man," she suddenly whispered. "He never saved money, always spent it like water. His cousin still suspects we got something out of him. Heaven knows, we got nothing. He just spent it in his haphazard way. Buying something today, selling it tomorrow, or breaking it up — God knows what happened. When he died there was nothing left, all spent! Otherwise it would not be so dismal today...."

往，我把正屋也讓給他住了，自己便搬在這廂房裏。他也真是一走紅運，就與眾不同，我們就常常這樣說笑。要是你早來一個月，還趕得上看這裏的熱鬧，三日兩頭的猜拳行令，說的說，笑的笑，唱的唱，做詩的做詩，打牌的打牌……。

「他先前怕孩子們比孩子們見老子還怕，總是低聲下氣的。近來可也兩樣了，能說能鬧，我們的大良們也很喜歡和他玩，一有空，便都到他的屋裏去。他也用種種方法逗着玩；要他買東西，他就要孩子裝一聲狗叫，或者磕一個響頭。哈哈，真是過得熱鬧。前兩月二良要他買鞋，還磕了三個響頭哩，哪，現在還穿着，沒有破呢。」

一個穿白長衫的人出來了，她就住了口。我打聽連殳的病症，她卻不大清楚，只說大約是早已瘦了下去的罷，可是誰也沒理會，因為他總是高高興興的。到一個多月前，這才聽到他吐過幾回血，但似乎也沒有看醫生；後來躺倒了；死去的前三天，就啞了喉嚨，說不出一句話。十三大人從寒石山路遠迢迢地上城來，問他可有存款，他一聲也不響。十三大人疑心他裝出來的，也有人說有些生癆病死的人是要說不出話來的，誰知道呢……。

「可是魏大人的脾氣也太古怪，」她忽然低聲說，「他就不肯積蓄一點，水似的化錢。十三大人還疑心我們得了甚麼好處。有甚麼屁好處呢？他就冤裏冤枉糊裏糊塗地化掉了。譬如買東西；今天買進，明天又賣出，弄破，真不知道是怎麼一回事。待到死了下來，甚麼也沒有，都糟掉了。要不然，今天也不至於這樣地冷靜……。

"He just fooled about, not wanting to do the proper thing. I had thought of that, and spoken to him. At his age, he should have got married; it would have been easy for him then. And if no suitable family could be found, at least he could have bought a few concubines to go on with. People should keep up appearances. But he would laugh whenever I brought it up. 'Old bitch, you are always worrying about such things for other people,' he would say. He was never serious, you see; he wouldn't listen to good advice. If he had listened to me, he wouldn't be wandering lonely in the nether world now; at least there would be wailing from his dear ones...."

A shop assistant arrived, bringing some clothes with him. The three relatives of the dead picked out the underwear, then disappeared behind the curtain. Soon, the curtain was lifted; the new underwear had been put on the corpse, and they proceeded to put on his outer garments. I was surprised to see them dress him in a pair of khaki military trousers with broad red stripes, and a tunic with glittering epaulettes. I could not say what rank these indicated, or how he acquired it. Then the body was placed in the coffin. Wei lay there awkwardly, a pair of brown leather shoes beside his feet, a paper sword at his waist, and beside his lean and ashen face a military cap with a gilt band.

The three relatives wailed beside the coffin, then stopped and wiped their tears. The boy with hemp attached to his hair withdrew, as did the old woman's third grandchild — no doubt they had been born under the wrong stars.

As the labourers lifted the coffin lid, I stepped forward to see Wei for the last time.

In his awkward costume he lay placidly, with closed mouth and eyes. There seemed to be an ironical smile on his lips, mocking the ridiculous corpse.

「他就是胡鬧,不想辦一點正經事。我是想到過的,也勸過他。這麼年紀了,應該成家;照現在的樣子,結一門親很容易;如果沒有門當戶對的,先買幾個姨太太也可以:人是總應該像個樣子的。可是他一聽到就笑起來,說道,『老傢伙,你還是總替別人惦記着這等事麼?』你看,他近來就浮而不實,不把人的好話當好話聽。要是早聽了我的話,現在何至於獨自冷清清地在陰間摸索,至少,也可以聽到幾聲親人的哭聲……。」

一個店伙背了衣服來了。三個親人便檢出裏衣,走進幃後去。不多久,孝幃揭起了,裏衣已經換好,接着是加外衣。這很出我意外。一條土黃的軍褲穿上了,嵌着很寬的紅條,其次穿上去的是軍衣,金閃閃的肩章,也不知道是甚麼品級,那裏來的品級。到入棺,是連殳很不妥帖地躺着,腳邊放一雙黃皮鞋,腰邊放一柄紙糊的指揮刀,骨瘦如柴的灰黑的臉旁,是一頂金邊的軍帽。

三個親人扶着棺沿哭了一場,止哭拭淚;頭上絡麻線的孩子退出去了,三良也避去,大約都是屬「子午卯酉」之一的。

粗人扛起棺蓋來,我走近去最後看一看永別的連殳。

他在不妥帖的衣冠中,安靜地躺着,合了眼,閉着嘴,口角間彷彿含着冰冷的微笑,冷笑着這可笑的死屍。

When the nails began to be hammered in, the wailing started afresh. I could not stand it very long, so withdrew to the courtyard; then, somehow, I was out of the gate. The damp road glistened, and I looked up at the sky where the cloud banks had scattered and a full moon hung, shedding a cool light.

I walked with quickened steps, as if eager to break through some heavy barrier, but finding it impossible. Something struggled in my ears, and, after a long, long time, burst out. It was like a long howl, the howl of a wounded wolf crying in the wilderness in the depth of night, anger and sorrow mingled in its agony.

Then my heart felt lighter, and I paced calmly on along the damp cobbled road under the moon.

October 17, 1925

　　敲釘的聲音一響，哭聲也同時迸出來。這哭聲使我不能聽完，只好退到院子裏；順腳一走，不覺出了大門了。潮濕的路極其分明；仰看太空，濃雲已經散去，掛着一輪圓月，散出冷靜的光輝。

　　我快步走着，彷彿要從一種沉重的東西中衝出，但是不能夠。耳朵中有甚麼掙扎着，久之，久之，終於掙扎出來了，隱約像是長嗥，像一匹受傷的狼，當深夜在曠野中嗥叫，慘傷裏夾雜着憤怒和悲哀。

　　我的心地就輕鬆起來，坦然地在潮濕的石路上走，月光底下。

　　　　　　　　　　　　　　一九二五年十月十七日畢。

傷 逝

Regret for the Past

REGRET FOR THE PAST

Juansheng's Notes

I want, if I can, to record my remorse and grief, for Zijun's sake as well as for my own.

How silent and empty it is, this shabby room in a forgotten corner of the hostel. Time certainly flies. A whole year has passed since I fell in love with Zijun and, thanks to her, escaped from this silence and emptiness. On my return here, as ill luck would have it, this was the only room vacant. The broken window with the half-withered locust tree and old wistaria outside it and the square table in front of it are unchanged. Unchanged too are the mouldering wall and wooden bed beside it. At night I lie alone, just as I did before living with Zijun. The past year has been blotted out as if it had never been, as if I had never moved out of this shabby room to set up house, in a small way but with high hopes, in Lucky Lane.

Nor is that all. A year ago there was a difference in this silence and emptiness for it held expectancy, the expectancy of Zijun's arrival. The tapping of high heels on the brick pavement, cutting into my long, restless waiting, would galvanize me into life. Then I would see her pale round face dimpling in a smile, her thin white arms, striped cotton blouse and black skirt. And she would bring in to show me a new leaf from the half-withered locust tree outside the window, or clusters of the mauve

傷　　逝

——涓生的手記

如果我能夠，我要寫下我的悔恨和悲哀，為子君，為自己。

會館裏的被遺忘在偏僻裏的破屋是這樣地寂靜和空虛。時光過得真快，我愛子君，仗着她逃出這寂靜和空虛已經滿一年了。事情又這麼不湊巧，我重來時，偏偏空着的又只有這一間屋。依然是這樣的破窗，這樣的窗外的半枯的槐樹和老紫藤，這樣的窗前的方桌，這樣的敗壁，這樣的靠壁的板床。深夜中獨自躺在床上，就如我未曾和子君同居以前一般，過去一年中的時光全被消滅，全未有過，我並沒有曾經從這破屋子搬出，在吉兆胡同創立了滿懷希望的小小的家庭。

不但如此。在一年之前，這寂靜和空虛是並不這樣的，常常含着期待；期待子君的到來。在久待的焦躁中，一聽到皮鞋的高底尖觸着磚路的清響，是怎樣地使我驟然生動起來呵！於是就看見帶着笑渦的蒼白的圓臉，蒼白的瘦的臂膊，布的有條紋的衫子，玄色的裙。她又帶了窗外的半枯的槐樹的新葉來，使我看見，還有掛在鐵

wistaria flowers that hung from a vine which looked as if made of iron.

But now there is only silence and emptiness. Zijun will never come back — never, never again.

When Zijun was not here, I could see nothing in this shabby room. Out of sheer boredom I would pick up a book — science or literature, it was all the same to me — and read on and on till it suddenly dawned on me that I had turned a dozen pages without taking in a word. My sense of hearing, however, was so acute that I seemed able to hear all the footsteps outside the gate, including those of Zijun, gradually approaching — but all too often they faded away again to be lost at last in the medley of other footfalls. I hated the steward's son who wore cloth-soled shoes which sounded quite different from those of Zijun. I hated the little wretch next door who used face-cream, often wore new leather shoes, and whose steps sounded all too like those of Zijun.

Could her rickshaw have been upset? Could she have been run over by a tram?...

I would want to put on my hat to go and find her, but her uncle had cursed me to my face.

Then, abruptly, I would hear her draw nearer, step by step, so that by the time I went out to meet her she would already have passed the wistaria trellis, her face dimpling in a smile. Probably she wasn't badly treated after all in her uncle's home. I would calm down and, after we had gazed at each other in silence for a moment, the shabby room would gradually be filled with the sound of my pronouncements on the tyranny of the family, the need to break with tradition, the equality of men and women, Ibsen, Tagore and Shelley.... She would nod her head, smiling, her eyes filled with a childlike look of wonder. On the wall was pinned a copper-plate reproduction of a bust of Shelley, cut out from a magazine. It was one of the best-looking likenesses of

似的老幹上的一房一房的紫白的藤花。

然而現在呢，只有寂靜和空虛依舊，子君卻決不再來了，而且永遠，永遠地！……

子君不在我這破屋裏時，我甚麼也看不見。在百無聊賴中，隨手抓過一本書來，科學也好，文學也好，橫豎甚麼都一樣；看下去，看下去，忽而自己覺得，已經翻了十多頁了，但是毫不記得書上所說的事。只是耳朵卻分外地靈，彷彿聽到大門外一切往來的履聲，從中便有子君的，而且橐橐地逐漸臨近，——但是，往往又逐漸渺茫，終於消失在別的步聲的雜沓中了。我憎惡那不像子君鞋聲的穿布底鞋的長班的兒子，我憎惡那太像子君鞋聲的常常穿着新皮鞋的鄰院的搽雪花膏的小東西！

莫非她翻了車麼？莫非她被電車撞傷了麼？……

我便要取了帽子去看她，然而她的胞叔就曾經當面罵過我。

驀然，她的鞋聲近來了，一步響於一步，迎出去時，卻已經走過紫藤棚下，臉上帶着微笑的酒窩。她在她叔子的家裏大約並未受氣；我的心寧帖了，默默地相視片時之後，破屋裏便漸漸充滿了我的語聲，談家庭專制，談打破舊習慣，談男女平等，談伊孛生，談泰戈爾，談雪萊……。她總是微笑點頭，兩眼裏瀰漫着稚氣的好奇的光澤。壁上就釘着一張銅板的雪萊半身像，是從雜誌上裁下來

him, but when I pointed it out to her she only gave it a hasty glance, then hung her head as if in embarrassment. In matters like this, Zijun had probably not freed herself completely from the trammels of old ideas. It occurred to me later that it might be better to substitute a picture of Shelley drowning at sea, or a portrait of Ibsen. But I never got round to it. And now even this print has vanished.

"I'm my own mistress. None of them has any right to interfere with me."

She came out with this statement clearly, firmly and gravely after a thoughtful silence, following a conversation about her uncle who was here and her father in the country. We had known each other then for half a year. By that time I had told her all my views, all about myself, and what my failings were. I had hidden very little, and she understood me completely. These few words of hers stirred me to the bottom of my heart and rang in my ears for many days afterwards. I was unspeakably happy to know that Chinese women were not as hopeless as the pessimists made out, and that we should see in the not too distant future the splendour of the dawn.

Each time I saw her out, I kept several paces behind her. And each time the old wretch's face, bewhiskered as if with fish tentacles, would be pressed so hard against the dirty window-pane that the tip of his nose was flattened. And each time we reached the outer courtyard, against the bright glass window there was the little wretch's face, plastered with facecream. But looking neither right nor left as she walked proudly out, she did not see them. And I walked proudly back.

"I'm my own mistress. None of them has any right to interfere with me." Her mind was completely made up on this point. She was by far the more thoroughgoing and resolute of the two of us. What

的，是他的最美的一張像。當我指給她看時，她卻只草草一看，便低了頭，似乎不好意思了。這些地方，子君就大概還未脫盡舊思想的束縛，——我後來也想，倒不如換一張雪萊淹死在海裏的記念像或是伊孛生的罷；但也終於沒有換，現在是連這一張也不知那裏去了。

「我是我自己的，他們誰也沒有干涉我的權利！」

這是我們交際了半年，又談起她在這裏的胞叔和在家的父親時，她默想了一會之後，分明地，堅決地，沉靜地說了出來的話。其時是我已經說盡了我的意見，我的身世，我的缺點，很少隱瞞；她也完全了解的了。這幾句話很震動了我的靈魂，此後許多天還在耳中發響，而且說不出的狂喜，知道中國女性，並不如厭世家所說那樣的無法可施，在不遠的將來，便要看見輝煌的曙色的。

送她出門，照例是相離十多步遠；照例是那鮎魚鬚的老東西的臉又緊帖在髒的窗玻璃上了，連鼻尖都擠成一個小平面；到外院，照例又是明晃晃的玻璃窗裏的那小東西的臉，加厚的雪花膏。她目不邪視地驕傲地走了，沒有看見；我驕傲地回來。

「我是我自己的，他們誰也沒有干涉我的權利！」這徹底的思想就在她的腦裏，比我還透澈，堅強得多。半瓶雪花膏和鼻尖的小平

did she care about the half pot of facecream or the flattened nose tip?

I cannot remember clearly how I expressed my true, passionate love for her. Not only now: my impression just after the event itself was hazy. Thinking back that night, I recollected only a few disjointed scraps; while a month or two after we started living together, even these vanished like dreams without a trace. All I can remember is that for about a fortnight beforehand I had considered very carefully what attitude to take, how to make my declaration, and how to behave if turned down. But when the time came it was all in vain. In my nervousness, something constrained me to use a method seen in films. The thought of this makes me thoroughly ashamed, yet it is the only thing I remember clearly. Even today it is like a solitary lamp in a dark room, showing me clasping her hand with tears in my eyes and going down on one knee....

At the time I did not even notice Zijun's reaction clearly. All I knew was that she accepted my proposal. However, I seem to remember that her face first turned pale then gradually flushed red, redder than I ever saw it before or after. Sadness and joy mingled with apprehension flashed from her childlike eyes, although she tried to avoid my gaze, looking ready in her confusion to fly out of the window. Then I knew she accepted my proposal, although not knowing what she said or whether she said anything at all.

She, however, remembered everything. She could reel off the speech I made as if she had learned it by heart. She described my conduct in detail, to the life, like a film unfolding itself before her eyes, including of course that trashy scene from the movies which I was only too anxious to forget. The night, when all was still, was our time for review. I was often interrogated and examined, or ordered to repeat everything said on that occasion; yet she often had to fill in gaps

面，於她能算甚麼東西呢？

　　我已經記不清那時怎樣地將我的純真熱烈的愛表示給她。豈但現在，那時的事後便已模糊，夜間回想，早只剩了一些斷片了；同居以後一兩月，便連這些斷片也化作無可追蹤的夢影。我只記得那時以前的十幾天，曾經很仔細地研究過表示的態度，排列過措辭的先後，以及倘或遭了拒絕以後的情形。可是臨時似乎都無用，在慌張中，身不由己地竟用了在電影上見過的方法了。後來一想到，就使我很愧恧，但在記憶上卻偏只有這一點永遠留遺，至今還如暗室的孤燈一般，照見我含淚握着她的手，一條腿跪了下去……。

　　不但我自己的，便是子君的言語舉動，我那時就沒有看得分明；僅知道她已經允許我了。但也還彷彿記得她臉色變成青白，後來又漸漸轉作緋紅，──沒有見過，也沒有再見的緋紅；孩子似的眼裏射出悲喜，但是夾着驚疑的光，雖然力避我的視線，張皇地似乎要破窗飛去。然而我知道她已經允許我了，沒有知道她怎樣説或是沒有説。

　　她卻是甚麼都記得：我的言辭，竟至於讀熟了的一般，能夠滔滔背誦；我的舉動，就如有一張我所看不見的影片掛在眼下，敘述得如生，很細微，自然連那使我不願再想的淺薄的電影的一閃。夜闌人靜，是相對溫習的時候了，我常是被質問，被考驗，並且被命覆述當時的言語，然而常須由她補足，由她糾正，像一個丁等的學生。

and correct my mistakes as if I were a Grade D student.

Gradually these reviews became few and far between. But whenever I saw her gazing raptly into space, a tender look dawning on her dimpling face, I knew she was going over that old lesson again and feared she was visualizing my ridiculous act from the movies. I knew, though, that she must be visualizing it, that she insisted on visualizing it.

But she didn't find it ridiculous. Though I thought it laughable, even contemptible, to her it was no joke. And I knew this beyond a doubt because of her true, passionate love for me.

Late spring last year was our happiest and also our busiest time. I had calmed down by then, although bestirring my mental faculties in step with my physical activity. This was when we started walking side by side in the street. We went several times to the park, but most of our outings were in search of lodgings. On the road I was conscious of searching looks, sarcastic smiles or lewd and contemptuous glances which unless I was on my guard set me shivering, so that at every instant I had to summon all my pride and defiance to my support. She, however, was completely fearless and impervious to all this. She continued slowly and calmly on her way, as if there were no one in sight.

It was no easy matter finding lodgings. In most cases we were refused on some pretext or other, while we ourselves turned down a few places as unsuitable. To start with we were very particular — and yet not too particular either, because we saw that most of these lodgings did not look the sort of place where we could live. Later on, all we asked was to be tolerated. We had looked at over twenty places before we found one we could make do: two rooms with a northern exposure in a small house in Lucky Lane. The owner was a petty official but an intelligent man, who occupied only the central and the side

這溫習後來也漸漸稀疏起來。但我只要看見她兩眼注視空中，出神似的凝想着，於是神色越加柔和，笑窩也深下去，便知道她又在自修舊課了，只是我很怕她看到我那可笑的電影的一閃。但我又知道，她一定要看見，而且也非看不可的。

然而她並不覺得可笑。即使我自己以為可笑，甚而至於可鄙的，她也毫不以為可笑。這事我知道得很清楚，因為她愛我。是這樣地熱烈，這樣地純真。

去年的暮春是最為幸福，也是最為忙碌的時光。我的心平靜下去了，但又有別一部分和身體一同忙碌起來。我們這時才在路上同行，也到過幾回公園，最多的是尋住所。我覺得在路上時時遇到探索，譏笑，猥褻和輕蔑的眼光，一不小心，便使我的全身有些瑟縮，只得即刻提起我的驕傲和反抗來支持。她卻是大無畏的，對於這些全不關心，只是鎮靜地緩緩前行，坦然如入無人之境。

尋住所實在不是容易事，大半是被託辭拒絕，小半是我們以為不相宜。起先我們選擇得很苛酷，——也非苛酷，因為看去大抵不像是我們的安身之所；後來，便只要他們能相容了。看了二十多處，這才得到可以暫且敷衍的處所，是吉兆胡同一所小屋裏的兩間南屋；主人是一個小官，然而倒是明白人，自住着正屋和廂房。他

rooms. His household consisted simply of a wife, a baby girl not yet one year old, and a maidservant from the country. As long as the child didn't cry, it would be very quiet.

Our furniture, simple as it was, had already taken the greater part of the money I had raised; and Zijun had sold her only gold ring and earrings too. I tried to stop her, but when she insisted I didn't press the point. I knew that unless allowed to make a small investment in our home she would feel uncomfortable.

She had already quarrelled with her uncle, so enraging him in fact that he had disowned her. And I had broken with several friends who thought they were giving me good advice but were actually either afraid for me, or jealous. Still, this meant we were very quiet. Although it was getting on for dusk when I left the office and the rickshaw man always went slowly, at last the time came when we were together again. First we would look at each other in silence, then relax and talk intimately, and finally fall silent again. We both bowed our heads pensively then, without anything particular in mind. Little by little, body and soul alike, she became an open book to me. In the short space of three weeks I learned more about her, overcoming many impediments which I had fancied I understood but now discovered to have been real barriers.

As the days passed, Zijun became more lively. She had no liking for flowers though, and when I bought two pots of flowers at the market she left them unwatered for four days so that they died neglected in a corner. I hadn't the time to see to everything. She had a liking for animals, however, which she may have picked up from the official's wife; and in less than a month our household was greatly increased as four chicks of ours started picking their way across the courtyard with the landlady's dozen. But the two mistresses could tell them apart, each able to identify her own. Then there was a spotted

只有夫人和一個不到周歲的女孩子，僱一個鄉下的女工，只要孩子不啼哭，是極其安閒幽靜的。

我們的傢俱很簡單，但已經用去了我的籌來的款子的大半；子君還賣掉了她唯一的金戒指和耳環。我攔阻她，還是定要賣，我也就不再堅持下去了；我知道不給她加入一點股分去，她是住不舒服的。

和她的叔子，她早經鬧開，至於使他氣憤到不再認她做侄女；我也陸續和幾個自以為忠告，其實是替我膽怯，或者竟是嫉妒的朋友絕了交，然而這倒很清靜。每日辦公散後，雖然已近黃昏，車伕又一定走得這樣慢，但究竟還有二人相對的時候。我們先是沉默的相視，接着是放懷而親密的交談，後來又是沉默。大家低頭沉思着，卻並未想着甚麼事。我也漸漸清醒地讀遍了她的身體，她的靈魂，不過三星期，我似乎於她已經更加了解，揭去許多先前以為了解而現在看來卻是隔膜，即所謂真的隔膜了。

子君也逐日活潑起來。但她並不愛花，我在廟會時買來的兩盆小草花，四天不澆，枯死在壁角了，我又沒有照顧一切的閒暇。然而她愛動物，也許是從官太太那裏傳染的罷，不一月，我們的眷屬便驟然加得很多，四隻小油雞，在小院子裏和房主人的十多隻在一同走。但她們卻認識雞的相貌，各知道那一隻是自家的。還有一隻

peke, bought at the market. I believe he had a name of his own to begin with, but Zijun gave him another one — Asui. And I called him Asui too, though I didn't like the name.

It is true that love must be constantly renewed, must grow and create. When I spoke of this to Zijun, she nodded understandingly.

Ah, what peaceful, happy evenings those were!

Tranquillity and happiness will grow stale if unchanged, unrenewed. While in the hostel, we had occasional differences of opinion or misunderstandings; but even these vanished after we moved to Lucky Lane. We just sat facing each other in the lamplight, reminiscing, savouring again the joy of the new harmony which had followed our disputes.

Zijun grew plumper, her cheeks became rosier; the only pity was that she was too busy. Housekeeping left her no time even to chat, much less to read or go for walks. We often said we would have to get a maid.

Another thing that upset me on my return in the evening was her covert look of unhappiness, or the forced smile which depressed me even more. Luckily I discovered that this was owing to her secret feud with the petty official's wife, the bone of contention being the two families' chicks. But why wouldn't she tell me outright? People ought to have a home of their own. A lodging of this kind was no place to live in.

I had my routine too. Six days of the week I went from home to the bureau and from the bureau home. In the office I sat at my desk copying, copying endless official documents and letters. At home I kept her company or helped her light the stove, boil rice or steam rolls. This was when I learned to cook.

花白的叭兒狗，從廟會買來，記得似乎原有名字，子君卻給它另起了一個，叫作阿隨。我就叫它阿隨，但我不喜歡這名字。

這是真的，愛情必須時時更新，生長，創造。我和子君說起這，她也領會地點點頭。

唉唉。那是怎樣的寧靜而幸福的夜呵！

安寧和幸福是要凝固的，永久是這樣的安寧和幸福。我們在會館裏時，還偶有議論的衝突和意思的誤會，自從到吉兆胡同以來，連這一點也沒有了；我們只在燈下對坐的懷舊譚中，回味那時衝突以後的和解的重生一般的樂趣。

子君竟胖了起來，臉色也紅活了；可惜的是忙。管了家務便連談天的工夫也沒有，何況讀書和散步。我們常說，我們總還得僱一個女工。

這就使我也一樣地不快活，傍晚回來，常見她包藏着不快活的顏色，尤其使我不樂的是她要裝作勉強的笑容。幸而探聽出來了，也還是和那小官太太的暗鬥，導火線便是兩家的小油雞。但又何必硬不告訴我呢？人總該有一個獨立的家庭。這樣的處所，是不能居住的。

我的路也鑄定了，每星期中的六天，是由家到局，又由局到家。在局裏便坐在辦公桌前鈔，鈔，鈔些公文和信件；在家裏是和她相對或幫她生白爐子，煮飯，蒸饅頭。我的學會了煮飯，就在這時候。

Still, I ate much better here than in the hostel. Although cooking was not Zijun't forte, she threw herself into it heart and soul. Her ceaseless anxieties on this score made me anxious too, and in this way we shared the sweet and the bitter together. She kept at it so hard all day, perspiration made her short hair cling to her brows, and her hands began to grow rough.

And then she had to feed Asui and the chicks.... No one else could do this chore.

I told her I would rather go without food than see her work herself to the bone like this. She just glanced at me without a word, looking rather wistful, so that I couldn't very well say any more. But she went on working as hard as ever.

Finally the blow I had been expecting fell. The evening before the Double Tenth Festival, I was sitting idle while she washed the dishes when we heard a knock on the door. When I opened it, the messenger from our bureau handed me a mimeographed slip of paper. I had a good idea what it was and, when I took it to the lamp, sure enough it read:

> By order of the commissioner, Shi Juansheng is discharged.
>
> The secretariat, October 9th

I had foreseen this while we were still in the hostel. Face-Cream, being one of the gambling friends of the commissioner's son, was bound to have spread rumours and tried to make trouble. I was only surprised that this hadn't happened sooner. In fact this was really no blow, because I had already decided that I could work as a clerk somewhere else or teach, or even, though it was more difficult, do some translation work. I knew the editor of *Freedom's Friend,* and had corresponded with him a couple of months previously. But all the same,

　　但我的食品卻比在會館裏時好得多了。做菜雖不是子君的特長，然而她於此卻傾注着全力；對於她的日夜的操心，使我也不能不一同操心，來算作分甘共苦。況且她又這樣地終日汗流滿面，短髮都粘在腦額上；兩隻手又只是這樣地粗糙起來。

　　況且還要飼阿隨，飼油雞，……都是非她不可的工作。

　　我曾經忠告她：我不吃，倒也罷了；卻萬不可這樣地操勞。她只看了我一眼，不開口，神色卻似乎有點淒然；我也只好不開口。然而她還是這樣地操勞。

　　我所預期的打擊果然到來。雙十節的前一晚，我呆坐着，她在洗碗。聽到打門聲，我去開門時，是局裏的信差，交給我一張油印的約條。我就有些料到了，到燈下去一看，果然，印着的就是：

奉
局長諭史涓生着毋庸到局辦事
　　　　　　　　　　　　　　秘書處啟　十月九號

　　這在會館裏時，我就早已料到了；那雪花膏便是局長的兒子的賭友，一定要去添些謠言，設法報告的。到現在才發生效驗，已經要算是很晚的了。其實這在我不能算是一個打擊，因為我早就決定，可以給別人去鈔寫，或者教讀，或者雖然費力，也還可以譯點書，況且《自由之友》的總編輯便是見過幾次的熟人，兩月前還通過

my heart was thumping. What distressed me most was that even Zijun, fearless as she was, had turned pale. Recently she seemed to be weaker, more faint-hearted.

"What does it matter?" she said. "We can make a fresh start. We...."

Her voice trailed off and to my ears, it failed to carry conviction. The lamplight, too, seemed unusually dim. Men are really ludicrous creatures, so easily upset by trifles. First we gazed at each other in silence, then started discussing what to do. Finally we decided to live as economically as possible on the money we had, to advertise in the paper for a post as clerk or teacher, and to write at the same time to the editor of *Freedom's Friend* explaining my present situation and asking him to accept a translation from me to help tide me over this difficult period.

"Suit the action to the word! Let's make a fresh start."

I went straight to the table and pushed aside the bottle of sesame oil and saucer of vinegar, while Zijun brought over the dim lamp. First I drew up the advertisement; then I made a selection of books to translate. I hadn't looked at my books since we moved house, and each volume was thick with dust. Last of all I wrote the letter.

I hesitated for a long time over the wording of the letter. When I stopped writing to think, and glanced at her in the dusky lamplight, she was looking very wistful again. I had never imagined a trifle like this could cause such a striking change in someone so firm and fearless as Zijun. She really had grown much weaker lately; this wasn't something that had just started that evening. More put out than ever, I had a sudden vision of a peaceful life — the quiet of my shabby room in the hostel flashed before my eyes, and I was just about to take a good look at it when I found myself back in the dusky lamplight again.

It took me a long time to finished the letter, a very lengthy letter.

信。但我的心卻跳躍着。那麼一個無畏的子君也變了色，尤其使我痛心；她近來似乎也較為怯弱了。

「那算甚麼。哼，我們幹新的。我們……。」她說。

她的話沒有說完；不知怎地，那聲音在我聽去卻只是浮浮的；燈光也覺得格外黯淡。人們真是可笑的動物，一點極微末的小事情，便會受着很深的影響。我們先是默默地相視，逐漸商量起來，終於決定將現有的錢竭力節省，一面登「小廣告」去尋求鈔寫和教讀，一面寫信給《自由之友》的總編輯，說明我目下的遭遇，請他收用我的譯本，給我幫一點艱辛時候的忙。

說做，就做罷！來開一條新的路！

我立刻轉身向了書案，推開盛香油的瓶子和醋碟，子君便送過那黯淡的燈來。我先擬廣告；其次是選定可譯的書，遷移以來未曾翻閱過，每本的頭上都滿漫着灰塵了；最後才寫信。

我很費躊躕，不知道怎樣措辭好，當停筆凝思的時候，轉眼去一瞥她的臉，在昏暗的燈光下，又很見得凄然。我真不料這樣微細的小事情，竟會給堅決的，無畏的子君以這麼顯著的變化。她近來實在變得很怯弱了，但也並不是今夜才開始的。我的心因此更繚亂，忽然有安寧的生活的影像——會館裏的破屋的寂靜，在眼前一閃，剛剛想定睛凝視，卻又看見了昏暗的燈光。

許久之後，信也寫成了，是一封頗長的信；很覺得疲勞，彷彿

And I was so tired after writing it that I realized I must have grown weaker myself lately too. We decided to send in the advertisement and post the letter the next day. Then with one accord we straightened up silently, as if conscious of each other's fortitude and strength, able to see new hope growing from this fresh beginning.

Indeed, this blow from outside infused new spirit into us. While in the bureau I had been like a wild bird in a cage, given just enough bird-seed by its captor to keep alive but not to thrive; doomed as time passed to lose the use of its wings, so that if ever released it would be unable to fly. Now, at any rate, I had got out of the cage. I must soar anew through the boundless sky before it was too late, before I had forgotten how to flap my wings.

Of course we could not expect results from a small advertisement right away. However, translating is not so simple either. You read something and think you understand it, but when you come to translate it difficulties crop up everywhere, and progress is very slow. Still, I was determined to do my best. In less than a fortnight, the edge of a fairly new dictionary was black with my fingerprints, which shows how seriously I took my work. The editor of *Freedom's Friend* had said that his magazine would never ignore a good manuscript.

Unfortunately, there was no room where I could be undisturbed, and Zijun was not as quiet or considerate as she had been. Our place was so cluttered up with dishes and bowls, so filled with smoke, that it was impossible to work steadily there. But of course I had only myself to blame for not being able to afford a study. On top of this there were Asui and the chicks. The chicks, moreover, had now grown into hens and were more of a bone of contention than ever between the two families.

Then there was the never-ending business of eating every day. All Zijun's energies seemed to go to this. One ate to earn and earned to

近來自己也較為怯弱了。於是我們決定，廣告和發信，就在明日一同實行。大家不約而同地伸直了腰肢，在無言中，似乎又都感到彼此的堅忍倔強的精神，還看見從新萌芽起來的將來的希望。

外來的打擊其實倒是振作了我們的新精神。局裏的生活，原如鳥販子手裏的禽鳥一般，僅有一點小米維繫殘生，決不會肥胖；日子一久，只落得麻痺了翅子，即使放出籠外，早已不能奮飛。現在總算脫出這牢籠了，我從此要在新的開闊的天空中翱翔，趁我還未忘卻了我的翅子的扇動。

小廣告是一時自然不會發生效力的；但譯書也不是容易事，先前看過，以為已經懂得的，一動手，卻疑難百出了，進行得很慢。然而我決計努力地做，一本半新的字典，不到半月，邊上便有了一大片烏黑的指痕，這就證明着我的工作的切實。《自由之友》的總編輯曾經說過，他的刊物是決不會埋沒好稿子的。

可惜的是我沒有一間靜室，子君又沒有先前那麼幽靜，善於體帖了，屋子裏總是散亂着碗碟，瀰漫着煤煙，使人不能安心做事；但是這自然還只能怨我自己無力置一間書齋。然而又加以阿隨，加以油雞們。加以油雞們又大起來了，更容易成為兩家爭吵的引線。

加以每日的「川流不息」的吃飯；子君的功業，彷彿就完全建立

eat, while Asui and the hens had to be fed too. Apparently she had forgotten all she had ever learned, and did not realize that she was interrupting my train of thought when she called me to meals. And although I sometimes showed a little displeasure as I sat down, she paid no attention at all, just went on munching away quite unconcerned.

It took her five weeks to realize that my work would not be restricted by regular meal-times. When the realization came she was probably annoyed, but she said nothing. After that my work did go forward faster, and soon I had translated 50,000 words. I had only to polish the manuscript, and it could be sent in with two already completed shorter pieces to *Freedom's Friend*. Those meals were still a headache though. I didn't mind the dishes being cold, but there wasn't enough to go round. Although my appetite was much smaller than before now that I was sitting at home all day using my brain, even so there was't always even enough rice. It had been given to Asui, sometimes along with the mutton which I myself rarely had a chance of eating recently. Asui was so thin, she said, it was really pathetic; besides it made the landlady sneer at us. She couldn't stand being laughed at.

So there were only the hens to eat my left-lovers. It was a long time before I realized this. I was very conscious however that my "place in nature," as Huxley describes it, was only somewhere between the peke and the hens.

Later on, after much argument and insistence, the hens started appearing on our table and we and Asui were able to enjoy them for over the days. They were very thin though, because for a long time they had been fed only a few grains of sorghum a day. After that, life became much more peaceful. Only Zijun was very dispirited and often seemed sad and bored, or even sulky. How easily people change!

在這吃飯中。吃了籌錢，籌來吃飯，還要餵阿隨，飼油雞；她似乎將先前所知道的全都忘掉了，也不想到我的構思就常常為了這催促吃飯而打斷。即使在坐中給看一點怒色，她總是不改變，仍然毫無感觸似的大嚼起來。

使她明白了我的作工不能受規定的吃飯的束縛，就費去五星期。她明白之後，大約很不高興罷，可是沒有說。我的工作果然從此較為迅速地進行，不久就共譯了五萬言，只要潤色一回，便可以和做好的兩篇小品，一同寄給《自由之友》去。只是吃飯卻依然給我苦惱。菜冷，是無妨的，然而竟不夠；有時連飯也不夠，雖然我因為終日坐在家裏用腦，飯量已經比先前要減少得多。這是先去餵了阿隨了，有時還併那近來連自己也輕易不吃的羊肉。她說，阿隨實在瘦得太可憐，房東太太還因此嗤笑我們了，她受不住這樣的奚落。

於是吃我殘飯的便只有油雞們。這是我積久才看出來的，但同時也如赫胥黎的論定「人類在宇宙間的位置」一般，自覺了我在這裏的位置：不過是叭兒狗和油雞之間。

後來，經多次的抗爭和催逼，油雞們也逐漸成為肴饌，我們和阿隨都享用了十多日的鮮肥；可是其實都很瘦，因為它們早已每日只能得到幾粒高粱了。從此便清靜得多。只有子君很頹唐，似乎常覺得悽苦和無聊，至於不大願意開口。我想，人是多麼容易改變呵！

But we couldn't keep Asui either. We had stopped hoping for a letter from anywhere, and Zijun had long had not even a scrap of food with which to get him to beg or stand on his hindlegs. Besides, winter was fast approaching, and we didn't know what to do about a stove. His appetite had long been a heavy liability, of which we were all too conscious. So even the dog had to go.

If we had tied a tag to him and put him on sale in the market, we might have made a few coppers. But neither of us could bring ourselves to do this. Finally I muffled his head in a cloth and took him outside the West Gate, where I let him loose. When he ran after me, I pushed him into a pit — not a very deep one.

When I got home, I found the place much more peaceful; but Zijun's tragic expression quite staggered me. I had never seen such a look on her face before. Of course it was because of Asui, but why take it so to heart? And I hadn't told her about pushing him into the pit.

That night, something icy crept into her tragic expression.

"Really!" I couldn't help blurting out. "What's got into you today, Zijun?"

"What?" She didn't even glance at me.

"The way you look...."

"It's nothing — nothing at all."

Eventually I guessed from her behaviour that she considered me callous. Actually, when on my own I had managed all right, although too proud to mix much with family connections. Since my move I had become estranged from my former friends. But if I could only take wing and fly away, I still had plenty of ways to make a living. The wretchedness of my present life was largely due to her — getting rid of Asui was a case in point. But Zijun seemed too obtuse now even to understand that.

　　但是阿隨也將留不住了。我們已經不能再希望從甚麼地方會有來信，子君也早沒有一點食物可以引它打拱或直立起來。冬季又逼近得這麼快，火爐就要成為很大的問題；它的食量，在我們其實早是一個極易覺得的很重的負擔。於是連它也留不住了。

　　倘使插了草標到店市去出賣，也許能得幾文錢罷，然而我們都不能，也不願這樣做。終於是用包袱蒙着頭，由我帶到西郊去放掉了，還要追上來，便推在一個並不很深的土坑裏。

　　我一回寓，覺得又清靜得多了；但子君的淒慘的神色，卻使我很吃驚。那是沒有見過的神色，自然是為阿隨。但又何至於此呢？我還沒有說起推在土坑裏的事。

　　到夜間，在她的淒慘的神色中，加上冰冷的分子了。

　　「奇怪。——子君，你怎麼今天這樣兒了？」我忍不住問。

　　「甚麼？」她連看也不看我。

　　「你的臉色……。」

　　「沒甚麼，——甚麼也沒有。」

　　我終於從她言動上看出，她大概已經認定我是一個忍心的人。其實，我一個人，是容易生活的，雖然因為驕傲，向來不與世交來往，遷居以後，也疏遠了所有舊識的人，然而只要能遠走高飛，生路還寬廣得很。現在忍受着這生活壓迫的苦痛，大半倒是為她，便是放掉阿隨，也何嘗不如此。但子君的識見卻似乎只是淺薄起來，竟至於連這一點也想不到了。

When I took an opportunity to hint this to her, she nodded as if she understood. But judging by her later behaviour, she either didn't take it in or else she didn't believe me.

The cold weather and her cold looks made it impossible for me to be comfortable at home. But where could I go? I could get away from her icy looks in the street and parks, but the cold wind there cut like a knife. Finally I found a haven in the public library.

Admission was free, and there were two stoves in the reading room. Although the fires were very low, the mere sight of the stoves made one warmer. There were no books worth reading: the old ones were out of date, and there were no new ones to speak of.

But I didn't go there to read. There were usually a few other people there, sometimes as many as a dozen, all thinly clad like me. We kept up a pretence of reading in order to keep out of the cold. This suited me down to the ground. In the streets you were liable to meet people you knew who would glance at you contemptuously, but here there was no uncalled-for trouble of that kind, because my acquaintances were all gathered round other stoves or warming themselves at the stoves in their own homes.

Although there were no books for me to read there, I found quiet in which to think. As I sat there alone thinking over the past, I realized that during the last half year, for love — blind love — I had neglected all the other important things in life. First and foremost, livelihood. A man must make a living before there can be any place for love. There must be a way out for those who struggle, and I hadn't yet forgotten how to flap my wings, although I was much weaker than before....

The reading room and the readers gradually faded. I saw fisher-men on the angry sea, soldiers in the trenches, dignitaries in their cars, speculators at the stock exchange, heroes in mountain forests, teach-

我揀了一個機會，將這些道理暗示她；她領會似的點頭。然而看她後來的情形，她是沒有懂，或者是並不相信的。

天氣的冷和神情的冷，逼迫我不能在家庭中安身。但是往那裏去呢？大道上，公園裏，雖然沒有冰冷的神情，冷風究竟也刺得人皮膚欲裂。我終於在通俗圖書館裏覓得了我的天堂。

那裏無須買票；閱書室裏又裝着兩個鐵火爐。縱使不過是燒着不死不活的煤的火爐，但單是看見裝着它，精神上也就總覺得有些溫暖。書卻無可看：舊的陳腐，新的是幾乎沒有的。

好在我到那裏去也並非為看書。另外時常還有幾個人，多則十餘人，都是單薄衣裳，正如我，各人看各人的書，作為取暖的口實。這於我尤為合式。道路上容易遇見熟人，得到輕蔑的一瞥，但此地卻決無那樣的橫禍，因為他們是永遠圍在別的鐵爐旁，或者靠在自家的白爐邊的。

那裏雖然沒有書給我看，卻還有安閒容得我想。待到孤身枯坐，回憶從前，這才覺得大半年來，只為了愛，——盲目的愛，——而將別的人生的要義全盤疏忽了。第一，便是生活。人必生活着，愛才有所附麗。世界上並非沒有為了奮鬥者而開的活路；我也還未忘卻翅子的扇動，雖然比先前已經頹唐得多……。

屋子和讀者漸漸消失了，我看見怒濤中的漁夫，戰壕中的兵士，摩托車中的貴人，洋場上的投機家，深山密林中的豪傑，講台

ers on their platforms, night prowlers, thieves in the dark.... Zijun was nowhere near me. She had lost all her courage in her resentment over Asui and absorption in her cooking. The strange thing was that she didn't look particularly thin....

It grew colder. The few lumps of slow-burning hard coal in the stove had at last burnt out, and it was closing time. I had to go back to Lucky Lane to expose myself to that icy look. Of late I had sometimes been met with warmth, but this only upset me more. One evening, I remember, from Zijun's eyes flashed the childlike look I had not seen for so long, as she reminded me with a smile of something that happened at the hostel. But there was a constant look of fear in her eyes as well. I knew she was worried by the fact that my behaviour recently had been colder than her own; so sometimes, to comfort her, I forced myself to talk and laugh. But each forced laugh and remark at once rang hollow. And the way this hollowness immediately re-echoed in my ears, like a hateful sneer, was more than I could bear.

Zijun may have felt this too, for after this she lost her wooden calm and, though she tried her best to hide it, often showed anxiety. She treated me, however, much more tenderly.

I wanted to speak to her plainly, but lacked the courage. Whenever I made up my mind to speak, the sight of those childlike eyes compelled me, for the time being, to force a smile. But my smile turned straightway into a sneer at myself and made me lose my cold composure.

After that she revived the old questions and started new tests, forcing me to give all sorts of hypocritical answers to show my affection for her. Hypocrisy became branded on my heart, so filling it with falseness that it was hard to breathe. I often felt, in my depression, that really great courage was needed to tell the truth; for a man who lacked

上的教授，昏夜的運動者和深夜的偷兒……。子君，——不在近
旁。她的勇氣都失掉了，只為着阿隨悲憤，為着做飯出神；然而奇
怪的是倒也並不怎樣瘦損……。

冷了起來，火爐裏的不死不活的幾片硬煤，也終於燒盡了，已
是閉館的時候。又須回到吉兆胡同，領略冰冷的顏色去了。近來也
間或遇到溫暖的神情，但這卻反而增加我的苦痛。記得有一夜，子
君的眼裏忽而又發出久已不見的稚氣的光來，笑着和我談到還在會
館時候的情形，時時又很帶些恐怖的神色。我知道我近來的超過她
的冷漠，已經引起她的憂疑來，只得也勉力談笑，想給她一點慰
藉。然而我的笑貌一上臉，我的話一出口，卻即刻變為空虛，這空
虛又即刻發生反響，回向我的耳目裏，給我一個難堪的惡毒的冷
嘲。

子君似乎也覺得的，從此便失掉了她往常的麻木似的鎮靜，雖
然竭力掩飾，總還是時時露出憂疑的神色來，但對我卻溫和得多
了。

我要明告她，但我還沒有敢，當決心要說的時候，看見她孩子
一般的眼色就使我只得暫且改作勉強的歡容。但是這又即刻來冷嘲
我，並使我失卻那冷漠的鎮靜。

她從此又開始了往事的溫習和新的考驗，逼我做出許多虛偽的
溫存的答案來，將溫存示給她，虛偽的稿便寫在自己的心上。我的
心漸被這些草稿填滿了，常覺得難於呼吸。我在苦惱中常常想，說
真實自然須有極大的勇氣的；假如沒有這勇氣，而苟安於虛偽，那

courage and reconciled himself to hypocrisy could never open up a new path in life. What's more, he just could not exist.

Then Zijun started looking resentful. This happened for the first time one morning, one bitterly cold morning, or so I imagined. I laughed up my sleeve with freezing indignation. All the ideas and intelligent, fearless phrases she had learned were empty after all; yet she had no inkling of their emptiness. She had given up reading long ago, so did not understand that the first thing in life is to make a living and that to do this people must advance hand in hand, or else soldier on alone. All she could do was cling to someone else's clothing, making it hard for even a fighter to struggle, and bringing ruin on both.

I felt that our only hope lay in parting. She ought to make a clean break. The thought of her death occurred to me abruptly, but at once I reproached myself and felt remorse. Happily it was morning, and there was plenty of time for me to tell her the truth. Whether or not we could make a fresh start depended on this.

I deliberately brought up the past. I spoke of literature, then of foreign authors and their works, of Ibsen's *A Doll's House* and *The Lady from the Sea*. I praised Nora for being strong-minded.... All this had been said the previous year in the shabby room in the hostel, but now it rang hollow. As the words left my mouth I could not free myself from the suspicion that an unseen urchin behind me was maliciously parroting everything I said.

She listened, nodding agreement, then was silent. And I wound up abruptly, the last echo of my voice vanishing in the emptiness.

"Yes," she said presently, after another silence. "But.... Juansheng, I feel you're a different person these days. Is that true? Tell me honestly."

This was a head-on blow. But taking a grip of myself, I explained

也便是不能開闢新的生路的人。不獨不是這個，連這人也未嘗有！

　　子君有怨色，在早晨，極冷的早晨，這是從未見過的，但也許是從我看來的怨色。我那時冷冷地氣憤和暗笑了；她所磨練的思想和豁達無畏的言論，到底也還是一個空虛，而對於這空虛卻並未自覺。她早已甚麼書也不看，已不知道人的生活的第一着是求生，向着這求生的道路，是必須攜手同行，或奮身孤往的了，倘使只知道捶着一個人的衣角，那便是雖戰士也難於戰鬥，只得一同滅亡。

　　我覺得新的希望就只在我們的分離；她應該決然捨去，——我也突然想到她的死，然而立刻自責，懺悔了。幸而是早晨，時間正多，我可以說我的真實。我們的新的道路的開闢，便在這一遭。

　　我和她閒談，故意地引起我們的往事，提到文藝，於是涉及外國的文人，文人的作品：《諾拉》，《海的女人》。稱揚諾拉的果決……。也還是去年在會館的破屋裏講過的那些話，但現在已經變成空虛，從我的嘴傳入自己的耳中，時時疑心有一個隱形的壞孩子，在背後惡意地刻毒地學舌。

　　她還是點頭答應着傾聽，後來沉默了。我也就斷續地說完了我的話，連餘音都消失在虛空中了。

　　「是的。」她又沉默了一會，說，「但是，……涓生，我覺得你近來很兩樣了。可是的？你，——你老實告訴我。

　　我覺得這似乎給了我當頭一擊，但也立即定了神，說出我的意

my views and proposals: only by making a fresh start and building a new life could we both avoid ruin.

To clinch the matter I said firmly:

"... Besides, you can go boldly ahead now without any scruples. You asked me for the truth. You're right: we shouldn't be hypocritical. Well the truth is it's because I don't love you any more. Actually, this makes it much better for you, because it'll be easier for you to go ahead without any regret...."

I was expecting a scene, but all that followed was silence. Her face turned ashen pale, as pale as death; but in a moment her colour came back and that childlike look darted from her eyes. She gazed around like a hungry or thirsty child searching for its kindly mother. But she only stared into space, fearfully avoiding my eyes.

The sight was more than I could stand. Fortunately it was still early. Braving the cold wind, I hurried to the public library.

There I saw *Freedom's Friend,* with my short articles in it. This took me by surprise and breathed a little fresh life into me. "There are plenty of ways open to me," I reflected. "But things can't go on like this."

I started calling on old friends with whom I had long been out of touch, but didn't go more than once or twice. Naturally their rooms were warm, yet I felt chilled to the marrow. And in the evenings I huddled in a room colder than ice.

An icy needle was piercing my heart so that it kept aching numbly. "There are plenty of ways open to me," I reflected. "I haven't forgotten how to flap my wings." The thought of her death occurred to me abruptly, but at once I reproached myself and felt remorse.

In the library the new path ahead of me often flashed before my

見和主張來：新的路的開闢，新的生活的再造，為的是免得一同滅亡。

臨末，我用了十分的決心，加上這幾句話：

「……況且你已經可以無須顧慮，勇往直前了。你要我老實說；是的，人是不該虛偽的。我老實說罷：因為，因為我已經不愛你了！但這於你倒好得多，因為你更可以毫無掛念地做事……。」

我同時預期着大的變故的到來，然而只有沉默。她臉色陡然變成灰黃，死了似的；瞬間便又甦生，眼裏也發了稚氣的閃閃的光澤。這眼光射向四處，正如孩子在飢渴中尋求着慈愛的母親，但只在空中尋求，恐怖地迴避着我的眼。

我不能看下去了，幸而是早晨，我冒着寒風逕奔通俗圖書館。

在那裏看見《自由之友》，我的小品文都登出了。這使我一驚，彷彿得了一點生氣。我想，生活的路還很多，——但是，現在這樣也還是不行的。

我開始去訪問久已不相聞問的熟人，但這也不過一兩次；他們的屋子自然是暖和的，我在骨髓中卻覺得寒冽。夜間，便蜷伏在比冰還冷的冷屋中。

冰的針刺着我的靈魂，使我永遠苦於麻木的疼痛。生活的路還很多，我也還沒有忘卻翅子的扇動，我想。——我突然想到她的死，然而立刻自責，懺悔了。

在通俗圖書館裏往往瞥見一閃的光明，新的生路橫在前面。她

eyes. She had faced up bravely to the facts and boldly left this icy home. Left it, what's more, without any sense of grievance. Then light as a cloud I floated through the void, the blue sky above me and, below, mountain ranges, mighty oceans, skyscrapers, battlefields, motor-cars, thoroughfares, rich men's mansions, bright busy shopping centres, and the dark night....

What's more, indeed, I foresaw that this new life was just around the corner.

Somehow we managed to live through the fearful winter, a bitter Beijing winter. But like dragonflies caught by mischievous boys who tie them up to play with and torment at will, although we had come through alive we were prostrate — the end was only a matter of time.

I wrote three letters to the editor of *Freedom's Friend* before receiving a reply. The envelope contained nothing but two book tokens, one for twenty cents, the other for thirty cents. So my nine cents spent on postage to press for payment and my whole day without food had all gone for nothing.

Then what I had been expecting finally happened.

As winter gave place to spring and the wind became less icy, I spent more time roaming the streets, not getting home generally before dark. On one such dark evening I came home listlessly as usual and, as usual, grew so depressed at the sight of our gate that my feet began to drag. Eventually, however, I reached my room. It was dark inside. As I groped for the matches and struck a light, the place seemed extraordinarily quiet and empty.

I was standing there in bewilderment, when the official's wife called me outside.

"Zijun's father came today and took her away," she said simply.

勇猛地覺悟了，毅然走出這冰冷的家，而且，——毫無怨恨的神色。我便輕如行雲，漂浮空際，上有蔚藍的天，下是深山大海，廣廈高樓，戰場，摩托車，洋場，公館，晴明的鬧市，黑暗的夜⋯⋯。

而且，真的，我預感得這新生面便要來到了。

我們總算度過了極難忍受的冬天，這北京的冬天就如蜻蜓落在惡作劇的壞孩子的手裏一般，被繫着細線，盡情玩弄，虐待，雖然幸而沒有送掉性命，結果也還是躺在地上，只爭着一個遲早之間。

寫給《自由之友》的總編輯已經有三封信，這才得到回信，信封裏只有兩張書券：兩角的和三角的。我卻單是催，就用了九分的郵票，一天的飢餓，又都白挨給於己一無所得的空虛了。

然而覺得要來的事，卻終於來到了。

這是冬春之交的事，風已沒有這麼冷，我也更久地在外面徘徊；待到回家，大概已經昏黑。就在這樣一個昏黑的晚上，我照常沒精打采地回來，一看見寓所的門，也照常更加喪氣，使腳步放得更緩。但終於走進自己的屋子裏了，沒有燈；摸火柴點起來時，是異樣的寂寞和空虛！

正在錯愕中，官太太便到窗外來叫我出去。

「今天子君的父親來到這裏，將她接回去了。」她很簡單地說。

This was not what I had expected. I felt as if hit on the back of the head, and stood speechless.

"She went?" I finally managed to ask.

"Yes."

"Did — did she say anything?"

"No. Just asked me to tell you when you came back that she'd gone."

I couldn't believe it; yet the room was extraordinarily quiet and empty. I gazed around in search of Zijun, but all I could see were some shabby sticks of furniture scattered sparsely about the room, as if to prove their inability to conceal anyone or anything. It occurred to me that she might have left a letter or at least jotted down a few words, but no. Only salt, dried chilli, flour and half a cabbage had been placed together, with a few dozen coppers at the side. These were all our worldly goods, and now she had solemnly left these all to me, mutely bidding me to use them to eke out my existence a little longer.

As if repelled by my surroundings, I hurried out to the middle of the courtyard where all around me was dark. Bright lamplight showed on the window-paper of the central room, where they were teasing the baby to make her laugh. My heart grew calmer as by degrees I glimpsed a way out of this heavy oppression: high mountains and marshlands, thoroughfares, brightly lit banquets, trenches, pitch-black night, the thrust of a sharp knife, utterly noiseless footsteps....

Relaxing, I thought about travelling expenses and sighed.

As I lay with closed eyes I conjured up a picture of the future, but before the night was half over it had vanished. In the gloom I suddenly seemed to see a pile of groceries, then Zijun's ashen face appeared

這似乎又不是意料中的事，我便如腦後受了一擊，無言地站着。

「她去了麼？」過了些時，我只問出這樣一句話。

「她去了。」

「她，——她可說甚麼？」

「沒說甚麼。單是託我見你回來時告訴你，說她去了。」

我不信；但是屋子裏是異樣的寂寞和空虛。我遍看各處，尋覓子君；只見幾件破舊而黯淡的傢俱，都顯得極其清疏，在證明着它們毫無隱匿一人一物的能力。我轉念尋信或她留下的字跡，也沒有；只是鹽和乾辣椒，麵粉，半株白菜，卻聚集在一處了，旁邊還有幾十枚銅元。這是我們兩人生活材料的全副，現在她就鄭重地將這留給我一個人，在不言中，教我藉此去維持較久的生活。

我似乎被周圍所排擠，奔到院子中間，有昏黑在我的周圍；正屋的紙窗上映出明亮的燈光，他們正在逗着孩子玩笑。我的心也沉靜下來，覺得在沉重的迫壓中，漸漸隱約地現出脫走的路徑：深山大澤，洋場，電燈下的盛筵，壕溝，最黑最黑的深夜，利刃的一擊，毫無聲響的腳步……。

心地有些輕鬆，舒展了；想到旅費，並且噓一口氣。

躺着，在合着的眼前經過的預想的前途，不到半夜已經現盡；暗中忽然彷彿看見一堆食物，這之後，便浮出一個子君的灰黃的臉

to gaze at me beseechingly with childlike eyes. But as soon as I pulled myself together, there was nothing there.

However, my heart was still heavy. Why couldn't I have waited a few days instead of blurting out the truth to her like that? Now she knew all that was left to her was the blazing fury of her father — to his children he was a heartless creditor — and the cold looks of bystanders, colder than frost or ice. Apart from this there was only emptiness. What a fearful thing it is to bear the heavy burden of emptiness, walking what is called one's path in life amid cold looks and blazing fury! This path ends, moreover, in nothing but a grave without so much as a tombstone.

I ought not to have told Zijun the truth. Since we had loved each other, I should have indulged her to the last with lies. If truth is precious, it should not have proved such a heavy burden of emptiness to Zijun. Of course lies are empty too, but at least they would not have proved so crushing a burden in the end.

I had imagined that if I told Zijun the truth she could go forward boldly without scruples, just as when we started living together. But I must have been wrong. Her courage and fearlessness then were owing to love.

Lacking the courage to shoulder the heavy burden of hypocrisy, I thrust the burden of the truth on to her. Because she had loved me she would have to bear this heavy burden amid cold looks and blazing fury to the end of her days.

I had thought of her death.... I saw that I was a weakling who deserved to be cast out by the strong, honest men and hypocrites both. Yet she, from first to last, had hoped that I could eke out my existence....

I must leave Lucky Lane, which was so extraordinarily empty and

來，睜了孩子氣的眼睛，懇託似的看着我。我一定神，甚麼也沒有了。

但我的心卻又覺得沉重。我為甚麼偏不忍耐幾天，要這樣急急地告訴她真話的呢？現在她知道，她以後所有的只是她父親——兒女的債主——的烈日一般的嚴威和旁人的賽過冰霜的冷眼。此外便是虛空。負着虛空的重擔，在嚴威和冷眼中走着所謂人生的路，這是怎麼可怕的事呵！而況這路的盡頭，又不過是——連墓碑也沒有的墳墓。

我不應該將真實說給子君，我們相愛過，我應該永久奉獻她我的說謊。如果真實可以寶貴，這在子君就不該是一個沉重的空虛。謊語當然也是一個空虛，然而臨末，至多也不過這樣地沉重。

我以為將真實說給子君，她便可以毫無顧慮，堅決地毅然前行，一如我們將要同居時那樣。但這恐怕是我錯誤了。她當時的勇敢和無畏是因為愛。

我沒有負着虛偽的重擔的勇氣，卻將真實的重擔卸給她了。她愛我之後，就要負了這重擔，在嚴威和冷眼中走着所謂人生的路。

我想到她的死……。我看見我是一個卑怯者，應該被擯於強有力的人們，無論是真實者，虛偽者。然而她卻自始至終，還希望我維持較久的生活……。

我要離開吉兆胡同，在這裏是異樣的空虛和寂寞。我想，只要

lonely. To my mind, if only I could get away, it would be as if Zijun were still at my side; or at least as if she were still in town and might drop in on me at any time, as she had when I lived in the hostel.

However, all my letters went unanswered, as did applications to friends to find me a post. There was nothing for it but to seek out a family connection whom I had not visited for a long time. This was an old classmate of my uncle's, a highly respected senior licentiate who had lived in Beijing for many years and had a wide circle of acquaintances.

The gatekeeper eyed me scornfully, no doubt on account of my shabby clothes. When finally I was admitted, my uncle's friend still acknowledged our acquaintance but treated me very coldly. He knew all about us.

"Obviously you can't stay here," he told me coldly, after being asked to recommend me to a job elsewhere. "But where will you go? It's extremely difficult.... That, h'm, that friend of yours, Zijun, I suppose you know, is dead."

I was dumbfounded.

"Are you sure?" I blurted out at last.

He laughed drily. "Of course I am. My servant Wang Sheng comes from the same village as her family."

"But — how did she die?"

"Who knows? At any rate, she's dead."

I have forgotten how I took my leave and went home. I knew he wouldn't tell a lie. Zijun would never come back as she had last year. Although she had thought to bear the burden of emptiness amid cold looks and blazing fury till the end of her days, it had been too much

離開這裏，子君便如還在我的身邊；至少，也如還在城中，有一天，將要出乎意表地訪我，像住在會館時候似的。

然而一切請託和書信，都是一無反響；我不得已，只好訪問一個久不問候的世交去了。他是我伯父的幼年的同窗，以正經出名的拔貢，寓京很久，交遊也廣闊的。

大概因為衣服的破舊罷，一登門便很遭門房的白眼。好容易才相見，也還相識，但是很冷落。我們的往事，他全都知道了。

「自然，你也不能在這裏了，」他聽了我託他在別處覓事之後，冷冷地說，「但那裏去呢？很難。——你那，甚麼呢，你的朋友罷，子君，你可知道，她死了。」

我驚得沒有話。

「真的？」我終於不自覺地問。

「哈哈。自然真的。我家的王升的家，就和她家同村。」

「但是，——不知道是怎麼死的？」

「誰知道呢。總之是死了就是了。」

我已經忘卻了怎樣辭別他，回到自己的寓所。我知道他是不說謊話的；子君總不會再來的了，像去年那樣。她雖是想在嚴威和冷眼中負着虛空的重擔來走所謂人生的路，也已經不能。她的命運，

for her. Fate had decreed that she should die believing the truth I had told her — die in a world without love.

Obviously I could not stay there. But where could I go?

Around me was a great void and deathlike silence. I seemed to see the darkness before the eyes of those, each one in turn, who died unloved; to hear all their bitter, despairing cries as they struggled.

I was waiting for something new, something nameless and unexpected. But day after day passed in the same deathlike silence.

I went out much less than before, sitting or lying in the great void, allowing this deathlike silence to eat away my soul. Sometimes the silence itself seemed afraid, seemed to recoil. At such times there flashed into my mind nameless, unexpected new hope.

One overcast morning when the sun had failed to struggle out from behind the clouds and the very air was tired, sounds of pattering paws and snuffling made me open my eyes. A glance around the room revealed nothing, but looking down I saw a tiny creature perambulating the floor. It was thin, covered with dust, more dead than alive....

When I took a closer look, my heart missed a beat. I jumped up.

It was Asui. He had come back.

I left Lucky Lane not just because of the cold glances of my landlord, his wife and their maid, but largely on account of Asui. But where could I go? There were many ways open to me of course, this I knew, and sometimes I glimpsed them stretching out before me. What I didn't know was how to take the first step.

After much cogitation and weighing of pros and cons, I decided that the hostel was the only possible lodging place for me. Here is the same shabby room as before, the same wooden bed, half-withered locust

已經決定她在我所給與的真實——無愛的人間死滅了！

自然我不能在這裏了；但是，「那裏去呢？」

四圍是廣大的空虛，還有死的寂靜。死於無愛的人們的眼前的黑暗，我彷彿一一看見，還聽得一切苦悶和絕望的掙扎的聲音。

我還期待着新的東西到來，無名的，意外的。但一天一天，無非是死的寂靜。

我比先前已經不大出門，只坐臥在廣大的空虛裏，一任這死的寂靜侵蝕着我的靈魂。死的寂靜有時也自己戰慄，自己退藏，於是在這絕續之交，便閃出無名的，意外的，新的期待。

一天是陰沉的上午，太陽還不能從雲裏面掙扎出來，連空氣都疲乏着。耳中聽到細碎的步聲和咻咻的鼻息，使我睜開眼。大致一看，屋子裏還是空虛；但偶然看到地面，卻盤旋着一匹小小的動物，瘦弱的，半死的，滿身灰土的……。

我一細看，我的心就一停，接着便直跳起來。

那是阿隨。它回來了。

我的離開吉兆胡同，也不單是為了房主人們和他家女工的冷眼，大半就為着這阿隨。但是，「那裏去呢？」新的生路自然還很多，我約略知道，也間或依稀看見，覺得就在我面前，然而我還沒有知道跨進那裏去的第一步的方法。

經過許多回的思量和比較，也還只有會館是還能相容的地方。依然是這樣的破屋，這樣的板床，這樣的半枯的槐樹和紫藤，但那

tree and wistaria vine. But all that formerly gave me love and life, hope and happiness, has vanished. Nothing remains but emptiness, the empty existence I exchanged for the truth.

There are many ways open to me and I must take one of them, because I am still living. I still don't know, though, how to take the first step. Sometimes the road seems like a great grey serpent, writhing and darting at me. I wait and wait, watching it approach, but it always vanishes suddenly in the darkness.

The early spring nights are as long as ever. Sitting idle as the time drags, I recall a funeral procession I saw in the street this morning. There were paper figures and paper horses in front and, behind, weeping like singing. Now I see how clever they are — this is so simple.

Then Zijun's funeral springs to my mind. She bore the heavy burden of emptiness alone, advancing down the long grey road only to be swallowed up amid cold looks and blazing fury.

If only there really were ghosts, really were a hell! Then, no matter how the infernal whirlwind roared, I would seek out Zijun to tell her of my remorse and grief, to beg for her forgiveness. Failing this, the poisonous flames of hell would engulf me and fiercely consume all my remorse and grief.

In the whirlwind and flames I would put my arms round Zijun and ask her pardon, or let her take her revenge....

However, this is emptier than my new life. I have nothing now but the early spring night which is still as long as ever. Since I am living, I must make a fresh start. And the first step is just to record my remorse and grief, for Zijun's sake as well as for my own.

All I have is weeping like singing as I mourn for Zijun, burying her in oblivion.

時使我希望，歡欣，愛，生活的，卻全都逝去了，只有一個虛空，我用真實去換來的虛空存在。

新的生路還很多，我必須跨進去，因為我還活着。但我還不知道怎樣跨出那第一步。有時，彷彿看見那生路就像一條灰白的長蛇，自己蜿蜒地向我奔來，我等着，等着，看看臨近，但忽然便消失在黑暗裏了。

初春的夜，還是那麼長。長久的枯坐中記起上午在街頭所見的葬式，前面是紙人紙馬，後面是唱歌一般的哭聲。我現在已經知道他們的聰明了，這是多麼輕鬆簡截的事。

然而子君的葬式卻又在我的眼前，是獨自負着虛空的重擔，在灰白的長路上前行，而又即刻消失在周圍的嚴威和冷眼裏了。

我願意真有所謂鬼魂，真有所謂地獄，那麼，即使在孽風怒吼之中，我也將尋覓子君，當面說出我的悔恨和悲哀，祈求她的饒恕；否則，地獄的毒焰將圍繞我，猛烈地燒盡我的悔恨和悲哀。

我將在孽風和毒焰中擁抱子君，乞她寬容，或者使她快意……。

但是，這卻更虛空於新的生路；現在所有的只是初春的夜，竟還是那麼長。我活着，我總得向着新的生路跨出去，那第一步，——卻不過是寫下我的悔恨和悲哀，為子君，為自己。

我仍然只有唱歌一般的哭聲，給子君送葬，葬在遺忘中。

I want to forget. For my own sake, I do not want to remember the oblivion I gave Zijun for her burial.

I must make a fresh start in life. Hiding the truth deep in my wounded heart, I must advance silently, taking oblivion and falsehood as my guide....

October 21, 1925

　　我要遺忘；我為自己，並且要不再想到這用了遺忘給子君送葬。

　　我要向着新的生路跨進第一步去，我要將真實深深地藏在心的創傷中，默默地前行，用遺忘和說謊做我的前導……。

　　　　　　　　　　一九二五年十月二十一日畢。

鑄劍

Forging the Swords

FORGING THE SWORDS

I

Mei Jian Chi had no sooner lain down beside his mother than rats came out to gnaw the wooden lid of the pan. The sound got on his nerves. The soft hoots he gave had some effect at first, but presently the rats ignored him, crunching and munching as they pleased. He dared not make a loud noise to drive them away, for fear of waking his mother, so tired by her labours during the day that she had fallen asleep as soon as her head touched the pillow.

After a long time silence fell. He was dozing off when a sudden splash made him open his eyes with a start. He heard the rasping of claws against earthenware.

"Good! I hope you drown!" he thought gleefully and sat up quietly.

He got down from the bed and picked his way by the light of the moon to the door. He groped for the fire stick behind it, lit a chip of pine wood and lighted up the water vat. Sure enough, a huge rat had fallen in. There was too little water inside for it to get out. It was just swimming round, scrabbling at the side of the vat.

"Serves you right!" the boy exulted. This was one of the creatures that kept him awake every night by gnawing the furniture. He stuck the torch into a small hole in the mud wall to gloat over the sight, till the beady eyes revolted him and reaching for a dried reed he pushed

鑄　　劍

一

眉間尺剛和他的母親睡下，老鼠便出來咬鍋蓋，使他聽得發煩。他輕輕地叱了幾聲，最初還有些效驗，後來是簡直不理他了，格支格支地徑自咬。他又不敢大聲趕，怕驚醒了白天做得勞乏，晚上一躺就睡着了的母親。

許多時光之後，平靜了；他也想睡去。忽然，撲通一聲，驚得他又睜開眼。同時聽到沙沙地響，是爪子抓着瓦器的聲音。

「好！該死！」他想着，心裏非常高興，一面就輕輕地坐起來。

他跨下床，借着月光走向門背後，摸到鑽火傢伙，點上松明，向水甕裏一照。果然，一匹很大的老鼠落在那裏面了；但是，存水已經不多，爬不出來，只沿着水甕內壁，抓着，團團地轉圈子。

「活該！」他一想到夜夜咬傢俱，鬧得他不能安穩睡覺的便是它們，很覺得暢快。他將松明插在土牆的小孔裏，賞玩着；然而那圓睜的小眼睛，又使他發生了憎恨，伸手抽出一根蘆柴，將它直按到

the creature under the water. After a time he removed the reed and the rat, coming to the surface, went on swimming round and scrabbling at the side of the vat, but less powerfully than before. Its eyes were under water — all that could be seen was the red tip of a small pointed nose, snuffling desperately.

For some time he had had an aversion to red-nosed people. Yet now this small pointed red nose struck him as pathetic. He thrust his reed under the creature's belly. The rat clutched at it, and after catching its breath clambered up it. But the sight of its whole body — sopping black fur, bloated belly, wormlike tail — struck him again as so revolting that he hastily shook the reed. The rat dropped back with a splash into the vat. Then he hit it several times over the head to make it sink.

Now the pine chip had been changed six times. The rat, exhausted, was floating submerged in the middle of the vat, from time to time straining slightly towards the surface. Once more the boy was seized with pity. He broke the reed in two and, with considerable difficulty, fished the creature up and put it on the floor. To begin with, it didn't budge; then it took a breath; after a long time its feet twitched and it turned over, as if meaning to make off. This gave Mei Jian Chi a jolt. He raised his left foot instinctively and brought it heavily down. He heard a small cry. When he squatted down to look, there was blood on the rat's muzzle — it was probably dead.

He felt sorry again, as remorseful as if he had committed a crime. He squatted there, staring, unable to get up.

By this time his mother was awake.

"What are you doing, son?" she asked from the bed.

"A rat...." He rose hastily and turned to her, answering briefly.

"I know it's a rat. But what are you doing? Killing it or saving it?"

水底去。過了一會，才放手，那老鼠也隨着浮上了來，還是抓着甕壁轉圈子。只是抓勁已經沒有先前似的有力，眼睛也淹在水裏面，單露出一點尖尖的通紅的小鼻子，咻咻地急促地喘氣。

他近來很有點不大喜歡紅鼻子的人。但這回見了這尖尖的小紅鼻子，卻忽然覺得它可憐了，就又用那蘆柴，伸到它的肚下去，老鼠抓着，歇了一回力，便沿着蘆幹爬了上來。待到他看見全身，——濕淋淋的黑毛，大的肚子，蚯蚓似的尾巴，——便又覺得可恨可憎得很，慌忙將蘆柴一抖，撲通一聲，老鼠又落在水甕裏，他接着就用蘆柴在它頭上搗了幾下，叫它趕快沉下去。

換了六回松明之後，那老鼠已經不能動彈，不過沉浮在水中間，有時還向水面微微一跳。眉間尺又覺得很可憐，隨即折斷蘆柴，好容易將它夾了出來，放在地面上。老鼠先是絲毫不動，後來才有一點呼吸；又許多時，四隻腳運動了，一翻身，似乎要站起來逃走。這使眉間尺大吃一驚，不覺提起左腳，一腳踏下去。只聽得吱的一聲，他蹲下仔細看時，只見口角上微有鮮血，大概是死掉了。

他又覺得很可憐，彷彿自己作了大惡似的，非常難受。他蹲着，呆看着，站不起來。

「尺兒，你在做甚麼？」他的母親已經醒來了，在床上問。

「老鼠……」。他慌忙站起，回轉身去，卻只答了兩個字。

「是的，老鼠。這我知道。可是你在做甚麼？殺它呢，還是在救它？」

He made no answer. The torch had burned out. He stood there silently in the darkness, accustoming his eyes to the pale light of the moon.

His mother sighed.

"After midnight you'll be sixteen, but you're still the same — so lukewarm. You never change. It looks as if your father will have no one to avenge him."

Seated in the grey moonlight, his mother seemed to be trembling from head to foot. The infinite grief in her low tones made him shiver. The next moment, though, hot blood raced through his veins.

"Avenge my father? Does he need avenging?" He stepped forward in amazement.

"He does. And the task falls to you. I have long wanted to tell you, but while you were small I said nothing. Now you're not a child any longer though you still act like one. I just don't know what to do. Can a boy like you carry through a real man's job?"

"I can. Tell me, mother. I'm going to change...".

"Of course. I can only tell you. And you'll have to change.... Well, come over here."

He walked over. His mother was sitting upright in bed, her eyes flashing in the shadowy white moonlight.

"Listen!" she said gravely. "Your father was famed as a forger of swords, the best in all the land. I sold his tools to keep us from starving, so there's nothing left for you to see. But he was the best sword-maker in the whole world. Twenty years ago, the king's concubine gave birth to a piece of iron which they said she conceived after embracing an iron pillar. It was pure, transparent iron. The king, realizing that this

他沒有回答。松明燒盡了；他默默地立在暗中，漸看見月光的皎潔。

「唉！」他的母親嘆息說，「一交子時，你就是十六歲了，性情還是那樣，不冷不熱地，一點也不變。看來，你的父親的仇是沒有人報的了。」

他看見他的母親坐在灰白色的月影中，彷彿身體都在顫動；低微的聲音裏，含着無限的悲哀，使他冷得毛骨悚然，而一轉眼間，又覺得熱血在全身中忽然騰沸。

「父親的仇？父親有甚麼仇呢？」他前進幾步，驚急地問。

「有的。還要你去報。我早想告訴你的了；只因為你太小，沒有說。現在你已經成人了，卻還是那樣的性情。這教我怎麼辦呢？你似的性情，能行大事的麼？」

「能。說罷，母親。我要改過……。」

「自然。我也只得說。你必須改過……。那麼，走過來罷。」

他走過去；他的母親端坐在床上，在暗白的月影裏，兩眼發出閃閃的光芒。

「聽哪！」她嚴肅地說，「你的父親原是一個鑄劍的名工，天下第一。他的工具，我早已都賣掉了來救了窮了，你已經看不見一點遺迹；但他是一個世上無二的鑄劍的名工。二十年前，王妃生下了一塊鐵，聽說是抱了一回鐵柱之後受孕的，是一塊純青透明的鐵。大

was a rare treasure, decided to have it made into a sword with which to defend his kingdom, kill his enemies and ensure his own safety. As ill luck would have it, your father was chosen for the task, and in both hands he brought the iron home. He tempered it day and night for three whole years, until he had forged two swords.

"What a fearful sight when he finally opened his furnace! A jet of white vapour billowed up into the sky, while the earth shook. The white vapour became a white cloud above this spot; by degrees it turned a deep scarlet and cast a peach-blossom tint over everything. In our pitch-black furnace lay two red-hot swords. As your father, sprinkled them drop by drop with clear well water, the swords hissed and spat and little by little turned blue. So seven days and seven nights passed, till the swords disappeared from sight. But if you looked hard, they were still in the furnace, pure blue and transparent as two icicles.

"Great happiness flashed from your father's eyes. Picking up the swords, he stroked and fondled them. Then lines of sadness appeared on his forehead and at the corners of his mouth. He put the swords in two caskets.

"'You've only to look at the portents of the last few days to realize that everybody must know the swords are forged,' he told me softly. 'Tomorrow I must go to present one to the king. But the day that I present it will be the last day of my life. I am afraid we shall never meet again.'

"Horrified, uncertain what he meant, I didn't know what to reply. All I could say was: 'But you've done such fine work.'

"'Ah, you don't understand! The king is suspicious and cruel. Now I've forged two swords the like of which have never been seen, he is bound to kill me to prevent my forging swords for any of his rivals who might oppose or surpass him.'

王知道是異寶，便決計用來鑄一把劍，想用它保國，用它殺敵，用
它防身。不幸你的父親那時偏偏入了選，便將鐵捧回家裏來，日日
夜夜地鍛煉，費了整三年的精神，煉成兩把劍。

　　「當最末次開爐的那一日，是怎樣地駭人的景象呵！嘩拉拉地騰
上一道白氣的時候，地面也覺得動搖。那白氣到天半便變成白雲，
罩住了這處所，漸漸現出緋紅顏色，映得一切都如桃花。我家的漆
黑的爐子裏，是躺着通紅的兩把劍。你父親用井華水慢慢地滴下
去，那劍嘶嘶地吼着，慢慢轉成青色了。這樣地七日七夜，就看不
見了劍，仔細看時，卻還在爐底裏，純青的，透明的，正像兩條
冰。

　　「大歡喜的光采，便從你父親的眼睛裏四射出來；他取起劍，拂
拭着，拂拭着。然而悲慘的皺紋，卻也從他的眉頭和嘴角出現了。
他將那兩把劍分裝在兩個匣子裏。

　　「『你只要看這幾天的景象，就明白無論是誰，都知道劍已煉就
的了。』他悄悄地對我說。『一到明天，我必須去獻給大王。但獻劍
的一天，也就是我命盡的日子。怕我們從此要長別了。』

　　「『你……。』我很駭異，猜不透他的意思，不知怎麼說的好。我
只是這樣地說：『你這回有了這麼大的功勞……』

　　「『唉！你怎麼知道呢！』他說。『大王是向來善於猜疑，又極殘
忍的。這回我給他煉成了世間無二的劍，他一定要殺掉我，免得我
再去給別人煉劍，來和他匹敵，或者超過他。』

"I shed tears.

"'Don't grieve,' he said. 'There's no way out. Tears can't wash away fate. I've been prepared for this for some time.' His eyes seemed to dart lightning as he placed a sheath on my knee.' This is the male sword,' he told me. 'Keep it. Tomorrow I shall take the female to the king. If I don't come back, you'll know I'm dead. Won't you be brought to bed in four or five months? Don't grieve, but bear our child and bring him up well. As soon as he's grown, give him his sword and tell him to cut off the king's head to avenge me!'"

"Did my father come back that day?" demanded the boy.

"He did not," she replied calmly. "I asked everywhere, but there was no news of him. Later someone told me that the first to stain with his blood the sword forged by your father was your father himself. For fear his ghost should haunt the palace, they buried his body at the front gate, his head in the park at the back."

Mei Jian Chi felt as if he were on fire and sparks were flashing from every hair of his head. He clenched his fists in the dark till the knuckles cracked.

His mother stood up and lifted aside the board at the head of the bed. Then she lit a torch, took a hoe from behind the door and handed it to her son with the order:

"Dig!"

Though the lad's heart was pounding, he dug calmly, stroke after stroke. He scooped out yellow earth to a depth of over five feet, when the colour changed to that of rotten wood.

"Look! Careful now!" cried his mother.

Lying flat beside the hole he had made, he reached down gingerly

「我掉淚了。

「『你不要悲哀。這是無法逃避的。眼淚決不能洗掉運命。我可是早已有準備在這裏了！』他的眼裏忽然發出電火似的光芒，將一個劍匣放在我膝上。『這是雄劍。』他説。『你收着。明天，我只將這雌劍獻給大王去。倘若我一去竟不回來了呢，那是我一定不再在人間了。你不是懷孕已經五六個月了麼？不要悲哀；待生了孩子，好好地撫養。一到成人之後，你便交給他這雄劍，教他砍在大王的頸子上，給我報仇！』」

「那天父親回來了沒有呢？」眉間尺趕緊問。

「沒有回來！」她冷靜地説。「我四處打聽，也杳無消息。後來聽得人説，第一個用血來飼你父親自己煉成的劍的人，就是他自己——你的父親。還怕他鬼魂作怪，將他的身首分埋在前門和後苑了！」

眉間尺忽然全身都如燒着猛火，自己覺得每一枝毛髮上都彷彿閃出火星來。他的雙拳，在暗中捏得格格地作響。

他的母親站起了，揭去床頭的木板，下床點了松明，到門背後取過一把鋤，交給眉間尺道：「掘下去！」

眉間尺心跳着，但很沉靜的一鋤一鋤輕輕地掘下去。掘出來的都是黃土，約到五尺多深，土色有些不同了，似乎是爛掉的材木。

「看罷！要小心！」他的母親説。

眉間尺伏在掘開的洞穴旁邊，伸手下去，謹慎小心地撮開爛

to shift the rotted wood till the tips of his fingers touched something as cold as ice. It was the pure, transparent sword. He made out where the hilt was, grasped it, and lifted it out.

The moon and stars outside the window and the pine torch inside the room abruptly lost their brightness. The world was filled with a blue, steely light. And in this steely light the sword appeared to melt away and vanish from sight. But when the lad looked hard he saw something over three feet long which didn't seem particularly sharp — in fact the blade was rounded like a leek.

"You must stop being soft now," said his mother. "Take this sword to avenge your father!"

"I've already stopped being soft. With this sword I'll avenge him!"

"I hope so. Put on a blue coat and strap the sword to your back. No one will see it if they are the same colour. I've got the coat ready here." His mother pointed at the shabby chest behind the bed. "You'll set out tomorrow. Don't worry about me."

Mei Jian Chi tried on the new coat and found that it fitted him perfectly. He wrapped it around the sword which he placed by his pillow, and lay down calmly again. He believed he had already stopped being soft. He determined to act as if nothing were on his mind, to fall straight asleep, to wake the next morning as usual, and then to set out confidently in search of his mortal foe.

However, he couldn't sleep. He tossed and turned, eager all the time to sit up. He heard his mother's long, soft, hopeless sighs. Then he heard the first crow of the cock and knew that a new day had dawned, that he was sixteen.

樹，待到指尖一冷，有如觸着冰雪的時候，那純青透明的劍也出現了。他看清了劍靶，捏着，提了出來。

窗外的星月和屋裏的松明似乎都驟然失了光輝，惟有青光充塞宇內。那劍便溶在這青光中，看去好像一無所有。眉間尺凝神細視，這才彷彿看見長五尺餘，卻並不見得怎樣鋒利，劍口反而有些渾圓，正如一片韭葉。

「你從此要改變你的優柔的性情，用這劍報仇去！」他的母親說。

「我已經改變了我的優柔的性情，要用這劍報仇去！」

「但願如此。你穿了青衣，背上這劍，衣劍一色，誰也看不分明的。衣服我已經做在這裏，明天就上你的路去罷。不要記念我！」她向床後的破衣箱一指，說。

眉間尺取出新衣，試去一穿，長短正很合式。他便重行疊好，裹了劍，放在枕邊，沉靜地躺下。他覺得自己已經改變了優柔的性情；他決心要並無心事一般，倒頭便睡，清晨醒來，毫不改變常態，從容地去尋他不共戴天的仇讎。

但他醒着。他翻來覆去，總想坐起來。他聽到他母親的失望的輕輕的長嘆。他聽到最初的雞鳴；他知道已交子時，自己是上了十六歲了。

II

Mei Jian Chi, his eyelids swollen, left the house without a look behind. In the blue coat with the sword on his back, he strode swiftly towards the city. There was as yet no light in the east. The vapours of night still hid in the dew that clung to the tip of each fir leaf. But by the time he reached the far end of the forest, the dew drops were sparkling with lights which little by little took on the tints of dawn. Far ahead he could just see the outline of the dark grey, crenellated city walls.

Mingling with the vegetable vendors, he entered the city. The streets were already full of noise and bustle. Men were standing about idly in groups. Every now and then women put their heads out from their doors. Most of their eyelids were swollen from sleep too, their hair was uncombed and their faces were pale as they had had no time to put on rouge.

Mei Jian Chi sensed that some great event was about to take place, something eagerly yet patiently awaited by all these people.

As he advanced, a child darted past, almost knocking into the point of the sword on his back. He broke into a cold sweat. Turning north not far from the palace, he found a press of people craning their necks towards the road. The cries of women and children could be heard from the crowd. Afraid his invisible sword might hurt one of them, he dared not push his way forward; but new arrivals were pressing up from behind. He had to move out of their way, till all he could see was the backs of those in front and their craning necks.

All of a sudden, the people in front fell one by one to their knees.

二

　　當眉間尺腫着眼眶，頭也不回的跨出門外，穿着青衣，背着青劍，邁開大步，徑奔城中的時候，東方還沒有露出陽光。杉樹林的每一片葉尖，都掛着露珠，其中隱藏着夜氣。但是，待到走到樹林的那一頭，露珠裏卻閃出各樣的光輝，漸漸幻成曉色了。遠望前面，便依稀看見灰黑色的城牆和雉堞。

　　和挑葱賣菜的一同混入城裏，街市上已經很熱鬧。男人們一排一排的呆站着；女人們也時時從門裏探出頭來。她們大半也腫着眼眶；蓬着頭；黃黃的臉，連脂粉也不及塗抹。

　　眉間尺預覺到將有巨變降臨，他們便都是焦躁而忍耐地等候着這巨變的。

　　他徑自向前走；一個孩子突然跑過來，幾乎碰着他背上的劍尖，使他嚇出了一身汗。轉出北方，離王宮不遠，人們就擠得密密層層，都伸着脖子。人叢中還有女人和孩子哭嚷的聲音。他怕那看不見的雄劍傷了人，不敢擠進去；然而人們卻又在背後擁上來。他只得宛轉地退避；面前只看見人們的背脊和伸長的脖子。

　　忽然，前面的人們都陸續跪倒了；遠遠地有兩匹馬並着跑過

In the distance appeared two riders galloping forward side by side. They were followed by warriors carrying batons, spears, swords, bows and flags, who raised a cloud of yellow dust. After them came a large cart drawn by four horses, bearing musicians sounding gongs and drums and blowing strange wind instruments. Behind were carriages with courtiers in bright clothes, old men or short, plump fellows, their faces glistening with sweat. These were followed by outriders armed with swords, spears and halberds. Then the kneeling people prostrated themselves and Mei Jian Chi saw a great carriage with a yellow canopy drive up. In the middle of this was seated a fat man in bright clothes with a grizzled moustache and small head. He was wearing a sword like the one on the boy's back.

Mei Jian Chi gave an instinctive shudder, but at once he felt burning hot. Reaching out for the hilt of the sword on his back, he picked his way forward between the necks of the kneeling crowd.

But he had taken no more than five or six steps when someone tripped him up and he fell headlong on top of a young fellow with a wizened face. He was getting up nervously to see whether the point of his sword had done any damage, when he received two hard punches in the ribs. Without stopping to protest he looked at the road. But the carriage with the yellow canopy had passed. Even the mounted attendants behind it were already some distance away.

On both sides of the road everyone got up again. The young man with the wizened face had seized Mei Jian Chi by the collar and would not let go. He accused him of crushing his solar plexus, and ordered the boy to pay with his own life if he died before the age of eighty. Idlers crowded round to gape but said nothing, till a few taking the side of the wizened youth let fall some jokes and curses. Mei Jian Chi could neither laugh at such adversaries nor lose his temper. Annoying as they were, he could not get rid of them. This went on for about

來。此後是拿着木棍、戈、刀、弓弩、旌旗的武人，走得滿路黃塵滾滾。又來了一輛四匹馬拉的大車，上面坐着一隊人，有的打鐘擊鼓，有的嘴上吹着不知道叫甚麼名目勞什子。此後又是車，裏面的人都穿畫衣，不是老頭子，便是矮胖子，個個滿臉油汗。接着又是一隊拿刀槍劍戟的騎士。跪着的人們便都伏下去了。這時眉間尺正看見一輛黃蓋的大車馳來，正中坐着一個畫衣的胖子，花白鬍子，小腦袋；腰間還依稀看見佩着和他背上一樣的青劍。

　　他不覺全身一冷，但立刻又灼熱起來，像是猛火焚燒着。他一面伸手向肩頭捏住劍柄，一面提起腳，便從伏着的人們的脖子的空處跨出去。

　　但他只走得五六步，就跌了一個倒栽葱，因為有人突然捏住了他的一隻腳。這一跌又正壓在一個乾癟臉的少年身上；他正怕劍尖傷了他，吃驚地起來看的時候，肋下就挨了很重的兩拳。他也不暇計較，再望路上，不但黃蓋車已經走過，連擁護的騎士也過去了一大陣了。

　　路旁的一切人們也都爬起來。乾癟臉的少年卻還扭住了眉間尺的衣領，不肯放手，說被他壓壞了貴重的丹田，必須保險，倘若不到八十歲便死掉了，就得抵命。閒人們又即刻圍上來，呆看着，但誰也不開口；後來有人從旁笑罵了幾句，卻全是附和乾癟臉少年的。眉間尺遇到了這樣的敵人，真是怒不得，笑不得，只覺得無

the time it takes to cook a pan of millet. He was afire with impatience. Still the onlookers, watching as avidly as ever, refused to disperse.

Then through the throng pushed a dark man, lean as an iron rake, with a black beard and black eyes. Without a word, he smiled coldly at Mei Jian Chi, then raised his hand to flick the jaw of the youngster with the wizened face and looked steadily into his eyes. For a moment the youth returned his stare, then let go of the boy's collar and made off. The dark man made off too, and the disappointed spectators drifted away. A few came up to ask Mei Jian Chi his age and address, and whether he had sisters at home. But he ignored them.

He walked south, reflecting that in the bustling city it would be easy to wound someone by accident. He had better wait outside the South Gate for the king's return, to avenge his father. That open, deserted space was the best place for his purpose. By now the whole city was discussing the king's trip to the mountain. What a retinue! What majesty! What an honour to have seen the king! They had prostrated themselves so low that they should be considered as examples to all the nation! They buzzed like a swarm of bees. Near the South Gate, however, it became quieter.

Having left the city, he sat down under a big mulberry tree to eat two rolls of steamed bread. As he ate, the thought of his mother brought a lump to his throat, but presently that passed. All around grew quieter and quieter, until he could hear his own breathing quite distinctly.

As dusk fell, he grew more and more uneasy. He strained his eyes ahead, but there was not a sign of the king. The villagers who had taken vegetables to the city to sell were one by one going home with empty baskets.

Long after all these had passed, the dark man came darting out from the city.

聊，卻又脫身不得。這樣地經過了煮熟一鍋小米的時光，眉間尺早已焦躁得渾身發火，看的人卻仍不見減，還是津津有味似的。

前面的人圈子動搖了，擠進一個黑色的人來，黑鬚黑眼睛，瘦得如鐵。他並不言語，只向眉間尺冷冷地一笑，一面舉手輕輕地一撥乾癟臉少年的下巴，並且看定了他的臉。那少年也向他看了一會，不覺慢慢地鬆了手，溜走了；那人也就溜走了；看的人們也都無聊地走散。只有幾個人還來問眉間尺的年紀，住址，家裏可有姊姊。眉間尺都不理他們。

他向南走着；心裏想，城市中這麼熱鬧，容易誤傷，還不如在南門外等候他回來，給父親報仇罷，那地方是地曠人稀，實在很便於施展。這時滿城都議論着國王的遊山，儀仗，威嚴，自己得見國王的榮耀，以及俯伏得有怎麼低，應該採作國民的模範等等，很像蜜蜂的排衙。直至將近南門，這才漸漸地冷靜。

他走出城外，坐在一株大桑樹下，取出兩個饅頭來充了飢；吃着的時候忽然記起母親來，不覺眼鼻一酸，然而此後倒也沒有甚麼。周圍是一步一步地靜下去了，他至於很分明地聽到自己的呼吸。

天色愈暗，他也愈不安，盡目力望着前方，毫不見有國王回來的影子。上城賣菜的村人，一個個挑着空擔出城回家去了。

人迹絕了許久之後，忽然從城裏閃出那一個黑色的人來。

"Run, Mei Jian Chi! The king is after you!" His voice was like the hoot of an owl.

Mei Jian Chi trembled from head to foot. Spellbound, he followed the dark man, running as if he had wings. At last, stopping to catch breath, he realized they had reached the edge of the fir-wood. Far behind were the silver rays of the rising moon; but in front all he could see were the dark man's eyes gleaming like will-o'-the-wisps.

"How did you know me?" asked the lad in fearful amazement.

"I've always known you." The man laughed. "I know you carry the male sword on your back to avenge your father. And I know you will fail. Not only so, but today someone has informed against you. Your enemy went back to the palace by the East Gate and has issued an order for your arrest."

Mei Jian Chi began to despair.

"Oh, no wonder mother sighed," he muttered.

"But she knows only half. She doesn't know that I'm going to take vengeance for you."

"You? Are you willing to take vengeance for me, champion of justice?"

"Ah, don't insult me by giving me that title."

"Well, then, is it out of sympathy for widows and orphans?"

"Don't use words that have been sullied, child," he replied sternly. "Justice, sympathy and such terms, which once were clean, have now become capital for fiendish usurers. I have no place for these in my heart. I want only to avenge you!"

「走罷，眉間尺！國王在捉你了！」他説，聲音好像鴟鴞。

眉間尺渾身一顫，中了魔似的，立即跟着他走；後來是飛奔。他站定了喘息許多時，才明白已經到了杉樹林邊。後面遠處有銀白的條紋，是月亮已從那邊出現；前面卻僅有兩點燐火一般的那黑色人的眼光。

「你怎麼認識我？……」他極其惶駭地問。

「哈哈！我一向認識你。」那人的聲音説。「我知道你背着雄劍，要給你的父親報仇，我也知道你報不成。豈但報不成；今天已經有人告密，你的仇人早從東門還宮，下令捕拿你了。」

眉間尺不覺傷心起來。

「唉唉，母親的嘆息是無怪的。」他低聲説。

「但她只知道一半。她不知道我要給你報仇。」

「你麼？你肯給我報仇麼，義士？」

「阿，你不要用這稱呼來冤枉我。」

「那麼，你同情於我們孤兒寡婦？……」

「唉，孩子，你再不要提這些變了污辱的名稱。」他嚴冷地説，「仗義，同情，那些東西，先前曾經乾淨過，現在卻都成了放鬼債的資本。我的心裏全沒有你所謂的那些。我只不過要給你報仇！」

"Good. But how will you do it!"

"I want two things only from you." His voice sounded from beneath two burning eyes. "What two things? First your sword, then your head!"

Mei Jian Chi thought the request a strange one. But though he hesitated, he was not afraid. For a moment he was speechless.

"Don't be afraid that I want to trick you out of your life and your treasure," continued the implacable voice in the dark. "It's entirely up to you. If you trust me, I'll go; if not, I won't."

"But why are you going to take vengeance for me? Did you know my father?"

"I knew him from the start, just as I've always known you. But that's not the reason. You don't understand, my clever lad, how I excel at revenge. What's yours is mine, what concerns him concerns me too. I bear on my soul so many wounds inflicted by others as well as by myself, that now I hate myself."

The voice in the darkness was silent. Mei Jian Chi raised his hand to draw the blue sword from his back and with the same movement swung it forward from the nape of his neck. As his head fell on the green moss at his feet, he handed the sword to the dark man.

"Aha!" The man took the sword with one hand, with the other he picked up Mei Jian Chi's head by the hair. He kissed the warm dead lips twice and burst into cold, shrill laughter.

His laughter spread through the fir-wood. At once, deep in the forest, flashed blazing eyes like the light of the will-o'-the-wisp which the next instant came so close that you could hear the snuffling of famished wolves. With one bite, Mei Jian Chi's blue coat was torn to shreds; the next disposed of his whole body, while the blood was in-

「好。但你怎麼給我報仇呢？」

「只要你給我兩件東西。」兩粒燐火下的聲音說。「那兩件麼？你聽着：一是你的劍，二是你的頭！」

眉間尺雖然覺得奇怪，有些狐疑，卻並不吃驚。他一時開不得口。

「你不要疑心我將騙取你的性命和寶貝。」暗中的聲音又嚴冷地說。「這事全由你。你信我，我便去；你不信，我便住。」

「但你為甚麼給我去報仇的呢？你認識我的父親麼？」

「我一向認識你的父親，也如一向認識你一樣。但我要報仇，卻並不為此。聰明的孩子，告訴你罷。你還不知道，我怎麼地善於報仇。你的就是我的；他也就是我。我的魂靈上是有這麼多的人，我所加的傷，我已經憎惡了我自己！」

暗中的聲音剛剛停止，眉間尺便舉手向肩頭抽取青色的劍，順手從後項窩向前一削，頭顱墜在地面的青苔上，一面將劍交給黑色人。

「呵呵！」他一手接劍，一手提着頭髮，提起眉間尺的頭來，對着那熱的死掉的嘴唇，接吻兩次，並且冷冷地尖利地笑。

笑聲即刻散佈在杉樹林中，深處隨着有一群燐火似的眼光閃動，倏忽臨近，聽到咻咻的餓狼的喘息。第一口撕盡了眉間尺的青

stantaneously licked clean. The only sound was the soft crunching of bones.

The huge wolf at the head of the pack hurled itself at the dark man. But with one sweep of the blue sword, its head fell on the green moss at his feet. With one bite the other wolves tore its skin to shreds, then next disposed of its whole body, while the blood was instantaneously licked clean. The only sound was the soft crunching of bones.

The dark man picked up the blue coat from the ground to wrap up Mei Jian Chi's head. Having fastened this and the blue sword on his back, he turned on his heel and swung off through the darkness towards the capital.

The wolves stood stock-still, hunched up, tongues lolling, panting. They watched him with green eyes as he strode away.

He swung through the darkness towards the capital, singing in a shrill voice as he went:

Sing hey, sing ho!

The single one who loved the sword

Has taken death as his reward.

Those who go single are galore,

Who love the sword are alone no more!

Foe for foe, ha! Head for head!

Two men by their own hands are dead.

衣，第二口便身體全都不見了，血痕也頃刻舔盡，只微微聽得咀嚼骨頭的聲音。

最先頭的一匹大狼就向黑色人撲過來。他用青劍一揮，狼頭便墜在地面的青苔上。別的狼們第一口撕盡了它的皮，第二口便身體全都不見了，血痕也頃刻舔盡，只微微聽得咀嚼骨頭的聲音。

他已經掣起地上的青衣，包了眉間尺的頭，和青劍都背在背脊上，回轉身，在暗中向王城揚長地走去。

狼們站定了，聳着肩，伸出舌頭，咻咻地喘着，放着綠的眼光看他揚長地走。

他在暗中向王城揚長地走去。發出尖利的聲音唱着歌：——

哈哈愛兮愛乎愛乎！

愛青劍兮一個仇人自屠。

伙頤連翩兮多少一夫。

一夫愛青劍兮嗚呼不孤。

頭換頭兮兩個仇人自屠。

一夫則無兮愛乎嗚呼！

愛乎嗚呼兮嗚呼阿呼，

阿呼嗚呼兮嗚呼嗚呼！

III

The king had taken no pleasure in his trip to the mountain, and the secret report of an assassin lying in wait on the road sent him back even more depressed. He was in a bad temper that night. He complained that not even the ninth concubine's hair was as black and glossy as the day before. Fortunately, perched kittenishly on the royal knee, she wriggled over seventy times till at last the wrinkles on the kingly brow were smoothed out.

But on rising after noon the next day the king was in a bad mood again. By the time lunch was over, he was furious.

"I'm bored!" he cried with a great yawn.

From the queen down to the court jester, all were thrown into a panic. The king had long since tired of his old ministers' sermons and the clowning of his plump dwarfs; recently he had even been finding insipid the marvellous tricks of rope-walkers, pole-climbers, jugglers, somersaulters, sword-swallowers and fire-spitters. He was given to bursts of rage, during which he would draw his sword to kill men on the slightest pretext.

Two eunuchs just back after playing truant from the palace, observing the gloom which reigned over the court, knew that dire trouble was impending again. One of them turned pale with fear. The other, however, quite confident, made his way unhurriedly to the king's presence to prostrate himself and announce:

"Your slave begs to inform you that he has just met a remarkable man with rare skill, who should be able to amuse Your Majesty."

"What?" The king was not one to waste words.

三

遊山並不能使國王覺得有趣；加上了路上將有刺客的密報，更使他掃興而還。那夜他很生氣，說是連第九個妃子的頭髮，也沒有昨天那樣的黑得好看了。幸而她撒嬌坐在他的御膝上，特別扭了七十多回，這才使龍眉之間的皺紋漸漸地舒展。

午後，國王一起身，就又有些不高興，待到用過午膳，簡直現出怒容來。

「唉唉！無聊！」他打一個大呵欠之後，高聲說。

上自王后，下至弄臣，看見這情形，都不覺手足無措。白鬚老臣的講道，矮胖侏儒的打諢，王是早已聽厭的了；近來便是走索、緣竿、拋丸、倒立、吞刀、吐火等等奇妙的把戲，也都看得毫無意味。他常常要發怒；一發怒，便按着青劍，總想尋點小錯處，殺掉幾個人。

偷空在宮外閒遊的兩個小宦官，剛剛回來，一看見宮裏面大家的愁苦的情形，便知道又是照例的禍事臨頭了，一個嚇得面如土色；一個卻像是大有把握一般，不慌不忙，跑到國王的面前，俯伏着，說道：

「奴才剛才訪得一個異人，很有異術，可以給大王解悶，因此特來奏聞。」

「甚麼？！」王說。他的話是一向很短的。

"He's a lean, dark fellow who looks like a beggar. He's dressed in blue, has a round blue bundle on his back and sings snatches of strange doggerel. When questioned, he says he can do a wonderful trick the like of which has never been seen, unique in the world and absolutely new. The sight will end all care and bring peace to the world. But when we asked for a demonstration, he wouldn't give one. He says he needs a golden dragon and a golden cauldron...."

"A golden dragon? That's me. A golden cauldron? I have one."

"That's just what your slave thought...."

"Bring him in!"

Before the king's voice had died away, four guards hurried out with the eunuch. From the queen down to the court jester, all beamed with delight, hoping this conjuror would end all care and bring peace to the world. And even if the show fell flat, there would be the lean, dark, beggarly-looking fellow to bear the brunt of the royal displeasure. If they could last till he was brought in, all would be well.

They did not have long to wait. Six men came hurrying towards the golden throne. The eunuch led the way, the four guards brought up the rear, and in the middle was a dark man. On nearer inspection they could see his blue coat, black beard, eyebrows and hair. He was so thin that his cheekbones stood out and his eyes were sunken. As he knelt respectfully to prostrate himself, on his back was visible a small round bundle, wrapped in blue cloth patterned in a dark red.

"Well!" shouted the king impatiently. The simplicity of this fellow's paraphernalia did not augur well for his tricks.

"Your subject's name is Yan-zhi-ao-zhe, born in Wenwen Village. I wasn't bred to any trade, but when I was grown I met a sage who taught me how to conjure with a boy's head. I can't do this alone, though. It must be in the presence of a golden dragon, and I must

「那是一個黑瘦的，乞丐似的男子。穿一身青衣，背着一個圓圓的青包裹；嘴裏唱着胡謅的歌。人問他。他説善於玩把戲，空前絕後，舉世無雙，人們從來就沒有看見過；一見之後，便即解煩釋悶，天下太平。但大家要他玩，他卻又不肯。説是第一須有一條金龍，第二須有一個金鼎。……」

「金龍？我是的。金鼎？我有。」

「奴才也正是這樣想。……」

「傳進來！」

話聲未絕，四個武士便跟着那小宦官疾趨而出。上自王后，下至弄臣，個個喜形於色。他們都願意這把戲玩得解愁解悶，天下太平；即使玩不成，這回也有了那乞丐似的黑瘦男子來受禍，他們只要能挨到傳了進來的時候就好了。

並不要許多工夫，就望見六個人向金階趨進。先頭是宦官，後面是四個武士，中間夾着一個黑色人。待到近來時，那人的衣服卻是青的，鬚、眉、頭髮都黑；瘦得顴骨、眼圈骨、眉稜骨都高高地突出來。他恭敬地跪着俯伏下去時，果然看見背上有一個圓圓的小包袱，青色布，上面還畫上一些暗紅色的花紋。

「奏來！」王暴躁地説。他見他傢伙簡單，以為他未必會玩甚麼好把戲。

「臣名叫宴之敖者；生長汶汶鄉。少無職業；晚遇明師，教臣把戲，是一個孩子的頭。這把戲一個人玩不起來，必須在金龍之前，

have a golden cauldron filled with clear water and heated with charcoal. Then when the boy's head is put in and the water boils, the head will rise and fall and dance all manner of figures. It will laugh and sing too in a marvellous voice. Whoever hears its song and sees its dance will know an end to care. When all men see it, the whole world will be peace."

"Go ahead!" the king ordered loudly.

They did not have long to wait. A great golden cauldron, big enough to boil an ox, was set outside the court. It was filled with clear water, and charcoal was lit beneath it. The dark man stood at one side. When the charcoal was red he put down his bundle and undid it. Then with both hands he held up a boy's head with fine eyebrows, large eyes, white teeth and red lips. A smile was on its face. Its tangled hair was like faint blue smoke. The dark man raised it high, turning round to display it to the whole assembly. He held it over the cauldron while he muttered something unintelligible, and finally dropped it with a splash into the water. Foam flew up at least five feet high. Then all was still.

For a long time nothing happened. The king lost patience, the queen, concubines, ministers and eunuchs began to feel alarmed, while the plump dwarfs started to sneer. These sneers made the king suspect that he was being made to look a fool. He turned to the guards to order them to have this oaf who dared deceive his monarch thrown into the great cauldron and boiled to death.

But that very instant he heard the water bubbling. The fire burning with all its might cast a ruddy glow over the dark man, turning him the dull red of molten iron. The king looked round. The dark man, stretching both hands towards the sky, stared into space and danced, singing in a shrill voice:

擺一個金鼎，注滿清水，用獸炭煎熬。於是放下孩子的頭去，一到水沸，這頭便隨波上下，跳舞百端，且發妙音，歡喜歌唱。這歌舞為一人所見，便解愁釋悶，為萬民所見，便天下太平。」

「玩來！」王大聲命令說。

並不要許多工夫，一個煮牛的大金鼎便擺在殿外，注滿水，下面堆了獸炭，點起火來。那黑色人站在旁邊，見炭火一紅，便解下包袱，打開，兩手捧出孩子的頭來，高高舉起。那頭是秀眉長眼，皓齒紅唇；臉帶笑容；頭髮蓬鬆，正如青煙一陣。黑色人捧着向四面轉了一圈，便伸手擎到鼎上，動着嘴唇說了幾句不知甚麼話，隨即將手一鬆，只聽得撲通一聲，墜入水中去了。水花同時濺起，足有五尺多高，此後是一切平靜。

許多工夫，還無動靜。國王首先暴躁起來，接着是王后和妃子、大臣、宦官們也都有些焦急，矮胖的侏儒們則已經開始冷笑了。王一見他們的冷笑，便覺自己受愚，回顧武士，想命令他們就將那欺君的莠民擲入牛鼎裏去煮殺。

但同時就聽得水沸聲；炭火也正旺，映着那黑色人變成紅黑，如鐵的燒到微紅。王剛又回過臉來，他也已經伸起兩手向天，眼光向着無物，舞蹈着，忽地發出尖利的聲音唱起歌來：

Sing hey for love, for love heigh ho!

Ah, love! Ah, blood! Who is not so?

Men grope in dark, the king laughs loud,

Ten thousand heads in death have bowed.

I only use one single head,

For one man's head let blood be shed!

Blood — let it flow!

Sing hey, sing ho!

As he sang, the water in the cauldron seethed up like a small cone-shaped mountain, flowing and eddying from tip to base. The head bobbed up and down with the water, skimming round and round, turning nimble somersaults as it went. They could just make out the smile of pleasure on its face. Then abruptly it gave this up to start swimming against the stream, circling, weaving to and fro, splashing water in all directions so that hot drops showered the court. One of the dwarfs gave a yelp and rubbed his nose. Scalded, he couldn't suppress a cry of pain.

The dark man stopped singing. The head remained motionless in the middle of the water, a grave expression on its face. After a few seconds, it began bobbing up and down slowly again. From bobbing it put on speed to swim up and down, not quickly but with infinite grace. Three times it circled the cauldron, ducking up and down. Then, its eyes wide, the jet-black pupils henomenally bright, it sang:

The sovereign's rule spreads far and wide,

He conquers foes on every side.

The world may end, but not his might,

哈哈愛兮愛乎愛乎！

愛兮血兮兮誰乎獨無。

民萌冥行兮一夫壺盧。

彼用百頭顱，千頭顱兮用萬頭顱！

我用一頭顱兮而無萬夫。

愛一頭顱兮血乎嗚呼！

血乎嗚呼兮嗚呼阿呼，

阿呼嗚呼兮嗚呼嗚呼！

　　隨着歌聲，水就從鼎口湧起，上尖下廣，像一坐小山，但自水尖至鼎底，不住地迴旋運動。那頭即隨水上上下下，轉着圈子，一面又滴溜溜自己翻筋斗，人們還可以隱約看見他玩得高興的笑容。過了些時，突然變了逆水的游泳，打旋子夾着穿梭，激得水花向四面飛濺，滿庭灑下一陣熱雨來。一個侏儒忽然叫了一聲，用手摸着自己的鼻子。他不幸被熱水燙了一下，又不耐痛，終於免不得出聲叫苦了。

　　黑色人的歌聲才停，那頭也就在水中央停住，面向王殿，顏色轉成端莊。這樣的有十餘瞬息之久，才慢慢地上下抖動；從抖動加速而為起伏的游泳，但不很快，態度很雍容。繞着水邊一高一低地游了三匝，忽然睜大眼睛，漆黑的眼珠顯得格外精采，同時也開口唱起歌來：

王澤流兮浩洋洋；

克服怨敵，怨敵克服兮，赫兮強！

宇宙有窮止兮萬壽無疆。

So here I come all gleaming bright.

Bright gleams the sword — forget me not!

A royal sight, but sad my lot.

Sing hey, sing ho, a royal sight!

Come back, where gleams the bright blue light.

The head stopped suddenly at the crest of the water. After several somersaults, it started plying up and down again, casting bewitching glances to right and to left as it sang once more:

Heigh ho, for the love we know!

I cut one head, one head, heigh ho!

I use one single head, not more,

The heads he uses are galore! ...

By the last line of the song the head was submerged, and since it did not reappear the singing became indistinct. As the song grew fainter, the seething water subsided little by little like an ebbing tide, until it was below the rim of the cauldron. From a distance nothing could be seen.

"Well?" demanded the king impatiently, tired of waiting.

"Your Majesty!" The dark man went down on one knee. "It's dancing the most miraculous Dance of Union at the bottom of the cauldron. You can't see this except from close by. I can't make it come up, because this Dance of Union has to be performed at the bottom of the cauldron."

The king stood up and strode down the steps to the cauldron. Regardless of the heat, he bent forward to watch. The water was smooth

　　幸我來也兮青其光！

　　青其光兮永不相忘。

　　異處異處兮堂哉皇！

　　堂哉皇哉兮嗳嗳唷，

　　嗟來歸來，嗟來陪來兮青其光！

　　頭忽然升到水的尖端停住；翻了幾個筋斗之後，上下升降起來，眼珠向着左右瞥視，十分秀媚，嘴裏仍然唱着歌：

　　阿呼嗚呼兮嗚呼嗚呼！

　　愛乎嗚呼兮嗚呼阿呼！

　　血一頭顱兮愛乎嗚呼。

　　我用一頭顱兮而無萬夫！

　　彼用百頭顱，千頭顱……

　　唱到這裏，是沉下去的時候，但不再浮上來；歌詞也不能辨別。湧起的水，也隨着歌聲的微弱，漸漸低落，像退潮一般，終至到鼎口以下，在遠處甚麼也看不見。

　　「怎了？」等了一會，王不耐煩地問。

　　「大王，」那黑色人半跪着說。「他正在鼎底裏作最神奇的團圓舞，不臨近是看不見的。臣也沒有法術使他上來，因為作團圓舞必須在鼎底裏。」

　　王站起身，跨下金階，冒着炎熱立在鼎邊，探頭去看。只見水

as a mirror. The head, lying there motionless, looked up and fixed its eyes on the king. When the king's glance fell on its face, it gave a charming smile. This smile made the king feel that they had met before. Who could this be? As he was wondering, the dark man drew the blue sword from his back and swept it forward like lightning from the nape of the king's neck. The king's head fell with a splash into the cauldron.

When enemies meet they know each other at a glance, particularly at close quarters. The moment the king's head touched the water, Mei Jian Chi's head came up to meet it and savagely bit its ear. The water in the cauldron boiled and bubbled as the two heads engaged upon a fight to the death. After about twenty encounters, the king was wounded in five places, Mei Jian Chi in seven. The crafty king contrived to slip behind his enemy, and in an unguarded moment Mei Jian Chi let himself be caught by the back of his neck, so that he could not turn round. The king fastened his teeth into him and would not let go, like a silkworm burrowing into a mulberry leaf. The boy's cries of pain could be heard outside the cauldron.

From the queen down to the court jester, all who had been petrified with fright before were galvanized into life by this sound. They felt as if the sun had been swallowed up in darkness. But even as they trembled, they knew a secret joy. They waited, round-eyed.

The dark man, rather taken aback, did not change colour. Effortlessly he raised his arm like a withered branch holding the invisible sword. He streched forward as if to peer into the cauldron. Of a sudden his arm bent, the blue sword thrust down and his head fell into the cauldron with a plop, sending snow-white foam flying in all directions.

As soon as his head hit the water, it charged at the king's head and took the royal nose between its teeth, nearly biting it off. The king gave a cry of pain and Mei Jian Chi seized this chance to get away,

平如鏡，那頭仰面躺在水中間，兩眼正看着他的臉。待到王的眼光射到他臉上時，他便嫣然一笑。這一笑使王覺得似曾相識，卻又一時記不起是誰來。剛在驚疑，黑色人已經掣出了背着的青色的劍，只一揮，閃電般從後項窩直劈下去，撲通一聲，王的頭就落在鼎裏了。

仇人相見，本來格外眼明，況且是相逢狹路。王頭剛到水面，眉間尺的頭便迎上來，狠命在他耳輪上咬了一口。鼎水即刻沸湧，澎湃有聲；兩頭即在水中死戰。約有二十回合，王頭受了五個傷，眉間尺的頭上卻有七處。王又狡猾，總是設法繞到他的敵人的後面去。眉間尺偶一疏忽，終於被他咬住了後項窩，無法轉身。這一回王的頭可是咬定不放了，他只是連連蠶食進去；連鼎外面也彷彿聽到孩子的失聲叫痛的聲音。

上自王后，下至弄臣，駭得凝結着的神色也應聲活動起來，似乎感到暗無天日的悲哀，皮膚上都一粒一粒地起粟；然而又夾着秘密的歡喜，瞪了眼，像是等候着甚麼似的。

黑色人也彷彿有些驚慌，但是面不改色。他從從容容地伸開那捏着看不見的青劍的臂膊，如一段枯枝；伸長頸子，如在細看鼎底。臂膊忽然一彎，青劍便騰地從他後面劈下，劍到頭落，墜入鼎中，溯的一聲，雪白的水花向着空中同時四射。

他的頭一入水，即刻直奔王頭，一口咬住了王的鼻子，幾乎要咬下來。王忍不住叫一聲「阿唷」，將嘴一張，眉間尺的頭就乘機掙

whirling round to cling with a vice-like grip to his jaw. They pulled with all their might in opposite directions, so that the king could not keep his mouth shut. Then they fell on him savagely, like famished hens pecking at rice, till the king's head was mauled and savaged out of all recognition. To begin with, he lashed about frantically in the cauldron; then he simply lay there groaning; and finally he fell silent, having breathed his last.

Presently the dark man and Mei Jian Chi stopped biting. They left the king's head and swam once round the edge of the cauldron to see whether their enemy was shamming or not. Assured that the king was indeed dead, they exchanged glances and smiled. Then, closing their eyes, their faces towards the sky, they sank to the bottom of the water.

IV

The smoke drifted away, the fire went out. Not a ripple remained on the water. The extraordinary silence brought high and low to their senses. Someone gave a cry, and at once they were all calling out together in horror. Someone walked over to the golden cauldron, and the others pressed after him. Those crowded at the back could only peer between the necks of those in front.

The heat still scorched their cheeks. The water, smooth as a mirror, was coated with oil which reflected a sea of faces: the queen, the concubines, guards, old ministers, dwarfs, eunuchs....

"Heavens! Our king's head is still in there! Oh, horrors! " The sixth concubine suddenly burst into frantic sobbing.

脱了，一轉臉倒將王的下巴下死勁咬住。他們不但都不放，還用全力上下一撕，撕得王頭再也合不上嘴。於是他們就如餓雞啄米一般，一頓亂咬，咬得王頭眼歪鼻塌，滿臉鱗傷。先前還會在鼎裏面四處亂滾，後來只能躺着呻吟，到底是一聲不響，只有出氣，沒有進氣了。

黑色人和眉間尺的頭也慢慢地住了嘴，離開王頭，沿鼎壁游了一匝，看他可是裝死還是真死。待到知道了王頭確已斷氣，便四目相視，微微一笑，隨即合上眼睛，仰面向天，沉到水底裏去了。

四

煙消火滅；水波不興。特別的寂靜倒使殿上殿下的人們警醒。他們中的一個首先叫了一聲，大家也立刻疊連驚叫起來；一個邁開腿向金鼎走去，大家便爭先恐後地擁上去了。有擠在後面的，只能從人脖子的空隙間向裏面窺探。

熱氣還炙得人臉上發燒。鼎裏的水卻一平如鏡，上面浮着一層油，照出許多人臉孔：王后、王妃、武士、老臣、侏儒、太監。……

「啊呀，天哪！咱們大王的頭還在裏面哪，哴哴哴！」第六個妃子忽然發狂似的哭嚷起來。

From the queen down to the court jester, all were sized by consternation. They scattered in panic, at a loss, running round in circles. The wisest old councillor went forward alone and put out a hand to touch the side of the cauldron. He winced, snatched back his hand and put two fingers to his mouth to blow on them.

Finally regaining control, they gathered outside the palace to discuss how best to recover the king's head. They consulted for the time it would take to cook three pans of millet. Their conclusion was: collect wire scoops from the big kitchen and order the guards to retrieve the royal head.

Soon the implements were ready: wire scoops, strainers, golden plates and dusters were all placed by the cauldron. The guards rolled up their sleeves. Some with wire scoops, some with strainers, they respectfully set about bringing up the remains. The scoops clashed against each other and scraped the edge of the cauldron, while the water eddied in their wake. After some time, one of the guards, with a grave face, raised his scoop slowly and carefully in both hands. Drops of water like pearls were dripping from the utensil, in which could be seen a snow-white skull. As the others cried out with astonishment, he deposited the skull on one golden plate.

"Oh, dear! Our king!" The queen, concubines, ministers and even the eunuchs burst out sobbing. They soon stopped, however, when another guard fished out another skull identical with the first.

They watched dully with tear-filled eyes as the sweating guards went on with their salvaging. They retrieved a tangled mass of white hair and black hair, and several spoonfuls of some shorter hair no doubt from white and black moustaches. Then another skull. Then three hairpins.

They stopped only when nothing but clear soup was left in the cauldron, and divided what they had on to three golden plates: one of skulls, one of hair, one of hairpins.

上自王后，下至弄臣，也都恍然大悟，倉皇散開，急得手足無措，各自轉了四五個圈子。一個最有謀略的老臣獨又上前，伸手向鼎邊一摸，然而渾身一抖，立刻縮了回來，伸出兩個指頭，放在口邊吹個不住。

大家定了定神，便在殿門外商議打撈辦法。約略費去了煮熟三鍋小米的工夫，總算得到一種結果，是：到大廚房去調集了鐵絲勺子，命武士協力撈起來。

器具不久就調集了，鐵絲勺、漏勺、金盤、擦桌布，都放在鼎旁邊。武士們便揎起衣袖，有用鐵絲勺的，有用漏勺的，一齊恭行打撈。有勺子相觸的聲音，有勺子刮着金鼎的聲音；水是隨着勺子的攪動而旋繞着。好一會，一個武士的臉色忽而很端莊了，極小心地兩手慢慢舉起了勺子，水滴從勺孔中珠子一般漏下，勺裏面便顯出雪白的頭骨來。大家驚叫了一聲；他便將頭骨倒在金盤裏。

「阿呀！我的大王呀！」王后、妃子、老臣、以至太監之類，都放聲哭起來。但不久就陸續停止了，因為武士又撈起了一個同樣的頭骨。

他們淚眼模糊地四顧，只見武士們滿臉油汗，還在打撈。此後撈出來的是一團糟的白頭髮和黑頭髮；還有幾勺很短的東西，似乎是白鬍鬚和黑鬍鬚。此後又是一個頭骨。此後是三枝簪。

直到鼎裏面只剩下清湯，才始住手；將撈出的物件分盛了三金盤：一盤頭骨，一盤鬚髮，一盤簪。

"His Majesty had only one head. Which is his?" demanded the ninth concubine frantically.

"Quite so...." The ministers looked at each other in dismay.

"If the skin and flesh hadn't boiled away, it would be easy to tell," said one kneeling dwarf.

They forced themselves to examine the skulls carefully, but the size and colour were about the same. They could not even distinguish which was the boy's. The queen said the king had a scar on his right temple as the result of a fall while still crown prince, and this might have left a trace on the skull. Sure enough, a dwarf discovered such a mark on one skull, and there was general rejoicing until another dwarf discovered a similar mark on the right temple of a slightly yellower skull.

"I know!" exclaimed the third concubine happily. "Our king had a very high nose."

The eunuchs hastened to examine the noses. To be sure, one of them was relatively high, though there wasn't much to choose between them; but unfortunately that particular skull had no mark on the right temple.

"Besides," said the ministers to the eunuchs, "could the back of His Majesty's skull have been so protuberant?"

"We never paid any attention to the back of His Majesty's skull...."

The queen and the concubines searched their memories. Some said it had been protuberant, some flat. When they questioned the eunuch who had combed the royal hair, he would not commit himself to an answer.

That evening a council of princes and ministers was held to deter-

「咱們大王只有一個頭。那一個是咱們大王的呢？」第九個妃子焦急地問。

「是呵⋯⋯。」老臣們都面面相覷。

「如果皮肉沒有煮爛，那就容易辨別了。」一個侏儒跪着説。

大家只得平心靜氣，去細看那頭骨，但是黑白大小，都差不多，連那孩子的頭，也無從分辨。王后説王的右額上有一個疤，是做太子時候跌傷的，怕骨上也有痕迹。果然，侏儒在一個頭骨上發見了；大家正在歡喜的時候，另外的一個侏儒卻又在較黃的頭骨的右額上看出相仿的瘢痕來。

「我有法子。」第三個王妃得意地説，「咱們大王的龍準是很高的。」

太監們即刻動手研究鼻準骨，有一個確也似乎比較地高，但究竟相差無幾；最可惜的是右額上卻並無跌傷的瘢痕。

「況且，」老臣們向太監説，「大王的後枕骨是這麼尖的麼？」

「奴才向來就沒有留心看過大王後枕骨⋯⋯。」

王后和妃子們也各自回想起來，有的説是尖的，有的説是平的。叫梳頭太監來問的時候，卻一句話也不説。

當夜便開了一個王公大臣會議，想決定那一個是王的頭，但結

mine which head was the king's, but with no better result than during the day. In fact, even the hair and moustaches presented a problem. The white was of course king's, but since he had been grizzled it was very hard to decide about the black. After half a night's discussion, they had just eliminated a few red hairs when the ninth concubine protested. She was sure she had seen a few brown hairs in the king's moustache; in which case how could they be sure there was not a single red one? They had to put them all together again and leave the case unsettled.

They had reached no solution by the early hours of the morning. They prolonged the discussion, yawning, till the cock crowed a second time, before fixing on a safe and satisfactory solution: All three heads should be placed in the golden coffin beside the king's body for interment.

The funeral took place a week later. The whole city was agog. Citizens of the capital and spectators from far away flocked to the royal funeral. As soon as it was light, the road was thronged with men and women. Sandwiched in between were tables bearing sacrificial offerings. Shortly before midday horsemen cantered out to clear the roads. Some time later came a procession of flags, batons, spears, bows, halberds and the like, followed by four cartloads of musicians. Then, rising and falling with the uneven ground, a yellow canopy drew near. It was possible to make out the hearse with the golden coffin in which lay three heads and one body.

The people knelt down, revealing rows of tables of offerings. Some loyal subjects gulped back tears of rage to think that the spirits of the two regicides were enjoying the sacrifice now together with the king. But there was nothing they could do about it.

Then followed the carriages of the queen and concubines. The crowd stared at them and they stared at the crowd, not stopping their

果還同白天一樣。並且連鬚、髮也發生了問題。白的自然是王的，然而因為花白，所以黑的也很難處置。討論了小半夜，只將幾根紅色的鬍子選出；接着因為第九個王妃抗議，說她確曾看見王有幾根通黃的鬍子，現在怎麼能知道決沒有一根紅的呢。於是也只好重行歸併，作為疑案了。

到後半夜，還是毫無結果。大家卻居然一面打呵欠，一面繼續討論，直到第二次雞鳴，這才決定了一個最慎重妥善的辦法，是：只能將三個頭骨都和王的身體放在金棺裏落葬。

七天之後是落葬的日期，合城很熱鬧。城裏的人民，遠處的人民，都奔來瞻仰國王的「大出喪」。天一亮，道上已經擠滿了男男女女；中間還夾着許多祭桌。待到上午，清道的騎士才緩轡而來。又過了不少工夫，才看見儀仗，甚麼旌旗、木棍、戈戟、弓弩、黃鉞之類；此後是四輛鼓吹車。再後面是黃蓋隨着路的不平而起伏着，並且漸漸近來了，於是現出靈車，上載金棺，棺裏面藏着三個頭和一個身體。

百姓都跪下去，祭桌便一列一列地在人叢中出現。幾個義民很忠憤，咽着淚，怕那兩個大逆不道的逆賊的魂靈，此時也和王一同享受祭禮，然而也無法可施。

此後是王后和許多王妃的車。百姓看她們，她們也看百姓，但

wailing. After them came the ministers, eunuchs and dwarfs, all of whom had assumed a mourning air. But no one paid the least attention to them, and their ranks were squeezed out of all semblance of order.

October 1926

哭着。此後是大臣、太監、侏儒等輩，都裝着哀戚的顏色。只是百姓已經不看他們，連行列也擠得亂七八糟，不成樣子了。

一九二六年十月作。